VAMPIRE RITES TRILOGY

THE SAGA OF DARREN SHAN

D1149798

DARREN SHAN

VAMPIRE RITES TRILOGY

THE SAGA OF DARREN SHAN

VAMPIRE MOUNTAIN
TRIALS OF DEATH
THE VAMPIRE PRINCE

HarperCollins *Children's Books*

If your trip to Vampire Mountain leaves you bloodthirsty
for more, visit Shanville
– home of Darren Shan –
at www.darrenshan.com

Vampire Mountain first published in Great Britain by Collins 2001
Trials of Death first published in Great Britain by Collins 2001
The Vampire Prince first published in Great Britain by Collins 2002

First published in this three-in-one edition by HarperCollins *Children's Books* 2004

HarperCollins *Children's Books* is a division of HarperCollins *Publishers* Ltd,
77-85 Fulham Palace Road, Hammersmith,
London W6 8JB

The HarperCollins *Children's Books* website address is:
www.harpercollins.co.uk

14

ISBN-13   978 0 00 714375 7

Printed and bound in England by
Clays Ltd, St Ives plc

DARREN SHAN

VAMPIRE MOUNTAIN

THE SAGA OF DARREN SHAN
BOOK 4

For:

The Freaky Fitzes: Ronan, Lorcan, Kealan, Tiernan & Meara
— viva the Shack Pack!!!

OBEs (Order of the Bloody Entrails) to:
Ann "the monstervator" Murphy
Moira "the mediatrix" Reilly
Tony "giggsy" Purdue

Partners In Crime:
Liam & Biddy
Gillie & Zoë
Emma & Chris

PROLOGUE

"PACK YOUR bags," Mr Crepsley said late one night, as he was heading for his coffin. "We leave for Vampire Mountain tomorrow."

I was used to the vampire making declarations out of the blue – he didn't believe in consulting me when making up his mind – but this was extraordinary, even for him.

"*Vampire Mountain?*" I shrieked, racing after him. "Why are we going *there?*"

"To present you to the Council," he said. "It is time."

"The Council of Vampire Generals?" I asked. "Why do we have to go? Why now?"

"We go because it is proper," he said. "And we go now because the Council only meets once every twelve years. If we miss this year's gathering, we will have a long wait until the next."

And that was all he'd say about it. He turned a deaf ear to

the rest of my questions and tucked himself into his coffin before the sun rose, leaving me to fret the day away.

*   *   *

My name's Darren Shan. I'm a half-vampire. I used to be human until eight or so years ago, when my destiny clashed with Mr Crepsley's and I reluctantly became his assistant. I had a hard time adapting to the vampire and his ways — especially when it came to drinking human blood — but finally I resigned myself, accepted my lot, and got on with the business of living.

We were part of a travelling band of amazing circus performers, led by a man called Hibernius Tall. We toured the world, putting on incredible shows for customers who appreciated our strange and magical talents.

Six years had passed since Mr Crepsley and me had last been separated from the Cirque Du Freak. We'd left to put a stop to a mad vampaneze by the name of Murlough, who was terrorizing the vampire's home city. The vampaneze are a breakaway group of vampires who kill humans when they feed on them. Vampires don't — we just take a bit of blood and move on, leaving those we sup from unharmed. Most of the vampire myths you read about in books or see in films actually originated with the vampaneze.

They'd been a good six years. I'd become a regular performer at the Cirque, going on with Madam Octa — Mr Crepsley's poisonous spider — every night to amaze and frighten audiences. I'd also learnt a few magic tricks, which I'd worked into the act. I got on well with the rest of the Cirque troupe. I'd grown accustomed to the wandering lifestyle and had been enjoying myself.

Now, after six years of stability, we were about to journey into the unknown again. I knew a small bit about the Council and Vampire Mountain. Vampires were ruled by soldiers called Vampire Generals who made sure their laws were enforced. They killed mad or evil vampires and kept the rest of the walking un-dead in line. Mr Crepsley used to be a Vampire General, but quit long ago, for reasons he'd never revealed.

Every so often — I now knew it was twelve years — the Generals gathered at a secret fortress to discuss whatever it was that blood-sucking creatures of the night discussed when they got together. Not only Generals attended — I'd heard that ordinary vampires could go as well — but they made up the majority. I didn't know where the fortress was, or how we'd get there, or why I had to be presented to the Council — but I was about to find out!

CHAPTER ONE

I WAS excited but anxious about the journey — I was venturing into the unknown, and I'd a feeling it wouldn't prove to be a smooth trip — so I spent the day busily packing rucksacks for myself and Mr Crepsley, to make the time pass faster. (Full-vampires will die if exposed to the sun for more than a few hours, but half-vampires aren't affected by it.) Since I didn't know where we were going, I didn't know what to take or leave. If Vampire Mountain was icy and wintry, I'd need thick clothes and boots; if it was somewhere hot and tropical, T-shirts and shorts would be more in order.

I asked some of the Cirque people about it but they knew nothing, except Mr Tall, who said I should pack for snow. Mr Tall was one of those people who seem to know something about everything.

Evra agreed about the snow. "I doubt if sun-shy vampires would make their base in the Caribbean!" he snorted.

Evra Von was a snake-boy, with scales instead of skin. Rather, he *used* to be a snake-boy — now he was a snake-*man*. Evra had grown these last six years, got taller and broader and older-looking. I hadn't. As a half-vampire, I aged at one-fifth the normal rate. So, though eight years had passed since Mr Crepsley blooded me, I only looked a year or so older.

I hated not being able to grow normally. Evra and me used to be best buddies, but not any more. We were still good friends and shared a tent, but he was a young man now, more interested in people — particularly women! — his own age. In reality I was only a couple of years younger than Evra, but I looked like a kid, and it was difficult for him to treat me as an equal.

There were benefits to being a half-vampire — I was stronger and faster than any human, and would live longer — but I'd have given them all up if it meant looking my real age and being able to lead an ordinary life.

Even though Evra and me were no longer as close as we'd once been, he was still my friend, and was worried about me heading off for Vampire Mountain. "From what I know, that journey's no joke," he warned in the deep voice which hit him a few years ago. "Maybe I should come with you."

I'd have loved to jump at his offer, but Evra had his own life to lead. It wouldn't be fair to drag him away from the Cirque Du Freak. "No," I told him. "Stay and keep my hammock warm. I'll be OK. Besides, snakes don't like the cold, do they?"

"That's true," he laughed. "I'd most likely fall asleep and hibernate till spring!"

Even though Evra wouldn't be coming, he helped me pack. I didn't have much to take: spare clothes, a thick pair of boots, special cooking utensils which folded up neatly so they were easier to carry, my diary — that went everywhere with me — and other bits and pieces. Evra told me to take a rope — he said it might come in handy, especially when it came to climbing.

"But vampires are great climbers," I reminded him.

"I know," he said, "but do you really want to hang off the side of a mountain with only your fingertips for support?"

"Of course he does!" someone boomed behind us before I could answer. "Vampires thrive on danger."

Turning to see who it was, I found myself face to face with the sinister being known as Mr Tiny, and my insides instantly froze with fright.

Mr Tiny was a small, plump man, with white hair, thick glasses and a pair of green wellies. He often toyed with a heart-shaped watch. He looked like a kindly old uncle but was in fact a cruel, dark-hearted man, who'd cut your tongue out as soon as say "hello". Nobody knew much about him, but everyone was afraid of him. His first name was Desmond, and if you shortened it and put it together with his surname you got *Mr Destiny*.

I hadn't seen Mr Tiny since shortly after joining the Cirque Du Freak, but I'd heard many tales about him — how he ate children for breakfast, and burned down towns to warm his feet. My heart tightened when I saw him standing a few metres away, eyes twinkling, hands wrapped behind his back, eavesdropping on Evra and me.

"Vampires are peculiar creatures," he said, stepping forward, as though he'd been part of the conversation all along. "They love a challenge. I knew one once who walked himself to death in sunlight, merely because someone had sneered at him for only being able to come out at night."

He stuck out a hand and, scared as I was, I automatically shook it. Evra didn't — when Mr Tiny extended his hand to the snake-man, he stood, quivering, shaking his head furiously. Mr Tiny merely smiled and withdrew the hand.

"So, you're off to Vampire Mountain," he said, picking up my rucksack and peering inside without asking. "Take matches, Master Shan. The way is long and the days are cold. The winds that gust around Vampire Mountain would cut even a tough-skinned young man like you to the bone."

"Thanks for the advice," I said.

That was the confusing thing about Mr Tiny: he was always polite and amiable, so even if you knew he was the sort of man who wouldn't blink in the face of great evil, you couldn't help liking him at least some of the time.

"Are my Little People near?" he asked. The Little People were short creatures who dressed in blue robes with hoods, never spoke, and ate anything that moved (including humans!). A handful of the mysterious beings almost always travelled with the Cirque Du Freak, and there were eight of them with us at that time.

"They're probably in their tent," I said. "I took them in some food an hour or so ago and I think they're still eating." One of my jobs was to hunt for the Little People. Evra used

16

to do it with me, until he grew up and demanded less messy chores. Nowadays I was helped by a couple of young humans, children of the Cirque helpers.

"Excellent," Mr Tiny beamed, and started away. "Oh," he paused, "one last thing. Tell Larten not to leave until I've had a word with him."

"I think we're in a hurry," I said. "We might not have time to—"

"Just tell him I want a word," Mr Tiny interrupted. "I'm sure he'll make time for *me*." With that, he tipped his glasses at us, waved farewell and moved on. I shared a worried look with Evra, found some matches and stuck them in my bag, then hurried off to wake Mr Crepsley.

CHAPTER TWO

MR CREPSLEY was snappish when I woke him — he hated rising before the sun went down — but stopped complaining when I explained why I'd disturbed his sleep. "Mr Tiny," he sighed, scratching the long scar which ran down the left side of his face. "I wonder what *he* wants?"

"I don't know," I answered, "but he said not to leave until he'd had a word with you." I lowered my voice and whispered, "We could sneak away without being seen if we hurried. Twilight's not far off. You could stand an hour or so of sunlight if we kept to the shadows, couldn't you?"

"I could," Mr Crepsley agreed, "were I given to fleeing like a dog with its tail between its legs. But I am not. I will face Desmond Tiny. Bring me my finest cloak — I like to look my best for visitors." That was as close to a joke as the vampire was likely to come — he didn't have much of a sense of humour.

An hour later, with the sun setting, we made our way to Mr Tall's caravan, where Mr Tiny was regaling the owner of the Cirque Du Freak with tales of what he'd seen in a recent earthquake.

"Ah, Larten!" Mr Tiny boomed. "Prompt as ever."

"Desmond," Mr Crepsley replied stiffly.

"Have a seat," Mr Tiny said.

"Thank you, but I will stand." Nobody liked sitting when Mr Tiny was around – in case they needed to make a quick getaway.

"I hear you're casting off for Vampire Mountain," Mr Tiny said.

"We leave presently," Mr Crepsley confirmed.

"This is the first Council you've been to in nearly fifty years, isn't it?"

"You are well informed," Mr Crepsley grunted.

"I keep an ear to the ground."

There was a knock at the door, and Mr Tall admitted two of the Little People. One walked with a slight limp. He'd been with the Cirque Du Freak almost as long as me. I called him Lefty, though that was only a nickname — none of the Little People had real names.

"Ready, boys?" Mr Tiny asked. The Little People nodded. "Excellent!" He smiled at Mr Crepsley. "The path to Vampire Mountain is as hazardous as ever, isn't it?"

"It is not easy," Mr Crepsley agreed cagily.

"Dangerous for a young snip of a thing like Master Shan, wouldn't you say?"

"Darren can look after himself," Mr Crepsley said, and I grinned proudly.

"I'm sure he can," Mr Tiny responded, "but it's unusual for one so young to make the journey, isn't it?"

"Yes," Mr Crepsley said curtly.

"That's why I'm sending these two along as guards." Mr Tiny waved a hand at the Little People.

"*Guards?*" Mr Crepsley barked. "We do not need any. I have made the trip many times. I can look after Darren myself."

"You can indeed," Mr Tiny cooed, "but a little help never went astray, did it?"

"They would get in the way," Mr Crepsley growled. "I do not want them."

"My Little People? Get in the way?" Mr Tiny sounded shocked. "They exist only to serve. They'll be like shepherds, watching over the two of you while you sleep."

"Nevertheless," Mr Crepsley insisted, "I do not want—"

"This is not an offer," Mr Tiny interrupted. Though he spoke softly, the menace in his voice was unmistakable. "They're going with you. End of story. They'll hunt for themselves and see to their own sleeping arrangements. All you have to do is make sure you don't 'lose' them in the snowy wastelands on the way."

"And when we get there?" Mr Crepsley snapped. "Do you expect me to take them inside? That is not permitted. The Princes will not stand for it."

"Yes they will," Mr Tiny disagreed. "Don't forget by

whose hands the Hall of Princes was built. Paris Skyle and the rest know on which side their blood is buttered. They won't object."

Mr Crepsley was furious – practically shaking with rage – but the anger seeped out of him as he stared into Mr Tiny's eyes and realized there was no arguing with the little man. In the end he nodded and averted his gaze, ashamed at having to bow to the demands of this interfering man.

"I knew you'd see it my way," Mr Tiny beamed, then turned his attention to me. "You've grown," he noted. "Inside, where it matters. Your battles with the Wolf Man and Murlough have toughened you."

"How do you know about that?" Mr Crepsley gasped. It was common knowledge that I'd had a run-in with the fearsome Wolf Man, but nobody was meant to know of our fight with Murlough. If the vampaneze ever found out, they'd hunt us to the ends of the Earth and kill us.

"I know all manner of things," Mr Tiny cackled. "This world holds no secrets from me. You've come a long way," he addressed me again, "but there's a long way yet to go. The path ahead isn't easy, and I'm not just talking about the route to Vampire Mountain. You must be strong, and keep faith in yourself. Never admit defeat, even when it seems inevitable."

I hadn't expected such a speech, and I listened in a daze, numbly wondering why he was sharing such words with me.

"That's all I have to say," he finished, standing and rubbing his heart-shaped watch. "Time's ticking. We've all got places to be and deadlines to meet. I'll be on my way.

Hibernius, Larten, Darren." He bowed briefly to each of us in turn. "We'll meet again, I'm sure." He turned, headed for the door, shared a look with the Little People, then let himself out. In the silence which followed, we stared at one another speechlessly, wondering what all that had been about.

*   *   *

Mr Crepsley wasn't happy but he couldn't postpone leaving — making it to the Council on time was more important than anything else, he told me. So, while the Little People stood waiting outside his van, I helped him pack.

"Those clothes will not do," he said, referring to my bright pirate costume which still fitted me after all the years of wear and tear. "Where we are going, you would stand out like a peacock. Here," he thrust a bundle at me. I unrolled it to reveal a light grey jumper and trousers, along with a woolly cap.

"How long have you been preparing for this?" I asked.

"Some time now," he admitted, pulling on clothes of a similar colour to mine, in place of his usual red attire.

"Couldn't you have told me about it earlier?"

"I could have," he replied in that infuriating way of his.

I slipped into my new clothes, then looked for socks and shoes. Mr Crepsley shook his head when he saw me searching. "No footwear," he said. "We go barefoot."

"Over snow and ice?" I yelped.

"Vampires have harder feet than humans," he said. "You will barely feel the cold, especially when we are walking."

"What about stones and thorns?" I grumbled.

"They will toughen your soles up even more," he grinned, then took off his slippers. "It is the same for all vampires. The way to Vampire Mountain is not just a journey — it is a test. Boots, jackets, ropes: such items are not permitted."

"Sounds crazy to me," I sighed, but took the rope, spare clothes and boots out of my bag. When we were ready, Mr Crepsley asked where Madam Octa was. "You're not bringing *her*, are you?" I grumbled — I knew who'd have to look after her if she came, and it wouldn't be Mr Crepsley!

"There is someone I wish to show her to," he said.

"Someone who eats spiders, I hope," I sniffed, but fetched her from behind his coffin, where I kept her between shows. She shuffled around while I lifted the cage and placed it in my bag, but settled down once she found herself in the dark again.

Then it was time to go. I'd said goodbye to Evra earlier — he was taking part in that night's show and had to prepare — and Mr Crepsley had bid farewell to Mr Tall. Nobody else would miss us.

"Ready?" Mr Crepsley asked.

"Ready," I sighed.

Leaving the safety of the van, we cleared the camp, let the two silent Little People fall into place behind us, and set off on what would prove to be a wild, peril-filled adventure into lands cold and foreign and steeped in blood.

CHAPTER THREE

I WOKE shortly before nightfall, stretched the stiffness out of my bones — what I wouldn't have given for a bed or hammock! — then left the confines of the cave to study the barren land we were journeying through. I didn't get much chance to study the countryside while we travelled at night. It was only during quiet moments such as these that I could pause and take everything in.

We hadn't hit the snowlands yet, but already we'd left most of civilization behind. Humans were few and far between out here where the ground was rocky and forbidding. Even animals were scarce, though some were strong enough to eke out a living — mostly deer, wolves and bears.

We'd been travelling for weeks, maybe a month — I lost track of time after the first handful of nights. Whenever I asked Mr Crepsley how many kilometres were left, he'd smile and say, "We are some way off yet."

My feet cut up badly when we reached the hard ground. Mr Crepsley applied the sap of herbal plants that he found along the way to my soles, carried me for a few nights while my skin grew back (I healed quicker than a human would), and I'd been OK since.

I said one night that it was a pity the Little People were with us, or he could have carried me on his back and flitted. (Vampires are able to run at an extra-fast speed, a magic kind of running, where they slip through space like eels through a net. They call it 'flitting'.) He said our slow pace had nothing to do with the Little People. "Flitting is not permitted on the way to Vampire Mountain," he explained. "The journey is a way of weeding out the weak from the strong. Vampires are ruthless in certain aspects. We do not believe in supporting those who are incapable of supporting themselves."

"That's not very nice," I observed. "What about somebody who's old or injured?"

Mr Crepsley shrugged. "Either they do not attempt the journey, or they die trying."

"That's stupid," I said. "If I could flit, I would. No one would know."

The vampire sighed. "You still do not understand our ways," he said. "There is no nobility in pulling the wool over the eyes of one's comrades. We are proud beings, Darren, who live by exacting codes. From our point of view it is better to lose one's life than lose one's pride."

Mr Crepsley often spoke about pride and nobility and being true to oneself. Vampires were a stern lot, he said, who lived as close to nature as they could. Their lives were rarely easy, and that was the way they liked it — "Life is a challenge," he once told me, "and only those who rise to the challenge truly know what it means to live."

I'd grown accustomed to the Little People, who trailed along behind us at night, silent, aloof, precise. They hunted for their own food during the day, while we slept. By the time we woke, they'd eaten and grabbed a few hours sleep and were ready to go. Their pace never changed. They marched behind us like robots, a few metres to the rear. I thought the one with the limp might struggle, but he'd yet to show signs that he was feeling any strain.

Mr Crepsley and me fed mostly on deer. Their blood was hot, salty and good. We had bottles of human blood to keep us going — vampires need regular doses of human blood to remain healthy, and though they prefer to drink directly from the vein, they can bottle blood and store it — but we drank from them sparingly, saving them in case of an emergency.

Mr Crepsley wouldn't let me light a fire in the open — it might attract attention — but it was allowed in way-stations. Way-stations were caves or underground caverns where bottles of human blood and coffins were stored. They were resting places, where vampires could hole up for a day or two. There weren't many of them — it took about a week to make it from one to another — and some had been taken over or destroyed by animals since Mr Crepsley had last come this way.

"How come they allow way-stations but no shoes or

ropes?" I asked one day as we warmed our feet by a fire and tucked into roast venison (we ate it raw most of the time).

"The way-stations were introduced after our war with the vampaneze seven hundred years ago," he said. "We lost many of our clan in the fight with the vampaneze, and humans killed even more of us. Our numbers were dangerously low. The way-stations were set up to make it easier to get to Vampire Mountain. Some vampires object to them and never use them, but most accept them."

"How many vampires *are* there?" I asked.

"Between two and three thousand," he answered. "Maybe a few hundred more or less."

I whistled. "That's a lot!"

"Three thousand is nothing," he snorted. "Think about the billions of humans."

"It's more than I expected," I said.

"Once, we numbered more than a hundred thousand," Mr Crepsley said. "And this was long ago, when that was a huge amount."

"What happened to them?" I asked.

"They were killed," he sighed. "Humans with stakes; disease; fights — vampires love to fight. In the centuries before the vampaneze broke away and provided us with a real foe, we fought amongst ourselves, many dying in duels. We came close to extinction, but kept our heads above water, just about."

"How many Vampire Generals are there?" I asked curiously.

"Between three and four hundred."

"And vampaneze?"

"Maybe two hundred and fifty, or three hundred — I cannot say for sure."

As I was remembering this old conversation, Mr Crepsley emerged from the cave behind me and watched the sun sinking. It looked the same colour as his cropped orange hair. The vampire was in great form — the nights were growing longer the closer to Vampire Mountain we got, so he was able to move about more than usual.

"It is always nice to see it go down," Mr Crepsley said, referring to the sun.

"I thought it was going to snow earlier," I said.

"There will be snow aplenty soon," he replied. "We should reach the snow drifts this week." He glanced down at my feet. "Will you be able to survive the harsh cold?"

"I've made it this far, haven't I?"

"This has been the easy part," he smiled, then clapped me on the back when he saw my dismayed frown. "Do not worry — you will be fine. But let me know if your feet cut up again. There are rare bushes which grow along the trail, the sap of which can seal the pores of one's skin."

The Little People came out of the cave, hoods covering their faces. The one without a limp was carrying a dead fox.

"Ready?" Mr Crepsley asked me.

I nodded and swung my rucksack on to my back. Looking ahead over the rocky terrain, I asked the usual question: "Is it much further?"

Mr Crepsley smiled, began walking, and said over his shoulder, "We are some way off yet."

Muttering darkly, I glanced back at the relatively comfortable cave, then faced front and followed the vampire. The Little People fell in behind, and after a while I heard brittle snapping sounds as they chewed on the bones of the fox.

* * *

Four nights later we ran into heavy snow. For a few nights we travelled over country that was one long unbroken blanket of freezing white, where nothing lived, but after that trees, plants and animals appeared again.

My feet felt like two blocks of ice as we trudged through the belt of snow, but I gritted my teeth and walked off the effects of the cold. The worst bit was getting up at dusk, having slept with my feet tucked beneath me all day. There was always an hour or two after waking when my toes tingled and I thought they'd drop off. Then the blood would circulate and everything would be fine — until the next night.

Sleeping outside was dreadfully uncomfortable. The two of us would lie down together in our clothes – which we hadn't changed out of since reaching the snow – and pull rough blankets we'd made from deer skins over our bodies. But even with our shared warmth it was freezing. Madam Octa had it easy — she slept safe and snug in her cage, only waking to feed every few days. I often wished I could change places with her.

If the Little People felt the cold, they gave no indication. They didn't bother with blankets, just lay down beneath a bush or against a rock when they wanted to sleep.

Almost three weeks after we'd last stopped at a way-station, we came to another. I couldn't wait to sit beside a fire and eat cooked meat again. I was even looking forward to sleeping in a coffin — anything was better than hard, cold earth! This way-station was a cave set low in a cliff, above a forest ring and a large stream. Mr Crepsley and me aimed directly for it – a strong moon in the clear night sky lit the way – while the Little People went off to hunt. The climb only took ten minutes. I pushed ahead of Mr Crepsley as we approached the mouth of the cave, eager to get the fire started, only for him to lay a hand on my shoulder. "Hold," he said softly.

"What?" I snapped. I was irritable after three weeks of sleeping rough.

"I smell blood," he said.

Pausing, I sniffed the air, and after a few seconds I got the whiff too, strong and sickly.

"Stay close behind me," Mr Crepsley whispered. "Be prepared to run the instant I give the order." I nodded obediently, then trailed after him as he crept to the opening and slid inside.

The cave was dark, especially after the brightness of the moonlit night, and we entered slowly, giving our eyes time to adjust. It was a deep cave, turning off to the left and going back twenty or more metres. Three coffins had been placed on stands in the middle, but one was lying on the floor, its lid hanging off, and another had been smashed to pieces against the wall to our right.

The wall and floor around the shattered coffin were dark with blood. It wasn't fresh, but by its smell it wasn't more than a couple of nights old. Having checked the rest of the cave — to ensure we were alone — Mr Crepsley edged over to the blood and crouched to examine it, dipping a finger into the dried pool, then tasting it.

"*Well?*" I hissed, as he stood, rubbing his finger and thumb together.

"It is the blood of a vampire," he said quietly.

My insides tightened —— I'd been hoping it was the blood of a wild animal. "What do you think—" I started to ask, when there was a sudden rushing sound behind me. A strong arm wrapped around my middle, a thick hand clutched my throat, and — as Mr Crepsley shot forward to help — my attacker grunted triumphantly: "*Hah!*"

CHAPTER FOUR

As I stiffened helplessly, my life in the hands of whoever had hold of me, Mr Crepsley leapt, the fingers of his right hand outstretched like a blade. He sliced the hand over the top of my head. My assailant released me and ducked in the same movement, dropping heavily to the floor as Mr Crepsley sailed by. As the vampire rolled to his feet and spun to strike a second blow, the man who'd snatched me roared, "Stop, Larten! It's me — Gavner!"

Mr Crepsley paused and I got to my feet, coughing from the fright, but no longer afraid. Turning, I saw a burly man with a scarred, patchy face and dark rims around both his eyes. He was dressed in similar clothes to ours, with a cap pulled down over his ears. I recognized him instantly — Gavner Purl, a Vampire General. I'd met him years ago, shortly before my run-in with Murlough.

"You bloody fool, Gavner!" Mr Crepsley shouted. "I

would have killed you if I had connected! Why did you sneak up on us?"

"I wanted to surprise you," Gavner said. "I've been shadowing you most of the night, and this seemed like the perfect time to close in. I didn't expect to almost lose my head in the process," he grumbled.

"You should have been paying more attention to your surroundings and less to Darren and I," Mr Crepsley said, pointing towards the blood-stained wall and floor.

"By the blood of the vampaneze!" Gavner hissed.

"Actually, it is the blood of a vampire," Mr Crepsley corrected him dryly.

"Any idea whose?" Gavner asked, hurrying over to test the blood.

"None," Mr Crepsley said.

Gavner prowled around the confines of the cave, studying the blood and broken coffin, searching for further clues. Finding none, he returned to where we were standing and scratched his chin thoughtfully. "He was probably attacked by a wild animal," he mused aloud. "A bear – maybe more than one – caught him during the day, while he was sleeping."

"I am not so sure of that," Mr Crepsley disagreed. "A bear would have caused great damage to the cave and its contents, but only the coffins have been disturbed."

Gavner ran his eyes over the cave again, noting the tidy state of the rest of it, and nodded. "What do you think happened?" he asked.

"A fight," Mr Crepsley suggested. "Between two vampires, or between the dead vampire and somebody else."

"Who'd be out here in the middle of nowhere?" I asked.

Mr Crepsley and Gavner exchanged a troubled look. "Vampire hunters, perhaps," Gavner muttered.

My breath caught in my throat — I'd grown so used to the vampire way of life, I'd all but forgotten that there were people in the world who thought we were monsters and made it their business to hunt us down and kill us.

"Or maybe humans who chanced upon him by accident and panicked," Mr Crepsley said. "It has been a long time since vampire hunters aggressively trailed us. This may have been a case of mere misfortune."

"Either way," Gavner said, "let's not hang around and wait for it to happen again. I was looking forward to resting, but now I think it's best we don't cage ourselves in."

"Agreed," Mr Crepsley replied, and after one last sweep of the cave, we retreated, senses alert to the slightest hint of an attack.

*   *   *

We made our base for the night in the middle of a ring of thick trees, and lit a rare fire — all of us felt chilled to the bone after our experience in the cave. While we were discussing the dead vampire and whether we should search the surrounding area for his body, the Little People returned, carrying a young deer they'd captured. They stared suspiciously at Gavner, who stared just as suspiciously back.

"What are *they* doing with you?" he hissed.

"Mr Tiny insisted I bring them," Mr Crepsley said, then raised a quieting hand as Gavner swivelled to ask more questions. "Later," he promised. "Let us eat first and dwell upon the death of our comrade."

The trees sheltered us from the rising sun, so we sat up long after dawn, discussing the dead vampire. Since there wasn't anything we could do about him – the vampires decided against a search, on the grounds that it would slow us down – talk eventually turned to other matters. Gavner asked about the Little People again, and Mr Crepsley told him how Mr Tiny had appeared and sent them with us. Then he asked Gavner why he'd been trailing us.

"I knew you'd be presenting Darren to the Princes," Gavner said, "so I located your mental pattern and traced you through it." (Vampires are able to bond mentally with each other.) "I had to cut up from a hundred miles south, but I hate travelling alone — it's boring having no one to chat with."

As we talked, I noticed a couple of toes were missing from Gavner's left foot and asked about them. "Frostbite," he answered cheerfully, wriggling the three remaining toes. "I broke my leg coming here a couple of Councils back. Had to crawl for five nights to reach a way-station. It was only by the luck of the vampires that I didn't lose more than a few toes."

The vampires talked a lot about the past, old friends and previous Councils. I thought they'd mention Murlough – Gavner had alerted Mr Crepsley to the mad vampaneze's whereabouts – but they didn't, not even in passing.

"How have *you* been?" Gavner asked me.

"Fine," I said.

"Life with this sour buzzard hasn't got you down?"

"I've coped so far," I smiled.

"Any intentions of topping up?" he asked.

"Pardon?"

He raised his fingers so I could see the ten scars on the tips, the usual sign of a vampire. "Do you plan to become a full-vampire?"

"No," I said quickly, then looked sideways at Mr Crepsley. "I *don't* have any such plans, do I?" I asked suspiciously.

"No," Mr Crepsley smiled. "Not until you have come of human age. If we made a full-vampire of you now, it would be sixty or seventy years before you were fully grown."

"I bet it's horrible ageing so slowly when you're a kid," Gavner noted.

"It is," I sighed.

"Things will improve with time," Mr Crepsley said.

"Sure," I said sarcastically, "when I'm all grown up — thirty years from now!" I rose and shook my head, disgusted. I often got downhearted when my thoughts turned to the decades I'd have to spend on the road to maturity.

"Where are you going?" Mr Crepsley asked as I headed towards the trees.

"To the stream," I said, "to fill our canteens."

"Maybe one of us should go with you," Gavner said.

"Darren is not a child," Mr Crepsley answered before I could. "He will be fine."

I hid a grin – I enjoyed the rare occasions when the vampire passed a compliment about me – and continued down to the stream. The chilly water was fast-flowing and gurgled loudly as I filled the canteens, splashing around the rims and my fingers. If I'd been human I might have got frostbite, but vampires are a lot sturdier.

As I was corking the second canteen, a tiny cloud of steamy breath drifted across from the other side of the stream. I glanced up, surprised that a wild animal had ventured this close, and found myself staring into the flaming eyes of a fierce, hungry-looking, sharp-fanged wolf.

CHAPTER FIVE

THE WOLF studied me silently, its nose crinkling over its jagged canines as it sniffed my scent. I gently laid my canteen aside, not sure what to do. If I called for help, the wolf might panic and flee — then again, it might attack. If I stayed as I was, it might lose interest and slink away — or it might take it as a sign of weakness and move in for the kill.

I was desperately trying to decide when the wolf tensed its hind legs, lowered its head and pounced, crossing the stream with one mighty bound. It crashed into my chest, knocking me to the ground. I tried scrambling away but the wolf had perched on top of me and was too heavy to throw off. My hands searched frantically for a rock or stick, something to beat the animal with, but there was nothing to grab except snow.

The wolf was a terrifying sight up close, with its dark grey face and slanting yellow eyes, its black muzzle and bared white teeth, some five or six centimetres long. Its tongue lolled out the side of its mouth and it was panting slowly. Its breath stank of blood and raw animal flesh.

I knew nothing about wolves – except vampires couldn't drink from them – so I didn't know how to react: attack its face or go for its body? Lie still and hope it went away, or shout and maybe scare it off? While my brain was spinning, the wolf lowered its head, extended its long wet tongue, and ...*licked me!*

I was so stunned, I just lay there, staring up at the jaws of the fearsome animal. The wolf licked me again, then got off, faced the stream, went down on its paws and lapped at the water. I lay where I was a few moments more, then pulled myself up and sat watching it drink, noting that it was a male.

When the wolf had drunk his fill, he stood, lifted his head and howled. From the trees on the opposite side of the stream, three more wolves emerged and crept down to the bank, where they drank. Two were females and one was a young cub, darker and smaller than the others.

The male watched the others drinking, then sat beside me. He snuggled up to me like a dog and, before I knew what I was doing, I'd reached around and was tickling him behind his ear. The wolf whined pleasantly and cocked his head so I could scratch behind the other ear.

One of the she-wolves finished drinking and jumped the stream. She sniffed my feet, then sat on the other side of me and offered her head to be scratched. The male growled at her jealously but she took no notice.

The other two weren't long joining the couple on my side of the stream. The female was shyer than her mates and hovered several metres away. The cub had no such fears and crawled over my legs and belly, sniffing like a hound-dog. He cocked a leg to mark my left thigh, but before he could, the male wolf snapped at him and sent him tumbling. He barked angrily, then slunk back and climbed over me again. This time he didn't try to mark his territory — thankfully!

I sat there for ages, playing with the cub and tickling the bigger pair of wolves. The male rolled over on to his back, so that I could rub his belly. His hair was lighter underneath, except for a long streak of black hair which ran part-way up his middle. 'Streak' seemed like a good name for a wolf, so that's what I called him.

I wanted to see if they knew any tricks, so I found a stick and threw it. "Fetch, Streak, fetch!" I shouted, but he didn't budge. I tried getting him to sit to attention. "Sit, Streak!" I ordered. He stared at me. "Sit — like this." I squatted on my haunches. Streak moved back a little, as though he thought I might be mad. The cub was delighted and jumped on me. I laughed and stopped trying to teach them tricks.

After that I headed back to camp to tell the vampires about my new friends. The wolves followed, though only Streak walked by my side — the others trailed behind.

Mr Crepsley and Gavner were asleep when I got back, tucked beneath thick deer blankets. Gavner was snoring loudly. With only their heads showing, they looked like the ugliest pair of babies in the world! I wished I had a camera capable of photographing vampires, so that I could snap them.

I was about to join them beneath the blankets when I had an idea. The wolves had stopped at the trees. I coaxed them in. Streak came first and examined the copse, making sure it was safe. When he was satisfied, he growled lightly and the other wolves entered, keeping away from the sleeping vampires.

I lay down on the far side of the fire and held a blanket up, inviting the wolves to lie down with me. They wouldn't go beneath the blanket — the cub tried, but its mother jerked it back by the scruff of its neck — but once I lay down and covered myself with it, they crept up and lay on top, even the shy she-wolf. They were heavy, and the scent of their hairy bodies was overbearing, but the warmth of the wolves was heavenly, and despite the fact that I was resting so close to the cave where a vampire had been killed recently, I slept in complete comfort.

*　*　*

I was awakened by angry growls. Jolting upright, I found the three adult wolves spread in a semicircle in front of my bed, the male in the middle. The cub was cowering behind me. Ahead stood the Little People. Their grey hands were flexing by their sides and they were moving in on the wolves.

"Stop!" I roared, leaping to my feet. On the other side of the fire — which had died out while I was sleeping — Mr Crepsley and Gavner snapped awake and rolled out from under their blankets. I jumped in front of Streak and snarled at the Little People. They stared at me from beneath their blue hoods. I glimpsed the large green eyes of the one closest me.

"What's happening?" Gavner shouted, blinking rapidly.

The nearest Little Person ignored Gavner, pointed at the wolves, then at his belly, and rubbed it. That was the sign that he was hungry. I shook my head. "Not the wolves," I told him. "They're my friends." He made the rubbing motion again. "No!" I shouted.

The Little Person began to advance, but the one behind him – Lefty – reached out and touched his arm. The Little Person locked gazes with Lefty, stood still a moment, then shuffled away to where he'd left the rats they'd caught while hunting. Lefty lingered a moment, his hidden green eyes on mine, before joining his brother (I always thought of them as brothers).

"I see you have met some of our cousins," Mr Crepsley said, stepping slowly over the remains of the fire, holding his hands palms-up so the wolves wouldn't be alarmed. They growled at him, but once they caught his scent they relaxed and sat, though they kept a wary eye on the munching Little People.

"*Cousins?*" I asked.

"Wolves and vampires are related," he explained. "Legends claim that once we were the same, just as man and ape were originally one. Some of us learned to walk on two legs and became vampires — the others remained wolves."

"Is that true?" I asked.

Mr Crepsley shrugged. "Where legends are concerned, who knows?" He crouched in front of Streak and studied him silently. Streak sat up straight and ruffled his head to make his ears and mane erect. "A fine specimen," Mr Crepsley said, stroking the wolf's long snout. "A born leader."

"I call him Streak, because he's got a streak of black hair on his belly," I said.

"Wolves have no need of names," the vampire informed me. "They are not dogs."

"Don't be a spoilsport," Gavner said, stepping up beside his friend. "Let him give them names if he wants. It can't do any harm."

"I suppose not," Mr Crepsley agreed. He held out a hand to the she-wolves and they stepped forward to lick his palm, including the shy one. "I always had a way with wolves," he said, unable to keep the pride out of his voice.

"How come they're so friendly?" I asked. "I thought wolves shied away from people."

"From humans," Mr Crepsley said. "Vampires are different. Our scent is similar to their own. They recognize us as kindred spirits. Not all wolves are amiable – these must have had dealings with our kind before – but none would ever attack a vampire, not unless they were starving."

"Did you see any more of them?" Gavner asked. I shook my head. "Then they're probably journeying towards Vampire Mountain to join up with other packs."

"Why would they be going to Vampire Mountain?" I asked.

"Wolves come whenever there's a Council," he explained. "They know from experience that there will be plenty of scraps for them to feed on. The guardians of Vampire Mountain spend years stocking up for Councils. There's always food left over, which they dump outside for the creatures of the wild to dispose of."

"It's a long way to go for a few scraps," I commented.

"They go for more than food," Mr Crepsley said. "They gather for company, to salute old friends, find new mates and share memories."

"Wolves can communicate?" I asked.

"They are able to transmit simple thoughts to one another. They do not actually talk – wolves have no words – but can share pictures and pass on maps of where they have been, letting others know where hunting is plentiful or scarce."

"Talking of which, we'd better make *ourselves* scarce," Gavner said. "The sun's sinking and it's time we got a move on. You chose a long, roundabout route to come by, Larten, and if we don't pick up the pace, we'll arrive late for Council."

"There are other paths?" I asked.

"Of course," he said. "There are dozens of ways. That's why – except for the remains of the dead one – we haven't run into other vampires — each comes by a different route."

We rolled up our blankets and departed, Mr Crepsley and Gavner keeping a close eye on the trail, scouring it for signs of whoever had killed the vampire in the cave. The wolves followed us through the trees and ran beside us for a couple of hours, keeping clear of the Little People, before vanishing ahead of us into the night.

"Where are they going?" I asked.

"To hunt," Mr Crepsley replied.

"Will they come back?"

"It would not surprise me," he said, and, come dawn, as we were making camp, the four wolves re-appeared like ghosts out of the snow and made their beds beside and on top of us. For the second day running, I slept soundly, disturbed only by the cold nose of the cub when he snuck in under the blanket during the middle of the day to cuddle up beside me.

CHAPTER SIX

WE PROCEEDED with caution for the first few nights after finding the blood-spattered cave. But when we encountered no further signs of the vampire killer, we put our concerns on hold and enjoyed the rough pleasures of the trail as best we could.

Running with wolves was fascinating. I learnt lots by watching them and asking questions of Mr Crepsley, who fancied himself something of a wolf expert.

Wolves aren't fast, but they're tireless, sometimes roaming forty or fifty kilometres a day. They usually pick on small animals when hunting, but occasionally go after larger victims, working as a team. Their senses – sight, hearing, smell – are strong. Each pack has a leader, and they share food equally. They're great climbers, able to survive any sort of conditions.

We hunted with them often. It was exhilarating to race alongside them on bright star-speckled nights, over the gleaming snow — chasing a deer or fox and sharing the hot, bloody kill. Time passed quicker with the wolves around, and the kilometres slipped by almost unnoticed.

*　*　*

One cold, clear night, we came upon a thick briar patch which covered the floor of a valley sheltered between two towering mountains. The thorns were extra thick and sharp, capable of pricking the skin of even a full-vampire. We paused at the mouth of the valley while Mr Crepsley and Gavner decided how to proceed.

"We could climb the side of one of the mountains," Mr Crepsley mused, "but Darren is not as strong a climber as us — he could be damaged if he slipped."

"How about going around?" Gavner suggested.

"It would take too long."

"Could we dig a way under?" I asked.

"Again," Mr Crepsley said, "it would take too long. We will just have to pick our way through as carefully as we can."

He removed his jumper and so did Gavner.

"What are you getting undressed for?" I asked.

"Our clothes would protect us a bit," Gavner explained, "but we'd come out the other end in tattered rags. Best to keep them intact."

When Gavner took off his trousers, we saw he was wearing a pair of yellow boxer shorts with pink elephants stitched into them. Mr Crepsley stared at the shorts incredulously. "They were a present," Gavner mumbled, blushing furiously.

"From a human female you were romantically involved with, I presume," Mr Crepsley said, the corners of his normally stern mouth twitching upwards, threatening to split into a rare unrestrained smile.

"She was a lovely woman," Gavner sighed, tracing the outline of one of the elephants. "She just had very poor taste in underwear..."

"And in boyfriends," I added impishly. Mr Crepsley burst into laughter at that and doubled over, tears streaming down his face. I'd never seen the vampire laugh so much – I'd never guessed he could! Even Gavner looked surprised.

It took Mr Crepsley a long time to recover from his laughing fit. When he'd wiped the tears away and was back to his normal sombre self, he apologized (as though laughing were a crime). He then rubbed some foul-smelling lotion into my skin, which sealed the pores, making it harder to cut. Without wasting any more time, we advanced. The going was slow and painful. No matter how careful I was, every few metres I'd step on a thorn or scratch myself. I protected my face as best I could, but by the time we were halfway into the valley, my cheeks were specked with shallow red rivulets.

The Little People hadn't removed their blue robes, even though the cloth was being cut to ribbons. After a while, Mr Crepsley told them to walk in front, so they endured the worst of the thorns while beating a path for the rest of us. I almost felt sorry for the silent, uncomplaining pair.

The wolves had the easiest time. They were built for terrain like this, and slinked through the briars swiftly. But they weren't happy. They'd been acting strangely all night, creeping along beside us, low of spirit, sniffing the air suspiciously. We could sense their anxiety, but didn't know what was causing it.

I was watching my feet, stepping carefully over a row of glinting thorns, when I ran into Mr Crepsley, who'd come to a sudden stop. "What's up?" I asked, peering over his shoulder.

"Gavner!" he snapped, ignoring my question.

Gavner shuffled past me, breathing heavily (we often teased him about his heavy breathing). I heard him utter a choked cry as he reached Mr Crepsley.

"What is it?" I asked. "Let me see." The vampires parted and I saw a tiny piece of cloth snagged on a briar bush. A few drops of dried blood had stained the tips of the thorns.

"What's the big deal?" I asked.

The vampires didn't answer immediately — they were gazing around worriedly, much the same way that the wolves were.

"Can't you smell it?" Gavner finally replied quietly.

"What?"

"The blood."

I sniffed the air. There was only the faintest of scents because the blood was dry. "What about it?" I asked.

"Think back six years," Mr Crepsley said. He picked the cloth off the briar – the wolves were growling loudly now – and thrust it under my nostrils. "Breathe deeply. Ring any bells?"

It didn't straightaway – my senses weren't as sharp as a full-vampire's – but then I recalled that long-ago night in

Debbie Hemlock's bedroom, and the smell of the insane Murlough's blood as he lay dying on the floor. My face turned white as I realized — it was the blood of a *vampaneze*!

CHAPTER SEVEN

WE MADE quick time through the remainder of the briar patch, taking no notice of the cutting thorns. On the far side we stopped to get dressed, then hurried on without pause. There was a way-station nearby that Mr Crepsley was determined to reach before the break of day. The journey would normally have taken several hours but we made it in two. Once inside and secure, the vampires fell into a heated discussion. They'd never encountered evidence of vampaneze activity in this part of the world before — there was a treaty between the two clans, preventing such acts of trespass.

"Maybe it's a mad wanderer," Gavner suggested.

"Even the most insane vampaneze knows better than to come here," Mr Crepsley disagreed.

"What other explanation could there be?" Gavner asked.

Mr Crepsley considered the problem. "He could be a spy."

"You think the vampaneze would risk war?" Gavner sounded dubious. "What could they learn that would justify such a gamble?"

"Maybe it's *us* they're after," I said quietly. I didn't want to interrupt but felt I had to.

"What do you mean?" Gavner asked.

"Maybe they found out about Murlough."

Gavner's face paled and Mr Crepsley's eyes narrowed. "How could they have?" he snapped.

"Mr Tiny knew," I reminded him.

"Mr Tiny knows about Murlough?" Gavner hissed.

Mr Crepsley nodded slowly. "But even if he had told the vampaneze, how would they know we were coming *this* way? We could have chosen any number of paths. They could not have second-guessed us."

"Perhaps they're covering all the paths," Gavner said.

"No," Mr Crepsley said confidently. "It is too far-fetched. Whatever the vampaneze's reason for being here, I am sure it has nothing to do with *us*."

"I hope you're right," Gavner grumbled, unconvinced.

We discussed it some more, including the question of whether the vampaneze had killed the vampire in the previous way-station, then grabbed a few hours of shut-eye, taking turns to remain on watch. I barely slept as I was worrying about being attacked by the purple-faced killers.

When night came, Mr Crepsley said we should progress no further until we were sure the way was safe. "We cannot risk running into a pack of vampaneze," he said. "We will scout the area, make sure we are not in danger, then carry on as before."

"Have we time to go scouting?" Gavner asked.

"We must make time," Mr Crepsley insisted. "Better to waste a few nights than run into a trap."

I stayed in the cave while they went scouting. I didn't want to – I kept thinking about what had happened to that other vampire – but they said I'd be in the way if I came — a vampaneze would hear me coming a hundred metres away.

The Little People, she-wolves and cub stayed with me. Streak went with the vampires — the wolves had sensed the vampaneze presence before we did, so it would be helpful for them to have one along.

It was lonely without the vampires and Streak. The Little People were aloof as always – they spent a lot of the day stitching their blue robes back into shape – and the she-wolves lay out and snoozed. Only the cub provided me with company. We spent hours playing together, in the cave and among the trees of a nearby small forest. I'd called the cub Rudi, after Rudolf the red-nosed reindeer, because of his fondness for rubbing his cold nose into my back while I was asleep.

I caught a couple of squirrels in the forest and cooked them, so they were ready in the morning when the vampires returned. I served hot berries and roots with them — Mr Crepsley had taught me which wild foods were safe to eat. Gavner thanked me for the food but Mr Crepsley was distant and didn't say much. They'd discovered no further trace of the vampaneze, and that worried them — a mad vampaneze couldn't have covered his tracks so expertly. That meant we were dealing with one – or more – in full control of his senses.

Gavner wanted to flit ahead to consult with the other vampires, but Mr Crepsley wouldn't let him — the laws against flitting on the way to Vampire Mountain were more important than our safety, he insisted.

It was strange how Gavner went along with most of what Mr Crepsley said. As a General, he could have ordered us to do whatever he pleased. But I'd never seen him pull rank on Mr Crepsley. Maybe it was because Mr Crepsley had once been a General of high ranking. He'd been on the verge of becoming a Vampire Prince when he quit. Perhaps Gavner still considered Mr Crepsley his superior.

After a full day's sleep, the vampires set off to scout the land ahead again. If the way was clear, we'd start back on the trail to Vampire Mountain the next night.

I ate a simple breakfast, then Rudi and me headed down to the forest to play. Rudi loved being away from the adult wolves. He was able to explore freely, with no one to snap at him or cuff him round the head if he misbehaved. He tried climbing trees but was too short for most. Finally he found one with low-hanging branches and he clambered halfway up. Once there, he looked down and whimpered.

"Come on," I laughed. "You're not *that* high up. There's no need to be afraid." He ignored me and went on whimpering. Then he bared his fangs and growled.

I stepped closer, puzzled by his behaviour. "What's wrong?" I asked. "Are you stuck? Do you want help?" The cub yapped. He sounded genuinely frightened. "OK, Rudi," I said, "I'm coming up to—"

I was silenced by a bone-shattering roar. Turning, I saw a huge dark bear lurching over the top of a snow-drift. It landed heavily, shook its snout, snarled, fixed its gaze upon me — then lunged, teeth flashing, claws exposed, intent on cutting me down!

CHAPTER EIGHT

THE BEAR would have killed me, if not for Rudi. The cub leapt from the tree, landing on top of the bear's head, momentarily blinding it. The bear roared and swiped at the cub, who ducked and bit one of its ears. The bear roared again and shook its head viciously from side to side. Rudi held on for a couple of seconds, before he was sent flying into a thicket.

The bear resumed its attack on me, but in the time the cub had bought, I'd ducked round the tree and was racing for the cave as fast as I could. The bear lurched after me, realized I was too far ahead, bellowed angrily, turned and went looking for Rudi.

I stopped when I heard frightened yapping. Glancing over my shoulder, I saw that the cub had made it back up the tree, the bark of which the bear was now ripping to pieces with its claws. Rudi was in no immediate danger, but sooner or later he'd slip or the bear would shake him down, and that would be the end of him.

I paused no more than a second, then turned, picked up a rock and the thickest stick I could find, and sped back to try and save Rudi.

The bear let go of the tree when it saw me coming, dropped to its haunches and met my challenge. It was a huge beast, maybe a metre and a half high; it had black fur, a white quarter-moon mark across its chest and a whitish face. Foam flecked its jaws and its eyes were wild, as though touched by rabid madness.

I stopped in front of the bear and whacked the ground with my stick. "Come on, Grizzly," I growled. It snarled and tossed its head. I glanced up at Rudi, hoping he'd have enough sense to slink down the tree and retreat to the cave, but he stayed where he was, petrified, unable to let go.

The bear swiped at me but I ducked out of the way of its massive paw. Rearing up on its hind legs, it collapsed flat upon me, trying to crush me with the weight of its body. I avoided it again, but it was a closer call this time.

I was prodding at the bear's face with the end of the stick, aiming for its eyes, when the she-wolves rushed on to the scene — they must have heard Rudi's yapping. The bear howled as one of the wolves leapt and bit deep into its shoulder, while the other attached herself to its legs, tearing at them with her teeth and claws. It shook off the uppermost wolf and bent to deal with the lower one, which was when I darted in with my stick and jabbed at its left ear.

I must have hurt it, because it lost interest in the wolves and hurled itself at me. I ducked out of the way of its body but one of its burly forelegs connected with the side of my head and knocked me to the ground.

The bear rolled to its feet and made for me, scattering the wolves with swipes of its claws. I scrabbled backwards, but not fast enough. Suddenly the bear was above me, standing erect, bellowing triumphantly — it had me exactly where it wanted! I slammed the stick against its stomach, then the rock, but it took no notice of such feeble blows. Leering, it started to fall...

...which was when the Little People barrelled into its back and knocked it off balance. Their timing couldn't have been any sweeter.

The bear must have thought the entire world was conspiring against it. Every time it had me in its sights, something new got in the way. Roaring loudly at the Little People, it threw itself at them madly. The one with the limp stepped out of its way but the other got trapped beneath it.

The Little Person raised his short arms, jammed them against the bear's torso and tried to shove it aside. The Little Person was strong, but he stood no chance against such a massive foe, and the bear came crashing down and flattened him. There was a horrible crunching sound and when the bear got to its feet, I saw the Little Person lying in pieces, broken bones jutting out of his body at crooked red angles.

The bear lifted its head and bellowed at the sky, then fixed its eyes on me and leered hungrily. Dropping to all fours, it advanced. The wolves leapt at it but it shook them loose as though they were fleas. I was still dazed from the blow, not able to get to my feet. I began crawling through the snow.

As the bear closed in for the kill, the second Little Person – the one I called Lefty – stepped in front of it, caught it by its ears, and *head-butted* it! It was the craziest thing I'd ever seen, but it did a remarkably effective job. The bear grunted and blinked dumbly. Lefty head-butted it again and was rearing his head back for a third blow when the bear struck at him with its right paw, like a boxer.

It hit Lefty in the chest and knocked him down. His hood had fallen off during the struggle and I could see his grey stitched-together face and round green eyes. There was a mask over his mouth, like the sort doctors wear during surgery. He stared up at the bear, unafraid, waiting for the killer blow.

"No!" I screamed. Stumbling to my knees, I threw a punch at the bear. It snarled at me. I punched it again, then grabbed a handful of snow and threw it into the beast's eyes.

While the bear cleared its vision, I looked for a weapon. I was desperate — anything was better than my bare hands. At first I saw nothing I could use, but then my eyes fell on the bones sticking out of the dead Little Person's body. Acting on instinct, I rolled across to where the Little Person lay, took hold of one of the longer bones, and pulled. It was covered in blood and my fingers slipped off. Trying again, I got a firmer hold and worked it from side to side. After a few tugs it snapped near the base and suddenly I wasn't defenceless any longer.

The bear had regained its sight and was pounding towards me. Lefty was still on the ground. The wolves were barking furiously, unable to do anything to deter the charging bear. The cub yapped from its perch in the tree.

I was on my own. Me against the bear. No one could help me now.

Spinning, using all my extra-sharp vampire abilities, I rolled beneath the clutching claws of the bear, jumped to my feet, picked my spot, and rammed the tip of the bone deep into the bear's unprotected neck.

The bear came to a halt. Its eyes bulged. Its forelegs dropped by its sides. For a moment it stood, gasping painfully, the bone sticking out of its neck. Then it crashed to the ground, shook horribly for a few seconds — and died.

I fell on top of the dead bear and lay there. I was shaking and crying, more from fright than pain. I'd looked death in the eye before, but never had I been involved in a fight as savage as this.

Eventually, one of the she-wolves — the normally shy one — cuddled up to me and licked around my face, making sure I was all right. I patted her to show I was OK, and buried my face in her neck, drying my tears on her hair. When I felt able, I stood and gazed at the area around me.

The other she-wolf was by the tree, coaxing Rudi down — the cub was even more shaken than me. The dead Little Person lay not far away, his blood seeping into the snow, turning it crimson. Lefty was sitting up, checking himself for injuries.

I made my way over to Lefty to thank him for saving my life. He was incredibly ugly without his hood: he had grey skin, and his face was a mass of scars and stitches. He had no ears or nose that I could see, and his round green eyes were set near the top of his head, not in the middle of his face like they are with most people. He was completely hairless.

Any other time I might have been frightened, but this creature had risked his life to save mine, and all I felt was gratitude. "Are you OK, Lefty?" I asked. He looked up and nodded. "That was a close call," I half-laughed. Again he nodded. "Thanks for coming to my rescue. I'd have been a goner if you hadn't stepped in." I sank to the ground beside him and gazed at the bear, then at the dead Little Person. "Sorry about your partner, Lefty," I said softly. "Shall we bury him?"

The Little Person shook his large head, started to rise, then paused. He stared into my eyes and I stared back questioningly. By the expression on his face, I almost expected him to speak.

Reaching up, Lefty gently tugged down the mask which covered the lower half of his face. He had a wide mouth full of sharp, yellow teeth. He stuck out his tongue – which was a strange grey colour, like his skin – and licked his lips. When they were wet, he flexed and stretched them a few times, then did the one thing I was sure the Little People could never do. In a creaky, slow, mechanical tone — he *spoke*.

"Name ... not Lefty. Name ... Harkat ... Harkat Mulds." And his lips spread into a jagged gash which was as close to a smile as he could come.

CHAPTER NINE

MR CREPSLEY, Gavner and Streak had been checking a maze of cliff-top tunnels when they heard faint echoes of the fight. They raced back, arriving fifteen minutes or so after I'd killed the bear. They were stunned when I explained what had happened and told them about Harkat Mulds. The Little Person had replaced his robes and hood, and when they asked him if it was true that he could talk, there was a long moment of silence during which I thought he wasn't going to say anything. Then he nodded and croaked, "Yes."

Gavner actually jumped back a few steps when he heard the Little Person speak. Mr Crepsley shook his head, amazed. "We will discuss this later," he said. "First there is the bear to deal with." He crouched beside the dead bear and studied it from top to bottom. "Describe how it attacked you," he said, and I told of the bear's sudden appearance and savage attack. "It makes no sense," Mr Crepsley frowned. "Bears do not behave in such a fashion unless agitated or starving. It was not hunger which motivated it — look at its round stomach — and if you did nothing to upset it..."

"It was foaming at the mouth," I said. "I think it had rabies."

"We shall soon see." The vampire used his sharp nails to cut open the bear's belly. He stuck his nose close to the cut and sniffed the blood that was oozing out. After a few seconds he pulled a face and stood up.

"Well?" Gavner asked.

"The bear *was* mad," Mr Crepsley said, "but not with rabies — it had consumed the blood of a vampaneze!"

"How?" I gasped.

"I am not sure," Mr Crepsley replied, then glanced up at the sky. "We have time before dawn. We will trace this bear's trail and perhaps learn more along the way."

"What about the dead Little Person?" Gavner asked. "Should we bury him?"

"Do you want to bury him ... *Harkat*?" Mr Crepsley asked, echoing my earlier question.

Harkat Mulds shook his head. "Not really."

"Then leave him," the vampire snapped. "Scavengers and birds will pick his bones clean. We do not have time to waste."

The path of the bear was easy to follow — even an untrained tracker like me could have traced it by the deep footprints and broken twigs.

Night was drawing to a close as we pulled up at a small mound of stones and found what had driven the bear mad.

Half-buried beneath the stones was a purple body with a red head of hair — a vampaneze!

"By the way his skull is crushed, he must have died in a fall," Mr Crepsley said, examining the dead man. "The bear found him after he was buried and dug him up. See the chunks that have been bitten out of him?" He pointed to the gaping holes in the vampaneze's belly. "That is what drove it mad — the blood of vampaneze and vampires is poisonous. Had you not killed it, it would have died in another night or two anyway."

"So that's where our mystery vampaneze was," Gavner grunted. "No wonder we couldn't find him."

"We don't have to worry about him any more, do we?" I sighed happily.

"Quite the contrary," Mr Crepsley snapped. "We have more reason to worry now than before."

"Why?" I asked. "He's dead, isn't he?"

"He is," Mr Crepsley agreed, then pointed to the stones which had been laid over the vampaneze. "*But who buried him?*"

* * *

We made camp at the base of a cliff, using branches and leaves to create a shelter where the vampires could sleep, safe from the sun. Once they were inside, Harkat and me sat by the entrance and the Little Person told his incredible story. The wolves had gone off hunting, except for Rudi, who curled up in my lap and dozed.

"My memories ... are not ... complete," said Harkat.

Speaking wasn't easy for him and he had to pause for breath often. "Much is ... clouded. I will tell ... you what ... I remember. First — I am a ... ghost."

Our jaws dropped.

"A ghost!" Mr Crepsley shouted. "Absurd!"

"Absolutely," Gavner agreed with a grin. "Vampires don't believe in crazy things like ghosts, do we, Larten?"

Before Mr Crepsley could reply, Harkat corrected himself. "What I should ... have said ... is, I ... *was* a ghost. All ... Little People ... were ghosts. Until ... they agreed terms ... with Mr Tiny."

"I don't understand," Gavner said. "Agree what terms? How?"

"Mr Tiny can ... talk with ... dead," Harkat explained. "I did not ... leave Earth ... when I died. Soul ... could not. I was ... stuck. Mr Tiny found ... me. Said he'd give ... me a ... body, so I ... could live again. In return ... I'd serve him, as a ... Little Person."

According to Harkat, each of the Little People had struck a deal with Mr Tiny, and each deal was different. They didn't have to serve him forever. Sooner or later, they would be freed, some to live on in their grey, short bodies, some to be reborn, others to move on to Heaven or Paradise or wherever it is that dead souls go.

"Mr Tiny has that much power?" Mr Crepsley asked.

Harkat nodded.

"What deal did *you* strike with him?" I asked curiously.

"I do not ... know," he said. "I cannot ... remember."

There were lots of things he couldn't remember. He didn't know who he'd been when he was alive, when or where he'd lived, or how long he'd been dead. He didn't even know if he'd been a man or a woman! The Little People were genderless, which meant they were neither male nor female.

"So how do we refer to you?" Gavner asked. "He? She? It?"

"*He* will ... do fine," Harkat said.

Their blue robes and hoods were for show. Their masks, on the other hand, were necessary, and they carried several spares, some stitched under their skin for extra safe-keeping! Air was lethal to them — if they breathed normal air for ten or twelve hours, they'd die. There were chemicals in their masks which purified the air.

"How can you die if you're already dead?" I asked, confused.

"My body can ... die, like anyone ... else's. If it does ... my soul goes ... back to the way ... it was."

"Could you agree another contract with Mr Tiny?" Mr Crepsley asked.

Harkat shook his head. "Not sure. But don't ... think so. One shot at ... extra life is ... all I think ... we get."

The Little People could read each other's minds. That's why they never spoke. He wasn't sure if the others were able to speak or not. When asked why he'd never spoken before, he pulled a crooked grin and said he'd never had cause to.

"But there must be a reason," Mr Crepsley pressed. "In all the hundreds of years that we have known them, no Little Person has ever spoken, even when dying or in great pain. Why have *you* broken that long silence? And *why*?"

Harkat hesitated. "I have a ... message," he finally said. "Mr Tiny ... gave me it ... to give to ... Vampire Princes. So I'd ... have had to speak ... soon anyway."

"A *message*?" Mr Crepsley leant forward intently, but pulled back into the shadows of the shelter when the sun hit him. "What sort of message?"

"It is for ... Princes," Harkat said. "I do not ... think I should ... tell you."

"Go on, Harkat," I urged him. "We won't tell them you told us. You can trust us."

"You will ... not tell?" he asked Mr Crepsley and Gavner.

"My lips are sealed," Gavner promised.

Mr Crepsley was slower to make his pledge, but finally nodded.

Harkat took a deep, shuddering breath. "Mr Tiny told ... me to tell ... Princes that the ... night of the ... Vampaneze Lord ... is at hand. That is ... all."

"The night of the Vampaneze Lord is at hand?" I repeated. "What kind of a message is that?"

"I do not ... know what ... it means," Harkat said. "I'm just ... the messenger."

"Gavner, do you—" I started to ask, but stopped when I saw the expressions of the vampires. Though Harkat's message meant nothing to me, it obviously meant a great deal to them. Their faces were even paler than usual, and they were trembling with fear. In fact, they couldn't have looked more terrified if they'd been staked to the ground out in the open and left for the sun to rise!

CHAPTER TEN

MR CREPSLEY and Gavner wouldn't explain the meaning of Harkat's message straightaway — they were too stunned to speak — and the story only trickled out over the next three or four nights, most of it coming from Gavner Purl.

It had to do with something Mr Tiny told the vampires hundreds of years ago, when the vampaneze broke away. Once the fighting had died down, he'd visited the Princes at Vampire Mountain and told them that the vampaneze were not hierarchically structured (Mr Crepsley's phrase), which meant there were no Vampaneze Generals or Princes. Nobody gave orders or bossed the others about.

"That was one of the reasons they broke away," Gavner said. "They didn't like the way things worked with vampires. They thought it was unfair that ordinary vampires had to answer to the Generals, and the Generals to the Princes."

Lowering his voice so that Mr Crepsley couldn't hear, he

said, "To be honest, I agree with some of that. There *is* room for change. The vampire system has worked for hundreds of years, but that doesn't mean it's perfect."

"Are you saying you'd rather be a vampaneze?" I asked, shocked.

"Of course not!" he laughed. "They kill, and allow mad vampaneze like Murlough to run around and do as they please. It's far better to be a vampire. But that doesn't mean that *some* of their ideas aren't worth taking on board.

"Not flitting on the way to Vampire Mountain, for example — that's a ridiculous rule, but it can only be changed by the Princes, who don't have to change anything they don't want to, regardless of what the rest of us think. Generals have to do everything the Princes say, and ordinary vampires have to do everything Generals say."

Though the vampaneze didn't believe in leaders, Mr Tiny said that one night a champion would step forward. He would be known as the Vampaneze Lord and the vampaneze would follow him blindly and do everything he said.

"What's so bad about that?" I asked.

"Wait till you hear the next bit," Gavner said gravely. Apparently, not long after the Vampaneze Lord came to power, he would lead the vampaneze into war against the vampires. It was a war, Mr Tiny warned, that the vampires couldn't win. They would be wiped out.

"Is that true?" I asked, appalled.

Gavner shrugged. "We've been asking ourselves that for seven hundred years. Nobody doubts Mr Tiny's powers – he's proved before that he can see into the future – but sometimes he tells lies. He's an evil little worm."

"Why didn't you go after the vampaneze and kill them all?" I asked.

"Mr Tiny said that some vampaneze would survive, and the Vampaneze Lord would come as promised. Besides, war with the vampaneze was exacting too heavy a toll. Humans were hunting us down and might have made an end of us. It was best to declare a truce and let matters lie."

"Is there no way the vampires could beat the vampaneze?" I asked.

"I'm not sure," Gavner replied, scratching his head. "There are more vampires than vampaneze, and we're as strong as they are, so I can't see why we shouldn't be able to get the better of them. But Mr Tiny said numbers wouldn't matter.

"There's one hope," he added. "The Stone of Blood."

"What's that?"

"You'll see when we get to Vampire Mountain. It's a magic icon, sacred to us. Mr Tiny said that if we prevented it from falling into the hands of the vampaneze, one night, long after the battle has been fought and lost, there's a chance that vampires might rise from the ashes and prosper again."

"How?" I asked, frowning.

Gavner smiled. "*That* question has puzzled vampires for as long as it's been asked. Let me know if you figure it out," he said with a wink, and drew the conversation to a troubling close.

*   *   *

A week later, we arrived at Vampire Mountain.

It wasn't the highest mountain in the region, but it was steep and rocky, and looked like it would be almost impossible to climb. "Where's the palace?" I asked, squinting up at the snowy peak, which seemed to point directly at the three-quarter moon overhead.

"Palace?" Mr Crepsley replied.

"Where the Vampire Princes live." Mr Crepsley and Gavner burst out laughing. "What's so funny?" I snapped.

"How long do you think we would escape detection if we built a palace on the side of a mountain?" Mr Crepsley asked.

"Then where...?" Understanding dawned. "It's *inside* the mountain!"

"Of course," Gavner smiled. "The mountain's a giant hive of caves and chambers. Everything a vampire could wish for is stored within — coffins, vats of human blood, food and wine. The only time you see vampires on the outside is when they're arriving or departing or going to hunt."

"How do we get in?" I asked.

Mr Crepsley tapped the side of his nose. "Watch and see."

We walked around the rocky base of the mountain. Mr Crepsley and Gavner were full of excitement, though only Gavner let it show — the older vampire acted as dryly as ever, and it was only when he thought nobody was looking that he'd grin to himself and rub his hands together in anticipation.

We reached a stream which was six or seven metres wide. The water flowed swiftly through it and gushed away down to the flat plains beyond. While we were working our way upstream, a lone wolf appeared in the near distance and howled. Streak and the other wolves came to an immediate stop. Streak's ears pricked up, he listened a moment, then howled back. His tail was wagging when he looked at me.

"He is saying goodbye," Mr Crepsley informed me, but I'd guessed that already.

"Do they have to go?" I asked.

"This is what they came for — to meet others of their kind. It would be cruel to ask them to stay with us."

I nodded glumly and reached down to scratch Streak's ears. "Nice knowing you, Streak," I said. Then I patted Rudi. "I'll miss you, you miserable little runt."

The adult wolves started away. Rudi hesitated, looking from me to the departing wolves. For a second I thought he might choose to stick with me, but then he barked, rubbed his wet nose over the tops of my bare feet, and set off after the others.

"You'll see him again," Gavner promised. "We'll look them up when we leave."

"Sure," I sniffed, pretending I wasn't bothered. "I'll be OK. They're just a pack of dumb old wolves. I don't care."

"Of course you don't," Gavner smiled.

"Come," Mr Crepsley said, heading upstream. "We cannot stand here all night, pining over a few mangy wolves." I glared at him and he coughed uncomfortably. "You know," he added softly, "wolves never forget a face. The cub will remember you even when it is old and grey."

"Really?" I asked.

"Yes," he said, then turned and resumed walking. Gavner and Harkat fell in behind him. I glanced over my shoulder one last time at the departing wolves, sighed resignedly, then I picked up my bag and followed.

CHAPTER ELEVEN

WE CROSSED above the opening where the stream came tumbling out of the mountain. The noise was deafening, especially for super-sensitive vampire ears, so we hurried on as quickly as possible. The rocks were slippery and in some spots we had to form a chain. At one extra-icy patch, Gavner and me both slipped. I was in front, holding on to Mr Crepsley, but the force of the fall broke our grip. Luckily, Harkat held on to Gavner and pulled the two of us up.

We reached the mouth of a tunnel a quarter of an hour later. We hadn't climbed very far up the mountain, but it was a steep drop when I looked down. I was glad we weren't climbing any higher.

Mr Crepsley entered first. I went in after him. It was dark inside the tunnel. I was going to ask Mr Crepsley if we should stop to set torches, when I realized that the further in we crept, the brighter the tunnel became.

"Where's the light coming from?" I asked.

"Luminous lichen," Mr Crepsley replied.

"Is that a tongue-twister or an answer?" I grumbled.

"It's a form of fungus which gives off light," Gavner explained. "It grows in certain caves and on the floors of some oceans."

"Oh, right. Does it grow all over the mountain?"

"Not everywhere. We use torches where it doesn't." Ahead of us, Mr Crepsley stopped and cursed. "What's wrong?" Gavner asked.

"Cave-in," he sighed. "There is no way through."

"Does that mean we can't get in?" I asked, alarmed at the thought of having trekked all this way for nothing, only to have to turn back at the very end.

"There are other ways," Gavner said. "The mountain's riddled with tunnels. We'll just have to backtrack and find another."

"We had better hurry," Mr Crepsley said. "Dawn is fast approaching."

We shuffled back the way we'd come, Harkat in the lead this time. Outside, we moved as quickly as we could – which wasn't very fast, given the treacherous footing – and made it to the mouth of the next tunnel a few minutes after the sun had started to rise. This new tunnel wasn't as large as the other and the two full-vampires had to walk bent double. Harkat and me just had to duck our heads. The luminous lichen didn't grow strongly here, though there was enough of it for our extra-sharp eyes to see by.

After a while I noticed that we were sloping downwards instead of up. I asked Gavner about this. "It's just the way the tunnel goes," he said. "It'll lead upwards eventually."

About half an hour later, we cut up. At one stage the tunnel veered upwards almost vertically and we faced a difficult climb. The walls pressed tightly about us and I'm sure I wasn't the only one whose mouth dried up with nerves. Shortly after the tunnel levelled out, it opened on to a small cave, where we stopped to rest. I could hear the stream we'd crossed earlier churning along not far beneath our feet.

There were four tunnels leading out of the cave. I asked Gavner how Mr Crepsley knew which to take. "The correct tunnel's marked," he said, leading me over to them and pointing to a tiny arrow which had been scratched into the wall at the bottom of one tunnel.

"Where do the others lead?" I asked.

"Dead ends, other tunnels, or up to the Halls." The Halls were what they called the parts of the mountain where the vampires lived. "Many of the tunnels haven't been explored and there are no maps. Never wander off by yourself," he warned. "You could get lost very easily."

While the others were resting, I checked on Madam Octa, to see if she was hungry. She'd slept through most of the journey – she didn't like the cold – but woke every now and then to eat. As I was taking the cloth off her cage, I saw a spider creeping towards us. It wasn't as large as Madam Octa, but it looked dangerous.

"Gavner!" I called, stepping away from the cage.

"What's wrong?"

"A spider."

"Oh," he grinned. "Don't worry — the mountain's full of them."

"Are they poisonous?" I asked, bending down to study the spider, which was examining the cage with great interest.

"No," he answered. "Their bite's no worse than a bee sting."

I removed the cloth, curious to see what Madam Octa would do when she spotted the strange spider. She took no notice of it, just sat where she was, while the other spider crawled over the cage. I knew a lot about spiders — I'd read many books about arachnids and watched wildlife programmes when I was younger — but hadn't seen any quite like this one before. It was hairier than most, and a curious yellow colour.

Once the spider had departed, I fed Madam Octa a few insects and replaced the cloth. I lay down with the others and napped for a few hours. At one stage I thought I heard children giggling in one of the tunnels. I sat up, ears strained, but the sound didn't come to me again.

"What's wrong?" Gavner groaned softly, half-opening an eye.

"Nothing," I said uncertainly, then asked Gavner if any vampire children lived in the mountain.

"No," he said, closing his eye. "You're the only blooded kid, as far as I know."

"Then I must have been imagining things," I yawned, and lay down again, though I kept one ear cocked while I dozed.

*　　*　　*

Later we rose and proceeded further up the mountain, taking the tunnels marked with arrows. After what seemed an age we came to a large wooden door blocking the tunnel. Mr Crepsley made himself presentable, then knocked loudly with his bare knuckles. There was no immediate answer, so he knocked again, then again.

Finally there were sounds of life on the far side of the door and it opened. Torchlight flared from within. It was blinding to us after so long in the tunnels and we shielded our eyes until they'd adjusted.

A lean vampire in dark green clothes emerged and cast an eye over us. He frowned when he saw Harkat and me, and took a firmer grip on the long spear he was holding. I could see others behind him, dressed in green as well, none lacking a weapon.

"Address yourselves to the gate," the guard barked. The vampires had told me this was how newcomers were greeted.

"I am Larten Crepsley, come to seek Council," Mr Crepsley said. It was the standard reply.

"I am Gavner Purl, come to seek Council," Gavner said.

"I am Darren Shan, come to seek Council," I told the guard.

"I ... Harkat Mulds. Come ... seek Council," Harkat wheezed.

"Larten Crepsley is recognized by the gate," the guard said. "And Gavner Purl is recognized. But these other two..." He pointed his spear at us and shook his head.

"They are our travelling companions," Mr Crepsley said. "The boy is my assistant, a half-vampire."

"Do you vouch for him?" the guard asked.

"I do."

"Then Darren Shan is recognized by the gate." The tip of his spear pointed firmly at Harkat now. "But *this* is no vampire. What business has he at Council?"

"His name is Harkat Mulds. He is a Little Person. He—"

"A Little Person!" the guard gasped, lowering his spear. He crouched and made a rude study of Harkat's face (Harkat had removed his hood soon after we entered the tunnels, the better to see by). "He's an ugly specimen, isn't he?" the guard remarked. If he hadn't been carrying a spear, I'd have ticked him off for speaking so inconsiderately. "I thought the Little People couldn't speak."

"We all thought that," Mr Crepsley said. "But they can. At least, this one can. He has a message for the Princes, to be delivered in person."

"A message?" The guard scratched his chin with the tip of the spear. "From who?"

"Desmond Tiny," Mr Crepsley replied.

The guard blanched, stood to attention and said quickly, "The Little Person known as Harkat Mulds is recognized by the gate. The Halls are open to all of you. Enter and fare well."

He stepped aside and let us pass. Moments later the door closed behind us and our journey to the Halls of Vampire Mountain was at an end.

CHAPTER TWELVE

ONE OF the green-clad guards escorted us to the Hall of Osca Velm, which was a Hall of welcome (most of the Halls were named after famous vampires). This was a small cavern, the walls knobbly and black with the grime and soot of decades. It was warmed and lit by several open fires, the air pleasantly thick with smoke (the smoke slowly exited the cavern through natural cracks and holes in the ceiling). There were several roughly-carved tables and benches where arriving vampires could rest and eat (the legs of the tables had been fashioned from the bones of large animals). There were hand-woven baskets full of shoes on the walls, which newcomers were free to pick from. You could also find out who was in attendance at the Council — a large black stone was set in one of the walls, and the name of every vampire who'd arrived was etched upon it. As we sat at a long wooden table, I saw a vampire climb a ladder and add our names to the list. After Harkat's, he put in brackets, 'A Little Person'.

There weren't many vampires in the quiet, smoky Hall — ourselves, a few more who'd recently arrived, and several green-uniformed guards. A vampire with long hair, wearing no top, came over to us with two round barrels. One was packed to the top with loaves of hard bread, the other was half-full of gristly bits of both raw and cooked meat.

We took as much as we wished to eat and set it down on the table (there were no plates), using our fingers and teeth to break off chunks. The vampire returned with three large jugs, filled with human blood, wine and water. I asked for a mug, but Gavner told me you had to pour straight from the jug. It was difficult – I soaked my chin and chest with water the first time I tried – but it was more fun than drinking out of a cup.

The bread was stale, but the vampire brought bowls of hot broth (the bowls were carved from the skulls of various beasts), and the bread was fine if you tore a piece off and dipped it in the thick, dark broth for a few seconds. "This is great," I said, munching away at my third slice.

"The best," Gavner agreed. He was already on his fifth.

"How come you're not having any broth?" I asked Mr Crepsley, who was eating his bread plain.

"Bat broth does not agree with me," he replied.

My hand froze on its way to my mouth. The soaked piece of bread I'd been holding fell to the table. "*Bat* broth?" I yelped.

"Of course," Gavner said. "What did you think it was made of?"

I stared down into the dark liquid of the bowl. The light was poor in the cavern, but now that I focused, I spotted a thin, leathery wing sticking out of the broth. "I think I'm going to be sick!" I moaned.

"Don't be stupid," Gavner chortled. "You loved it when you didn't know what it was. Just get it down you and pretend it's nice fresh chicken soup — you'll eat a lot worse than bat broth before your stay in Vampire Mountain's over!"

I pushed the bowl away. "Actually, I feel quite full," I muttered. "I'll leave it for now." I glanced at Harkat, who was mopping up the last of his broth with a thick slice of bread. "You don't mind eating bats?" I asked.

Harkat shrugged. "I've no taste ... buds. Food is ... all the same ... to me."

"You can't taste *anything*?" I asked.

"Bat ... dog ... mud — no difference. I have no ... sense of smell ... either. That's why ... no nose."

"That's something I meant to ask about," Gavner said. "If you're not able to smell without a nose, how can you hear without ears?"

"I have ... ears," Harkat said. "They're under ... skin." He pointed to two spots on either side of his round green eyes. (He'd left his hood down.)

Gavner leant over the table to examine Harkat's ears. "I see them!" he exclaimed and we all leaned over to gawk. Harkat didn't mind — he liked the attention. His 'ears' looked like dry dates, barely visible beneath the grey skin.

"You can hear in spite of the skin stretched over them?" Gavner asked.

"Quite well," Harkat replied. "Not as ... good as vampires. But better ... than humans."

"How come you've got ears but no nose?" I asked.

"Mr Tiny ... didn't give me ... nose. Never asked ... why not. Maybe because ... of air. Would need ... another mask ... for nose."

It was strange to think that Harkat couldn't smell the musky air of the Hall or taste the bat broth. No wonder the Little People never complained when I brought them rotting, stinking animals that had been dead for ages!

I was about to ask Harkat more about his limited senses when an ancient-looking vampire dressed in red sat down opposite Mr Crepsley and smiled. "I was expecting you weeks ago," he said. "What took you so long?"

"Seba!" Mr Crepsley roared, and lunged across the table to clasp the older vampire's shoulders. I was surprised — I'd never seen him behave so warmly towards another person. He was beaming when he let the vampire go. "It has been a long time, old friend."

"Too long," the older vampire agreed. "I have often searched for you mentally, in the hope that you were near. When I sensed you coming, I hardly dared believe it."

The older vampire ran an eye over Harkat and me. He was wrinkled and shrunken with age, but the light of a younger man burned brightly in his eyes. "Are you going to introduce me to your friends, Larten?" he asked.

"Of course," Mr Crepsley said. "You know Gavner Purl."

"Gavner," the vampire nodded.

"Seba," Gavner replied.

"This is Harkat Mulds," Mr Crepsley said.

"A Little Person," Seba noted. "I have not seen one of those since Mr Tiny visited us when I was a boy. Greetings, Harkat Mulds."

"Hello," Harkat replied.

Seba blinked slowly. "He *talks?*"

"Wait until you hear what he has to say!" Mr Crepsley said sombrely. Then, turning to me, he said, "And this is Darren Shan — my assistant."

"Greetings, Darren Shan," Seba smiled at me. He looked at Mr Crepsley strangely. "You, Larten — with an assistant?"

"I know," Mr Crepsley coughed. "I always said I would never take one."

"And so young," Seba murmured. "The Princes will not approve."

"Most probably not," Mr Crepsley agreed miserably. Then he shook off his gloom. "Darren, Harkat — this is Seba Nile, the quartermaster of Vampire Mountain. Do not let his age fool you — he is as sly, cunning and quick as any vampire, and will get the better of those who try and best him."

"As you know from experience," Seba chuckled. "Do you remember when you set out to steal half a vat of my finest wine and replace it with a lesser vintage?"

"Please," Mr Crepsley said, looking pained. "I was young

and foolish. There is no need to remind me."

"What happened?" I asked, delighted by the vampire's discomfort.

"Tell him, Larten," Seba said, and Mr Crepsley obeyed sullenly, like a child.

"He got to the wine first," he muttered. "Emptied the vat and replaced the wine with vinegar. I had swallowed half a bottle before I realized. I spent the rest of the night retching."

"No!" Gavner burst out laughing.

"I was young," Mr Crepsley growled. "I did not know better."

"But I taught you, Larten, did I not?" Seba remarked.

"Yes," Mr Crepsley smiled. "Seba was my tutor. I learned most of what I know at his hands."

The three vampires got to talking about old times and I sat listening. Most of what they said sailed clean over my head – names of people and places which meant nothing to me – and after a while I sat back and gazed around the cavern, studying the flickering lights of the fires and the shapes the smoke made in the air. I only realized I was dozing off when Mr Crepsley shook me gently and my eyes snapped open.

"The boy is tired," Seba noted.

"He has never made the journey before," Mr Crepsley said. "He is not accustomed to such hardship."

"Come," Seba said, standing. "I will find rooms for you. He is not the only one who needs to rest. We will talk more tomorrow."

As the quartermaster of Vampire Mountain, Seba was in charge of the stores and living quarters. It was his job to make sure there was enough food and drink and blood for everyone, and that every vampire had a place to sleep. There were other vampires working for him, but he was the main man. Aside from the Princes, Seba was the most respected vampire in the mountain.

Seba bid me walk beside him as we made our way from the Hall of Osca Velm to our sleeping quarters. He pointed out various Halls as we passed, and told me their names — most of which I couldn't pronounce, never mind remember — and what they were used for.

"It will take a while to adjust," he said, noting my dazed gaze. "For the first few nights you may feel lost. But in time you will grow accustomed to the place."

The network of tunnels connecting the Halls to the sleeping quarters were cold and damp, despite the torches, but the tiny rooms — niches carved out of the rocks — were bright and warm, each lit by a powerful torch. Seba asked if we wanted one big room between us, or if we'd prefer separate quarters.

"Separate," Mr Crepsley immediately replied. "I had enough of Gavner's snoring on the trail."

"Charming!" Gavner huffed.

"Harkat and me don't mind doubling up, do we?" I said, not liking the idea of being left on my own in such a strange place.

"That's fine ... by me," Harkat agreed.

All the rooms boasted coffins instead of beds, but when Seba saw my gloomy face, he laughed and said I could have a hammock if I preferred. "I will send one of my staff to you tomorrow," he promised. "Tell him what you need and he will get it — I look after my guests!"

"Thank you," I said, glad that I wouldn't have to sleep in the coffin every day.

Seba started to leave. "Wait," Mr Crepsley called him back. "I have something to show you."

"Oh?" Seba smiled.

"Darren," Mr Crepsley said, "fetch Madam Octa."

When Seba Nile saw the spider, his breath caught in his throat and he gazed at it as though mesmerized. "Oh, Larten," he sighed, "what a beauty!" He took the cage from me – holding it tenderly – and opened the door.

"Stop!" I hissed. "Don't let her out — she's poisonous!"

Seba only smiled and reached into the cage. "I have never met a spider I have not been able to charm," he said.

"But—" I began.

"It is all right, Darren," Mr Crepsley said. "Seba knows what he is doing."

The old vampire coaxed the spider on to his fingers and lifted her out of the cage. She squatted comfortably in the palm of his hand. Seba bent his face over her and whistled softly. The spider's legs twitched, and from her intent look, I knew he must be communicating mentally with her.

Seba stopped whistling and Madam Octa crawled up his arm. Upon reaching his shoulder, she nestled up to his chin and relaxed. I couldn't believe it! I'd always had to whistle continuously – with a flute, not my lips – and concentrate fiercely to keep her from biting me, but with Seba she was completely docile.

"She is marvellous," Seba said, stroking her. "You must tell me more about her when you have a chance. I thought I knew of all the spiders in existence, but this one is new to me."

"I thought you would like her," Mr Crepsley beamed. "That is why I brought her. I wish to make you a present of her."

"You would part with such a wonderful spider?" Seba asked.

"For you, old friend — anything."

Seba smiled at Mr Crepsley, then looked at Madam Octa. Sighing regretfully, he shook his head. "I must refuse," he said. "I am old, and not as sprightly as I used to be. I am kept busy trying to keep up with jobs I once zipped through. I do not have the time to care for such an exotic pet."

"Are you sure?" Mr Crepsley asked, disappointed.

"I would love to take her but I cannot." He placed Madam Octa back in her cage and handed it to me. "Only the young have the energy to tend to the needs of spiders of such calibre. Look after her, Darren — she is beautiful and rare."

"I'll keep my eye on her," I promised. I once thought the spider was beautiful too, until she bit my best friend and led to me becoming a half-vampire.

"Now," Seba said, "I must go. You are not the only new arrivals. Until we meet again — fare well."

There were no doors on the tiny rooms. Mr Crepsley and Gavner bid us goodnight, before heading for their coffins. Harkat and me stepped into our room and studied our two caskets.

"I don't think you'll fit in that," I said.

"That is ... OK. I can sleep ... on floor."

"In that case, see you in the morning." I glanced around the cave. "Or will it be night? Impossible to tell in here."

I didn't like getting into the coffin but took comfort in the fact that it was for one time only. Lying back, I left the lid open and stared up at the rocky grey ceiling. I thought that with the excitement of having arrived at Vampire Mountain, it'd take ages to fall asleep, but within minutes I'd dropped off and slept as soundly as I would have in my hammock back at the Cirque Du Freak.

CHAPTER THIRTEEN

HARKAT WAS standing by his coffin when I awoke, his green eyes wide open. I stretched and said good morning. There was a brief pause, then he shook his head and looked at me. "Good morning," he replied.

"Been awake long?" I asked.

"Just woke ... now. When you ... spoke to me. Fell asleep ... standing up."

I frowned. "But your eyes were open."

He nodded. "Always open. No lids ... or lashes. Can't shut them."

The more I learned about Harkat, the stranger he got! "Does that mean you can see things while you're asleep?"

"Yes, but I ... take no ... notice of them."

Gavner appeared at the entrance to our room. "Rise and shine, boys," he boomed. "Night's wearing on. There's work to be done. Anybody for bat broth?"

I asked to use the toilet before we went to eat. Gavner led me to a small door with the letters WC carved into it. "What does that stand for?" I asked.

"Water Closet," he informed me, then added, "Don't fall in!"

I thought that was a joke, but when I stepped inside, I realized it was a genuine warning — there was no toilet in the water closet, just a round hole in the ground which led to a gurgling mountain stream. I stared down the hole — it wasn't large enough for an adult to fall through, but somebody my size might just fit — and shivered when I saw dark, gushing water at the bottom. I didn't like the idea of squatting over the hole, but there was no other option, so I got on with it.

"Are all the toilets like that?" I asked when I came out.

"Yes," Gavner laughed. "It's the easiest way to get rid of the waste. There are several big streams leading out of the mountain and the toilets are built over them. The streams wash everything away."

Gavner led Harkat and me to the Hall of Khledon Lurt. Seba Nile had pointed out the Hall to me the day before and said it was where meals were served. He also told me a bit about Khledon Lurt; he had been a General of great standing, who'd died saving other vampires in the fight with the vampaneze, when they broke away.

Vampires loved telling tales of their ancestors. They kept few written records, opting instead to keep their history alive by word of mouth, passing on stories and legends around fires or over tables, one generation to another.

Red drapes hung from the ceiling, covering the walls, and there was a large statue of Khledon Lurt at the centre of the Hall. (Like most of the mountain's sculptures, it had been carved from the bones of animals.) The Hall was lit by strong torches, and it was nearly full when we arrived. Gavner, Harkat and me sat at a table with Mr Crepsley, Seba Nile and a load of vampires I didn't know. Talk was loud and raucous. Much of it had to do with fighting and feats of endurance.

This was my first good look at a crowd of vampires and I spent more time gazing around than I did eating. They didn't look that different to humans, except many were scarred from battle and hard living, and not a single one – it goes without saying! – was sun-tanned.

They were a smelly lot. They didn't use deodorants, though a few had strings of wild flowers or naturally scented herbs around their necks and wrists. Though vampires took care to wash in the world of humans – a foul stench could lead a vampire hunter to his prey – here in the mountain hardly any of them bothered with such luxuries. With all the soot and dirt of the Halls, they didn't see the point — it was impossible to keep clean.

I noticed virtually no women. After lengthy scanning, I spotted one sitting at a table in a corner, and another serving food. Otherwise, the vampires were all men. There were very few old people either; Seba seemed to be the oldest vampire present. I asked him about this.

"Very few vampires live to be a ripe old age," he replied.

"While vampires live far longer than humans, very few of us make it to our vampiric sixties or seventies."

"What do you mean?" I asked.

"Vampires measure age in two ways — earth years and vampire years," he explained. "The vampiric age is the age of the body — physically, I am in my eighties. The earth age refers to how many years a vampire has been alive — I was a young boy when I was blooded, so I am seven hundred earth years old."

Seven *hundred*! It was an incredible age.

"Though many vampires live for hundreds of earth years," Seba went on, "hardly any make it to their vampiric sixties."

"Why not?" I asked.

"Vampires live hard. We push ourselves to the limit, undergoing many tests of strength, wit and courage. Hardly any sit around in pyjamas and slippers, growing old quietly. Most, when they grow too old to care for themselves, meet death on their feet, rather than let their friends look after them."

"How come you've lived so long then?" I asked.

"Darren!" Mr Crepsley snapped, shooting me a piercing glare.

"Do not chastise the boy," Seba smiled. "His open curiosity is refreshing. I have lived to this long age because of my position," he said to me. "I was asked many decades ago to become the quartermaster of Vampire Mountain. It is not an enviable job, since it means living inside — hardly ever going hunting or fighting. But quartermasters are essential and much honoured — it would have been impolite of me to refuse. If I was free, I would have been long dead by now, but one who does not exert oneself tends to live longer than those who do."

"It seems crazy to me," I said. "Why do you push yourselves so hard?"

"It is our way," Seba answered. "Also, we have more time on our hands than humans, so it is less precious to us. If, in vampire years, a sixty-year-old man was blooded when he was twenty, he will have lived for more than four hundred earth years. A man grows tired of life when he has lived so much of it."

I was trying to see it from their point of view, but it was hard. Maybe I'd think differently when I'd been around a century or two!

Gavner rose before we'd finished eating and said he had to leave. He asked Harkat to accompany him.

"Where are you going?" I asked.

"The Hall of Princes," he said. "I must present myself to the Princes and tell them about the dead vampire and vampaneze we discovered. I also want to introduce Harkat, so he can pass on his message. The sooner the better, I think."

When they left, I asked Mr Crepsley why we hadn't gone with them. "It is not our place to present ourselves to the Princes," he said. "Gavner is a General, so he has the right to ask to see the Princes. As ordinary vampires, we must wait to be invited before them."

"But you used to be a General," I reminded him. "They wouldn't mind if you popped in to say hello, would they?"

"Of course they would," Mr Crepsley scowled, then turned to Seba and sighed. "He is slow to learn our ways."

Seba laughed. "And *you* are slow to learn the ways of the teacher. You forget how eagerly you questioned our way of life when you were blooded. I recall the night you stormed into my chambers and swore you would never become a General. You said Generals were backward imbeciles, and we should be looking to the future, not dwelling in the past."

"I never said that!" Mr Crepsley gasped.

"You certainly did," Seba insisted. "And more! You were a fiery youth, and there were times when I thought you would never calm down. I was often tempted to dismiss you, but I did not. I let you ask your questions and air your rage, and in time you learned that yours was not the wisest head in the world, and that the old ways might indeed be best.

"Students never appreciate their teachers while they are learning. It is only later, when they know more of the world, that they understand how indebted they are to those who instructed them. Good teachers expect no praise or love from the young. They wait for it, and in time, it comes."

"Are you scolding me?" Mr Crepsley asked.

"Yes," Seba smiled. "You are a fine vampire, Larten, but you have much to learn about teaching. Do not be so quick to criticize. Accept Darren's questions and stubbornness. Answer patiently and do not scold him for his opinions. Only in this way can he mature and develop as you did."

I extracted a guilty pleasure out of watching Mr Crepsley being hauled down a peg or two. I was extremely close to the vampire, but his pomposity sometimes got on my nerves. It was fun to see him have his wrists slapped!

"Stop smirking!" he snapped when he saw me.

"Now, now," I scolded him. "You heard what Mr Nile said — be *patient* — strive to *understand* me."

Mr Crepsley was puffing himself up to roar at me when Seba coughed discreetly. The vampire glanced at his old teacher, the air wheezed out of him, and he grinned sheepishly. Instead of giving out, he politely asked me to pass him a loaf of bread.

"My pleasure, Larten," I responded wryly, and the three of us shared a quiet laugh while the other vampires in the Hall of Khledon Lurt bellowed, told stories and cracked ribald jokes around us.

CHAPTER FOURTEEN

AFTER BREAKFAST, Mr Crepsley and me went to shower as we were filthy from the trek. He said we wouldn't wash often while here, but a shower at the start was a good idea. The Hall of Perta Vin-Grahl was a huge cavern with modest stalactites and two natural waterfalls, set close together to the right of the door. The water fell from high up into a vampire-made pond, and flowed to a hole near the back of the cavern, through which it disappeared and joined up with other streams underground.

"What do you think of the waterfalls?" Mr Crepsley asked, raising his voice to be heard over the noise of the running water.

"Beautiful," I said, admiring the way the torchlight reflected in the cascading water. "But where are the showers?"

Mr Crepsley grinned sadistically and I clicked to where we were meant to wash.

"No way!" I shouted. "The water must be freezing!"

"It is," Mr Crepsley agreed, slipping off his clothes, "but there are no other bathing facilities in Vampire Mountain."

I started to protest, but he laughed, walked to the nearest waterfall and immersed himself in the spray. I felt chilly just looking at the vampire showering, but I'd been eager to wash, and I knew he'd mock me for the rest of our stay if I backed out. So, wriggling free of my clothes, I walked to the edge of the pond, tested the water with my toes – *yowch!* – then leapt forward and surrendered myself to the flow of the second waterfall.

"Oh my lord!" I roared with ice-cold shock. "This is torture!"

"Aye!" Mr Crepsley shouted. "Now you understand why so few vampires bother to wash while at Council!"

"Is there a law against hot water?" I screeched, furiously scrubbing my chest, back and under my arms, in a hurry to finish with the shower.

"Not as such," Mr Crepsley replied, stepping out of his waterfall and running a hand through his short crop of orange hair, before shaking it dry like a dog. "But cold water is good enough for nature's other creatures of the wilds — we prefer not to heat it, at least not here, in the heart of our homeland."

Rough, prickly towels had been laid out close to the pond, and I wrapped myself in two of them as soon as I got out from under the waterfall. For a few minutes I felt as though my blood had turned to ice, but then my sensations returned and I was able to enjoy the warmth of the thick towels.

"Bracing," Mr Crepsley commented, rubbing himself dry.

"Murder, more like," I grumbled, though secretly I'd rather enjoyed the originality of the primitive shower.

While we were dressing, I stared at the rocky ceiling and walls and wondered how old the Halls were. I asked Mr Crepsley.

"Nobody knows exactly when vampires first came here or how they found it," he said. "The oldest discovered artefacts date back about three thousand years, but it is likely that for a long time it was only used occasionally, by small bands of wandering vampires.

"As far as we know, the Halls were established as a permanent base about fourteen hundred years ago. That is when the first Princes moved in and the Councils began. The Halls have grown since then. There are vampires at work on the structure all the time, hollowing out new rooms, extending old ones, building tunnels. It is long, tiring work – no mechanical equipment is allowed – but we have plenty of time to attend to it."

By the time we emerged from the Hall of Perta Vin-Grahl, word of Harkat's message had spread. He had told the Princes that the night of the Vampaneze Lord was at hand, and the vampires were in an uproar. They milled around the mountain like ants, passing on the word to those who hadn't heard, discussing it hotly and making absurd plans to set out and kill all the vampaneze they could find.

Mr Crepsley had promised to take me on a tour of the

Halls, but postponed it because of the commotion. He said we'd go when things quietened down — I might be trampled underfoot by agitated vampires if we set off now. I was disappointed, but knew he was right. This was no time to go exploring.

When we got back to my sleeping niche, a young vampire had taken away our coffins and was stringing up hammocks. He offered to find new clothes for Mr Crepsley and me if we wanted. We thanked him and accompanied him to one of the store-rooms to be kitted out. The stores of Vampire Mountain were full of treasures — food and blood vats and weapon caches — but I only got a brief look at these: the young vampire took us directly to the rooms where spare clothes were stored, and left us alone to pick whatever we liked.

I searched for a costume like my old one, but there were no pirate suits, so I chose a brown jumper and dark trousers, with a pair of soft shoes. Mr Crepsley dressed all in red – his favourite colour – though these robes were less fanciful than the ones he normally wore.

It was while he was adjusting his cape that I realized how similar his dress sense and Seba Nile's were. I mentioned it to him and he smiled. "I have copied many of Seba's ways," he said. "Not just his way of dressing, but also his way of speaking. I did not always use these precise, measured tones. When I was your age, I ran my words together the same as anybody. Years spent in the company of Seba taught me to slow down and consider my words before speaking."

"You mean I might end up like you one day?" I asked, alarmed at the thought of sounding so serious and stuffy.

"You might," Mr Crepsley said, "though I would not bet on it. Seba commanded my utmost respect, so I tried hard to copy what he did. You, on the other hand, seem to be determined to do the opposite of everything I say."

"I'm not *that* bad," I grinned, but there was some grain of truth in his words. I'd always been stubborn. I admired Mr Crepsley more than he knew, but hated the idea of looking like a pushover who did everything he was told. Sometimes I disobeyed the vampire just so he wouldn't think I was paying attention to what he said!

"Besides," Mr Crepsley added, "I have neither the heart nor the will to punish you when you make mistakes, as Seba punished me."

"Why?" I asked. "What did he do?"

"He was a fair but hard teacher," Mr Crepsley said. "When I told him of my desire to mimic him, he began paying close attention to my punctuation. Whenever I said 'don't' or 'it's' or 'can't' — he would pluck a hair from inside my nose!"

"No way!" I hooted.

"It is true," he said glumly.

"Did he use tweezers?"

"No — his fingernails."

"Ow!"

Mr Crepsley nodded. "I asked him to stop — I said I no longer cared to copy him — but he would not — he believes in finishing what one starts. After several months of having the hairs ripped from inside my nostrils, I had a brainwave, and singed them with a red-hot rod — not something I recommend you try! — so they would not grow back."

"What happened?"

Mr Crepsley blushed. "He began plucking hairs from an even more tender spot."

"Where?" I quickly asked.

The vampire's blush deepened. "I will not say — it is far too embarrassing."

(Later, when I got Seba by himself and put the question to him, he chortled wickedly and told me: "His *ears!*")

While we were slipping on our shoes, a slender, blond vampire in a bright blue suit barged into the room and slammed the door behind him. He stood panting by the door, unaware of us, until Mr Crepsley called to him. "Is that you, Kurda?"

"No!" the vampire yelled and grabbed for the handle. Then he paused and glanced over his shoulder. "Larten?"

"Yes," Mr Crepsley replied.

"That's different." The vampire sauntered over. When he got closer, I saw that he had three small red scars on his left cheek. They looked somehow familiar, though I couldn't think why. "I was hoping to run into you. I wanted to ask about this Harkat Mulds person and his message. Is it true?"

Mr Crepsley shrugged. "I have only heard the rumour. He said nothing to us about it on our way here." Mr Crepsley hadn't forgotten our promise to Harkat.

"Not a word of it?" the vampire asked, sitting on an upturned barrel.

"He told us the message was for the Vampire Princes only," I said.

The vampire eyed me curiously. "You must be the Darren Shan I've been hearing about." He shook my hand. "I'm Kurda Smahlt."

"What were you running from?" Mr Crepsley asked.

"Questions," Kurda groaned. "As soon as word of the Little Person and his message circulated, everyone ran to me to ask if it was true."

"Why should they ask *you*?" Mr Crepsley enquired.

"Because I know more about the vampaneze than most. And because of my investiture — it's amazing how much more you're expected to know when you move up in the world."

"Gavner Purl told me about that. Congratulations," Mr Crepsley said rather stiffly.

"You don't approve," Kurda noted.

"I did not say that."

"You didn't have to. It's written all over your face. But I don't mind. You're not the only one who objects. I'm used to the controversy."

"Excuse me," I said, "but what's an 'investiture'?"

"That's what they call it when you move up in the organization," Kurda explained. He had a light way of speaking, and a smile was never far from his lips and eyes. He reminded me of Gavner and I took an immediate shine to him.

"Where are you moving to?" I asked.

"The top," he smiled. "I'm being made a Prince. There'll

be a big ceremony and a lot of to-do." He grimaced. "It'll be a dull affair, I'm afraid, but there's no way around it. Centuries of tradition, standards to uphold, etcetera."

"You should not speak dismissively of your investiture," Mr Crepsley growled. "It is a great honour."

"I know," Kurda sighed. "I just wish people wouldn't make such a big deal of it. It's not like I've done anything wondrous."

"How *do* you become a Vampire Prince?" I asked.

"Why?" Kurda replied, a twinkle in his eye. "Thinking of applying for the job?"

"No," I chuckled. "Just curious."

"There's no fixed way," he said. "To become a General, you study for a set number of years and pass regular tests. Princes, on the other hand, are elected sporadically and for different reasons.

"Usually a Prince is someone who's distinguished himself in many battles, earning the trust and admiration of his colleagues. One of the established Princes nominates him. If the other Princes agree, he's automatically elevated up the ranks. If one objects, the Generals vote and the majority decision decides his fate. If two or more Princes object, the motion's rejected.

"I squeezed in by the vote," he grinned. "Fifty-four per cent of the Generals think I'll make a fitting Prince. Which means that near enough one in two think I won't!"

"It was the tightest vote ever," Mr Crepsley said. "Kurda is only a hundred and twenty earth years old, making him one of the youngest Princes ever, and many Generals believe he is too young to command their respect. They will follow him once he is elected – there is no question of that – but they are not happy about it."

"Come now," Kurda clucked. "Don't cover up for me and leave the boy thinking it's my age they object to. Here, Darren." When I was standing beside him, he bent his right arm so that the biceps were bulging. "What do you think?"

"They're not very big," I answered truthfully.

Kurda howled gleefully. "May the gods of the vampires save us from honest children! But you're right — they're *not* big. Every other Prince has muscles the size of bowling balls. The Princes have always been the biggest, toughest, bravest vampires. I'm the first to be nominated because of *this*." He tapped his head. "My *brain*."

"You mean you're smarter than everybody else?"

"Way smarter," he said, then pulled a face. "Not really," he sighed. "I just use my brains more than most. I don't believe vampires should stick to the old ways as rigidly as they do. I think we should move forward and adapt to life in the twenty-first century. More than anything else, I believe we should strive to make peace with our estranged brothers — the vampaneze."

"Kurda is the first vampire since the signing of the peace treaty to consort with the vampaneze," Mr Crepsley said gruffly.

"Consort?" I asked uncertainly.

"I've been meeting with them," Kurda explained. "I've spent much of the last thirty or forty years tracking them down, talking, getting to know them. That's where I got my scars." He tapped the left side of his face. "I had to agree to let them mark me — it was a way of offering myself to them and placing myself at their mercy."

Now I knew why the scars looked familiar — I'd seen similar marks on a human that the mad vampaneze Murlough had targeted six years earlier! Vampaneze were traditionalists and marked their prey in advance of a kill, always the same three scratches on the left cheek.

"The vampaneze aren't as different to us as most vampires believe," Kurda continued. "Many would jump at the chance to return to the fold. Compromises will have to be made — both sides must back down on certain issues — but I'm sure we can come to terms and live together again, as one."

"That is why he is being invested," Mr Crepsley said. "A lot of the Generals — fifty-four per cent, in any case — think it is time we were reunited with the vampaneze. The vampaneze trust Kurda but are reluctant to commit to negotiations with other Generals. When Kurda is a Prince, he will have total control over the Generals, and the vampaneze know no General would disobey the order of a Prince. So if he sends a vampire along to discuss terms, the vampaneze will trust him and sit down to talk. Or so the reasoning goes."

"You don't agree with it, Larten?" Kurda asked.

Mr Crepsley looked troubled. "There is much about the vampaneze which I admire, and I have never been opposed to talks designed to bridge the gap between us. But I would not be so quick to give them a voice among the Princes."

"You think they might use me to force more of their beliefs on us than we force on them?" Kurda suggested.

"Something like that."

Kurda shook his head. "I'm looking to create a tribe of equals. I won't force any changes through that the other Princes and Generals don't agree with."

"If that is so, luck to you. But things are happening too fast for my liking. Were I a General, I would have campaigned as hard as I could against you."

"I hope I live long enough to prove your distrust of me ill-founded," Kurda sighed, then turned to me. "What do *you* think, Darren? Is it time for a change?"

I hesitated before answering. "I don't know enough about the vampires or vampaneze to offer an opinion," I said.

"Nonsense," Kurda huffed. "Everyone's entitled to an opinion. Go on, Darren, tell me what you think. I like to know what's on people's minds. The world would be a simpler and safer place if we all spoke our true thoughts."

"Well," I said slowly, "I'm not sure I like the idea of doing a deal with the vampaneze – I think it's wrong to kill humans when you drink from them – but if you could persuade them to stop killing, it might be a good thing."

"This boy has brains," Kurda said, winking at me. "What you said just about sums up my own arguments in a nutshell. The killing of humans *is* deplorable and it's one of the concessions the vampaneze will have to make before a deal can be forged. But unless we draw them into talks and earn their trust, they'll never stop. Wouldn't it be worth giving up a few of our ways if we could stop the bloody murder?"

"Absolutely," I agreed.

"Hurm!" Mr Crepsley grunted, and would be drawn no further on the subject.

"Anyway," Kurda said, "I can't stay hidden forever. Time to return and fend off more questions. You're sure there's nothing you can tell me about the Little Person and his message?"

"Afraid not," Mr Crepsley said curtly.

"Oh well. I suppose I'll find out when I report to the Hall of Princes and see him myself. I hope you enjoy your stay in Vampire Mountain, Darren. We must get together once the chaos has died down and have a proper chat."

"I'd like that," I said.

"Larten," he saluted Mr Crepsley.

"Kurda."

He let himself out.

"Kurda's nice," I remarked. "I like him."

Mr Crepsley glanced at me sideways, stroked the long scar on his own left cheek, gazed thoughtfully at the door Kurda had left by, and again went, "Hurm!"

CHAPTER FIFTEEN

A COUPLE of long, quiet nights passed. Harkat had been kept in the Hall of Princes to answer questions. Gavner had General business to attend to and we only saw him when he crawled back to his coffin to sleep. I hung out with Mr Crepsley in the Hall of Khledon Lurt most of the time – he had a lot of catching up to do with old friends he hadn't seen in many years – or down in the stores with him and Seba Nile.

The elderly vampire was more disturbed by Harkat's message than most. He was the second oldest vampire in the Mountain – the oldest was a Prince, Paris Skyle, who was more than eight hundred – and the only one who'd been here when Mr Tiny visited and made his announcement all those centuries ago.

"A lot of today's vampires do not believe the old myths," he said. "They think Mr Tiny's warning was something we made up to frighten young vampires. But I remember how he looked. I recall the way his words echoed around the Hall of Princes, and the fear they instilled in everyone. The Vampaneze Lord is no mere figure of legend. He is real. And now, it seems, he is coming."

Seba lapsed into silence. He'd been drinking a mug of warm ale but had lost interest in it.

"He has not come yet," Mr Crepsley said spiritedly. "Mr Tiny is as old as time itself. When he says the night is at hand, he might mean hundreds or thousands of years from now."

Seba shook his head. "We have had our hundreds of years — seven centuries to make a stand and tackle the vampaneze. We should have finished them off, regardless of the consequences. Better to have been driven to the point of extinction by humans than wiped out entirely by the vampaneze."

"That is foolish talk," Mr Crepsley snapped. "I would rather take my chances with a mythical Vampaneze Lord than a real, stake-wielding human. So would you."

Seba nodded glumly and sipped at his ale. "You are probably right. I am old. My brain does not work as sharply as it used to. Perhaps my worries are those of an old man who has lived too long. Still..."

Such pessimistic words were on everybody's lips. Even those who scoffed outright at the idea of a Vampaneze Lord always seemed to end with a 'still...' or 'however...' or 'but...' The tension was clogging the dusty mountain air of the tunnels and Halls, constantly building, stifling all present.

The only one who didn't seem troubled by the rumours was Kurda Smahlt. He turned up outside our chambers, as upbeat as ever, the third night after Harkat had delivered his message.

"Greetings," he said. "I've had a hectic two nights, but things are calming down at last and I've a few free hours. I thought I'd take Darren on a tour of the Halls."

"Great!" I beamed. "Mr Crepsley was going to take me but we never got round to it."

"You don't mind if I escort him, Larten?" Kurda asked.

"Not in the slightest," Mr Crepsley said. "I am overwhelmed that one of your eminence has found the time to act as a guide so close to your investiture." He said it cuttingly, but Kurda ignored the elder vampire's sarcasm.

"You can tag along if you want," Kurda offered cheerfully.

"No thank you," Mr Crepsley smiled thinly.

"OK," Kurda said. "Your loss. Ready, Darren?"

"Ready," I said, and off we set.

*   *   *

Kurda took me to see the kitchens first. They were huge caves, built deep beneath most of the Halls. Large fires burned brightly. The cooks worked in shifts around the clock during times of Council. They had to in order to feed all the visitors.

"It's quieter the rest of the time," Kurda said. "There are usually no more than thirty vampires in residence. You often have to cook for yourself if you don't eat with the rest at the set times."

From the kitchens we progressed to the breeding Halls, where sheep, goats and cows were kept and bred. "We'd never be able to ship in enough milk and meat to feed all the vampires," Kurda explained when I asked why live animals were kept in the mountain. "This isn't an hotel, where you can ring a supplier and re-stock any time you please. Shipping in food is an enormous hassle. It's easier to rear the animals ourselves and butcher them when we need to."

"What about human blood?" I asked. "Where does that come from?"

"Generous donors," Kurda winked, and led me on. (I only realized much later that he'd side-stepped the question.)

The Hall of Cremation was our next stop. It was where vampires who died in the mountain were cremated. "What if they don't want to be cremated?" I asked.

"Oddly enough, hardly any vampires ask to be buried," he mused. "Perhaps it has something to do with all the time they spend in coffins while they're alive. However, if someone requests a burial, their wishes are respected.

"Not so long ago, we'd lower the dead into an underground stream, and let the water wash them away. There's a cave, far below the Halls, where one of the larger streams opens up. It's called the Hall of Final Voyage, though it's never used now. I'll show it to you if we're ever down that way."

"Why should we be down there?" I asked. "I thought those tunnels were only used to get in and out of the mountain."

"One of my hobbies is map-making," Kurda said. "I've been trying to make accurate maps of the mountain for decades. The Halls are easy but the tunnels are much more difficult. They've never been mapped and a lot are in poor shape. I try to get down to them whenever I return, to map out a few more unknown regions, but I don't have as much time to work on them as I'd like. I'll have even less when I'm a Prince."

"It sounds like an interesting hobby," I said. "Could I come with you the next time you go mapping? I'd like to see how it's done."

"You're really interested?" He sounded surprised.

"Why shouldn't I be?"

He laughed. "I'm used to vampires falling asleep whenever I start talking about maps. Most have no interest in such mundane matters. There's a saying among vampires: 'Maps are for humans'. Most vampires would rather discover new territory for themselves, regardless of the dangers, than follow directions on a map."

The Hall of Cremation was a large octagonal room with a high ceiling full of cracks. There was a pit in the middle – where the dead vampires were burnt – and a couple of long, gnarly benches on the far side, made out of bones. Two women and a man were sitting on the benches, whispering to each other, and a young child was at their feet, playing with a scattering of animal bones. They didn't have the appearance of vampires – they were thin and ill-looking, with lank hair and rags for clothes; their skin was deathly pale and dry, and their eyes were an eerie white colour. The adults stood when we entered, grabbed the child and withdrew through a door at the back of the room.

"Who were they?" I asked.

"The Guardians of this chamber," Kurda replied.

"Are they vampires?" I pressed. "They didn't look like vampires. And I thought I was the only child vampire in the mountain."

"You are," Kurda said.

"Then who—"

"Ask me later!" Kurda snapped with unusual briskness. I blinked at his sharp tone, and he smiled an immediate apology. "I'll tell you about them when our tour is complete," he said softly. "It's bad luck to talk about them here. Though I'm not superstitious by nature, I prefer not to test the fates where the Guardians are concerned."

(Although he'd aroused my curiosity, I wasn't to learn more about the strange, so-called Guardians until much later, as by the end of our tour I was in no state to ask any questions, and had forgotten about them entirely.)

Letting the matter of the Guardians drop, I examined the cremation pit, which was just a hollow dip in the ground. There were leaves and sticks in the bottom, waiting to be lit. Large pots were set around the hole, a club-like stick in each. I asked what they were for.

"Those are pestles, for the bones," Kurda said.

"What bones?"

"The bones of the vampires. Fire doesn't burn bones.

Once a fire's burnt out, the bones are extracted, put in the pots, and ground down to dust with the pestles."

"What happens to the dust?" I asked.

"We use it to thicken bat broth," Kurda said earnestly, then burst out laughing as my face turned green. "I'm joking! The dust is thrown to the winds around Vampire Mountain, setting the spirit of the dead vampire free."

"I'm not sure I'd like that," I commented.

"It's better than burying a person and leaving them to the worms," Kurda said. "Although, personally speaking, I want to be stuffed and mounted when my time comes." He paused a moment, then burst out laughing again.

Leaving the Hall of Cremation, we set off for the three Halls of Sport (individually they were called the Hall of Basker Wrent, the Hall of Rush Flon'x, and the Hall of Oceen Pird, though most vampires referred to them simply as the Halls of Sport). I was eager to see the gaming Halls, but as we made our way there, Kurda paused in front of a small door, bowed his head, closed his eyes and touched his eyelids with his fingertips.

"Why did you do that?" I asked.

"It's the custom," he said, and moved on. I stayed, staring at the door.

"What's this Hall called?" I asked.

Kurda hesitated. "You don't want to go in there," he said.

"Why not?" I pressed.

"It's the Hall of Death," he said quietly.

"Another cremation Hall?"

He shook his head. "A place of execution."

"*Execution?*" I was really curious now. Kurda saw this and sighed.

"You want to go in?" he asked.

"Can I?"

"Yes, but it's not a pretty sight. It would be better to proceed directly to the Halls of Sport."

A warning like that only made me more eager to see what lurked behind the door! Noting this, Kurda opened it and led me in. The Hall was poorly lit, and at first I thought it was deserted. Then I spotted one of the white-skinned Guardians, sitting in the shadows of the wall at the rear. He didn't rise or give any sign that he saw us. I started to ask Kurda about him, but the General shook his head instantly and hissed quietly, "I'm definitely not talking about them *here!*"

I could see nothing awful about the Hall. There was a pit in the centre of the floor and light wooden cages set against the walls, but otherwise it was bare and unremarkable.

"What's so bad about this place?" I asked.

"I'll show you," Kurda said, and guided me towards the edge of the pit. Looking down into the gloom, I saw dozens of sharpened poles set in the floor, pointing menacingly towards the ceiling.

"Stakes!" I gasped.

"Yes," Kurda said softly. "This is where the legend of the stake through the heart originated. When a vampire's brought to the Hall of Death, he's placed in a cage — that's what the cages against the walls are for — which is attached to ropes and hoisted above the pit. He's then dropped from a height and impaled on the stakes. Death is often slow and painful, and it's not unusual for a vampire to have to be dropped three or four times before he dies."

"But *why?*" I was appalled. "Who do they kill here?"

"The old or crippled, along with mad and treacherous vampires," Kurda answered. "The old or crippled vampires ask to be killed. If they're strong enough, they prefer to fight to the death, or wander off into the wilderness to die hunting. But those who lack the strength or ability to die on their feet ask to come here, where they can meet death face-on and die bravely."

"That's horrible!" I cried. "The elderly shouldn't be killed off!"

"I agree," Kurda said. "I think the nobility of the vampires is misplaced. The old and infirm often have much to offer, and I personally hope to cling to life as long as possible. But most vampires hold to the ancient belief that they can only lead worthwhile lives as long as they're fit enough to fend for themselves.

"It's different with mad vampires," he went on. "Unlike the vampaneze, we choose not to let our insane members run loose in the world, free to torment and prey on humans. Since they're too difficult to imprison – a mad vampire will claw his way through a stone wall – execution is the most humane way to deal with them."

"You could put them in straitjackets," I suggested.

Kurda smiled sourly. "There hasn't been a straitjacket

invented that could hold a vampire. Believe me, Darren, killing a mad vampire is a mercy, to the world in general and the vampire himself.

"The same goes for treacherous vampires," he added, "though there have been precious few of those — loyalty is something we excel at; one of the bonuses of sticking to the old ways so rigidly. Aside from the vampaneze — when they broke away, they were called traitors; many were captured and killed — there have been only six traitors executed in the fourteen hundred years that vampires have lived here."

I stared down at the stakes and shivered, imagining myself tied in a cage, hanging above the pit, waiting to fall.

"Do you give them blindfolds?" I asked.

"The mad vampires, yes, because it is merciful. Vampires who have *chosen* to die in the Hall of Death prefer to do without one — they like to look death in the eye, to show they're not afraid. Traitors, meanwhile, are placed in the cages face upwards, so their backs are to the stakes. It's a great dishonour for a vampire to die from stab wounds in the back."

"I'd rather get it in the back than the front," I snorted.

Kurda smiled. "Hopefully, you'll never get it in either!" Then, clapping my shoulder, he said, "This is a gloomy place, best avoided. Let's go play some games." And he swiftly ushered me out of the Hall, eagerly leaving behind its mysterious Guardian, the cages and the stakes.

CHAPTER SIXTEEN

THE HALLS of Sport were gigantic caverns, full of shouting, cheering, high-spirited vampires. They were exactly what I needed to perk me up after the disturbing visit to the Halls of Cremation and Death.

Various contests took place in each of the three Halls. They were mostly games of physical combat – wrestling, boxing, karate, weightlifting and so on – though speed chess was also strongly favoured, since it sharpened one's reactions and wits.

Kurda found seats for us near a wrestling circle and we watched as vampires tried to pin their opponents down or toss them out of the ring. You needed a quick eye to keep up with the action — vampires moved far faster than humans. It was like watching a fight on video while keeping the fast-forward button pressed.

The bouts weren't just faster than their human equivalents

— they were more violent too. Broken bones, bloody faces and bruises were the order of the night. Sometimes, Kurda told me, the damage was even worse — vampires could be killed taking part in these games, or injured so badly that a trip to the Hall of Death was all they had to look forward to.

"Why don't they wear protective clothing?" I asked.

"They don't believe in it," Kurda said. "They'd rather have their skulls cracked than wear helmets." He sighed morosely. "There are times when I think I don't know my people at all. Maybe I'd have been better off if I'd remained human."

We moved to another ring. In this one, vampires jabbed at each other with spears. It was a bit like fencing — you had to prick or cut an opponent three times to win — only a lot more dangerous and bloody.

"It's horrendous," I gasped as a vampire had half his upper arm sliced open, only to laugh and compliment his foe for making a good strike.

"You should see it when they play for real," someone said behind us. "They're just warming up at the moment." Turning, I saw a ginger-haired vampire who had only one eye. He was clad in a dark blue leather tunic and trousers. "They call this game the eye-baller," he informed me, "because so many people lose an eye or two playing it."

"Is that how you lost yours?" I asked, staring at his empty left eye socket and the scars around it.

"No," he chuckled. "I lost mine in a tussle with a lion."

"Honest?" I gasped.

"Honest."

"Darren, this is Vanez Blane," Kurda introduced us. "Vanez, this is—"

"—Darren Shan," Vanez nodded, shaking my hand. "I know him from the gossip. It's been a long time since one his age trod the Halls of Vampire Mountain."

"Vanez is a games master," Kurda explained.

"You're in charge of the games?" I asked.

"Hardly in charge," Vanez said. "The games are beyond the control of even the Princes. Vampires fight — it's in our blood. If not here, where their injuries can be tended to, then in the open, where they might bleed to death unaided. I keep an eye on things, that's all." He grinned.

"He also trains vampires to fight," Kurda said. "Vanez is one of our most valued instructors. Most Generals of the last hundred years have studied under him. Myself included." He rubbed the back of his head and grimaced.

"Still sore about that time I knocked you unconscious with a mace, Kurda?" Vanez enquired politely.

"You wouldn't have had the chance if I'd known what it was in advance," Kurda sulked. "I thought it was a bowl of incense!"

Vanez bellowed with laughter and slapped his knees. "You always were a bright one, Kurda — except when it came to the tools of war. One of my worst pupils," he told me. "Fast as an eel, and wiry, but he hated getting his hands bloody. A shame, as he would have been a wonder with a spear if he'd set his mind to it."

"There's nothing wonderful about losing an eye in a fight," Kurda huffed.

"There is if you win," Vanez disagreed. "Any injury's acceptable as long as you emerge victorious."

We watched the vampires cutting each other to pieces for another half an hour – nobody lost an eye while we were there – then Vanez led us round the Halls, explaining the games to me and how they served to toughen vampires up and prepare them for life in the outside world.

All manner of weapons hung from the walls of the Halls – some antiques, some for general use – and Vanez told me their names and how they were used; he even got a few down to demonstrate. They were fearsome instruments of destruction — jagged spears, sharp axes, long and glinting knives, heavy maces, blade-edged boomerangs which could kill from eighty metres, clubs with thick spikes sticking out of them, stone-head war hammers which could cave in a vampire's skull with one well-placed blow. After a while I noticed there were no guns or bows and arrows, and asked about their absence.

"Vampires only fight hand to hand," Vanez informed me. "We do not use missile devices, such as guns, bows or slings."

"Never?" I asked.

"Never!" he said firmly. "Our reliance on hand weapons is sacred to us – to the vampaneze as well. Any vampire who resorted to a gun or bow would be held in contempt for the rest of his life."

"Things used to be even more backwards," Kurda chipped in. "Until two hundred years ago, a vampire was only supposed to use a weapon of his own making. Every vampire had to fashion his own knives, spears and clubs. Now, thankfully, that's no longer the case, and we can use store-bought equipment; but many vampires still cling to the old ways, and most of the weapons used during Council are handmade."

Moving away from the weapons, we stopped beside a series of overlapping narrow planks. Vampires were balancing on the planks and crossing from one to another, trying to knock their opponents to the ground with long round-ended staffs. There were six vampires in action when we arrived. A few minutes later, only one remained aloft — a woman.

"Well done, Arra," Vanez clapped. "Your sense of balance is as awesome as ever."

The female vampire leapt from the plank and landed beside us. She was dressed in a white shirt and beige trousers. She had long dark hair, tied behind her back. She wasn't especially pretty – she had a hard, weathered face – but after so much time spent staring at ugly, scarred vampires, she looked like a movie star to me.

"Kurda, Vanez," she greeted the vampires, then fixed her cool grey eyes on me. "And you are Darren Shan." She sounded decidedly unimpressed.

"Darren, this is Arra Sails," Kurda said. I stuck out a hand but she ignored it.

"Arra doesn't shake the hands of those she doesn't respect," Vanez whispered.

"And she respects precious few of us," Kurda said aloud. "Still refusing to shake hands with *me*, Arra?"

"I will never shake the hand of one who does not fight," she grunted. "When you become a Prince, I will bow to you and do your bidding, but I will never shake your hand, even under threat of execution."

"I don't think Arra voted for me in the election," Kurda said humorously.

"*I* didn't vote for you either," Vanez said, with a wicked grin.

"See what an average day is like for me, Darren?" Kurda groaned. "Half the vampires here love to rub my nose in the fact that they didn't vote for me, while the half who *did* almost never admit it in public, for fear the others would look down their noses at them."

"Never mind," Vanez chuckled. "We'll all have to kow-tow to you when you're a Prince. We're just getting our digs in while we can."

"Is it illegal to make fun of a Prince?" I asked.

"Not as such," Vanez said. "It just isn't done."

I examined Arra while she was picking a splinter from one of the rounded ends of her staff. She seemed to be as tough as any male vampire, not as burly, but just as muscular. While studying her, I got to thinking about how few female vampires I'd seen, and asked about it.

There was a long silence. The two men looked embarrassed. I was going to let the matter drop when Arra glanced at me archly and said, "Women do not make good vampires. The entire clan's barren, so the life doesn't appeal to many of us."

"Barren?" I enquired.

"We can't have children," she said.

"What — *none* of you?"

"It's something to do with our blood," Kurda said. "No vampire can sire or bear a child. The only way we can add to our ranks is by blooding humans."

I was stunned. Of course, I should have long ago stopped to wonder why there were no vampire children, and why everyone was so surprised to meet a young half-vampire. But I'd so much else on my mind, I never really paused to consider it.

"Does that rule apply to half-vampires too?" I asked.

"I'm afraid so," Kurda said, frowning. "Larten never mentioned it?"

I shook my head numbly. I couldn't have children! It wasn't something I'd thought about much — seeing as how I aged at a fifth the human rate, it would be a long time before I was ready to become a parent — but I'd always assumed I'd have the choice. It was alarming to learn that I could never father a son or daughter.

"This is bad," Kurda muttered. "This is very, very bad."

"What do you mean?" I asked.

"Vampires are supposed to inform new recruits of such things before they blood them. It's one of the reasons we almost never blood children — we prefer new vampires to know what they're getting into and what they're giving up. To blood a boy your age was bad enough, but to do it without telling you all the facts..." Kurda shook his head glumly and shared an uncertain look with Arra and Vanez.

"You'll have to tell the Princes about this," Arra sniffed.

"They must be informed," Kurda agreed, "but I'm sure Larten means to tell them himself. I'll wait and let him speak. It would be unfair to jump in before he has a chance to put his side of the story forward. Will you two keep this to yourselves?"

Vanez nodded and, moments later, Arra did too. "But if he doesn't make mention of it soon..." Arra growled threateningly.

"I don't understand," I said. "Will Mr Crepsley get into trouble for blooding me?"

Kurda shared another glance with Arra and Vanez. "Probably not," he said, trying to make light of it. "Larten's a sly old vampire. He knows the ropes. I'm sure he'll be able to explain it away to the satisfaction of the Princes."

"Now," Vanez said before I could ask any more questions, "how would you like to try out the bars with Arra?"

"You mean have a go on the planks?" I asked, thrilled.

"I'm sure we can find a staff to suit you. How about it, Arra? Any objections to fighting a smaller opponent?"

"It will be a novel experience," the vampiress mused. "I'm accustomed to tackling men larger than myself. It will be interesting to fight one smaller."

She hopped up on to the planks and twirled her staff over her head and under her arms. It spun faster than my eyes could follow, and I began having second thoughts about getting up there with her; but I'd look like a coward if I backed out now.

Vanez found a staff small enough for me and spent a few minutes showing me how to use it. "Hold it in the middle," he instructed. "That way you can attack with either end. Don't swing too hard or you'll leave yourself open to a counterstrike. Jab at her legs and stomach. Forget about her head — you're too short to aim so high. Try tripping her. Go for her knees and toes — those are the soft points."

"What about defending himself?" Kurda interrupted. "I think that's more important. It's been eleven years since Arra was beaten on the bars. Show him how to stop her cracking his head open, Vanez, and forget the other stuff."

Vanez showed me how to block low jabs and sideswipes and overhead cuts. "The trick is keeping your balance," he said. "Fighting on the bars isn't like fighting on the ground. You can't just block a blow — you have to stay steady on your feet, so you're ready for the next. Sometimes it's better to take a strike than duck out of the way."

"Nonsense," Kurda snorted. "Duck all you like, Darren — I don't want to cart you back to Larten on a stretcher!"

"She won't really hurt me, will she?" I asked, alarmed.

Vanez laughed. "Of course not. Kurda's only winding you up. She won't go easy on you — Arra doesn't know how to take things easy — but I'm sure she won't set out to seriously harm you." He glanced up at Arra and muttered under his breath, "At least, I *hope* she won't!"

CHAPTER SEVENTEEN

I SLIPPED my shoes off and mounted the bars. I spent a minute or two getting used to them, shuffling around, focusing on my balance. It was easy without the staff — vampires have a great sense of balance — but awkward with it. I took a few practice swipes and almost fell off straightaway.

"Short jabs!" Vanez snapped, darting forward to steady me. "Broad swings will be the end of you."

I did as Vanez instructed and soon had the hang of it. A couple more minutes hopping from one bar to another, crouching and jumping, and I was ready.

We met in the middle of the bars and knocked our staffs together in salute. Arra was smiling — she obviously didn't think much of my chances. We nudged away from each other and Vanez clapped his hands to signal the start of the fight.

Arra attacked immediately and jabbed at my stomach with the end of her staff. As I pulled out of her way, she swept her staff round in a vicious circle and brought it down on top of me — a skull-cracker! I managed to raise my staff in time to divert the blow, but the jolt of the contact ran through the staff and my fingers to the rest of my body, and forced me to my knees. My grasp on the staff slipped, but I caught it before it fell.

"Are you out to kill him?" Kurda shouted angrily.

"The bars are no place for little boys who can't protect themselves," Arra sneered.

"I'm calling an end to this," Kurda huffed, striding towards me.

"As you wish," Arra said, lowering her staff and turning her back on me.

"No!" I grunted, getting to my feet and raising my staff.

Kurda stopped short. "Darren, you don't have to—" he began.

"I want to," I interrupted. Then, to Arra, "Come on — I'm ready."

Arra smiled as she faced me, but now it was an admiring smile, not a mocking one. "The half-vampire has spirit. It's good to know that the young aren't entirely spineless. Now let's see what it takes to drive the spirit out of you."

She attacked again, short chopping swipes, switching from left to right without warning. I blocked the blows as best I could, though I had to take some on my arms and shoulders. I retreated to the end of the plank, slowly, guarding myself, then leapt out of her way as she took a wide swing at my legs.

Arra hadn't anticipated the jump and was thrown off-balance. I used the moment to launch my first blow of the contest and hit her firmly on her left thigh. It didn't seem to hurt her much, but she hadn't been expecting it and let out a roar of surprise.

"A point to Darren!" Kurda whooped.

"We don't score this on points," Arra snarled.

"You'd better watch yourself, Arra," Vanez chuckled, his single eye a-gleam. "I think the boy has the beating of you. You'll never be able to show your face in the Halls again if a teenage half-vampire bests you on the bars."

"The night I'm bested by the likes of him is the night you can strap me into a cage in the Hall of Death and drop me on the stakes," Arra growled. She was angry now – she didn't like being baited by those on the ground – and when next she faced me, her smile had disappeared.

I moved cautiously. I knew that one good strike meant nothing. If I grew cocky and dropped my guard, she'd finish me off in no time. As she stepped across to face me, I edged backwards. I let her advance a couple of metres, then leapt to another bar. After a few retreating steps, I jumped to another bar, then another.

I was hoping to frustrate Arra. If I could drag the contest out, she might lose her temper and do something silly. But a vampire's patience is legendary and Arra was no exception. She trailed me like a cat after a bird, ignoring the jeers of those who'd gathered round the bars to observe the fight, taking her time, letting me play my evasive games, waiting for the right moment to strike.

Eventually she manoeuvred me into a corner and I had to fight. I got in a couple of low blows – hitting her toes and knees as Vanez had suggested – but there was no power in my shots and she took them without blinking. As I stooped to hit her toes again, she leapt to an adjoining bar and brought the flat of her staff down over my back. I roared with pain and dropped on to my belly. My staff fell to the floor.

"Darren!" Kurda shouted, rushing forward.

"Leave him!" Vanez snapped, holding the General back.

"But he's hurt!"

"He'll live. Don't disgrace him in front of all these vampires. Let him fight."

Kurda didn't like it, but he did as Vanez said.

Arra, meanwhile, had decided I was finished. Rather than strike me with her staff, she eased one of the rounded ends under my belly and tried rolling me off the bar. She was smiling again. I let my body roll, but held on tight to the bar with my hands and feet, so I didn't fall off. I swung right the way around, until I was hanging on upside down, snatched my staff off the ground and jabbed it between Arra's calves. With a sharp twist, I sent her sprawling. She shrieked, and for a split second I was sure I'd knocked her off and won, but she grabbed for the bar on her way down and held on, as I was doing. Her staff, however, struck the floor and spun away.

The vampires who'd gathered to watch – there were twenty or thirty around the bars now – clapped loudly as we hauled ourselves back to our feet and eyed each other warily. I lifted my staff and smiled. "Seems like *I* have the advantage now," I noted cockily.

"Not for long," Arra grunted. "I'm going to rip that staff out of your hands and smash your head in with it!"

"Is that so?" I grinned. "Come on then — let's see you try!"

Arra spread her hands and closed in on me. I hadn't really expected her to attack without her staff and wasn't sure what to do. I didn't like the idea of striking an unarmed opponent, especially a woman.

"You can pick your staff up if you want," I offered.

"Leaving the bars isn't allowed," she replied.

"Get someone to bring it to you then."

"That's not allowed either."

I retreated. "I don't want to hit you when you've nothing to defend yourself with," I said. "How about I throw away my staff as well and we fight hand to hand?"

"A vampire who abandons his weapon is a fool," Arra said. "If you throw the staff away, I'll ram it down your throat to teach you a lesson when we're through up here on the bars."

"OK!" I snapped irritably. "Have it your own way." I stopped retreating, raised my staff and laid into her.

Arra was hunched over — she had a lower centre of gravity that way and would be harder to knock off — so I was able to aim at her head. I jabbed at her face with the end of my staff. She avoided the first couple of blows, but I struck her cheek with the third. It didn't draw blood, but left a nasty welt.

Arra was retreating now. She gave ground grudgingly, standing up to my lesser strikes, taking them on her arms and hands, only backing up to avoid the heavier blows. Despite my earlier warning to myself, I grew over-confident. I thought I had her where I wanted. Instead of taking my time and finishing her off slowly, I went for the quick kill, and that proved my undoing.

I flicked the end of my staff towards the side of her head, planning to sting her ear. It was a casual swipe, neither as sharp nor as fast as it needed to be. I connected with her ear, but there was no power in the shot. Before I could draw back for my next, Arra's hands sprang into action.

Her right hand grasped the end of my staff and held it tight. Her left hand balled up into a fist and smashed into my jaw. She hit me again and I saw stars. As she drew back her fist for a third punch, I reacted automatically and stepped clear of her reach, which was when she gave a quick wrench and ripped my staff away from me.

"Now!" she hooted triumphantly, twirling the staff over her head. "Now who has the advantage?"

"Take it easy, Arra," I said nervously, backing away from her like crazy. "I offered to give you your staff back, remember?"

"And I refused," she snorted.

"Let him have a staff, Arra," Kurda said. "You can't expect him to defend himself with his bare hands. It isn't fair."

"How about it, *boy*?" she asked. "I'll let you call for a replacement staff if you wish." By her tone, I knew she wouldn't think much of me if I did.

I shook my head. I'd have traded anything I owned for a

staff, but I wasn't about to ask for special favours, not when Arra hadn't. "That's OK," I said. "I'll fight on like I am."

"Darren!" Kurda howled. "Don't be stupid. Call it off if you don't want another staff. You've fought bravely and proved your courage."

"There would be no shame in quitting now," Vanez agreed.

I stared into Arra's eyes, saw that she expected me to resign, and stopped. "No," I said. "No quitting. I won't get off these bars till I'm knocked off." I started forward, hunched over like Arra had been.

Arra blinked, surprised, then raised her staff and set about ending the contest. It didn't take long. I blocked her first jab with my left hand, took her second in the belly, ducked out of the way of her third, slapped away her fourth with my right hand. But I was caught square around the back of my head by her fifth. I dropped to my knees, groggy. There was the sound of rushing air, then the round end of Arra's staff connected cleanly with the left side of my face and I went crashing to the ground.

The next thing I knew, I was staring up at the roof, surrounded by concerned vampires. "Darren?" Kurda asked, worry in his voice. "Are you all right?"

"What ... happened?" I wheezed.

"She knocked you out," he said. "You've been unconscious for five or six minutes. We were about to send for help."

I sat up, wincing at the pain. "Why's the room spinning?" I groaned.

Vanez laughed and helped me to my feet. "He'll be fine," the games master said. "A bit of concussion never killed a vampire. A good day's sleep and he'll be right as night."

"How much further is it to Vampire Mountain?" I asked weakly.

"The poor child doesn't know whether he's coming or going!" Kurda snapped, and started to lead me away.

"Wait!" I shouted, my head clearing a bit. I looked for Arra Sails and spotted her sitting on one of the bars, applying a cream to her bruised cheek. Shaking free of Kurda, I stumbled across to the vampiress and stood as firmly as I could before her.

"Yes?" she asked, eyeing me guardedly.

I stuck out a hand and said, "Shake."

Arra stared at the hand, then into my unfocused eyes. "One good fight doesn't make you a warrior," she said.

"Shake!" I repeated angrily.

"And if I don't?" she asked.

"I'll get back up on the bars and fight you till you do," I growled.

Arra studied me at length, then nodded and took my hand. "Power to you, Darren Shan," she said gruffly.

"Power," I repeated weakly, then fainted into her arms and knew no more till I came to in my hammock the next night.

CHAPTER EIGHTEEN

TWO NIGHTS after my encounter with Arra Sails, Mr
Crepsley and me were called before the Vampire Princes. I
was still stiff from my fight and Mr Crepsley had to help me
dress. I groaned as I raised my arms over my head — they
were black and blue from where I'd taken Arra's blows.

"I cannot believe you were foolish enough to challenge
Arra Sails," Mr Crepsley tutted. He'd been teasing me about
my fight with the vampiress since learning of it, although
underneath his mocking front I could tell he was proud of
me. "Even *I* would hesitate at going one on one with her on
the bars."

"Guess that means I'm braver than you," I smirked.

"Stupidity and bravery are not the same thing," he chided
me. "You could have been seriously injured."

"You sound like Kurda," I sulked.

"I do not agree with Kurda's views on the fighting ways of

vampires – he is a pacifist, which runs contrary to our nature – but he is correct when he says that sometimes it is better not to fight. When a situation is hopeless, and there is nothing at stake, only a fool battles on."

"But it wasn't hopeless!" I exclaimed. "I almost beat her!"

Mr Crepsley smiled. "You are impossible to talk to. But so are most vampires. It is a sign that you are learning. Now finish dressing and make yourself presentable. We must not keep the Princes waiting."

✻ ✻ ✻

The Hall of Princes was situated at the highest internal point of Vampire Mountain. There was only one entrance to it, a long, wide tunnel guarded by a host of Mountain Guards. I hadn't been up here before — nobody could use the tunnel unless they had business in the Hall.

The green-garbed guards watched us every step of the way. You weren't allowed to take weapons into the Hall of Princes, or carry anything which might be used as a weapon. Shoes weren't permitted – too easy to hide a small dagger in the soles – and we were searched from head to foot at three different parts of the tunnel. The guards even ran combs through our hair, in case we had thin wires hidden inside!

"Why all the security?" I whispered to Mr Crepsley. "I thought the Princes were respected and obeyed by all vampires."

"They are," he said. "This is for tradition's sake more than anything else."

At the end of the tunnel we emerged into a huge cavern, in which a strange white dome stood gleaming. It was like no other building I'd ever seen — the walls pulsed, as though alive, and there were no joins or cracks that I could make out.

"What is it?" I asked.

"The Hall of Princes," Mr Crepsley said.

"What's it made of — rock, marble, iron?"

Mr Crepsley shrugged. "Nobody knows." He led me to the dome — the only guards on this side of the tunnel were grouped around the doors to the Hall — and told me to place my hands on it.

"It's warm!" I gasped. "And it throbs! What *is* it?"

"Long ago, the Hall of Princes was like any other," Mr Crepsley answered in his usual roundabout way. "Then, one night, Mr Tiny arrived and said he had gifts for us. This was shortly after the vampaneze had split from the vampires. The 'gifts' were the dome — which his Little People constructed, unseen by any vampire — and the Stone of Blood. The dome and Stone are magical artefacts. They—"

One of the guards at the doors hailed us. "Larten Crepsley! Darren Shan!" We hurried over. "You may be admitted now," the guard said, and struck the doors four times with the large spear he was carrying. The doors slid open — like electronic doors — and we entered.

Though no torches burned inside the Hall of Princes, it was as bright as day, far brighter than anywhere else in the mountain. The light originated in the walls of the dome itself, by means unknown to all but Mr Tiny. Long seats —

like pews – ran in circles around the dome. There was a large space at the centre, where four wooden thrones stood mounted on a platform. Three of the thrones were occupied by Vampire Princes. Mr Crepsley had told me that at least one Prince always skipped Council, in case anything happened to the others. Nothing hung from the walls, no paintings, portraits or flags. There were no statues either. This was a place for business, not pomp or ceremony.

Most of the seats were filled. Ordinary vampires sat at the rear; the middle sections were reserved for Mountain personnel, guards and the like. Vampire Generals occupied the front seats. Mr Crepsley and me made our way to the third row of seats from the front and slid in beside Kurda Smahlt, Gavner Purl and Harkat Mulds, who were waiting for us. I was glad to see the Little Person again, and asked what he'd been up to.

"Answering ... questions," he replied. "Saying same thing ... over and over ... and over ... again."

"Did any more of your memory come back?" I asked.

"No."

"But it's not for want of trying," Gavner laughed, leaning forward to squeeze my shoulder. "We've been practically torturing Harkat with questions, trying to get him to remember. And he hasn't complained once. If I was in his place, I'd have raised hell ages ago. He hasn't even been allowed to sleep!"

"Don't need ... much sleep," Harkat said shyly.

"Recovered from your bout with Arra yet?" Kurda asked.

Before I could answer, Gavner piped up. "I heard about that! What in Paradise were you thinking? I'd rather face a pit full of scorpions than hop on the bars with Arra Sails. I saw her make mincemeat of twenty seasoned vampires one night."

"It seemed like a good idea at the time," I grinned.

Gavner had to leave us to discuss something with a bunch of other Generals — vampires were forever debating serious issues in the Hall of Princes — and while we were waiting, Mr Crepsley explained a little more about the dome.

"The dome is magical. There is no way in except through the single set of doors. Nothing can penetrate its walls, no tool, explosive or acid. It is the toughest material known to man or vampire."

"Where did it come from?" I asked.

"We do not know. The Little People brought it in covered wagons. It took them months to haul it up, one sheet at a time. We were not allowed to watch as they assembled it. Our finest architects have been over it many times since, but not one can unravel its mysteries.

"The doors can only be opened by a Vampire Prince," he went on. "They can open them by laying their palms directly on the panels of the doors, or from their thrones, by pressing their palms down on the armrests."

"They must be electronic," I said. "The panels 'read' their fingerprints, right?"

Mr Crepsley shook his head. "The Hall was built centuries ago, long before electricity was even a thought in the minds of Man. It operates by paranormal means, or by a form of technology far advanced of anything we know.

"You see the red stone behind the Princes?" he asked. It was set on a pedestal five metres behind the platform, an oval stone, about twice the size of a football. "That is the Stone of Blood. That is the key, not only to the dome, but to the longevity of the vampire race itself."

"Long— what?" I asked.

"Longevity. It means long life."

"How can a stone have anything to do with a long life?" I asked, puzzled.

"The Stone serves several purposes," he said. "Every vampire, when accepted into the fold, must stand before the Stone and place his hands on it. The Stone looks as smooth as a ball of glass, but is ultra-sharp to the touch. It draws blood, which is absorbed by the Stone – hence its name – linking the vampire to the mental collective of the clan forever."

"Mental collective?" I repeated, wishing for the umpteenth time since I'd met Mr Crepsley that he'd use simple words.

"You know how vampires can mentally search for those they have bonded with?"

"Yes."

"Well, using the method of triangulation, we can also search for and find those we have *not* bonded with, via the Stone."

"Triangu— *what*?" I groaned, exasperated.

"Let us say you are a full-vampire whose blood has been absorbed by the Stone," he said. "When a vampire gives his blood, he also gives his name, by which the Stone and other vampires will thenceforth recognize him. If I want to search for you after you have been blooded, I merely place my hands on the Stone of Blood and think your name. Within seconds the Stone allows me to pinpoint your exact location anywhere on Earth."

"You could do this even if I didn't want to be found?" I asked.

"Yes. But pinpointing your location would be no good — by the time I got to where you had been when I made the search, you would have moved on. Hence the need for triangulation, which simply means three people are involved. If I wanted to find you, I could contact someone I was bonded with — Gavner, for instance — and mentally transmit your whereabouts to him. With me guiding him via the Stone of Blood, he could track you down."

I thought that over in silence a while. It was an ingenious system but I could see a few drawbacks. "Can anyone use the Stone of Blood to find a vampire?" I asked.

"Anyone with the ability to search mentally," Mr Crepsley said.

"Even a human or a vampaneze?"

"Very few humans have minds advanced enough to use the Stone," he said, "but the vampaneze have."

"Isn't the Stone dangerous then?" I asked. "If a vampaneze got his hands on it, couldn't he track every vampire down — at least all the ones he knew the names of — and guide his colleagues to them?"

Mr Crepsley smiled grimly. "Your battering at the hands of Arra Sails has not affected your powers of reasoning. You are correct — the Stone of Blood *would* mean the end of the vampire race if it fell into the wrong hands. The vampaneze would be able to hunt all of us down. They can also find those they do not know the names of – the Stone lets its user search for vampires by location as well as name, so they could scan for every vampire in England or America or wherever, then send out others to track them down. That is why we guard the Stone carefully and never let it leave the safety of the dome."

"Wouldn't it be simpler just to break it?" I asked.

Kurda, who'd been eavesdropping, laughed. "I put that proposal to the Princes several decades ago," he said. "The Stone could resist normal tools and explosives, the same as the walls of the dome, but that doesn't mean it's impossible to get rid of safely. 'Throw the damn thing down a volcano,' I pleaded, 'or toss it in the deepest sea.' They wouldn't hear of such a thing."

"Why not?" I asked.

"There are a number of reasons," Mr Crepsley answered before Kurda could reply. "First, the Stone can be used to locate vampires who are missing or in trouble, or those who are mad and on the loose. It is healthy to know that we are joined to the clan by more than tradition, that we can always rely on aid if we lead good lives, and punishment if we do not. The Stone keeps us in line.

"Second, the Stone of Blood is necessary to operate the

doors of the dome. When a vampire becomes a Prince, the Stone is a vital part of the ceremony. He forms a circle around it with two other Princes. They each use a hand to pump blood into him, while laying their other hand on the Stone. Blood flows from the old Princes to the new Prince, then to the Stone, and back again. By the end of the ceremony, the new Prince can control the doors of the Hall. Without the Stone, he would be a Prince in name only.

"There is a third reason why we do not destroy the Stone — the Lord of the Vampaneze." His face was dark. "The myth says that the Vampaneze Lord will wipe the vampire race from the face of the Earth when he comes to power, but through the Stone of Blood we might one night rise again."

"How's that possible?" I asked.

"We do not know," Mr Crepsley said. "But those were the words of Mr Tiny, and since the power of the Stone is also his, it makes sense to pay heed. Now more than ever, we must protect the Stone. Harkat's message concerning the Vampaneze Lord has struck at the hearts and spirits of many vampires. With the Stone, there is hope. To dispose of it now would be to surrender to fear."

"Charna's guts!" Kurda snorted. "I've no time for those old myths. We should get rid of the Stone, shut down the dome and build a new Hall of Princes. Apart from anything else, it's one of the main reasons the vampaneze are loathe to make a deal with us. They don't want to be hooked up to a magical tool of Mr Tiny's, and who can blame them? They're afraid of bonding with the Stone — they could never split from the vampire clan if they did, because we'd be able to use the Stone to hunt them down. If we removed the Stone, they might return to us, and then the vampaneze would be no more – there'd be one big family of vampires – and the threat of the Vampaneze Lord would evaporate."

"Does that mean you will be seeking to destroy the Stone when you are a Prince?" Mr Crepsley enquired.

"I'll mention the possibility," Kurda nodded. "It's a sensitive issue, and I don't expect the Generals to agree to it, but in time, as negotiations between ourselves and the vampaneze develop, I hope they'll come round to my way of thinking."

"Did you make this clear when you were seeking election?" Mr Crepsley asked.

Kurda shifted uncomfortably. "Well, no, but that's politics. Sometimes you have to hold things back. I didn't lie about it. If anyone had asked me for my views on the Stone, I'd have told them. They just ... didn't ... ask," he finished lamely.

"*Politics!*" Mr Crepsley huffed. "It is a sad day for vampires when our Princes voluntarily ensnare themselves in the despicable webs of politics." Sticking his nose in the air, he turned his back on Kurda and stared straight ahead at the platform.

"I've upset him," Kurda whispered to me.

"He's easily upset," I grinned. Then I asked if *I'd* have to bond with the Stone of Blood.

"Probably not until you become a full-vampire," Kurda said. "Half-vampires have been allowed to bond with it in the past, but not in the normal run of things."

I was going to ask more about the mysterious Stone of Blood and the dome, but then a serious-looking General banged the floor of the platform with a heavy staff and announced my name, along with Mr Crepsley's.

It was time to meet the Princes.

CHAPTER NINETEEN

THE THREE Vampire Princes in attendance were Paris Skyle, Mika Ver Leth, and Arrow. (The absent Prince was called Vancha March.)

Paris Skyle had a long grey beard, flowing white hair, no right ear, and he was the oldest living vampire at eight hundred earth years or more. He was revered by the others, not only for his immense age and position, but for his exploits when younger — according to the legends, Paris Skyle had been everywhere and done everything. Many of the tales were fanciful – he'd sailed with Columbus to America and introduced vampirism to the New World, fought beside Joan of Arc (a vampire sympathizer, apparently) and provided the inspiration for Bram Stoker's infamous *Dracula*. But that didn't mean the tales weren't true – vampires were, by their very existence, fanciful creatures.

Mika Ver Leth was the youngest Vampire Prince, a 'mere'

two hundred and seventy. He had shiny black hair and piercing eyes, like a raven's, and he dressed all in black. He looked even sterner than Mr Crepsley – his forehead was creased with wrinkles, as were the sides of his mouth – and I got the feeling he rarely smiled, if at all.

Arrow was a thickly-built bald man, with long tattoos of arrows adorning his arms and the sides of his head. He was a fearsome fighter, whose hatred of the vampaneze was legendary. He'd been married to a human before becoming a General, but she had been killed by a vampaneze who'd come to fight Arrow. He had returned to the fold, sullen and withdrawn, and trained to be a General. Since then he had devoted himself to his work, to the exclusion of all else.

All three Princes were burly, muscular men. Even the ancient Paris Skyle looked like he could toss an ox over his shoulder using a single hand.

"Greetings, Larten," Paris said to Mr Crepsley, stroking his long grey beard and studying the vampire with warm eyes. "It is good to see you in the Hall of Princes. I did not think I would look upon your face again."

"I vowed I would be back," Mr Crepsley replied, bowing before the Prince.

"I never doubted it," Paris smiled. "I just did not think I would be alive to welcome you. I have grown long of tooth, old friend. My nights are numbered."

"You will outlive us all, Paris," Mr Crepsley said.

"We shall see," Paris sighed. He fixed his gaze on me while Mr Crepsley bowed to the other Princes. When the vampire returned to my side, the old Prince said, "This must be your assistant — Darren Shan. Gavner Purl has spoken approvingly of him."

"He is of good blood and strong heart," Mr Crepsley said. "A fine assistant, who will one night make a first-rate vampire."

"'*One night*' indeed!" Mika Ver Leth snorted, squinting at me in a way I didn't like. "He's just a *boy!* This is no time for children to be admitted to our ranks. What possessed you to—"

"Please, Mika," Paris Skyle interrupted. "Let us not speak rashly. All here know the character of Larten Crepsley. We must treat him with the respect he has earned. I do not know why he chose to blood a child, but I am certain he can explain."

"I just think it's crazy, in this night and age." Mika Ver Leth grumbled his way to silence. When he was still, Paris turned to me and smiled.

"You must forgive us, Darren, if we seem discourteous. We are unused to children. It has been a long time since any were presented before us."

"I'm not really a child," I muttered. "I've been a half-vampire for eight years. It's not my fault my body hasn't aged."

"Precisely!" Mika Ver Leth snapped. "It's the fault of the vampire who blooded you. He—"

"Mika!" Paris snapped. "This vampire of noble standing and his assistant have come before us in good faith, to seek

150

our approval. Whether we grant it or not, they deserve to be heard politely, not challenged rudely in front of their colleagues."

Mika collected himself, stood and bowed to us. "Sorry," he said through gritted teeth. "I spoke out of turn. I will not do so again."

A murmur spread through the Hall. From the whispers, I gathered that it was most unusual for a Prince to apologize to an inferior, especially one who was no longer a General.

"Come, Larten," Paris said, as chairs were brought forward for us. "Sit and tell us what you have been up to since last we met."

Once we were seated, Mr Crepsley ran through his story. He told the Princes of his association with the Cirque Du Freak, the places he'd been, the people he'd met. When he came to the part about Murlough, he asked to speak to the Princes in private. He told them in whispers of the mad vampaneze, and how we'd killed him. They were disturbed by the news.

"This is worrisome," Paris mused aloud. "If the vampaneze find out, they could use it as an excuse to start a war."

"How could they?" Mr Crepsley responded. "I am no longer part of the clan."

"If they were suitably enraged, they could overlook that," Mika Ver Leth said. "If the rumour of the Vampaneze Lord is true, we must tread very carefully where our blood cousins are concerned."

"Still," Arrow said, contributing to the conversation for the first time, "I don't think Larten erred. It would be different if he were a General, but as a free agent, he is not bound by our laws. Were I in his position, I'd have done the same thing. He acted discreetly. I don't think we can fault him for that."

"No," Mika agreed. Glancing at me, he added, "Not for *that*."

With the matter of Murlough out of the way, we returned to our chairs and raised our voices so that all in the Hall could hear.

"Now," Paris Skyle said, adopting a grave expression. "It is time we returned to the business of your assistant. We all know that the world has changed vastly these last few centuries. Humans are more protective of one another and their laws are stricter than ever, particularly with regard to their young. That is why we no longer blood children. Even in the past, we blooded few of them. It has been ninety years since we last added a child to our ranks. Tell us, Larten, why you decided to break with recent tradition."

Mr Crepsley cleared his throat and locked eyes with the Princes, one after the other, until they settled on Mika. "I have no valid reason," he said calmly, and the Hall erupted into barely-contained shouts and muffled, hurried conversations.

"There will be quiet in the Hall!" Paris shouted, and all noise ceased at once. He looked troubled when he faced us. "Come, Larten, do not play games. You would not blood a boy out of simple fancy. There must be a reason. Did you kill his parents, perhaps, and decide it was your place to take care of him?"

"His parents are alive," Mr Crepsley said.

"Both of them?" Mika snapped.

"Yes."

"Then they are looking for him?" Paris asked.

"No. We faked his death. They buried him. They think he is dead."

"That much at least you did right," Paris murmured. "But why blood him in the first place?" When Mr Crepsley didn't answer, he turned to me and asked, "Darren? Do *you* know why he blooded you?"

Hoping to bail the vampire out of trouble, I said, "I found out the truth about him, so maybe part of it was to protect himself — he might have figured that he had to make me his assistant or kill me."

"That is a reasonable excuse," Paris noted.

"But not the truth," Mr Crepsley sighed. "I was never afraid of being exposed by Darren. In fact, the only reason he discovered the truth about me was because I tried to blood a friend of his, a boy his own age."

The Hall erupted into controversy, and it took the barking Princes several minutes to quiet the vampires. When order was finally restored, Paris resumed the questioning, more troubled than ever. "You tried to blood *another* boy?"

Mr Crepsley nodded. "But his blood was tainted with evil — he would not have made a good vampire."

"Let me get this straight," Mika growled. "You tried blooding one boy, but couldn't; his friend found out, so you blooded him instead?"

"That is about the sum of it," Mr Crepsley agreed. "I also blooded him in a rush, without revealing the full truth of our ways, which was unpardonable. In my defence I will add that I studied him at great length before blooding him, and was convinced of his honesty and strength of character when I did."

"What drew you to the first boy — the one with evil blood?" Paris asked.

"He knew who I was. He had seen a portrait of me in an old book, drawn long ago when I was using the name of Vur Horston. He asked to become my assistant."

"Didn't you explain our ways to him?" Mika asked. "Didn't you tell him we don't blood children?"

"I tried, but..." Mr Crepsley shook his head miserably. "It was as though I had no control over myself. I knew it was wrong, but I would have blooded him regardless, if not for his foul blood. I cannot explain why, because I do not understand it."

"You'll have to come up with a better argument than that," Mika warned him.

"I cannot," Mr Crepsley said softly, "because I have none."

There was a polite cough behind us and Gavner Purl stepped forward. "May I intervene on my friend's behalf?" he asked.

"By all means," Paris said. "We welcome your input, if it can clear things up."

"I don't know if it can do that," Gavner said, "but I'd like to note that Darren is an extraordinary boy. He made the trek to Vampire Mountain — no small feat for one his age — and fought a bear poisoned with vampaneze blood along the way. I'm sure you have heard of his contest with Arra Sails a few nights ago."

"We have," Paris chuckled.

"He is bright and brave, wily and honest. I believe he has the makings of a fine vampire. Given the chance, I think he'll excel. He's young, but younger vampires than him have come through the ranks. You were only two years old when you were blooded, weren't you, Sire?" he asked Paris Skyle.

"That's not the point!" Mika Ver Leth shouted. "This boy could be the next Khledon Lurt and it wouldn't make a blind bit of difference. Facts are facts — vampires no longer blood children. It will set a dangerous precedent if we let this pass without taking action."

"Mika is right," Arrow spoke softly. "The boy's courage and ability are not the issue. Larten acted poorly in blooding the boy and we must address that."

Paris nodded slowly. "They speak the truth, Larten. It would be wrong of us to ignore this. You yourself would never have tolerated such a breach of the rules were you in our position."

"I know," Mr Crepsley sighed. "I do not seek forgiveness, merely consideration. And I ask that no reprisals be taken against Darren. The fault is mine, and I alone should be punished."

"I don't know about *punishment*," Mika said uncomfortably.

"I'm not out to make an example of you. Dragging your good name through the muck is the last thing on my mind."

"None of us wish to do that," Arrow agreed. "But what option have we? He did wrong — we must address that wrong."

"But we must address it mercifully," Paris mused.

"I ask for no mercy," Mr Crepsley said stiffly. "I am not a young vampire who acted out of ignorance. I expect no special treatment. If you decide I am to be executed, I will accept your verdict without complaint. If—"

"They can't kill you because of *me!*" I gasped.

"—If you decide I must be tested," he continued, ignoring my outburst, "I will rise to any challenge you care to set, and die meeting it if I must."

"There will be no challenge," Paris huffed. "We reserve challenges for those who have not proven themselves in battle. I will say once again — your good standing is not in question."

"Perhaps..." Arrow said hesitantly, then lapsed into silence. A few seconds later, he resumed. "I think I have it. The talk of challenges gave me an idea. There *is* a way to resolve this without killing our old friend or soiling his good name." Pointing a finger at me, he said coolly, "Let's set a challenge for the *boy.*"

CHAPTER TWENTY

THERE WAS a long, thoughtful silence. "Yes," Paris Skyle finally murmured. "A challenge for the boy."

"I said I did not want to bring Darren into this!" Mr Crepsley objected.

"No," Mika contradicted him. "You said you didn't want him to be *punished*. Well, he won't be — a challenge is not a punishment."

"It is fair, Larten," Paris agreed. "If the boy proves himself in a test, your decision to blood him will be accepted and no more need be said about it."

"And the dishonour will be *his* if he fails," Arrow added.

Mr Crepsley scratched his long facial scar. "It is an honest solution," he mused, "but the decision is Darren's, not mine. I will not force a challenge on him." He turned to me. "Are you prepared to prove yourself to the clan and clear our names?"

I fidgeted uneasily on my chair. "Um ... what sort of a

challenge are we talking about exactly?" I asked.

"A good question," Paris said. "It would be unfair to pit him in battle against one of our warriors — a half-vampire is no match for a General."

"And a quest would take too long," Arrow said.

"That leaves the Trials," Mika muttered.

"No!" someone shouted behind us. Looking around, I spotted a red-faced Kurda striding towards the platform. "I won't stand for this!" he stormed. "The boy isn't ready for the Trials. If you insist on testing him, let him wait till he is older."

"There will be no waiting," Mika growled, rising to his feet and taking a few steps towards Kurda. "*We* wield the authority here, Kurda Smahlt — you're not a Prince yet, so don't act like one."

Kurda stopped and glowered at Mika, then dropped to one knee and bowed his head. "My apologies for speaking out of turn, Sire."

"Apology accepted," Mika grunted, returning to his seat.

"Have I the permission of the Princes to speak?" Kurda asked.

Paris checked with Mika, who shrugged curtly. "You have," he said.

"The Trials of Initiation are for experienced vampires," Kurda said. "They were not designed for children. It wouldn't be fair to subject him to them."

"Life for vampires has never been *fair*," Mr Crepsley said. "But it can be *just*. I do not enjoy the idea of submitting

Darren to the Trials, but it is a just decision and I shall stand by it if he agrees."

"Excuse me," I said, "but what *are* the Trials?"

Paris smiled kindly at me. "The Trials of Initiation are tests for vampires who wish to become Generals," he explained.

"What would I have to do?"

"Perform five acts of physical courage," he said. "The tests are picked at random and are different for each vampire. One involves diving to the bottom of a deep pool and retrieving a dropped medallion. In another you must dodge falling boulders. In another you must cross a hall filled with burning coals. Some tests are more difficult than others, but none are easy. The risk is great, and though most vampires survive, death by misadventure is not unheard of."

"You mustn't agree to this, Darren," Kurda hissed. "The Trials are for full-vampires. You aren't strong, quick or experienced enough. You'll be signing your death warrant if you say yes."

"I disagree," Mr Crepsley said. "Darren *is* capable of passing the Trials. It will not be easy, and he may struggle, but I would not let him step forward if I thought he would be completely out of his depth."

"Let's vote on it," Mika said. "I say it's the Trials. Arrow?"

"I agree — the Trials."

"Paris?"

The oldest living vampire shook his head uncertainly. "Kurda has a point when he says the Trials are not for children. I trust your judgement, Larten, but fear your optimism is misplaced."

"Can you suggest another way?" Mika snapped.

"No, but..." Paris sighed deeply. "What do the Generals think?" he asked, addressing those in the Hall. "We have heard from Kurda and Mika. Does anyone else have anything to add?"

The Generals muttered among themselves, until a familiar figure stood and cleared her throat — Arra Sails. "I respect Darren Shan," she said. "I have shaken his hand, and those who know me know how much that means to me. I believe Gavner Purl and Larten Crepsley when they say he will be a valuable addition to our ranks.

"But I also agree with Mika Ver Leth — Darren must prove himself. All of us have had to endure the Trials. They help make us what we are. As a woman, the odds were stacked against me, but I overcame them and took my place in this Hall as an equal. There must be no exceptions. A vampire who cannot pull his own weight is of no use to us. We have no place for children who need to be wet-nursed and tucked into their coffins at daybreak.

"Having said that," she concluded, "I don't think Darren will let us down. I believe he will pass the Trials and prove himself. I have every confidence in him." She smiled at me, then glared at Kurda. "And those who say otherwise – those who'd wrap him in blankets – should not be heeded. To deny Darren the right of Trials would be to shame him."

"Noble words," Kurda sneered. "Will you repeat them at his funeral?"

"Better to die with pride than live in shame," Arra retorted.

Kurda cursed quietly to himself. "How about it, Darren?" he asked. "Will you face death just to prove yourself to these fools?"

"No," I said, and saw a pained look cross Mr Crepsley's face. "But I'll face death to prove myself to *me*," I added. When the red-cloaked vampire heard that, he beamed proudly and raised a clenched fist in salute.

"Let us put it to the Hall," Paris said. "How many think Darren should undertake the Trials of Initiation?" Every arm went up. Kurda turned aside in disgust. "Darren? You are willing to proceed?"

I looked up at Mr Crepsley and made a sign for him to bend down. In a whisper, I asked him what would happen if I said no. "You would be disgraced and sent from Vampire Mountain in shame," he said solemnly.

"Would you be shamed too?" I asked, knowing how much his good name meant to him.

He sighed. "In the eyes of the Princes I would not be, but in my own eyes I would. Having chosen and blooded you, I feel any shame of yours would also be mine."

I gave that careful consideration. I'd learnt a lot about Mr Crepsley, how he thought and lived, during the eight years I'd served as his assistant. "You couldn't bear such shame, could you?" I asked.

His expression softened. "No," he said quietly.

"You'd go and chase an early death. Hunt wild animals and fight vampaneze, and push yourself until one of them killed you?"

"Something along those lines," he agreed with a quick nod.

I couldn't let that happen. Six years ago, when we'd gone after Murlough, the mad vampaneze had kidnapped Evra, and Mr Crepsley had offered to trade his life for the snake-boy's. He'd have done the same for me if I'd fallen into the killer's hands. I didn't like the sound of these Trials, but if undertaking them meant Mr Crepsley could carry on without shame, I owed it to him to place myself in the firing line.

Facing the Princes, I stood up straight and said solidly, "I agree to the Trials."

"Then it is decided," Paris Skyle smiled approvingly. "Return tomorrow and we shall draw the first Trial. You may leave now and rest."

That was the end of our meeting. I left the Hall with Gavner, Harkat and Kurda. Mr Crepsley stayed to discuss business with the Princes — I think it had to do with Mr Tiny, Harkat's message and the dead vampaneze and vampire we'd found on our way here.

"I'm glad ... to leave at ... last," Harkat said as we made our way back to the Halls. "I was ... growing bored of ... same old ... scenery."

I smiled, then glanced at Gavner worriedly. "How tough

are these Trials?" I asked.

"Very," he sighed.

"Try tough as the walls of the Hall of Princes," Kurda growled.

"They're not *that* difficult," Gavner said. "Don't exaggerate the dangers, Kurda — you'll frighten him."

"That's the last thing I want to do," Kurda said, smiling encouragingly at me. "But the Trials are meant for fully-grown vampires. I spent six years preparing for them, like most vampires do, yet I only barely scraped through."

"Darren will be OK," Gavner insisted, though the doubt in his voice was only barely concealed.

"Besides," I laughed, trying to cheer Kurda up, "I can always drop out if I get in over my head."

Kurda stared hard at me. "Weren't you listening? Didn't you understand?"

"What do you mean?" I asked.

"Nobody walks away from the Trials," Gavner said. "You might fail, but you can't quit — the Generals won't let you."

"So I'll fail," I shrugged. "I'll throw in the towel if things get hairy — pretend I've twisted an ankle or something."

"He *doesn't* understand!" Gavner groaned. "We should have explained it fully before we let him agree. He's given his word now, so there's no going back. Black blood of Harnon Oan!"

"*What* don't I understand?" I asked, confused.

"In the Trials, failure entails one fate only — death!" Kurda told me grimly. I stared at him wordlessly. "Most who fail, die in the attempt. But should you fail and not die, you will be taken to the Hall of Death, strapped into a cage, hoisted above the pit, and—" he gulped, averted his eyes, and finished in a terrible whisper, "—*dropped on the stakes until you are dead!*"

DARREN SHAN
TRIALS OF DEATH

THE SAGA OF DARREN SHAN
BOOK 5

For:

Nora & Davey – ever-gracious hosts

OBEs (Order of the Bloody Entrails) to:
The enormous, fearsome Emily Ford
Kellee "take no prisoners" Nunley

Mechanics of the Macabre:
Biddy & Liam
Gillie & Zoë
Emma & Chris

PROLOGUE

IF PEOPLE ever tell you vampires aren't real — don't believe them! The world's full of vampires. Not evil, shape-changing, cross-fearing creatures like in the legends, but honorable, long-living, extra-strong beings who need to drink blood to survive. They interfere as little as possible in the affairs of humans, and never kill those they drink from.

Hidden away in some snowy, barely accessible corner of the world, stands Vampire Mountain, where vampires meet every twelve years. The Council (as they call it) is presided over by the Vampire Princes – who are obeyed by all vampires – and most of those in attendance are Vampire Generals, whose job is to govern the walking undead.

In order to present me to the Princes, Mr Crepsley had dragged me along to Vampire Mountain and the Council. Mr Crepsley's a vampire. I'm his assistant, a half-vampire — my name's Darren Shan.

It was a long, hard journey. We travelled with a friend of ours — Gavner Purl — four wolves and two Little People, strange creatures who work for a mysterious master by the name of Mr Tiny. One of the Little People was killed on the way by a mad bear which had drunk the blood of a dead vampaneze (they're like vampires, except they have purple skin, red eyes, nails and hair — and they *always* kill when they feed). The other then spoke — the first time ever that a Little Person had communicated with anyone — and told us his name was Harkat Mulds. He also delivered a chilling message from Mr Tiny: a Vampaneze Lord would soon come into power and lead the purple-skinned killers into war against the vampires — and win!

Finally we arrived at Vampire Mountain, inside which the vampires lived in a warren of tunnels and large caves. There I made friends with a number of vampires, including Seba Nile, who'd been Mr Crepsley's teacher when he was younger; Arra Sails, one of the few female vampires; Vanez Blane, a one-eyed games master; and Kurda Smahlt, a General who was soon to become a Prince.

The Princes and most of the Generals weren't impressed with me. They said I was too young to be a vampire and criticized Mr Crepsley for blooding me. To prove myself worthy of being a half-vampire, I had to undertake the Trials of Initiation, a series of tough tests usually reserved for budding Generals. When I was making up my mind to accept the challenge, they told me that if I passed, I'd be accepted into the vampire ranks. What they neglected to tell me until afterwards (when it was too late to back out) was that if I failed — I'd be *killed!*

CHAPTER ONE

THE VAST cavern known as the Hall of Khledon Lurt was almost deserted. Apart from those sitting at my table — Gavner, Kurda and Harkat — there was only one other vampire present, a guard who sat by himself and sipped from a mug of ale, whistling tunelessly.

Roughly four hours had passed since I learned I was to be judged in the Trials of Initiation. I still didn't know very much about the Trials, but from the glum faces of my companions, and by what had been said in the Hall of Princes, I gathered my chances of emerging victorious were, at best, slim.

While Kurda and Gavner muttered on about my Trials, I studied Harkat, who I hadn't seen much of recently (he'd been cooped up in the Hall of Princes, answering questions). He was dressed in his traditional blue robes, although he now wore his hood down, no longer bothering to hide his grey, scarred, stitched-together face. Harkat had no nose, and his ears were sewn beneath the skin of his skull. He had a pair of large, round, green eyes, set near the top of his head. His mouth was jagged and full of sharp teeth. Normal air was poisonous to him — ten or twelve hours of it would kill him — so he wore a special mask which kept him alive. He moved it down over his chin when he was talking or eating, and back up to cover his mouth when he wasn't. Harkat had once been human, but had died and come back in this body, after striking a deal with Mr Tiny. He couldn't remember who he'd been or what sort of a deal he'd struck.

Harkat had carried a message to the Princes from Mr Tiny, to the effect that the night of the Vampaneze Lord was at hand. The Vampaneze Lord was a mythical figure whose arrival would supposedly signal the start of a war between the vampires and vampaneze, which — according to Mr Tiny — the vampaneze would win, wiping out the vampire forces in the process.

Catching my eye, Harkat lowered his mask and said, "Have you ... seen much of ... the Halls?"

"A fair bit of them," I replied.

"You must ... take me ... on a tour."

"Darren won't have much time for tours," Kurda sighed miserably. "Not with the Trials to prepare for."

"Tell me more about these Trials," I said.

"The Trials are part of our vampiric heritage, going back as long as any vampire can remember," Gavner told me.

Gavner Purl was a Vampire General. He was very burly, with short brown hair, and he had a scarred, beaten face. Mr Crepsley often teased him about his heavy breathing and snoring. "In the old nights they were held at every Council," Gavner continued, "and every vampire had to endure them, even if they'd passed a dozen times already.

"About a thousand years ago, the Trials were restructured. This was about the time that the Generals came into being. Before that, there were just Princes and ordinary vampires. Under the new terms, only those who wished to be Generals needed to undertake the Trials. A lot of ordinary vampires take the Trials even if they don't want to be a General — a vampire must usually pass the Trials of Initiation to earn the respect of his peers — but they aren't required to."

"I don't understand," I said. "I thought if you passed the Trials, you automatically became a General."

"No," Kurda answered ahead of Gavner, running a hand through his blond hair. Kurda Smahlt wasn't as muscular as most vampires — he believed in brains over brawn — and he bore less scar tissue than most, though he had three small red permanent scratches on his left cheek, marks of the vampaneze (Kurda's dream was to reunite the vampires and vampaneze, and he'd spent many decades discussing peace treaties with the murderous outcasts). "The Trials are only the first test for would-be Generals. There are other tests of strength, endurance and wisdom, which come later. Passing the Trials just means you're a vampire of good standing."

Good standing was a phrase I'd heard many times. Respect and honour were vitally important to vampires. If you were a vampire of good standing, it meant you were respected by your colleagues.

"What happens in the Trials?" I asked.

"There are many different tests," Gavner said, taking over again from Kurda. "You have to complete five of them. They'll be picked at random, one at a time. The challenges range from fighting wild boars to climbing perilous mountains to crawling through a pit filled with snakes."

"*Snakes?*" I asked, alarmed. My best friend at the Cirque Du Freak – Evra Von – kept a huge snake, which I'd grown accustomed to but never learned to like. Snakes gave me the shivers.

"There won't be any snakes in Darren's Trials," Kurda said. "Our last snake-keeper died nine years ago and hasn't been replaced. We still have a few snakes, but not enough to fill a tub, never mind a pit."

"The Trials take place one night after another," Gavner said. "A day's rest is all you're allowed in between. So you have to be especially careful at the start — if you get injured early on, you won't have much time to recover."

"Actually, he might get lucky there," Kurda mused. "The Festival of the Undead is almost upon us."

"What's that?" I asked.

"We celebrate with a huge feast when every vampire who's coming to Council has arrived," Kurda explained. "We used the Stone of Blood to search for latecomers a couple of nights ago, and only three more are on their way. When the last arrives, the Festival starts and no official business may take place for three nights and days."

"That's right," Gavner said. "If the Festival starts during your Trials, you'll have a three night break. That would be a great bonus."

"*If* the latecomers arrive in time," Kurda noted gloomily.

Kurda seemed to think I didn't stand a chance in the Trials. "Why are you so sure I'll fail?" I asked.

"It's not that I think poorly of you," Kurda said. "You're just too young and inexperienced. Apart from the fact that you're physically unprepared, you haven't had time to assess the different tasks and practise for them. You're being thrown in at the deep end and it isn't fair."

"Still harping on about fairness?" someone commented behind us — Mr Crepsley. Seba Nile — the quartermaster of Vampire Mountain — was with him. The pair sat and greeted us with silent nods.

"You were very quick to agree to the Trials, Larten," Kurda said disapprovingly. "Don't you think you should have explained the rules to Darren more thoroughly? He didn't even know that failure to complete the Trials means certain death!"

"Is that true?" Mr Crepsley asked me.

I nodded. "I thought I could quit if things weren't working out."

"Ah. I should have made it clearer. My apologies."

"A bit late for those now," Kurda sniffed.

"All the same," Mr Crepsley said, "I stand by my decision. It was a delicate situation. I did wrong to blood Darren — there was no hiding from that. It is important for both our sakes that one of us clears our names. Had I the choice, *I* would face the challenge, but the Princes elected Darren. Their word, as far as I am concerned, is law."

"Besides," Seba Nile added, "all is far from lost. When I heard the news, I hurried to the Hall of Princes and invoked the old and almost forgotten Period of Preparation clause."

"The what?" Gavner asked.

"Before the time of the Generals," Seba explained, "vampires did not spend years preparing for the Trials. They would draw a Trial at random — as they do now — but rather than tackle it immediately, they had a night and a day to prepare. This was to give them time to practise. Many chose to ignore the Period of Preparation — usually those who had undertaken the Trials before — but there was no dishonour in taking advantage of it."

"I never heard of that rule," Gavner said.

"*I* did," Kurda noted, "but I'd never have thought of it. Does it still apply? It hasn't been used in more than a thousand years."

"Just because it is unfashionable does not mean it is invalid," Seba chuckled. "The Period of Preparation was never formally abolished. Given that Darren is a special case, I went to the Princes and asked that he be allowed to avail himself of it. Mika objected, of course — that vampire was born to object — but Paris talked him round."

"So Darren has twenty-four hours to prepare for each Trial," Mr Crepsley said. "And twenty-four hours to rest afterwards — which adds up to a forty-eight hour gap between each test."

"That *is* good news," Gavner agreed, brightening up.

"There is more," Mr Crepsley said. "We also convinced the Princes to rule out some of the more foreboding Trials, those which are clearly beyond Darren's means."

"I thought you said you weren't going to ask for favours," Gavner noted with a grin.

"Nor did I," Mr Crepsley replied. "I merely asked that the Princes use their common sense. It would be illogical to ask a blind man to paint, or a mute man to sing. So too would it be senseless to expect a half-vampire to compete on even terms with a full-vampire. Many of the Trials remain, but those which are clearly impossible for one of Darren's stature have been eliminated."

"I still say it's unfair," Kurda complained. He faced the ancient Seba Nile. "Are there any other old laws we could make use of? Anything about children not being allowed to compete, or that they can't be killed if they fail?"

"None that I am aware of," Seba said. "The only vampires who cannot be killed for failing the Trials of Initiation are the Princes. All others are judged equally."

"Why would Princes be taking the Trials?" I asked.

"Long ago they had to participate in the Trials at every Council, like everybody else," Seba said. "Some still undertake them from time to time, if they feel they need to prove themselves. However, it is forbidden for a vampire to kill a Prince, so if a Prince fails and does not die during the Trial, nobody can execute him."

"What happens in cases like that?" I asked.

"There have not been many," Seba said. "Of the few that I know of, the Princes elected to leave Vampire Mountain and die in the wilds. Only one – Fredor Morsh – resumed his place in the Hall of Princes. That was when the vampaneze broke away, when we had need of all our leaders. Once the crisis had abated, he left to meet his fate."

"Come," Mr Crepsley said, rising and yawning. "I am tired. It is time to turn in for the day."

"I don't think I'll be able to sleep," I said.

"You must," he grunted. "Rest is vital if you are to complete the Trials. You will need to be fully alert, with all your wits about you."

"OK," I sighed, joining him. Harkat stood too. "See you all tomorrow," I said to the other vampires, and they nodded glumly in reply.

Back in my cell, I made myself as comfortable as possible in my hammock – most vampires slept in coffins, but I couldn't stand them – while Harkat climbed into his. It took ages to drift off, but finally I did, and though I didn't manage a full day's sleep, I was reasonably clear-headed when night rolled round and I had to report to the Hall of Princes to learn the nature of my first deathly Trial.

CHAPTER TWO

ARRA SAILS was waiting for Mr Crepsley and me outside the Hall of Princes. Arra was one of the rare female vampires at Vampire Mountain. She was a fierce fighter, the equal – or better – of most males. We'd fought a contest earlier during my stay and I'd won her hard-to-earn respect.

"How are you?" she asked, shaking my hand.

"Pretty good," I said.

"Nervous?"

"Yes."

"I was too, when facing my Trials," she smiled. "Only a fool goes into them without feeling anxious. The important thing is not to panic."

"I'll try not to."

Arra cleared her throat. "I hope you don't hold what I said in the Hall of Princes against me." Arra had urged the Princes to make me undertake the Trials. "I don't believe in going easy on vampires, even if they're children. Ours is a hard life, not suited to the weak. As I said in the Hall, I think you'll pass the Trials, but if you don't, I won't step in to plead for your life."

"I understand," I said.

"We're still friends?"

"Yes."

"If you need help preparing, call on me," she said. "I have been through the Trials three times, to prove to myself more than any other that I am a worthy vampire. There is very little that I don't know about them."

"We will bear that in mind," Mr Crepsley said, bowing to her.

"Courteous as ever, Larten," Arra noted. "And as handsome too."

I nearly laughed out loud. Mr Crepsley — *handsome*? I'd seen more appealing creatures in the monkey enclosures in zoos! But Mr Crepsley took the compliment in his stride, as though he was used to such flattery, and bowed again.

"And you are as beautiful as ever," he said.

"I know," she grinned, and left. Mr Crepsley watched her intently as she walked away, a faraway look on his normally solemn face. When he caught me smirking, he scowled.

"What are you grinning about?" he snapped.

"Nothing," I said innocently, then added slyly, "An old girlfriend?"

"If you must know," he said stiffly, "Arra was once my mate."

I blinked. "You mean she was your *wife*?"

"In a manner of speaking."

I stared, slack-jawed, at the vampire. "You never told me you were married!"

"I am not — any more — but I used to be."

"What happened — did you get a divorce?"

He shook his head. "Vampires neither marry nor divorce as humans do. We make temporary mating commitments instead."

I frowned. "Come again?"

"If two vampires wish to mate," he explained, "they agree to share their lives for a set amount of time, usually five or ten years. At the end of that time, they can agree to another five or ten years, or separate. Our relationships are not like those of humans. Since we cannot have children, and live such a long time, very few vampires stay mated for the whole of their lives."

"That sounds bizarre."

Mr Crepsley shrugged. "It is the vampire way."

I thought it over. "Do you still have feelings for Arra?" I asked.

"I admire and respect her," he answered cagily.

"That's not what I mean. Do you *love* her?"

"Oh, look," he said quickly, reddening around his throat. "It is time to present ourselves to the Princes. Hurry — we must not be late." And off he set at a rapid pace, as though scurrying ahead of any further personal questions.

*   *   *

Vanez Blane greeted us inside the Hall of Princes. Vanez was a games master, responsible for maintaining the three gaming Halls and watching over the contestants. He only had one eye, and from the left-hand side he looked quite frightful. But if you saw him from the front or right-hand side, you could tell at a glance that he was a kind, friendly vampire.

"How do you feel?" he asked. "Ready for the Trials?"

"Just about," I replied.

He took me to one side and spoke quietly. "You can say no if you want, but I've discussed it with the Princes, and they won't object if you ask me to be your Trials tutor. That means I'd tell you about the challenges and help you prepare for them. I'd be like a second in a duel, or a trainer in a boxing match."

"Sounds good to me," I said.

"You don't mind, Larten?" he asked Mr Crepsley.

"Not at all," Mr Crepsley said. "I had planned to be Darren's tutor, but you are much better suited to the job. You are sure it is not an inconvenience?"

"Of course it isn't," Vanez said firmly.

"Then it is agreed." We all shook hands and smiled at one another.

"It feels odd being the centre of so much attention," I said. "So many people are going out of their way to help me. Are you like this with all newcomers?"

"Most of the time — yes," Vanez said. "Vampires look out for each other. We have to — everybody else in the world hates or fears us. A vampire can always depend on help from those of his own." He winked and added, "Even that cowardly rogue, Kurda Smahlt."

Vanez didn't really think Kurda was a cowardly rogue – he just liked to tease the soon to be Prince – but many vampires in the mountain did. Kurda didn't like fighting or war, and believed in making peace with the vampaneze. To a lot of vampires, that was unthinkable.

A guard called my name and I stepped forward, past the circular benches to the platform where the thrones of the Princes were situated. Vanez stood just behind me, while Mr Crepsley stayed in his seat — only Trials tutors were allowed to accompany contestants to the platform.

Paris Skyle, a white-haired, grey-bearded Prince – he was also the oldest living vampire – asked if I was willing to accept whatever Trial came my way. I said I was. He announced to the Hall in general that the Period of Preparation had been invoked, and that some Trials had been withdrawn, on account of my size and youth. He asked if anyone objected. Mika Ver Leth – who'd suggested the Trials – looked unhappy about the concessions, and picked irritably at the folds of his black shirt, but said nothing. "Very well," Paris declared. "We shall draw the first Trial."

A bag of numbered stones was brought forward by a green-uniformed guard. I'd been told that there were seventeen stones in it, each with its own individual number. Each number corresponded to a Trial, and the one I picked would be the Trial I'd have to face.

The guard shook the bag and asked if anyone wanted to examine the stones. One of the Generals raised a hand. This was common practice — the stones were always examined — so I didn't worry about it, just focused on the floor and tried to stop the nervous rumblings of my belly.

When the stones had been checked and approved, the guard shook them up once more, then held the bag out to me. Closing my eyes, I dipped in a hand, grabbed the first stone I touched, and drew it out. "Number eleven," the guard shouted. "The Aquatic Maze."

The vampires in the Hall mumbled softly among themselves.

"Is that good or bad?" I asked Vanez while the stone was taken up for the Princes to verify.

"It depends," he said. "Are you able to swim?"

"Yes."

"Then it's as good a first Trial as any. Things could have been worse."

Once the stone had been checked and placed aside so that it couldn't be drawn again, Paris told me that I would be expected to report for the Trial at dusk tomorrow. He wished me luck — he said business would keep him away, though one of the other Princes would be present — then dismissed me. Leaving the Hall, I hurried away with Vanez and Mr Crepsley to prepare for my first testing brush with death.

CHAPTER THREE

THE AQUATIC Maze was man-made, built with a low ceiling and watertight walls. There were four doors in and out of it, one in each of its four external walls. From the centre, where I would be left, it normally took five or six minutes to find your way out, assuming you didn't get lost.

But in the Trial, you had to drag around a heavy rock – half your weight – which slowed you down. With the rock, eight or nine minutes was good going.

But as well as the rock, there was the water to contend with. As soon as the Trial commenced, the maze started to fill with water, which was pumped in via hoses from underground streams. The water slowed you down even more, and navigating the maze usually took about a quarter of an hour. If it took longer, you were in serious trouble — because the maze filled to the top in seventeen minutes exactly.

"It's vital not to panic," Vanez said. We were down in one of the practice mazes, a smaller replica of the Aquatic Maze. The route wasn't the same — the walls of the Aquatic Maze could be moved around, so the maze was different each time — but it served as a good learning experience. "Most who fail in the Maze do so because they panic," he went on. "It can be frightening when the water rises and the going gets slower and tougher. You have to fight that fear and concentrate on the route. If you let the water distract you, you'll lose your bearings — and then you're finished."

We spent the early part of the night walking through the maze, over and over, Vanez teaching me how to make a map inside my head. "Each wall of the maze looks the same," he said, "but they aren't. There are identifying marks — a discoloured stone, a jagged bit of floor, a crack. You must note these small differences and build your map from them. That way, if you find yourself in a passage where you've already been, you'll recognize it and can immediately start looking for a new way out, wasting no time in the process."

I spent hours learning how to make mental maps of the maze. It was a lot harder than it sounds. The first few passages were easy to remember — a chipped stone in the top left corner of one, a moss-covered stone in the floor of the next, a knobbly stone in the ceiling of the one after that — but the further on I got, the more I had to remember, and the more confusing it became. I had to find something new in every corridor, because if I used a mark which was similar to one I'd committed to memory already, I'd get the two confused and would wind up chasing my tail around.

"You're not concentrating!" Vanez snapped when I came to a standstill for the seventh or eighth time in quick succession.

"I'm trying," I grumbled, "but it's hard."

"*Trying* isn't good enough," he barked. "You have to tune out all other thoughts. Forget the Trials and the water and what will happen if you fail. Forget about dinner and breakfast and whatever else is distracting you. Think only about the maze. It must fill your thoughts completely, or you're doomed."

It wasn't easy, but I gave it my best shot, and within an hour had improved considerably. Vanez was right — cutting off all other trains of thought was the solution. It was boring, wandering through a maze for hours on end, but that boredom was what I had to learn to appreciate. In the Aquatic Maze, excitement could confuse and kill me.

Once my map-making skills were up to scratch, Vanez wrapped a long rope round my waist and attached a rock to the other end. "This rock is only a quarter of your weight," he said. "We'll try you with a heavier rock later, but I don't want to tire you out too much ahead of the Trial. We'll get you accustomed to this one first, move up to a rock that's a third your weight, then try you on the real thing for a short spell, to give you a taste of how it feels."

The rock wasn't especially heavy — as a half-vampire, I was much stronger than a human — but it was a nuisance. Apart from slowing me down, it also had a nasty habit of catching on corners or in cracks, which meant I had to stop and free it. "It's important to stop the instant you feel it snagging," Vanez said. "Your natural instinct will be to tug on the rope and free it quickly, but more often than not that worsens the situation, and you wind up taking even longer to sort it out. Seconds are vital in the maze. It's better to act methodically and lose four or five seconds freeing yourself, than act hastily and lose ten or twenty."

There were ways to stop the rock and rope from snagging so much. When I came to corners or bends, I had to seize the rope and pull the rock in close to me — that way it was less likely to get stuck. And it was helpful to give the rope a shake every few seconds — that kept it loose. "But you have to do these things automatically," Vanez said. "You must do them without pausing to think. Your brain should be fully occupied with mapping the maze. Everything else must be done by instinct."

"It's useless," I groaned, sinking to the floor. "It'd take months to get ready for this. I haven't a hope in hell."

"Of course you have!" Vanez roared. Squatting beside me, he poked me in the ribs. "Feel that?" he asked, jabbing a sharp finger into the soft flesh of my belly.

"Ow!" I slapped his hand away. "Quit it!"

"It's sharp?" he asked, jabbing me again. "It hurts?"

"Yes!"

He grunted, jabbed me one more time, then stood. "Imagine how much sharper the stakes in the Hall of Death are," he said.

Sighing miserably, I hauled myself to my feet and wiped sweat from my brow. Picking up the rope, I gave it a shake, then started back through the maze, dragging the rock and mapping out the walls, as Vanez had taught me.

*   *   *

Finally we broke for a meal and met up with Mr Crepsley and Harkat in the Hall of Khledon Lurt. I wasn't hungry – I felt too nervous to eat – but Vanez insisted I wolf my food down — he said I'd need every last bit of energy when it came to the Trial.

"How is he progressing?" Mr Crepsley asked. He'd wanted to watch me train, but Vanez had told him he'd be in the way.

"Remarkably well," Vanez said, chewing on the bones of a skewered rat. "To be honest, though I slapped on a brave face when the Trial was picked, I thought he'd be – excuse the pun – out of his depth. The Aquatic Maze isn't one of the more brutal Trials, but it's one you need a lot of time to prepare for. But he's a quick learner. We've still got a lot to cram in – we haven't tried him in water yet – but I'm a lot more hopeful now than I was a handful of hours ago."

Harkat had brought Madam Octa – Mr Crepsley's spider – to the Hall with him and was feeding her breadcrumbs soaked in bat broth. He'd agreed to take care of her while I was concentrating on my Trials. Moving away from the vampires, I struck up a conversation with the Little Person. "Managing her OK?" I asked.

"Yes. She is ... easy to ... take care of."

"Just don't let her out of her cage," I warned. "She looks cute, but her bite is lethal."

"I know. I have ... often watched ... you and her ... when you ... were on stage ... at the Cirque ... Du Freak."

Harkat's speech was improving – he slurred his words a lot less now – but he still had to take long pauses for breath in the middle of sentences.

"Do you think ... you will ... be ready ... for Trial?" he asked.

I shrugged. "Right now, the Trial's the last thing on my mind — I'm not even sure I'm going to get through the training! Vanez is working me hard. I suppose he has to, but I feel exhausted. I could slide under the table and sleep for a week."

"I have been ... listening to ... vampires talk," Harkat said. "Many are ... betting on you."

"Oh?" I sat up, taking an interest. "What sort of odds are they giving me?"

"They do not ... have actual ... odds. They bet ... clothes and ... pieces of ... jewellery. Most vampires ... are betting ... *against* you. Kurda and Gavner ... and Arra ... are accepting ... most of the ... bets. They ... believe in you."

"That's good to hear," I smiled. "What about Mr Crepsley?"

Harkat shook his head. "He said ... he does not ... bet. Especially not ... on children."

"That's the sort of thing the dry old buzzard would say," I huffed, trying not to sound disappointed.

"But I ... heard him talking ... to Seba Nile," Harkat added. "He said ... that if you ... failed, he would ... eat his cape."

I laughed, delighted.

"What are you two talking about?" Mr Crepsley asked.

"Nothing," I said, grinning up at him.

When we'd finished eating, Vanez and me headed back for the maze, where we practised with heavier rocks and in water. The next few hours were some of the most arduous of my life, and by the time he called it a night and sent me to my cell to rest, I was so tired that I collapsed halfway there and had to be carted back to my hammock by a couple of sympathetic guards.

CHAPTER FOUR

I WAS so stiff when I woke that I thought I wouldn't be able to make it to the maze, never mind find my way out of it! But after a couple of minutes of walking around, I worked off the stiffness and felt as fit as ever. I realized Vanez had pushed me exactly the right amount, and made a note not to doubt his tactics in future.

I was hungry but Vanez had told me not to eat anything when I woke — if things were tight, a few extra pounds could mean the difference between living and dying.

Mr Crepsley and Vanez fetched me when it was time. Both were clad in their finest clothes, Mr Crepsley resplendent in bright red robes, Vanez less flamboyant in a dull brown tunic and trousers.

"Ready?" Vanez asked. I nodded. "Hungry?"

"Starving!"

"Good," he smiled. "I'll treat you to the finest meal of

your life after the Trial. Think about that if you get into trouble — it helps to have something to look forward to."

We wound our way down through the torch-lit tunnels to the Aquatic Maze, Vanez walking in front of me, Mr Crepsley and Harkat just behind. Vanez carried a purple flag, the sign that he was escorting a vampire to Trial. Most of the vampires we passed made a strange gesture when they saw me coming: they put the tip of their right-hand middle finger to their forehead, placed the tips of the fingers to either side of it on their eyelids, and spread their thumb and little finger out wide to the sides.

"Why are they doing that?" I asked Vanez.

"It's a customary gesture," he explained. "We call it the death's touch sign. It means, 'Even in death, may you be triumphant'."

"I'd rather they just said, 'Good luck'," I muttered.

"That doesn't have quite the same resonance," Vanez chuckled. "We believe that the gods of the vampires respect those who die nobly. They bless us when a vampire meets death proudly, and curse us when one dies meekly or poorly."

"So they want me to die well for their own sakes," I said sarcastically.

"For the sake of the clan," Vanez corrected me seriously. "A vampire of good standing always puts the good of the clan before his own wellbeing. Even in death. The hand gesture is to remind you of that."

The Aquatic Maze was built in the pit of a large cavern. From the top it looked like a long square box. Around the sides of the pit were forty or fifty vampires, the most the cave could hold. Among them were Gavner and Kurda, Seba Nile and Arra Sails — and Mika Ver Leth, the Vampire Prince who'd sentenced me to the Trials.

Mika summoned us over, nodded gravely to Vanez and Mr Crepsley, then fixed his icy gaze on me. He was dressed in his customary black outfit and looked even sterner than Mr Crepsley. "You have prepared for the Trial?" he asked.

"I have."

"You know what lies ahead of you?"

"I do."

"Except for the four exits, there is no escape from the maze," he said. "Should you fail this Trial, you will not have to face the Hall of Death."

"I'd rather the stakes to drowning," I grunted.

"Most vampires would," he agreed. "But you need not worry — it is still water, not running."

I frowned. "What's that got to do with anything?"

"Still water cannot trap a vampire's soul," he explained.

"Oh, that old myth," I laughed. Many vampires believed that if you died in a river or stream, your soul remained trapped forever by the flowing water. "That doesn't bother me. It's the drowning I'm not fond of!"

"Either way, I wish you luck," Mika said.

"No you don't," I sniffed.

"Darren!" Mr Crepsley hissed.

"It's all right," Mika silenced him with a wave of his hand. "Let the boy speak his piece."

"*You* made me take the Trials," I said. "You don't think I'm good enough to be a vampire. You'll be happy if I fail, because it'll prove you were right."

"Your assistant has a low opinion of me, Larten," Mika remarked.

"He is young, Mika. He does not know his place."

"Don't apologize for him. The young *should* speak their thoughts." He addressed me directly again. "You are right in one thing only, Darren Shan — I *don't* think you have what it takes to make it as a vampire. As for the rest of what you say ..." He shook his head. "No vampire takes pleasure in seeing another fail. I sincerely hope you prove me wrong. We need vampires of good standing, now more than ever. I will raise a glass of blood to your name should you complete the Trials, and willingly admit in public that I misjudged you."

"Oh," I said, bemused. "In that case, I guess I'm sorry for what I said. No hard feelings?"

The black-haired, eagle-eyed Prince smiled tightly. "No hard feelings." Then he clapped his hands loudly, barked sharply: "May the gods bless you with the luck of the vampires!" — and the Trial commenced.

* * *

I was blindfolded, placed on a stretcher and carried into the heart of the maze by four guards — so I couldn't memorize the way. Once inside, I was set down and the blindfold was removed. I found myself in a narrow corridor, about a metre and a half wide, less than two metres high. My size would work in my favour in this Trial — tall vampires had to stoop, which made the going even harder.

"You are ready?" one of the guards asked.

"I'm ready," I said, glancing around the corridor to find my first marker. I spotted a whitish stone in the wall to my left and made a note of it, starting my mental map-making process.

"You must stay here till the water pours," the guard said. "That's the signal for the start of the Trial. Nobody can check on you once we leave, so there's nothing to prevent you cheating, apart from your conscience."

"I won't cheat," I snapped. "I'll wait for the water."

"I'm sure you will," the vampire smiled apologetically. "I had to say it anyway — tradition."

The four guards gathered up the stretcher and left. They were all wearing extra soft shoes, so their footsteps made no noise.

Small candles were set in glass bulbs in the roof of the maze, so I'd have plenty of light to see by, even when the water rose high.

My nerves gnawed at me while I was waiting for the water to gush. A cowardly voice inside my head niggled at me to make an early beginning. Nobody would ever know. Better to live with a little shame than die because of stupid pride.

I ignored the voice — I'd never be able to look Mr Crepsley, Gavner or the others in the eye if I cheated.

Finally there was a gurgling sound and water bubbled up out of a nearby pipe. Breathing a sigh of relief, I hurried for the end of the corridor, dragging my rock behind me, shaking the rope at regular intervals, as Vanez had taught me.

I made good time to start with. The water barely hindered me and there were plenty of striking stones to identify the different corridors by. I didn't panic when I came to a dead end or worked my way back to a corridor I'd already visited, just stuck my head down and kept walking, taking a new route.

The going got tough after five or six minutes. The water was up above my knees. Each step was an endeavour. The rock now felt like it weighed a tonne. I was having trouble breathing and my muscles ached, especially those in my legs and back.

Still I didn't panic. Vanez had prepared me for this. I had to accept the water, not fight it. I let my pace drop. The mistake many vampires made was to try walking quickly — they exhausted themselves early and never got anywhere near the end.

Another couple of minutes passed. I was growing anxious. There was no way to tell how close or far from the finish I was. I could be a single turn away from an exit door without knowing it — or nowhere near one. At least I'd recognize an exit if I saw it — a huge white X was painted on all four doors and a large black button was at the centre of the X. All I had to do was press that button and the door would open, the water would flood out, and I'd be safe.

The trouble was finding it. The water was up to my chest by this stage and the rock was getting heavier all the time. I'd stopped shaking the rope – it was too much of an effort –

and could feel it drifting along behind me, threatening to stick between my legs. That happened sometimes — vampires got knotted up in the rope and came to a standstill, drowning where they stood.

I was turning a corner when the rock snagged on something. I gave the rope a pull, trying to free it — to no avail. Taking a deep breath, I dived down to see what was wrong. I found the rock had jammed against a large crack in a wall. It only took a few seconds to prise it loose, but when I sprang up, I suddenly realized that my mind was a blank. Had I been in this tunnel before? I looked for a familiar sign but couldn't spot any. There was a yellow stone high up in one of the walls, and I thought I'd passed it earlier, but I didn't know for sure.

I was lost!

I lurched to the end of the corridor, then up another, desperately trying to establish my position. Panic flooded my system. I kept thinking, "I'm going to drown! I'm going to drown!" I could have passed a dozen markers and not recognized any of them, I was so stressed out.

The water was up to my chin. It splashed into my mouth. Sputtering, I slapped at the water, as though that would make it go away. I stumbled and fell. Came up spitting water and gasping. Terrified, I started to scream...

...and that stopped me. The sound of my roars snapped me back to my senses. I remembered Vanez's advice, stood perfectly still, shut my eyes and refused to budge until I had the panic under control. I concentrated on the thought of the feast that awaited me. Fresh meat, wild roots and fruit.

A bottle of human blood to perk me up. Dessert — mountain berries, hot and juicy.

I opened my eyes. My heart had stopped beating like a drum and the worst of the panic attack had passed. I waded slowly down the corridor, searching for a marker. If I could find one, I was sure I'd recall the rest of my mental map. I reached the end of the corridor — no markers. The next corridor was new to me as well. And the one after that. And the next.

I could feel the panic bubbling up again when I spotted a candle holder set in a pale grey circular stone — one of my markers! I stared at the candle and waited for my map to reform. For several long seconds my mind remained as terrifyingly blank as it had been — then the map fell back into place. It came to me in sections first, a piece at a time, then in a rush. I stood where I was for a few more seconds, making sure I had it clear in my head, before continuing.

The water was up to my lower lip now. The going was almost impossible. I had to proceed in sluggish jumps, lurching forward to keep my head above water, being extra careful not to bash it on the ceiling. How long before I ran out of air? Three minutes? Four? It couldn't be much more than that. I had to find the way out — and quick!

Concentrating on the map inside my head, I tried figuring out how far away I was from the spot where I'd started. By my reckoning, I should be near one of the border walls. If I was, and the exit door was close by, I stood a chance. Otherwise the Trial was as good as over.

Turning a corner, I ran into my first stretch of border wall. I knew it immediately, because the stones were darker and rougher than the rest of the maze. There was no X printed on it, but my heart gave a joyous leap all the same. Backtracking, I banished the map from my thoughts — it was no use to me any longer — and hurried along to the next turning, searching for that elusive X.

I found four different sections of border wall, none of which contained the exit. The water was almost up to the ceiling now. I was swimming more than walking, pressing my lips to the roof to draw in air. I'd have been OK if not for the wretched rock — it dragged behind me worse than ever when I tried to swim, slowing me down to a crawl.

As I paused to draw breath, I realized it was time to make a critical decision. Vanez had discussed this with me in the practice maze. He'd hoped things wouldn't reach this stage, but if they did, it was vital that I chose correctly.

If I continued as I was, I'd perish. I was making very little progress and in a minute or two the water would cover my face completely and I'd drown. The time had come to gamble. One last roll of the dice. If the luck of the vampires was with me, it would mean survival. If not...

I took several deep breaths, filling my lungs, then ducked under the water and dived to the floor. Picking up the rock, I turned over, so I was floating on my back, and placed the rock on my belly. Then I swam. It was awkward — streams of water forced themselves up my nose — but this was the only way to stop the rock from dragging on me.

Vampires can hold their breath longer than humans — five or six minutes, easily — but because I was on my back, I had to keep blowing air out through my nose, to stop the water going up it, so I'd have two, three minutes at most before I ran out of oxygen and drowned.

Swimming around another corner, I stared down a long corridor. I could spot the shape of what must be border wall at the end, but I was too far away to see if there was an X on it or not. I thought there might be, but that could be my mind playing tricks — Vanez had warned me about underwater mirages.

I swam up the corridor. About half-way, I realized there was no X — a long crack in the stones had fooled me — so I turned and quickly headed back the way I'd come. The weight of the rock was forcing me down. I stopped, put my feet on the floor and used them to push myself up, then straightened out and resumed swimming.

I searched in vain for another glimpse of border wall but the next two turnings both led to other corridors, not the wall. My oxygen was running out. It was getting harder and harder to move my arms and legs.

The next turn didn't lead to border wall either, but I had no time to swim ahead and look for another turning. Summoning all of my energy, I swam down the short corridor and took the right turn at the end. That led to another short corridor. As I started down it, the rock slipped off my belly, scratching me as it fell. I yelped without thinking. Water rushed in and air rushed out.

Coughing, I struck for the ceiling to draw more air, but when I reached it, I found the water had beaten me to the punch — there was no more air to be had!

I trod water, silently cursing the fates and vampire gods. This was the end. I'd given it my best shot but it wasn't to be. The best thing now would be to open my mouth, gulp in water and make as quick a finish of it as I could. I would have, too, except this corridor wasn't well lit, and I didn't like the idea of dying in darkness. So, painfully, I dived again to the floor, gathered the rock, turned over on to my back, placed the rock on my belly, and swam ahead to find somewhere brighter to die.

As I made the left turn at the end of corridor, I spotted the dark stone of border wall. I smiled weakly, remembering how excited that would have made me a few minutes ago. I rolled over on to my belly, so that I could die on my feet — then stopped.

There was an X on the wall!

I stared at it stupidly while precious air bubbles popped out of my mouth. Was this another trick of my mind? Another false crack? It must be. There was no way I could be this lucky. I should ignore it and...

No! It *was* an X!

I was out of air and strength, but the sight of that X gave me a new lease of life. Making use of resources I hadn't known I had, I kicked hard with my legs and shot towards the wall like a bullet. I bumped my head against it, recoiled, then rolled over and studied the large, rough X.

I was so delighted to find the X, I almost didn't think to push the button at its centre. What a farce that would have been — to come so far and fail at the very end! But, thankfully, I was spared that indignity. Of its own accord, my left hand crept out, ran its fingers over the button set in the X, then pressed it. The button slid inwards and the X vanished as the stone slid back into the wall.

With a huge slushing roar, water gushed out through the gap. I was carried along with it, coming to a jolt just beyond the door when my rock caught on something. My eyes and mouth were shut, and for a while it seemed like I was still submerged in the maze, as water flooded out over my head. Gradually, though, the level diminished, and I realized I could breathe.

Following the deepest single breath of my life, I opened my eyes and blinked. The cavern seemed a lot brighter than it had less than half an hour ago, when I'd been led down to it by Vanez Blane. I felt like I was sitting on a beach on a warm summer's day.

Cheers and hollers reached my ears. Staring around like a fish on dry land, I noticed delighted vampires streaming towards me, splashing through pools of water, whooping with excitement. I was too tired to identify their faces, but I recognized the orange crop of hair on the vampire leading the way — Mr Crepsley.

As the water subsided, I struggled to my feet and stood outside the door of the Aquatic Maze, smiling foolishly, rubbing the bump on my head where I'd connected with the wall. "You did it, Darren!" Mr Crepsley roared, reaching my side and throwing his arms around me in a rare display of affection.

Another vampire embraced me and yelled, "I thought you'd had it! So much time had passed, I was sure you'd failed!"

Blinking water from my eyes, I made out the features of Kurda and Gavner. And, close behind, Vanez and Arra. "Mr Crepsley? Kurda? Vanez? What are you doing on a beach in the middle of the day?" I asked. "You'll sizzle in the sunlight if you don't watch out."

"He's delirious!" someone laughed.

"Who would not be?" Mr Crepsley replied, hugging me proudly.

"Think I'll sit down a while," I muttered. "Call me when it's time to build sand castles." And, collapsing on my bottom, I stared up at the roof, convinced it was the wide open sky, and hummed merrily to myself while the vampires fussed around me.

CHAPTER FIVE

I WAS shivering like a bedraggled rat when I woke late the next day. I'd been asleep for fifteen hours or more! Vanez was there to bid me good morning. He handed me a small mug full of a dark liquid and told me to drink.

"What is it?" I asked.

"Brandy," he said. I hadn't tried brandy before. After the first mouthful, which made me gag, I decided I quite liked it. "Steady on," Vanez laughed as I poured it freely down my throat. "You'll get drunk!"

Laying aside the mug, I hiccuped and grinned. Then I remembered the Trial. "I did it!" I shouted, jumping up. "I found the way out!"

"You certainly did," Vanez agreed. "It was a close-run thing. You were in there just over twenty minutes. Did you have to swim towards the finish?"

"Yes," I said, then described all that had happened in the maze.

"You performed excellently," Vanez said when I finished. "Brains, strength and luck — no vampire lasts long without a healthy measure of each."

Vanez led me to the Hall of Khledon Lurt to get something to eat. The vampires there applauded when they saw me and crowded round to tell me how well I'd done. I made light of it and acted humble, but inside I felt like a hero. Harkat Mulds turned up while I was tucking into my third bowl of bat broth and fifth slice of bread. "I am ... glad you ... survived," he said in his simple, direct fashion.

"Me too," I laughed.

"The betting ... against you ... has dropped ... since you passed ... the first Trial. More vampires ... are betting ... on you to ... win, now."

"That's good to hear. Have *you* bet anything on me?"

"I have ... nothing to bet," Harkat said. "If I had ... I would."

While we were talking, a rumour spread through the Hall, upsetting the vampires around us. Listening closely, we learned that one of the last remaining vampires on their way to Council had arrived before dawn and immediately rushed to the Hall of Princes to inform them of vampaneze tracks he'd chanced across while travelling to the mountain.

"Maybe it's the same vampaneze we found on our way here," I said, referring to a dead vampaneze we'd stumbled upon during the course of our journey.

"Maybe," Vanez muttered, unconvinced. "I'll leave you for a while. Stay here. I won't be long." When he returned, the games master appeared troubled. "The vampire was Patrick Goulder," he said. "He came by an entirely different route, and the tracks were quite fresh. It's almost certain that this was a different vampaneze."

"What does it mean?" I asked, unsettled by the anxious rumblings of the vampires around us.

"I don't know," Vanez admitted. "But two vampaneze being on the paths to Vampire Mountain is hardly coincidence. And when you take Harkat's message about the Vampaneze Lord into consideration, it doesn't look promising."

I thought again of Harkat's message and Mr Tiny's long ago vow that the Vampaneze Lord would lead the vampaneze against the vampires and crush them. I'd had other things to worry about, and still had – my Trials were far from over – but it was hard to ignore this ominous threat to the entire vampire clan.

"Still," Vanez said, making light of it, "the doings of the vampaneze are of no interest to us. We must concentrate on the Trials. We'll leave the other business to those best equipped to deal with it."

But, try as we might to avoid the topic, the rumours followed us around the Halls all day long and my achievements of the night before went unremarked upon thereafter — nobody was interested in the fate of a single half-vampire while the future of the race itself hung in the balance.

✳   ✳   ✳

Hardly anyone paid attention to me when I turned up with Vanez Blane at the Hall of Princes at dusk. A few pressed their right-hand fingers to their forehead and eyelids when they saw the purple flag — the death's touch sign — but they were too preoccupied to discuss my first Trial with me. We had to wait a long time for the Princes to beckon us forward — they were arguing with their Generals, trying to decide what the vampaneze were up to and how many might be skulking around. Kurda was standing up for his alienated allies.

"If they meant to attack us," he shouted, "they would have done so on the trail, while we were coming singly or in pairs."

"Maybe they plan to attack us on the way back," someone retorted.

"Why should they?" Kurda challenged him. "They've never attacked before. Why start now?"

"Perhaps the Vampaneze Lord put them up to it," an old General suggested, and nervous growls of assent echoed round the Hall.

"Nonsense!" Kurda snorted. "I don't believe those old legends. Even if they *are* true, Mr Tiny said the night of his coming *was at hand* — not already upon us."

"Kurda is correct," Paris Skyle said. "Besides, attacking us in such a fashion — alone, on our way to or from Council — would be cowardly, and the vampaneze are no cowards."

"Then why are they here?" someone cried. "What are they up to?"

"It's possible," Kurda said, "that they came to see *me*."

Every vampire in the Hall stared at him.

"Why should they do that?" Paris asked.

"They are my friends." He sighed. "I don't believe this Vampaneze Lord myth, but many vampaneze do, and a lot are as troubled by it as us — they don't want a war any more than we do. It's possible that Mr Tiny sent word to the vampaneze as he did to us, and the pair found on the way here were coming to warn me, or to discuss the situation."

"But Patrick Goulder couldn't find the second vampaneze," Mika Ver Leth said. "If he's still alive, wouldn't he have contacted you by now?"

"How?" Kurda asked. "A vampaneze can't waltz up to the gates and ask for me by name. He'd be killed on sight. If he *is* a messenger, he's probably waiting somewhere nearby, hoping to catch me when I leave."

That made sense to a lot of the vampires, but others dismissed it out of hand — the idea of a vampaneze going out of his way to help a vampire was lunacy as far as they were concerned — and the argument reared up again and bubbled on for another couple of hours.

Mr Crepsley said little during the arguing. He just sat in his pew near the front, listening carefully, thinking hard. He was so absorbed in what was being said, he hadn't even noticed my arrival.

Finally, during a lull, Vanez crept forward and whispered to one of the guards, who advanced to the platform and had a word in the ear of Paris Skyle (his only good ear — his right had been chopped off many years before). Paris nodded, then clapped loudly for silence. "We have been overlooking our duties, my friends," he said. "The news of the vampaneze is worrying, but we must not let it interfere with regular Council affairs. There is a young half-vampire for whom time is precious. May we enjoy a few minutes of peace to deal with his more pressing concerns?"

When the vampires had settled back into their seats, Vanez escorted me up to the platform.

"Congratulations on passing the first of your Trials, Darren," Paris said.

"Thank you," I replied politely.

"As one who never learned to swim, I have extra reason to admire your narrow escape," said Arrow, the large, bald Prince, with tattoos of arrows on his arms and head. "Had I found myself in your position, I wouldn't have made it out alive."

"You did well, young Shan," Mika Ver Leth agreed. "A good start is half the battle. There's a long way to go, but I'm willing to accept that I might have been wrong about you."

"We would hear more of your exploits in the maze had we the time," Paris sighed, "but, alas, that is a tale you must save for another occasion. Are you ready to choose your next Trial?"

"I am."

The bag of numbered stones was produced. After they'd been checked, I reached in, dug down and picked one close to the bottom. "Number twenty-three," the guard called out, having examined the stone. "The Path of Needles."

"I thought there were only seventeen Trials," I muttered to Vanez as the stone was taken to the Princes.

"Seventeen for you," he agreed, "but there are more than sixty in total. A lot have been left out because they're not currently possible to host — like the pit of snakes — and others have been omitted to account for your size and age."

"Is it a difficult Trial?" I asked.

"It's easier than the Aquatic Maze," he said. "And your size will be an asset. It's as favourable as any we could have hoped for."

The Princes examined the stone, announced their approval, then set it aside and wished me well. They'd treated me rather curtly, but I understood their distraction and didn't feel slighted. As Vanez and me left, I heard the arguments about the vampaneze kick into life again, and the thick air of tension in the Hall was almost as suffocating as the water in the Aquatic Maze had been.

CHAPTER SIX

THE PATH of Needles was a long, narrow cavern filled with sharp-tipped stalactites and stalagmites. Vanez took me to see it before we set off to practice in another cave.

"All I have to do is walk across?" I asked.

"That's all."

"It isn't much of a Trial, is it?" I said confidently.

"We'll see if you think the same way tomorrow," he grunted. "The stalagmites are exceedingly slippery — one wrong move and you can impale yourself in the flicker of an eye. And many of the stalactites are precariously perched, hanging by a thread. Any sudden noise will result in some falling. If one hits you on the way down, it can cut clean through you."

Despite his warning, I still felt it was going to be easy. By the end of our first practice session, I'd revised my opinion.

We practised in a cave where the stalagmites weren't as sharp or as slippery as those on the Path of Needles, where the stalactites wouldn't break off and fall without warning. Yet, mild as this cave was in comparison, I came close to spearing myself on several occasions, rescued only by the quick hands of Vanez Blane.

"You're not gripping hard enough!" he growled after I'd almost gouged an eye out. I'd scratched my cheek on the stalagmite and Vanez was applying spit to the cut, to stop the flow of blood (as a half-vampire, my spit was no good for closing cuts).

"It's like trying to hold on to a buttered pole," I grumbled.

"That's why you must grip harder."

"But it hurts. I'll cut my hands to shreds if I—"

"Which would you rather?" Vanez interrupted. "Bloody hands or a stalagmite through your heart?"

"That's a stupid question," I groaned.

"Then stop acting stupidly!" he snapped. "You'll cut your palms to ribbons on the Path of Needles — there's no way to avoid that. You're a half-vampire, so the flesh will grow back quickly. You have to ignore the pain and focus on your grip. There will be plenty of time after the Trial to moan about your poor little fingers and how you'll never play the piano again."

"I can't play the piano anyway," I huffed, but did as he ordered and took a firmer grip on the treacherous mineral stakes.

At the end of the session, Vanez applied special herbs and leaves to my hands, to ease the worst of the pain and toughen up my palms for the ordeal ahead. It felt for a while as though my fingers were on fire, but gradually the pain seeped away, and by the time I had to report back for my second bout of training, it was just a dull throb at the end of my arms.

We concentrated on stealth this time. Vanez taught me to check each stalagmite before transferring my weight on to it. If one snapped off in the cave, it could send me plummeting to my death, or the sound could result in falling stalactites, which were just as hazardous.

"Keep one eye on the ceiling," Vanez said. "Most falling stalactites can be avoided by simply twisting out of the way."

"What if they can't be avoided?" I asked.

"Then you're in trouble. If one's coming for you and can't be dodged, you have to knock it sideways or catch it. Catching is harder but preferable — if you knock a stalactite out of the way, it'll crash and shatter. That sort of noise can bring the roof down."

"I thought you said this was going to be easier than the Aquatic Maze," I complained.

"It is," he assured me. "You need lots of luck to make it out of the Aquatic Maze. On the Path of Needles, you can exert more control over your fate — your life's in your own hands."

Arra Sails turned up during our third practice session, to help me work on my balance. She blindfolded me and made me crawl over a series of blunt stalagmites, so that I learnt to manoeuvre by touch alone. "He has an excellent sense of balance," she noted to Vanez. "As long as he doesn't flinch from the pain in his hands, he should sail through this test."

Finally, after many hours of practice, Vanez sent me back to my cell to grab some shuteye. Once again he'd worked me just the right amount. Tired, bruised and nicked though I was, after a few hours in my hammock I felt good as new and ready for anything.

* * *

There were hardly any vampires present at the Path of Needles to observe my second Trial. Most were locked away in the Hall of Princes, or had gathered in one of the mountain's many meeting chambers, to discuss the vampaneze. Mr Crepsley turned out to cheer me on, and so did Gavner Purl and Seba Nile. But Harkat was the only other familiar face in the tiny crowd of well-wishers.

A guard told me that the Princes sent their apologies, but couldn't preside over the Trial. Vanez complained – he said the Trial should be delayed if a Prince wasn't present – but the guard cited a couple of past cases where Princes hadn't been able to attend Trials, which had gone ahead without them. Vanez asked me if I wanted to push the point – he said, if we created a fuss, we could probably convince the Princes to postpone the Trial for a night or two, till one of them had time to come down and watch – but I said I'd rather get it over with.

The guard who'd been sent by the Princes checked to make sure I knew what I had to do, wished me luck, guided me to the mouth of the Path of Needles, and set me loose.

I climbed up on to the first of the stalagmites and stared at the sea and sky of glinting spikes. The cavern was aptly named — from this point it looked precisely like a pathway built of needles. Suppressing a shiver, I started ahead at a snail's crawl. There was no rushing on the Path of Needles. To survive, you had to move slowly and surely. I tested each stalagmite before settling upon it, shaking it gently from side to side, making sure it would hold my weight.

Bringing up my legs was tricky. There was no way of gripping the tips of the stalagmites with my toes, so I had to place my feet lower down, sometimes wedging them between two stalagmites. While this gave me a chance to take the weight off my arms and hands, it resulted in lots of scratching to my knees and thighs when it came time to drag my legs forward.

It was worst in the spots where the stalactites hung low over the stalagmites. There, I had to stretch out, so that I was lying almost flat on the stalagmites, in order to wriggle ahead. I picked up many nasty cuts to my chest, belly and back. After a while I found myself envying those fabulous Indian fakirs who can train themselves to lie on a bed of nails!

About a fifth of the way in, my left leg slipped and banged loudly against one of the stalagmites. There was a trembling, tingling sound overhead. Glancing up, I saw several nearby stalactites shaking. For a couple of seconds it seemed like they weren't going to fall, but then one snapped free and shattered on the ground. The noise of that shook others loose, and suddenly stalactites were dropping like nail-bombs all around me.

I didn't panic. Thankfully, hardly any of the stalactites fell close enough to damage me. One would have cut my right arm in two if I hadn't spotted it and shifted out of the way, and I had to suck my gut in quickly to avoid a small but sharp stalactite ripping a new bellybutton in my middle. But otherwise I stayed perched where I was, watching the ceiling closely for signs of danger, and waited out the avalanche.

Eventually the stalactites stopped falling and the echoes of their shattering died away. I waited a minute, for fear of late droppers – Vanez had warned me about those – but when all looked safe I proceeded at my same cautious, leisurely pace.

The falling stalactites had taken my mind off my torn, pricked body. Adrenalin had surged through me when I saw the shower of lethal needles and I was temporarily immune to pain. Sensation returned the further I progressed, but I remained numb to most of the cuts, only wincing every now and then, when an especially sharp point bit deeper into my flesh than usual.

I got a good grip with my feet at the half-way stage and rested for five or six minutes. The ceiling was quite high here, so I was able to stand at full stretch and rotate my arms and neck, working some of the stiffness out of my muscles. It was hot and I was sweating like crazy. I was wearing a tight leather outfit, which made me sweat even worse but which was necessary — loose clothes would have snagged on the stalactites.

Many vampires wore no clothes when going through the Path of Needles, but although I hadn't minded stripping to get through a valley full of sharp thorns on the way to Vampire Mountain, I wasn't about to take my clothes off in front of a load of strangers!

I wiped my hands on my trouser legs, but they were so stained with blood by this stage that my hands came away slippier than they'd been before. Looking around, I found a few pockets of dirt and used the muck to dry my palms. The dirt got in under my torn flesh and stung as if I'd grabbed two fistfuls of nettles, but the pain subsided after a while and I was ready to continue.

I was making good time, and had passed the three-quarters stage, when I made my first real mistake. Though the ceiling was high in this part of the cavern, the stalagmites grew close together and I had to stretch out to crawl over them. The tips were digging into my belly and chest, so I picked up speed, anxious to clear the vicious cluster.

Reaching ahead with my left hand, I tested a large stalagmite, but only slightly — it was so big, I felt sure it would support me. As I shifted my weight on to it, there was a sharp cracking sound and the tip broke away in my hand. I realized immediately what was happening and tried retreating, but it was too late. My weight snapped the tip clean off and my body dipped, slamming into a few neighbouring stalagmites.

The noise wasn't especially loud, but it built like thunder, and I could hear familiar tingling sounds overhead. Easing my head around, I glued my eyes to the ceiling and watched as several small stalactites fell and smashed. They didn't bother me — even if they'd been on target, they couldn't have done much harm — but the enormous stalactite directly above caused my guts to shrivel in fearful anticipation. For a while it looked like I was safe – the initial noise didn't even make the stalactite quiver – but, as smaller stalactites dropped and exploded, the larger one began to shake, gently at first, then alarmingly.

I tried scurrying out of its way, but I was snagged on the stalagmites. It would take a few seconds to free myself. I half rolled over, creating room to manoeuvre. I was staring up at the stalactite, judging how long I had to wriggle clear, when I thought about the stalactites around it. If the big one fell and smashed, the vibrations would bring pretty much every stalactite in this part of the cavern down on top of me!

While I was considering the problem, and trying to figure a way out of it, the large stalactite snapped abruptly in the middle and the lower half dropped upon me in a rush, its pin-sharp tip directed like an arrow at the soft flesh of my belly — it was going to run me through!

CHAPTER SEVEN

I HAD a split-second to think and react. For a human, it would have been curtains. As a half-vampire, I stood a chance. Wriggling out of the way was impossible — no time — so I flopped on to my back, bracing myself against the flat rim of the stalagmite whose tip I'd broken off. Letting go of the stalagmites around me, ignoring the pain as a dozen sharp tips dug into me, I raised my hands above my body and grabbed for the dropping stalactite.

I caught it in midair, several centimetres above the tip. It slid down through my hands, shedding tiny silver splinters all along the flesh of my palms. I had to bite down hard on my tongue to hold an agonized yell inside.

Ignoring the pain, I pressed my hands closer together, gripping the stalactite as tightly as I could, and the tip came to a stop a couple of centimetres above my belly. The muscles in my arms creaked at the effort it took to halt and hold the heavy piece of stalactite, but didn't let me down.

Gently, with trembling arms, I laid the stalactite to one side, careful not to make any noise, then prised myself off the stalagmites and blew on my bleeding palms, the lines of which had been severed in dozens of places by the sharp sides of the stake. By the luck of the vampires, none of my fingers had been amputated, but that was the only thing I had to feel grateful for.

The rest of my body had been similarly lacerated. I felt like I'd been stabbed all over. Blood was flowing freely from my back, arms and legs, and I could feel a deep impression in the skin of my lower back, where the rim of the big stalagmite had cut into me.

But I was alive!

I took my time going over the rest of the sharp cluster, hard as it was. Once clear, I paused, wiped the blood from my hands, licked my fingers and rubbed spit into the worst of my wounds. I wasn't able to close cuts like full-vampires could, but the damp saliva eased some of the pain. A few sorry tears crept down my cheeks, but I knew self-pity would get me nowhere, so I wiped them away and told myself to concentrate — I wasn't out of the cavern yet.

I thought about taking off my top and ripping it to pieces, wrapping the strips around my hands to give me a firmer grip. But that would have been cheating, and the vampire blood in me boiled angrily at the suggestion. Instead, I found more pockets of dirt and used them to dry my blood stained palms and fingers. I also rubbed lots of dirt into my feet and lower legs, since that was where much of the blood was flowing to.

After a short rest, I continued. The going wasn't so hard on this side of the cluster, but I was in such poor condition that it seemed difficult. I proceeded slowly, testing each stalagmite more thoroughly than was necessary, taking no chances whatsoever.

Finally, after more than an hour and a half on the Path of Needles – most vampires made it across in less than forty minutes – I crawled out, to be warmly greeted by the few vampires who'd gathered to cheer my success.

"Well?" Vanez asked, throwing a roughly woven towel around my shoulders. "Still think it isn't much of a Trial?"

I glowered at the games master. "If I ever say such a stupid thing again," I told him, "cut out my tongue and sew my lips closed!"

"Come on," he laughed. "We'll wash off that blood and dirt, then get busy with the balms and bandages."

Supported by Vanez and Mr Crepsley, I hobbled away from the Path of Needles, and said a silent prayer that the next Trial would have nothing to do with cramped caverns and razor-sharp obstacles. If I'd known how my prayer was going to be answered, I wouldn't have bothered!

*　*　*

As events transpired, I didn't have to worry about my next Trial immediately. While I was showering beneath an icy-cold waterfall in the Hall of Perta Vin-Grahl, word reached us that the final vampire had arrived at the mountain, which meant the Festival of the Undead would commence at the end of the next day, with the setting of the sun.

"There!" Vanez beamed. "Three nights and days to drink, be merry, recover and relax. Things couldn't have worked out better if we'd planned them."

"I don't know," I groaned, using my fingernails to dig dirt out of the cuts in my legs and feet. "I think I'll need a couple of weeks — at least!"

"Nonsense," Vanez said. "A few nights and you'll be good as ever. A little scarred and scratched, but nothing that will work against you in the later Trials."

"Will I have my extra allotted day to prepare for the Trial, on top of the three days allowed for the Festival?" I asked.

"Of course," he said. "There can be no official business during the Festival of the Undead. It's a time for rest and games and the swapping of old tales. Even the subject of the vampaneze must be put on ice for the next three nights and days.

"I've been looking forward to this for months," Vanez said, rubbing his hands together. "As a games master, I can have nothing to do with the organizing or administration of games during the Festival — so I can cut loose and really enjoy myself, without having to worry about what others are getting up to."

"Can you take part in the games with just one eye?" I asked.

"Certainly," he replied. "There are a few which require the use of both, but most don't. Wait and see — I'll crack many a head before the final ceremonies of the Festival. Dozens of vampires are going to leave the Council cursing my name and the night they crossed me."

When I finished showering, I stepped out of the waterfall and wrapped myself in several towels. I stood by a couple of strong torches to dry out, then Vanez bandaged over the worst of my wounds and I slipped into the light clothes he'd provided. Although the material was wafer-thin, I felt uncomfortable, and as soon as I was back in my cell I got rid of the clothes and lay down naked in my hammock.

I didn't get much sleep that night — I was too sore. Though I tried to lie still, I couldn't, and my tossing and turning kept me awake. Finally I got up, pulled on a pair of short trousers and went looking for Harkat. It turned out he was back in the Hall of Princes — they were questioning him about his message from Mr Tiny one last time, before the Festival of the Undead — so I returned to my cell, found a mirror and passed a few hours counting the scratches on the backs of my arms and legs.

As day rolled round — I was getting used to the passage of time inside the mountain; when I'd first arrived I hadn't been able to tell the difference between day and night — I got back on my hammock and gave sleep another try. This time I managed to doze off, and though my sleep was fitful, I squeezed in a handful of hours before the start of the much-anticipated Festival of the Undead.

CHAPTER EIGHT

THE FESTIVAL got under way in the immense Hall of Stahrvos Glen (also known as the Hall of Gathering). Every vampire in the mountain was present. Large as the Hall was, we were squeezed in like sardines. Looking around while we waited for sunset, I counted at least four hundred heads, possibly as many as five.

Everyone was decked out in brightly coloured clothes. The few female vampires in the Hall wore long flowing dresses, and most of the men sported dashing (but dusty) capes. Mr Crepsley and Seba Nile wore matching red costumes and looked like a father and son as they stood side by side. Even Harkat had borrowed new, bright blue robes for the occasion.

I was the only one who looked out of place. I was itching like mad from my cuts and scratches, and was still wearing the dull, thin shirt and short trousers that Vanez had given me in the Hall of Perta Vin-Grahl. Even that flimsy material irritated me — I kept reaching back and plucking it clear of my skin. Mr Crepsley told me several times to stop fidgeting, but I couldn't.

"Come see me later," Seba whispered as I tugged at my shirt for the thousandth time. "I have something which will ease much of the itching."

I started to thank the old quartermaster, but a gong sounded loudly and cut me off. Every vampire in the Hall stopped talking at the ringing of the gong. Moments later the three Vampire Princes appeared at the head of the Hall and mounted a platform so that all could see them clearly. The Festival of the Undead and the Ceremony of Conclusion — which would come at the end of Council — were the only times that all the Princes left their impregnable Hall at the top of the mountain. At least one of them was always present the rest of the time.

"It is good to see you, my friends," Paris Skyle beamed.

"We welcome you all to Vampire Mountain," Mika Ver Leth said.

"And wish you well during your stay," Arrow added.

"I know all of you have heard the rumours of the vampaneze," Paris said. "These are troubling times, and there is much to discuss and plan. But not these next three nights. Because this is the Festival of the Undead, where every vampire is equal, and all must enjoy themselves."

"I'm sure everyone's anxious to get the festivities rolling," Mika said. "But first the roll-call of those who've passed on to Paradise since last we met for Council."

Arrow called out the names of nine vampires who'd died during the past twelve years. As each name was announced, the vampires in the Hall made the death's touch sign and muttered in unison, 'Even in death, may he be triumphant.'"

When the last name had been called, Paris clapped his hands and said, "That is the last piece of official business out of the way. There shall be no more until the close of the Festival. Luck to you, my friends."

"Luck!" the vampires shouted, and then they were tossing their capes off, roughly hugging each other, and hollering at the tops of their voices, "Luck! Luck! Luck!"

* * *

The next several hours were so exciting, I almost managed to forget about my cuts and the itching. I was swept along to the gaming Halls by a wave of vampires eager to test themselves against old friends and foes. Some couldn't wait to reach the Halls and began wrestling and boxing in the tunnels on the way. They were prised apart by more level-headed vampires and carried – often struggling and protesting – down to the Halls, where they could fight in comfort and for the benefit of an audience.

It was sheer pandemonium in the three gaming Halls. Because none of the official games masters were on duty, there was nobody to bark commands or make sure everything proceeded in an orderly fashion. Vampires spilled around the Hall and over one another, challenging anyone who got in their way, lashing out with joyous gusto.

Mr Crepsley was no better than the rest. His customary dignity had disappeared in the mad rush and he dashed about like a wild man, yelling, throwing punches and leaping around. Even the Vampire Princes joined in the madness, including Paris Skyle, who was eight hundred years old if he was a night.

I bobbed along as best I could, trying to keep my head above the sea of writhing vampires. The initial burst of frenzied activity had scared me a little – I hadn't been expecting it – but I was soon having great fun, dodging between the legs of tussling vampires and knocking them over.

At one stage I found myself back to back with Harkat. He'd been caught up in the rush the same as the rest of us, and was busy tossing vampires over his shoulders, left and right, as if they were bags of cotton. The vampires loved it – they couldn't understand how one so little could be so strong – and were queuing up to test themselves against him.

I had a chance to catch my breath while I was standing behind Harkat — nobody was interested in a half-vampire when there was a Little Person to challenge. Once I'd recovered some of my spent energy, I slid away and rejoined the throng of battling vampires.

Gradually the chaos abated. A lot of vampires had been injured in the fighting, and while they dragged themselves away to be patched up, those left standing paused to wipe the sweat from their brows and sate their thirst with a good long drink.

After a while the games started for real. Vampires took to the mats, wrestling rings and bars, two or three at a time, the way they were meant to. Those too tired or too wounded to fight gathered around the sparring vampires and cheered them on.

I watched Mr Crepsley fighting. It was some form of karate and he was red-hot at it. His hands moved like lightning, fast even for a vampire, and he scythed down his opponents like flies, usually in a matter of seconds.

At another mat, Vanez was wrestling. The one-eyed games master was having the great time he'd predicted. While I was in attendance, he sent three vampires away with bloody noses and spinning heads, and was making short work of his fourth as I left.

I was passing a jousting ring when a laughing vampire grabbed me and pushed me forward to compete. I didn't protest — it was a law of the Festival that you never refused a challenge. "What are the rules?" I asked, shouting to be heard.

"See the two ropes hanging from the overhead bar?" the vampire who'd dragged me in asked. I nodded. "Grab one and stand on the platform on this side. Your opponent grabs the other and faces you. Then you swing out into the middle and kick and punch each other till one of you gets knocked off."

My opponent was a large, hairy vampire, who looked like a monster out of a comic book. I didn't stand a chance against him, but I gave it a fair try. Taking a firm hold of the rope, I swung out to meet him, and spent a few seconds avoiding his thrashing feet and fists. I managed to kick him in the ribs and slap him round the head, but my blows had no effect, and he soon caught my jaw a beauty and swatted me to the floor.

The vampires around the ring rushed forward to help me up. "Are you OK?" the one who'd volunteered me for the contest asked.

"Fine," I said, testing my teeth with my tongue to see if any were broken. "Is it the best out of three or five?"

The vampires cheered and slapped me on the back — they loved a trier. I was led back to the rope and went head to head with the gorilla again. I only lasted a few seconds, but nobody expected anything different. I was carried away like a champion and handed a mug of ale. I didn't like the taste, but it would have been rude to refuse, so I drained the mug, smiled as they cheered again, then wobbled away to look for a place to sit down and rest.

A lot of ale, wine, whisky and brandy was being consumed (as well as plenty of blood!), but hardly any vampires got drunk. This was because vampires had stronger metabolisms than humans. The average vampire had to drink a whole barrel of beer before he got tipsy. As a half-vampire, I wasn't as immune to the effects of alcohol as the rest. I felt quite light-headed after my mug of ale and made up my mind not to drink any more — at least not tonight!

Kurda joined me while I was resting. He was flushed and smiling. "Crazy, isn't it?" he said. "All these vampires, acting like unruly children. Think how embarrassing it would be if anyone saw us!"

"It's fun though, isn't it?" I laughed.

"Certainly," he agreed. "I'm just glad I only have to endure it once every twelve years."

"Kurda Smahlt!" someone yelled. Looking around, we spotted Arra Sails on her favourite set of bars, twirling a staff over her head. "How about it, Kurda — fancy your chances?"

Kurda grimaced. "I've a sore leg, Arra," he shouted.

The vampires around the bars jeered.

"Come on, Kurda," Arra called. "Not even a pacifist like yourself has the right to refuse a challenge during the Festival of the Undead."

Kurda sighed, took off his shoes and advanced. The vampires gave a roar of delight and word quickly spread that Kurda Smahlt was going into action against Arra Sails. Soon, a huge crowd had formed around the bars, most of them vampires who wanted to see Kurda wind up flat on his back.

"She hasn't been beaten on the bars in eleven years," I murmured to Kurda as he chose his staff.

"I know," he groaned.

"Try not to get too close to her," I advised him (speaking as though I was an expert, when in fact I'd only been on the bars once before). "The more you stay away, the longer you can drag it out."

"I'll bear that in mind."

"And be careful," I warned him. "She'll crack your head clean open if you give her the chance."

"Are you trying to *en*courage or *dis*courage me?" he snapped.

"Encourage, of course," I grinned.

"Well, you're doing a lousy job of it!"

He tested a staff, liked the feel of it, and hopped on to the bars. The vampires cheered and moved back, so there'd be plenty of room for him to fall.

"I've been waiting for decades to get you up here," Arra smiled, twirling her staff and advancing.

"I hope it proves worth the wait," Kurda said, blocking her first blow and dancing away from her on the bar.

"You managed to avoid me last time, but there's no escape now. I'm going to—"

Kurda launched a few blows of his own and Arra leapt backwards, surprised. "Are you here to talk or fight?" Kurda asked pleasantly.

"To fight!" Arra snarled, then concentrated.

The two sparred cautiously for a few minutes, testing each other. Then Arra's staff connected with one of Kurda's knees. It seemed an innocent enough blow, but he teetered on the bar and dropped his guard. Arra grinned and darted forward to finish him off. As she did, Kurda leapt across to a parallel bar and brought his staff around in a broad swing.

Arra was taken by complete surprise and there was nothing she could do as the staff swept her legs out from under her. She fell to the floor with a thump — *defeated*! There was a stunned silence, then the vampires roared their approval and surged forward to shake Kurda's hand. He thrust through them to check on Arra and see if she was OK. The vampiress slapped his hands away as he bent to help her up.

"Don't touch me!" she hissed.

"I was only trying—" he began.

"You cheated!" she interrupted. "You faked injury. I want to make it the best out of three."

"I beat you fair and square," Kurda said evenly. "There's no rule against feigning distress. You shouldn't have leapt in for the kill like you did. If you hadn't been so eager to disgrace me, my ploy wouldn't have worked."

Arra glared at the soon to be Vampire Prince, then dropped her gaze and muttered, "There is truth in your words." Lifting her eyes, she stared directly at Kurda. "I apologize for slighting you, Kurda Smahlt. I spoke in anger. Will you forgive me?"

"I will if you'll take my hand," Kurda smiled.

Arra shook her head shortly. "I cannot," she said miserably. "You beat me cleanly, and it shames me to refuse your hand — but I cannot bring myself to take it."

Kurda looked hurt but forced a smile. "That's OK," he said. "I forgive you anyway."

"Thank you," Arra said, then turned and ran from the Hall, her features contorted with the pain of overwhelming shame.

Kurda was heavy-hearted when he sat down beside me. "I feel sorry for her," he sighed. "It must be cruel to be so set in one's ways. Her refusal to shake my hand will haunt her the rest of her life. In her eyes, and the eyes of those who think like her, she's committed an unpardonable act. It doesn't matter much to me whether she shakes my hand or not, but she'll feel she's disgraced herself."

"Nobody could believe it when you beat her," I said, trying to cheer him up. "I thought you weren't supposed to be any good when it came to fighting."

Kurda laughed lightly. "I *choose* not to fight — it doesn't mean I *can't*! I'm no heroic, versatile vampire, but nor am I the useless coward many think I am."

"If you fought more often, they wouldn't think that," I noted.

"True," he admitted. "But their opinion doesn't matter." Kurda put his fingers on my chest and pressed softly down on my heart. "In here is where a man should judge himself, not on bars or in a ring or on a battlefield. If you know in your heart that you're true and brave, that should be enough.

"Of the nine vampires who've died since last Council, five could have been here tonight, alive and well, had they not been determined to prove themselves to others. They drove themselves to early graves, just so their companions would admire them." He lowered his head and sighed deeply. "It's stupid," he mumbled. "Pointless and sad. And one night it may prove to be the end of us all."

Rising, he drifted away, sullen and depressed. I sat where I was for a long time after he'd gone, studying the bloodied, battling vampires and mulling over the peaceful Kurda's solemn, troubling words.

CHAPTER NINE

As DAY rolled round and wore on, most vampires retired to their coffins. They'd have happily continued fighting and drinking, but the first of the formal balls was due at sunset and they had to prepare for it. There'd be three balls during the Festival of the Undead, one at the end of each day. Two large Halls were used for the balls, so all the vampires could be accommodated.

The ball was a strange event. Most of the vampires were dressed in their colourful clothes, as they had been earlier, but now their shirts, trousers and capes were torn, ripped and blood-specked, while their bodies and faces were scratched and bruised. Many had broken arms and legs, but every single one of them took to the dance floor, even those on crutches.

At the stroke of sunset, the vampires all raised their faces to the ceiling and howled like wild wolves. The howling went on for several minutes, each vampire holding his or her howl as long as possible. They called this the howl of the night, and it was performed at the first ball of each Festival. The aim was to outlast the others — the vampire who sustained his howl the longest would win the title "of the Howl," which he'd carry until the following Council. So, if I'd won, I'd have had to be addressed as Darren Shan of the Howl for the next twelve years.

Of course, I didn't come close to winning — since I was only a half-vampire, my voice was one of the weakest, and I was among the first to fall silent. Gradually, as the voices of the others cracked, they fell silent too, one by one, until in the end only a handful were howling, their faces red with the strain of such a fierce bellow. While the last few vampires howled themselves hoarse, the rest urged on their favourites – "Keep it up, Butra!", "Howl like a demon, Yebba!" – and pounded the floor with their feet and hands.

In the end the contest was won by a huge vampire called Yebba. He'd won it twice before — though not at the last Council – and was a popular victor. There was a short ceremony, in which he had to drink a tub of blood straight down without pause, then Paris Skyle dubbed him Yebba of the Howl. Almost as soon as the words had left the Prince's lips, the band began to play and the vampires started to dance.

The band consisted entirely of drummers, who kept up a slow, heavy beat. As the vampires danced stiffly – short steps, in time with the funereal music – they chanted the words of ancient songs, telling of great battles and vampire champions, praising those who'd died nobly, cursing those who'd betrayed or shamed the clan (though they didn't name them — it was a custom never to mention the names of traitors or vampires of poor standing).

I tried dancing — everybody had to have a go — but I wasn't much good at it. I could have jumped about to something fast and loud, but this was too precise. If you didn't know how to do it right, you looked stupid. Not knowing any of the words to the sombre songs was another drawback. Besides, the dancing made my itching worse than ever and I kept having to stop to scratch my back.

After a few minutes, I made my excuses and slipped away. I went looking for Seba Nile, who'd said he had something that would cure the itching. I found the quartermaster in the second chamber. He was dancing and leading the singing, so I took a seat and waited for him to finish.

Gavner Purl was in the Hall; he spotted me after a while and sat down beside me. He looked exhausted and was breathing heavier than ever. "I only got to my coffin an hour or so ago," he explained. "I was trapped by a couple of my old tutors and had to spend the entire day listening to their stories."

There was a break in the music, while the band drank blood and lined up their next song. Seba bowed to his companions and left the dance floor during the pause. I waved a hand in the air to grab his attention. He stopped to grab a mug of ale, then ambled over. "Gavner. Darren. Enjoying yourselves?"

"I would be if I had the energy," Gavner wheezed.

"How about you, Darren?" Seba asked. "What do you think of our Festival of the Undead?"

"It's weird," I answered honestly. "First you all howl like wild animals — then dance around like robots!"

Seba stifled a laugh. "You should not say such things out loud," he gently chided me. "You will hurt our feelings. Most vampires are proud of their dancing — they think they dance with great style."

"Seba," I said, scratching my legs, "do you remember saying you had something that would stop my itching?"

"I do."

"Would you mind giving it to me now?"

"It is not so easily fetched," Seba said. "We must make a short journey, down to the tunnels beneath the Halls."

"Will you take me when you have the time?" I asked.

"I have the time," he said. "But first find Kurda Smahlt. I promised I would let him accompany me when next I made the trip — he wants to map the region."

"Where will I tell him we're going?" I enquired.

"Tell him we go where the arachnids roam. He will know where I mean. Also, fetch that beautiful spider of yours — Madam Octa. I wish to bring her with us."

I found Kurda listening to vampires telling legendary stories from the past. Storytellers were in great demand at the Festival. Vampires didn't bother much with books. They preferred to keep the past alive orally. I don't think the full history of the vampires had ever been written down. I tugged on Kurda's elbow and whispered Seba's message to him. He said he'd accompany us, but asked me to give him a few minutes while he went and collected his map-making equipment. He said he'd meet us outside Seba's quarters, low in the mountain, close to the stores which the quartermaster was in charge of.

When I arrived back with Madam Octa, I learned that Gavner had also decided to join us. He felt he'd fall asleep if he stayed where he was, listening to the music, warmed by the glow of the torches and the press of vampires. "A stroll below decks is just what the captain ordered," he said, imitating a sailor's salty tones.

I looked around for Harkat — I thought he might like to see what the lower tunnels of Vampire Mountain were like — but he was surrounded by admiring vampires. Harkat's metabolism was even stronger than a vampire's and he could drink alcohol all day and night without being affected. The vampires were astonished by his capacity for drink and were cheering him on as he downed one mug of ale after another. I didn't like to take him away from his new-found friends, so I left him.

When we were ready, we gathered together outside Seba's rooms and set off for the tunnels. The guards on the gate connecting the tunnels to the Halls weren't regular guards — no vampire could carry out his normal duties during the Festival. They weren't dressed as neatly as the regular guards and some had been drinking, which they'd never do while on duty any other time. Seba told them where we were going and they waved us through, warning us not to get lost.

"We'd better not," Kurda smirked. "By the smell of you lot, you'd have trouble finding an apple at the bottom of a barrel of cider!"

The guards laughed and made mock threats not to let us back in. One of the more sober guards asked if we wanted torches but Seba said we'd be OK — the walls were coated with luminous lichen where we were going.

Kurda got his map-making equipment out when we reached tunnels where he'd never been before. It was just a sheet of grid-divided paper and a pencil. He paused every so often to add a tiny piece of line to the page, signifying the length of tunnel we'd traversed.

"Is that all there is to map-making?" I asked. "It looks easy."

"Tunnels aren't difficult to map," he agreed. "It's different if you're trying to map open land or a stretch of sea coast."

"Don't listen to him," Gavner said. "Even tunnels are difficult. I tried it once and made a mess of it. You have to work to scale and make sure you mark the length exactly right. If you're out by even the tiniest fraction, it throws the rest of the map off."

"It's just a knack," Kurda said. "You'd pick it up quickly if you gave it a proper try."

"No thanks," Gavner said. "I've no intention of spending my spare time trapped down a maze of tunnels, trying to map them out. I don't know what the appeal is."

"It's fascinating," Kurda said. "It gives you a clearer understanding of your environment, not to mention a great sense of achievement when you're finished. Apart from which, there's the practical aspect."

"'Practical aspect'!" Gavner snorted. "Nobody uses your maps except yourself!"

"Not so," Kurda corrected him. "Nobody's interested in helping me make maps, but plenty are willing to make use of them. Did you know we'll be building a new Hall, lower than any of the other levels, over the next few years?"

"A Hall of storage," Gavner nodded.

"That's being constructed out of a cave *I* discovered, which will connect to the rest of the Halls via a tunnel nobody knew about till *I* went snooping around."

"There are also the breach points," Seba noted.

"What are those?" I asked.

"Tunnels which open on to the Halls," Seba explained. "There are many ways into the Halls apart from the main gates of entry. Kurda has unearthed many of these and brought them to our attention, so that we might seal them off against attack."

"Who'd attack you up here?" I frowned.

"He's referring to animal attacks," Kurda said. "Stray wolves, rats and bats often crept in by breach points and went foraging for food. They were getting to be quite a nuisance. My maps helped put an end to most of their advances."

"OK," Gavner smiled. "I was wrong — your maps *do* serve a purpose. You still wouldn't get me down here helping you make them though."

We proceeded in silence for a time. The tunnels were narrow and the roofs were low-hanging, so it was hard going for the grown vampires. They enjoyed a few minutes of relief when the tunnels opened up briefly, but then they constricted again and it was back to crouching and shuffling along. It was dark too. We had just enough light to see by, but there wasn't enough for Kurda to make maps. He dug out a candle and started to light it, but Seba stopped him.

"No candles," the quartermaster said.

"But I can't see," Kurda complained.

"I am sorry, but you will have to make do as best you can."

Kurda grumbled, bent his head low over the sheet of paper, so his nose was almost touching it, and drew carefully as we progressed, stumbling often because he wasn't watching where he was going.

Finally, after crawling though an especially small tunnel, we found ourselves in a moderately large cave that was coated from base to ceiling in cobwebs. "Quiet now," Seba whispered as we stood. "It would not do to disturb the residents."

The "residents" were spiders. Thousands — possibly hundreds of thousands — of them. They filled the cave, dangling from the ceiling, hanging on cobwebs, scuttling across the floor. They were like the spider I'd spotted when I first arrived at Vampire Mountain, hairy and yellow. None was quite as large as Madam Octa but they were bigger than most ordinary spiders.

A number of the spiders scurried towards us. Seba dropped cautiously to one knee and whistled. The spiders hesitated, then returned to their corners. "Those were sentries," Seba said. "They would have defended the others had we come to cause mischief."

"How?" I asked. "I thought they weren't poisonous."

"Singly, they are harmless," Seba explained. "But if they attack in groups, they can be most troublesome. Death is an unlikely result – for a human, maybe, but not a vampire – but severe discomfort would certainly be in order, possibly even partial paralysis."

"I see why you wouldn't allow any candles," Kurda said. "One stray spark and this place would go up like dry paper."

"Precisely." Seba wandered into the centre of the cave. The rest of us followed slowly. Madam Octa had crept forward to the bars of her cage and was making a careful study of the spiders. "They have been here for thousands of years," Seba whispered, reaching up and letting some of the spiders crawl over his hands and up his arms. "We call them Ba'Halen's spiders, after the vampire who – if the legends are to be believed – first brought them here. No human knows of their existence."

I took no notice as the spiders crept up my legs – I was used to handling Madam Octa, and before her I'd studied spiders as a hobby – but Gavner and Kurda looked uneasy. "Are you sure they won't bite?" Gavner asked.

"I would be surprised if they did," Seba said. "They are docile, and usually only attack when threatened."

"I think I'm going to sneeze," Kurda said as a spider crawled over his nose.

"I would not advise it," Seba warned him. "They might interpret that as an act of aggression."

Kurda held his breath and shook from the effort of controlling the sneeze. His face had turned a bright shade of red by the time the spider moved on. "Let's beat it," he wheezed, letting out a long, shaky breath.

"Best suggestion I've heard all night," Gavner agreed.

"Not so fast, my friends," Seba smiled. "I did not bring you here for fun. We are on a mission. Darren — take off your top."

"*Here?*" I asked.

"You want to put a stop to the itching, do you not?"

"Well, yes, but..." Sighing, I did as Seba ordered.

When my back was bare, Seba found some old cobwebs which had been abandoned. "Bend over," he commanded, then held the cobwebs over my back and rubbed them between his fingers, so that they crumbled and sprinkled over my flesh.

"What are you doing?" Gavner asked.

"Curing an itch," Seba replied.

"With cobwebs?" Kurda said sceptically. "Really, Seba, I didn't think you believed in old wives' tales."

"It is no tale," Seba insisted, rubbing the webby ash into my broken skin. "There are chemicals in these cobwebs which aid the healing process and work against irritation. Within an hour, the itching will have ceased."

When I was covered in ash, Seba tied some thick, whole webs around the worst infected areas, including my hands. "We will take the webs off before we leave the tunnels," he said, "although I advise against washing for a night or two — the itching may return if you do."

"This is crazy," Gavner muttered. "It'll never work."

"Actually, I think it's working already," I contradicted him. "The backs of my legs were killing me when we came in, but now the itching is barely noticeable."

"If it's so effective," Kurda said, "why haven't we heard about it before?"

"I do not broadcast," Seba said. "If the curative powers of the webs were widely known, vampires would come down here to the caves all the time. They would disturb the natural routines of the spiders, forcing them further down into the mountain, and within years the supplies would dry up. I only bring people here when they truly need help, and always ask them to keep the secret to themselves. I trust none of you will betray my confidence?"

We all said we wouldn't.

Once I'd been seen to, Seba took Madam Octa out of her cage and laid her down on the floor. She squatted uncertainly while a crowd of inquisitive spiders gathered around her. One with light grey spots on its back ducked forward in a testing attack. She swatted it away with ease, and the rest withdrew. Once she'd familiarized herself with the terrain, she explored the cave. She climbed up the walls and on to the cobwebs, disturbing other spiders in the process. They reacted angrily to her intrusion, but calmed down once they saw how large she was and that she meant them no harm.

"They recognize majesty when they see it," Seba noted, pointing to lines of spiders following Madam Octa around. The one with grey spots was to the fore. "If we left her here, they would make a queen of her."

"Could she breed with them?" Kurda asked.

"Probably not," Seba mused. "But it would be interesting if she could. There has been no new blood introduced to the colony for thousands of years. I would be fascinated to study the offspring of such a union."

"Forget it," Gavner shivered. "What if the babies turned out to be as poisonous as their mother? We'd have thousands of them roaming the tunnels, killing at will!"

"Hardly," Seba smiled. "Spiders tend not to pick on those bigger than themselves, not while smaller and more vulnerable prey exists. Still, she is not my spider. It is for Darren to decide."

I watched her carefully for a couple of minutes. She looked happy out in the open, among those of her own kind. But I knew better than anyone the awful consequences of her bite. Better not to risk it. "I don't think we should leave her," I said.

"Very well," Seba agreed, pursed his lips and whistled softly. Madam Octa returned to her cage immediately in response, though once inside she kept close to the bars, as though lonely. I felt sorry for her, but reminded myself that she was just a spider and didn't have any real feelings as such.

Seba played for a while with the spiders, whistling and inviting them to crawl over him. I grabbed the flute — it was really just a fancy tin whistle — from Madam Octa's cage and joined him. It took a few minutes to tune my thoughts into the spiders' — they weren't as easy to make mental contact with as Madam Octa — but Seba and me had great fun once I was in control, letting them jump between our bodies and spin adjoining webs which connected us from head to foot.

Gavner and Kurda watched, bemused. "Could I control them too?" Gavner asked.

"I doubt it," Seba said. "It is more difficult than it looks. Darren is naturally gifted with spiders. Very few people have the ability to bond with spiders. You are a fortunate young man, Darren."

I'd gone off spiders since that nasty business between Madam Octa and my best friend, Steve Leopard, all those years ago, but at Seba's words I felt some of my old love for the eight-legged predators re-surfacing, and made myself a promise to take more of an interest in the webby world of spiders in the future.

When we were finished playing, Seba and me brushed off the cobwebs — being careful not to remove the curing webs he'd attached to my body — then the four of us crawled out to the tunnels. Some of the spiders followed us, but turned back when they realized we were leaving, all except the grey-spotted one, which trailed behind us almost to the end of the tunnel, as though smitten by Madam Octa and loathe to see her leave.

CHAPTER TEN

WE'D STARTED back for the Halls when I remembered the old burial site Kurda had told me about not long after I'd arrived at Vampire Mountain. I asked if we could see it. Seba was game and so was Kurda. Gavner wasn't so keen, but agreed to tag along. "Burial chambers make me feel morbid," he said as we wound our way through the tunnels.

"That's an odd view for a vampire," I noted. "Don't you sleep in a coffin?"

"Coffins are different," Gavner said. "I feel snug in a coffin. It's graveyards, morgues and crematoriums I can't stand."

The Hall of Final Voyage was a large cave with a domed roof. Luminous lichen grew thickly on the walls. A churning stream cut through the middle of the cave and exited via a tunnel which led it back underground. The stream was wide, fast and loud. We had to raise our voices to be heard above its roar as we stood at its edge.

"The bodies of the dead used to be carried down here," Kurda said. "They were stripped, placed in the water, and let loose. The stream swept them away, through the mountain and out to the wilderness beyond."

"What happened to them then?" I asked.

"They washed up on some far-off bank, where their bodies were devoured by animals and birds of prey." He chuckled when I blanched. "Not a pretty way to go, is it?"

"It is as good a way as any," Seba disagreed. "When *I* die, this is how I want to be disposed of. Dead bodies are an essential part of the natural food chain. Feeding flesh to fires is a waste."

"Why did they stop using the stream?" I asked.

"Bodies got stuck," Seba cackled. "They piled up a short way down the tunnel. The stench was unbearable. A team of vampires had to tie ropes around themselves and swim down the tunnel to hack the bodies free. They were pulled back by their colleagues, since nobody could swim against so furious a current.

"I was on that work detail," Seba continued. "Thankfully I only had to pull on the rope and did not have to venture into the water. Those who went down the tunnel to free the bodies could never bring themselves to talk of what they found."

As I gazed down at the dark water of the stream, shivering at the idea of swimming down the tunnel to pry loose stuck corpses, a thought struck me and I turned to Kurda. "You say the bodies washed up for animals and birds to feed on — but isn't vampire blood poisonous?"

"There wasn't any blood," Kurda said.

"Why not?" I frowned.

Kurda hesitated and Seba answered for him. "It had been drained by the Guardians of the Blood, who also removed most of their internal organs."

"Who are the Guardians of the Blood?" I asked.

"Do you remember the people we saw in the Hall of Cremation and the Hall of Death when I took you on a tour of the mountain?" Kurda said.

I cast my mind back and recalled the strange, ultra-pale people with the eerie white eyes, dressed in rags, sitting alone and quiet in the sombre Halls. Kurda had been reluctant to discuss them, and said he'd tell me about them later, but with all that had happened since, I'd forgotten to follow up on the mystery. "Who are they?" I asked. "What do they do?"

"They're the Guardians of the Blood," Kurda said. "They came to Vampire Mountain more than a thousand years ago — we don't know from where — and have resided here ever since, though small bands go off wandering every decade or so, sometimes returning with new members. They've separate living quarters beneath the Halls and rarely mix with us. They also have their own language, customs and beliefs."

"Are they humans?" I asked.

"They're ghouls!" Gavner grunted.

"That is unfair," Seba tutted. "They are loyal servants, deserving of our gratitude. They are in charge of the cremation ceremonies, and do a noble job of preparing the dead. Plus, they provide us with blood — that is where most of the human blood in our stores comes from. We could never ship in enough to supply the needs of all the vampires at Council, so we rely upon the Guardians. They do not let us feed directly from them, but they extract their blood themselves and pass it to us in jars."

"Why?" I asked, perplexed. "It can't be much fun, living inside a mountain and giving their blood away. What's in it for them?"

Kurda coughed uncomfortably. "Do you know what a saprotroph is?" I shook my head. "They're creatures – or small organisms – which feed on the waste or dead bodies of others. The Guardians are saprotrophs. They eat the internal organs – including the hearts and brains – of dead vampires."

I stared at Kurda, wondering if he was joking. But I saw by his grim expression that he wasn't. "Why do you let them?" I cried, my insides churning.

"We need them," Seba said plainly. "Their blood is necessary. Besides, they do us no harm."

"You don't think eating dead bodies is harmful?" I gasped.

"We haven't had any complaints from the dead yet," Gavner chortled, but his humour was forced — he looked as uncomfortable as I felt.

"They take great care with the bodies," Seba explained. "We are sacred to them. They drain the blood off first and store it in special casks of their own making – that is how they got their name – then delicately cut the torso open and remove the required organs. They also extract the brain, by inserting small hooks up the corpse's nose and pulling it out in little pieces."

"*What?*" Gavner roared. "I've never heard that before!"

"Most vampires are not aware of it," Seba said. "But I have studied the Guardians in some detail over the centuries. The skulls of vampires are precious to them, and they never slice them apart."

"That's somewhat unsettling," Kurda murmured distastefully.

"It's disgraceful!" Gavner snorted.

"Cool!" I cooed.

"Once the organs and brains have been removed," Seba went on, "they cook them to make them safe — our blood is as deadly to the Guardians as it is to any creature."

"And that's what they live on?" I asked, revolted but fascinated.

"No," Seba replied. "They would not survive very long if that was their only intake. They eat normal food, preserving and reserving our organs for special occasions — they eat them at marriages, funerals, and other such events."

"That's disgusting!" I shouted, torn between ghoulish laughter and moral outrage. "Why do they do it?"

"We're not sure what the appeal is," Kurda admitted, "but part of it may be that it keeps them alive longer. The average Guardian lives a hundred and sixty years or more. Of course, if they became vampires, they'd live even longer, but none do — accepting a vampire's blood is taboo as far as the Guardians are concerned."

"How can you let them do it?" I asked. "Why not send these monsters away?"

"They are not monsters," Seba disagreed. "They are people with peculiar feeding habits — much like ourselves! Besides, we drink their blood. It is a fair arrangement — our organs for their blood."

"'Fair' isn't the word I'd use," I muttered. "It's cannibalism!"

"Not really," Kurda objected. "They don't eat the flesh of their own, so they're not really cannibals."

"You're nit-picking," I grunted.

"It is a thin line," Seba agreed, "but there *is* a difference. I would not want to be a Guardian, and I do not socialize with them, but they are just odd humans getting along as best they can. Do not forget that *we* feed off people too, Darren. It would be wrong to despise them, just as it is wrong for humans to hate vampires."

"I told you this would turn morbid," Gavner chuckled.

"You were right," Kurda smiled. "This is a realm of the dead, not the living, and we should leave them to it. Let's get back to the Festival."

"Have you seen enough, Darren?" Seba asked.

"Yes," I shivered. "And heard enough too!"

"Then let us depart."

We set off, Seba in front, Gavner and Kurda fast on his heels. I hung back a moment, studying the stream, listening to the roar of the water as it entered and exited the cave, thinking about the Guardians of the Blood, imagining my dead, drained, hollowed body making the long descent down the mountain, tossed about like a rag doll from rock to rock.

It was a horrible image. Shaking my head, I thrust it from my thoughts and hurried after my friends, unaware that within a frighteningly short time I would be back at this same gruesome spot, not to mourn the passing of somebody else's life — but to fight desperately for my own!

CHAPTER ELEVEN

THE FESTIVAL of the Undead came to a grand, elaborate close on the third night. The celebrations started several hours before sunset, and though the Festival officially ended with the coming of night, a number of vampires kept the party spirit alive late into the following morning.

There was no fighting during the final day of the Festival. The time was given over to story-telling, music and singing. I learned much about our history and ancestors – the names of great vampire leaders, fierce battles we'd fought with humans and vampaneze – and would have stayed to listen right through the night had I not had to leave to learn of my next Trial.

This time I picked the Hall of Flames, and every vampire in attendance looked grim-faced when the Trial was called out.

"It's bad, isn't it?" I asked Vanez.

"Yes," the games master answered truthfully. "It will be your hardest Trial yet. We will ask Arra to help us prepare. With her help, you might pull through."

He placed a worrying amount of stress on the *might*.

*   *   *

I spent most of the following night and day learning to dodge fire. The Hall of Flames was a large metal room with lots of holes in the floor. Fierce fires would be lit outside the Hall when it was time for the Trial, and vampires would use bellows to pump flames into the room and up through the floor. Because there were so many pipes leading from the fires to the holes, it was impossible to predict the path the flames would follow and where they would emerge.

"You must use your ears as much as your eyes," Arra instructed. The vampiress had injured her right arm during the Festival and it was in a sling. "You can hear the flames coming before you see them."

One of the fires had been lit outside the Hall and a couple of vampires pumped flames from it into the room, so that I could learn to recognize the sound of the fire travelling through the pipes. Arra stood behind me, pushing me out of the way of the flames if I failed to react quickly enough. "You hear the hissing?" she asked.

"Yes."

"That is the sound of flames passing you by. It's when you hear a short whistling sound — like that!" she snapped, tugging me back as a pillar of fire sprouted from the floor at my feet. "Did you hear it?"

"Just about," I said, trembling nervously.

"That's not good enough," she frowned. "*Just about* will kill you. You have very little time to outmanoeuvre the flames. Every fraction of a second is precious. It's no good to react straightaway — you must react *in advance.*"

A few hours later, I had the hang of it and was darting around the Hall, avoiding the flames with ease. "That's good," Arra said as we rested. "But only one fire burns at the moment. Come the time of your Trial, all five will be lit. The flames will come quicker and in greater volume. You have much to learn before you are ready."

After more practice, Arra took me outside the Hall and over to the fire. She shoved me up close to it, grabbed a burning branch and ran it over the flesh of my legs and arms. "Stop!" I screeched. "You're burning me alive!"

"Be still!" she commanded. "You must accustom yourself to the heat. Your skin is tough — you can stand a lot of punishment. But you must be ready for it. Nobody makes it through the Hall of Flames unmarked. You *will* be burnt and singed. Your chances of emerging alive depend on how you react to your injuries. If you let yourself feel the pain, and panic — you'll die. If not, you might survive."

I knew she wouldn't say such things unless they were true, so I stood still and ground my teeth together while she ran the glowing tip of the branch over my flesh. The itching, which had all but disappeared following Seba's application of the cobwebs, flared into life again, adding to my misery.

During a break, I studied my flesh where Arra had run the flaming branch over it. It was a nasty pink colour and stung when touched, like a bad case of sunburn. "Are you sure this is a good idea?" I asked.

"You must grow used to the lick of flames," Arra said. "The more pain we subject your body to now, the easier it will be to cope later. Be under no illusions — this is one of the most testing Trials. You will suffer greatly before the end."

"You're not exactly filling me with confidence," I moaned.

"I'm not here to fill you with confidence," she replied archly. "I'm here to help you save your life."

After a short discussion between Vanez and Arra, it was decided that I should go without my usual few hours of sleep in the run up to the Trial. "We need those extra hours," Vanez said. "You've had three days and nights of rest. Right now, practice is more important than sleep."

So, after a brief break, it was back to the Hall and the fire, where I learned how to *narrowly* dodge flames. It was best to move about as little as possible during the Trial. That way you could listen more intently and concentrate on predicting where the next burst of flames was coming from. It meant getting singed and lightly burnt, but that was preferable to taking a wrong step and going up in a cloud of smoke.

We practised until half an hour before the start of the Trial. I nipped back to my cell to catch my breath and change clothes — I'd be wearing leather shorts, nothing else — then returned to the Hall of Flames, where many vampires had gathered to wish me well.

Arrow — the bald-headed, tattooed Prince — had come from the Hall of Princes to oversee the Trial. "I'm sorry none of us could make it last time," he apologized, making the death's touch sign.

"That's OK," I told him. "I don't mind."

"You are a gracious competitor," Arrow said. "Now, do you know the rules?"

I nodded. "I have to stay in there fifteen minutes and try not to get roasted."

"Well put," the Prince grinned. "Are you ready?"

"Almost," I said, knees knocking together. I turned to face Mr Crepsley. "If I don't pull through, I want you to—" I began, but he interrupted angrily.

"Do not talk like that! Think positively."

"I *am* thinking positively," I said, "but I know how difficult it will be. All I was going to say was, I've been thinking it over, and if I die, I'd like you to take my body home and bury it in my grave. That way I'll be close to Mum, Dad and Annie."

Mr Crepsley's eyes twitched (was he blinking back *tears?*) and he cleared his throat. "I will do as you request," he croaked, then offered me his hand. I brushed it aside and gave him a hug instead.

"I'm proud to have been your assistant," I whispered in his ear, then pulled away before he could say anything else, and entered the Hall of Flames.

The door clanging shut behind me cut off the sound of the fires being stoked up. I walked towards the centre of the room, sweating freely from the heat and fear. The floor was already hot. I wanted to rub some spit on to my feet, to cool them, but Arra had told me not to do that too soon. Things would get a whole lot hotter later — better to hold some spit back for when I really needed it.

There was a gurgling sound from the pipes below. I tensed, but it was only one of the pipes shaking. Relaxing, I closed my eyes and swallowed deep breaths while there was still clean air to breathe. That was another problem I'd have to face — although there were holes in the roof and walls, oxygen would be in short supply, and I'd have to find air pockets in amongst the flames, or risk suffocating.

As I was thinking about the air, I heard an angry hissing sound in the floor beneath me. Opening my eyes, I saw a jagged funnel of flame erupt several metres to my left.

The Trial had begun.

I ignored the spouting flames – they were too far away to harm me – and listened closely for the next burst. This time it came from one of the far corners of the room. I'd got off to a lucky start. Sometimes, according to Arra, flames struck at you right at the beginning and didn't let up for the entirety of the Trial. At least I had time to adjust gradually to the heat.

There was a whistling sound close to my right. I jumped aside as fire blossomed in the air nearby, then ticked myself off — that burst had been close, but it wouldn't have struck.

I should have stood my ground or edged carefully out of its way. Moving as I had, I could have stepped straight into trouble.

The flames were coming in quick bursts now, all around the Hall. I could feel a terrible heat building in the air and already it was hard to breathe. A hole a few centimetres from my right foot whistled. I didn't move as fire erupted and stung my leg — I could tolerate a small burn like that. A larger burst came out of a wider hole behind me. I shifted forward ever so slightly, rolling gently away from the worst of its bite. I felt the flames licking at the skin of my bare back, but none took hold.

The hardest times were when two or more funnels sprang from holes set close together. There was nothing I could do when trapped between a set of fiery pillars, except suck in my belly and step gingerly through the thinner wall of flames.

Within a few minutes my feet were in agony — they absorbed the worst of the flames. I spat on my palms and rubbed spit into my soles, which provided some measure of temporary relief. I would have stood on my hands to give my feet a rest, except that would have exposed my head of hair to the fire.

Most vampires, when preparing for the Trials, shaved their heads months in advance, so they were bald when the Trials began. That way, if they drew the Hall of Flames, they'd stand a better chance, since hair burns a lot easier than flesh. But you weren't allowed to shave your head *especially* for the Trial, and things had happened so quickly with me that nobody had thought to prepare me against the possibility of facing the flames.

There was no way to keep track of time. I had to focus every last ounce of my concentration on the floor and fire. The briefest of distractions could have lethal consequences.

Several holes in front of me spouted flames at the same time. I began edging backwards, when I heard pipes whistling savagely behind me. Sucking in my belly again, I nudged over to my left, away from the thickest sheets of fire.

The moment of danger passed, but I was getting trapped in a corner. Vanez had warned me about this, even before we'd tracked down Arra and asked her to train me. "Stay away from the corners," he'd said. "Stick to the middle as much as possible. If you find yourself backing into a corner, get out of it quickly. Most who perish in the Hall of Flames do so in corners, trapped by walls of fire, unable to break free."

I started back the way I'd come, but the fire was still shooting up through the holes, blocking my path. Reluctantly, I edged further towards the corner, ready to take the first opening as soon as one presented itself. The trouble was — none did.

The gurgling of pipes to my rear brought me to a halt. Flame burst out of the floor behind me, scorching my back. I grimaced but didn't move — there was nowhere to move *to*. The air was very poor in this region of the room. I waved my hands in front of my face, trying to create a draught which would suck some fresh air in, but it didn't work.

The pillars of flames in front of me had formed a wall of fire, at least two or three metres thick. I could barely see the rest of the room through the flickering flames. As I stood, waiting for a path to open, the mouths of the pipes at my feet hissed, several of them all at once. A huge ball of fire was on its way, about to explode directly underneath me! I had a split second to think and act.

Couldn't stand still — I'd burn.

Couldn't retreat — I'd burn.

Couldn't duck to the sides — I'd burn.

Forward, through the thick banks of fire? I'd probably burn, but there was open ground and air beyond — *if* I made it through. It was a lousy choice, but there was no time to complain. Closing my eyes and mouth, I covered my face with my arms and darted forward into the wall of crackling flames.

CHAPTER TWELVE

FIRE ENGULFED and billowed about me like a ferocious red-and-yellow locust cloud. I'd never in my worst nightmare imagined such heat. I almost opened my mouth to scream. If I had, fire would have gushed down my throat and torched me to a crisp from the inside out.

When I burst through the other side of the fiery wall, my hair was a burning bush and flames sprouted from my body like mushrooms. I dropped to the floor and rolled around, beating at my hair with my hands, extinguishing the flames. I paid no attention to the hisses and whistlings of the pipes. If flames had struck in those seconds of madness, they'd have devoured me. But I got lucky... lucky Darren Shan... the luck of the vampires.

Once I'd slapped out the worst of the flames, I got to my knees, groaning weakly. Sucking in hot, thin air, I prodded gently at the smouldering mess on top of my head, making sure there were no sparks waiting to flare back into life.

My entire body was black and red. Black from the soot, red from where the burns had eaten through my flesh. I was in bad shape but I had to go on. Sore as I was, and painful as it was to move, I had to. The ravenous demons of the fire would devour me if I didn't.

Standing, I tuned out the roars of the flames and listened for the sounds of the pipes. It wasn't easy — my ears had been savagely burnt affecting my sense of hearing — but I was able to detect the faintest hints of hissing and whistling, and after a few shaky steps I was back on course, anticipating the bursts of flames and moving to avoid them.

The one good thing about wading through the wall of fire was that it had burnt out much of the feelings in my feet. There was almost no pain now beneath my knees. That meant I was dangerously burnt, and part of me worried about what would happen after the Trial — if my feet were burnt beyond repair, they might have to be amputated! — but that was a worry for another time. Right now I was glad of the relief and took comfort from it.

My ears were seriously troubling me. I tried to rub some spit on them but my mouth had dried up completely. I caressed them gently between my fingers, but that made them worse. In the end I left them alone and just did my best to ignore them.

The flames were forcing me into another corner. Rather than let myself get trapped again, I ducked through a roaring bank of fire, back to open ground, enduring the ensuing pain.

I closed my eyes as often as possible, every time there was the slightest lull. The heat was dreadful for them. They'd dried up the same way my mouth had and I was afraid of losing my sight.

As I rolled away from yet another nasty burst of fire, the flames in the Hall began to die away. I paused suspiciously. Was this the start of an even worse assault? Could I expect a huge ball of fire to burst through the pipes and blow me away?

While I twitched and strained my ears, the door to the Hall swung open and vampires in heavy capes entered. I stared at them as though they were aliens. What were they doing? Were they firemen who'd lost their way? Someone should tell them they shouldn't be here. It was dangerous.

I backed away from the vampires as they converged on me. I'd have warned them to get out before the big ball of fire hit, except I had no voice. I couldn't even manage a squeak. "Darren, it is over," one of the vampires said. He sounded like Mr Crepsley, but it couldn't be — Mr Crepsley wouldn't wander into a Hall during the middle of a Trial.

I waved a singed hand at the vampires and mouthed the words, "Go away! Get out of here!"

"Darren," the lead vampire said again, "it is over. You won!"

I couldn't make sense of his words. All I knew was that a huge ball of fire was due, and if these heedless fools were blocking my way, I'd be incapable of dodging it. Hitting out at them, I tried weaving my way through their arms to safety.

I ducked the grasp of the lead vampire, but the next caught me by the scruff of the neck. His touch was painful and I dropped to the floor, screaming silently.

"Be careful!" the lead vampire snapped, then bent over me — it *was* Mr Crepsley! "Darren," he said softly, "it is all right. You did it. You are safe."

Shaking my head, unable to think clearly, I mouthed the same word over and over, "Fire! Fire! Fire!"

I was still mouthing it when they lifted me on to a stretcher and carted me from the Hall. And even when we were outside, clear of the flames, and medics were attending to my wounds, I couldn't stop my lips from forming the word of warning, or my eyes from rolling to the left and right, fearfully searching for the tell tale-signs of red and yellow terror.

CHAPTER THIRTEEN

MY CELL. Lying on my belly. Medics examining my back, rubbing cool lotions into my skin. Somebody lifting my charred feet, gasping, calling for help.

* * *

Gazing at the ceiling. Someone holding a torch up to my eyes, peering into my pupils. A razor running over my head, scalping me, removing the remains of my burnt hair. Gavner Purl stepping forward, worried. "I think he's—" he starts to say. Darkness.

* * *

Nightmares. The world on fire. Running. Burning. Screaming. Calling for help. Everybody else on fire too.

Jolt awake. Vampires around me. Nightmare still playing at the back of my mind. Convinced the cell's on fire. I try to break free. They hold me down. I curse them. Struggle. Pain gushes through me. Wince. Relax. Return to fire-plagued dreams.

*　*　*

Finally I drifted back from the lands of delirium. I was lying face down. I moved my head slightly to gaze around the cell. Mr Crepsley and Harkat Mulds were sitting nearby, monitoring me.

"Thought ... I saw ... Gavner," I wheezed.

Mr Crepsley and Harkat sprang forward, smiling worriedly. "He was here earlier," Mr Crepsley said. "So were Kurda, Vanez and Arra. The medics told them to leave."

"I ... made it?" I asked.

"Yes."

"How bad ... am I ... burnt?"

"Very bad," Mr Crepsley said.

"You look ... like an over ... cooked sausage," Harkat joked.

I laughed weakly. "I sound ... like you ... now," I told him.

"Yes," he agreed. "But you ... will get ... better."

"Will I?" I addressed the question to Mr Crepsley.

"Yes," he said, nodding firmly. "You have suffered a terrible ordeal, but the damage is not permanent. Your feet suffered the worst of the punishment, but the medics have saved them. It will take time to heal, and your hair might never grow back, but you are in no immediate danger."

"I feel ... terrible," I told him.

"Be glad you can feel at all," he replied bluntly.

"What about ... next Trial?"

"Do not think of such things now."

"I ... must," I gasped. "Will I ... have time ... to get ready ... for it?" Mr Crepsley didn't say anything. "Tell me ... the truth," I insisted.

"There will be no extra time," he sighed. "Kurda is in the Hall of Princes as we speak, arguing your case, but he will not be able to persuade them to postpone. There is no precedent for a delay between Trials. Those unfit to continue must..." He came to a halt.

"...be taken to ... the Hall of ... Death," I finished for him. While he sat there, trying to think of something comforting to say, Kurda returned, looking flushed with excitement. "Is he awake?" he asked.

"I am," I answered.

Crouching beside me, he said, "It's almost sunset. You must choose your next Trial or admit failure and be carted away for execution. If we carry you to the Hall of Princes, do you think you'll be able to stand upright for a couple of minutes?"

"I'm not... sure," I answered honestly. "My feet... hurt."

"I know," he said. "But it's important. I've found a way to buy us some time, but only if you can act as if you're fine."

"What *way*?" Mr Crepsley asked, astonished.

"No time for explanations," Kurda snapped. "Are you willing to give it a go, Darren?" I nodded weakly. "Good. Let's get him on a stretcher and up to the Hall of Princes. We mustn't be late."

Hurrying through the tunnels, we made it to the Hall just in time for sunset. Vanez Blane was outside, waiting with his purple flag. "What's going on, Kurda?" he asked. "There's no way Darren will be ready to face a Trial tomorrow."

"Trust me," Kurda said. "It was Paris' idea, but we can't let on. We have to act as if we're ready to continue. It all hinges on Darren standing up and drawing his Trial. Come on. And remember — we *have to* act like there's nothing wrong."

We were all mystified by Kurda's behaviour, but we had no choice but to do as he said. Entering the Hall of Princes, I heard the voices of the vampires within drop, as all eyes fixed upon us. Kurda and Mr Crepsley carried me to the platform of the Princes, Harkat and Vanez just behind.

"Is this young Master Shan?" Paris asked.

"It is, sire," Kurda answered.

"He looks terrible," Mika Ver Leth noted. "Are you sure he's fit to continue with the Trials?"

"He is merely resting, sire," Kurda said lightly. "He likes to feign injury, so that he may be carried around like a lord."

"Really?" Mika replied, smiling tightly. "If that is the case, let the boy step forward and choose his next Trial. You understand," he added ominously, "what we must do if he is unable?"

"We understand," Kurda said, and laid his end of the stretcher down. Mr Crepsley followed suit. The two vampires helped me to my feet, then slowly let go of me. I teetered dangerously and almost fell. I probably would have, if there hadn't been so many vampires present — but I didn't want to look frail in front of them.

Fighting the pain, I stumbled forward to the platform. It took a long time to make it up the steps, but I didn't falter. Nobody said anything while I was climbing, and when I got there the bag of numbered stones was produced and checked as normal. "Number four," the vampire clutching the bag announced once I'd drawn my stone. "The Blooded Boars."

"A tricky Trial," Paris Skyle mused as the stone was passed to the Princes to be certified. "Are you ready for it, Darren?"

"I don't ... know what it ... is," I said. "But ... I will be ... there to face it ... tomorrow, as ... scheduled."

Paris smiled warmly. "That is good to hear." He cleared his throat and widened his eyes innocently. "I, however, cannot make it. I have pressing business to attend to and regretfully must give this Trial a miss. My good colleague Mika will take my place."

Mika imitated Paris' innocent look. "Actually, I can't stir from the Hall tomorrow either. This Vampaneze Lord business takes up all my time. How about you, Arrow?"

The bald Prince shook his head glumly. "Alas, I also must make my excuses. My diary — so to speak — is full."

"Sires," Kurda said, quickly stepping forward. "You have already skipped one of Darren's Trials. We allowed for your absence on that occasion, but to neglect your post twice in the course of one set of Trials is unpardonable and does Darren a grave disservice. I must protest most strongly."

Paris started to smile, caught himself, and forced a scowl. "There is truth in your words," he muttered.

"We cannot miss another of the boy's Trials," Mika agreed.

"One way or another, one of us must be present," Arrow finished.

The three Princes huddled close together and discussed it quietly. By the way they smirked and winked at Kurda, I knew they'd something up their sleeves.

"Very well," Paris said out loud. "Darren has reported fit for his next Trial. Since we cannot be there to oversee it, we have decided to postpone it. We apologize for the inconvenience, Darren. Will you pardon us?"

"I'll let ... it pass ... this time," I grinned.

"How long must we wait, sires?" Kurda asked, feigning impatience. "Darren is anxious to conclude his Trials."

"Not long," Paris said. "One of us will be there for the Trial at sunset, seventy-two hours from now. Is that agreeable?"

"It is irksome, sire," Kurda sighed theatrically, "but if we must wait, we shall."

Bowing, Kurda led me from the platform, helped me back on to the stretcher, and carried me from the Hall with Mr Crepsley. Once outside, the vampires set me down and laughed loudly.

"You rogue, Kurda Smahlt!" Mr Crepsley roared. "How did you dream that one up?"

"It was Paris' idea," Kurda replied humbly. "The Princes wanted to help Darren, but they couldn't turn around and say they were giving him time to recover on account of his injuries. They needed an excuse in order to save face. This way, it looks as though Darren was ready and willing to proceed, so there's no shame in postponing it."

"That's why ... I had to stand," I noted. "So nobody would be ... suspicious."

"Correct," Kurda beamed. "Everyone in the Hall knows what's really happening, but as long as it *looks* like everything is in order, nobody will object."

"Three nights ... and days," I mused. "Will it be ... enough?"

"If not, it will not be for want of trying," Mr Crepsley said with fierce determination, and we set off down the tunnels at a cracking pace to find some medics capable of knocking me back into shape before I had to face the Blooded Boars.

CHAPTER FOURTEEN

TIME PASSED slowly while I was confined to my recovery hammock. Medics fussed over me, rubbing lotions into my charred flesh, changing bandages, cleaning the wounds, making sure infection didn't set in. They often commented on how fortunate I was. None of the damage was permanent, except maybe the hair loss. My feet would heal, my lungs were OK, most of my skin would grow back. All things considered, I was in great shape and should thank my lucky stars.

But I didn't *feel* in great shape. I was in pain the whole time. It was bad enough when I lay still, but grew unbearable when I moved. I cried into my pillow a lot, wishing I could fall asleep and not wake until the pain had passed, but even in sleep I was tortured by the after-effects of the fire, terrorized by nightmares, never more than a sharp twinge away from wakefulness.

I had plenty of visitors, who helped distract me from the pain. Seba and Gavner spent hours by my side, telling me stories and jokes. Gavner had started calling me Toastie, because he said I looked like a slice of burnt toast. And he offered to find a charred torch stub and draw fake ashen eyebrows on my forehead, since my own had been burnt off along with my head of hair. I told him where he could stick his torch stub — and the rest of the torch as well!

I asked Seba if he had any special cures for burns, hoping the old vampire would know of some traditional remedy which the medics were ignorant of. "Alas, no," he said, "but when your wounds have healed, we shall make another trip to the caves of Ba'Halen's spiders and find cobwebs to prevent further itching."

Arra often came to see me, though she spent more time talking with Mr Crepsley than me. The two spent a lot of time talking about the old nights and their life together when they were mates.

After a while I fell to wondering if the pair might be planning to mate again, and how that would affect my relationship with the vampire. When I asked Mr Crepsley about it, he coughed with embarrassment and snapped that I wasn't to bother him with such nonsense — Arra and he were just good friends.

"*Of course* you are," I chuckled, and goaded him with a knowing wink.

Kurda could only get down to see me a couple of times. Now that the Festival of the Undead was out of the way, there was a lot of business for the vampires to discuss, much of it connected to the vampaneze. As a senior General and vampaneze expert, he had to spend most of his waking hours in meetings and conferences.

Arra was with me on one of the rare occasions when Kurda came. She stiffened when she saw him and he made to withdraw, to avoid a confrontation. "Wait," she called him back. "I want to thank you for what you did for Darren."

"It was nothing," he smiled.

"It wasn't," she disagreed. "Many of us care about Darren but only you had sense enough to steer him to safety in his hour of need. The rest of us would have stood by and watched him die. I don't agree with your ways – there's a thin line between diplomacy and cowardice – but sometimes they *do* work better than our own."

Arra left and Kurda smiled lightly. "Do you know," he remarked, "that's the closest she'll ever get to saying she likes me."

Kurda fed me some water – I was on a liquids only diet – and told me what had been happening while I was out of action. A committee had been established to discuss the workings of the vampaneze and what to do in the event of the emergence of a Vampaneze Lord. "For the first time, they're seriously talking about making peace with the vampaneze," he said.

"That must make you happy."

He sighed. "If this had happened a few years ago, I'd have been whooping with glee. But time's running out. I think it's going to take more than a mere committee to unite the tribes and combat the threat of the Vampaneze Lord."

"I thought you didn't believe in the Vampaneze Lord," I said.

He shrugged. "Officially, I don't. Between you and me..." He lowered his voice. "The thought of him scares me witless."

"You think he's real?" I asked.

"If Mr Tiny says so — yes. Whatever else I believe or don't believe in, there's no doubting the powers of Mr Tiny. Unless we act quickly to prevent the possibility of a Vampaneze Lord arising, I'm sure he'll come. Stopping him before he gets started may involve a terrible sacrifice, but if that's the price of averting a war, so be it."

It was odd to hear Kurda making such a confession. If he — friend to the vampaneze — was worried, the other vampires must be terrified. I hadn't been paying a lot of attention to talk of the Vampaneze Lord, but I made up my mind to listen more closely in future.

The next night — the last before the start of my fourth Trial — Mr Crepsley came to see me after a meeting with Vanez Blane. Harkat was already by my hammock. The Little Person had spent more time with me than anyone else.

"I have discussed things with Vanez," Mr Crepsley said, "and we both agree that you would be better served in the run up to your next Trial by rest rather than practice. There are no special skills required in the Trial of the Blooded Boars. You simply have to face and kill two boars which have been infected with vampire blood. It is a straightforward fight to the death."

"If I can beat a wild bear, I can beat a couple of boars," I grinned, trying to sound upbeat — I'd killed a savage bear during our trek to Vampire Mountain.

"Most certainly you can," Mr Crepsley agreed. "Were it not for your wounds, I would even hazard a guess that you could do it with one arm tied behind your back."

I smiled, then coughed. I'd been coughing a lot since the Hall of Flames. It was a natural reaction to all the smoke I'd inhaled. My lungs hadn't suffered any serious damage, so the coughing should stop in another couple of days. Mr Crepsley handed me a glass of water and I sipped from it slowly. I was able to feed myself now, and had enjoyed my first meal since the Hall of Flames earlier in the night. I was still in pretty poor shape, but thanks to my vampire blood, I was recovering quickly.

"Do you feel ready for the Trial?" Mr Crepsley asked.

"I'd like another twenty-four hours," I sighed, "but I think I'll be OK. I walked about for nearly a quarter of an hour after breakfast, and I felt good. As long as my legs and feet hold, I should be fine — fingers crossed."

"I have been talking to Seba Nile," Mr Crepsley said, switching subjects. "He tells me he is thinking of retiring once Council has ended. He feels he has served long enough as the quartermaster of Vampire Mountain. He wants to see the world one last time before he dies."

"Maybe he can come with us to the Cirque Du Freak," I suggested.

"Actually," Mr Crepsley said, watching closely for my reaction, "we might not be returning to the Cirque Du Freak."

"Oh?" I frowned.

"Seba has offered me the job of quartermaster. I am thinking of accepting it."

"I thought nobody liked becoming quartermaster," I said.

"It is not much sought after," Mr Crepsley agreed, "but quartermasters are widely respected. The running of Vampire Mountain is a great responsibility. It can also be richly rewarding — for hundreds of years you are capable of influencing the lives of every new Vampire General."

"Why did he offer the job to you?" I asked. "Why not one of his assistants?"

"His assistants are young. They dream of being Generals or going out into the world and making a mark of their own. It would be unfair to tear one of them away from his dreams when I am at hand, ready and able to step into the breach."

"You want to do this, don't you?" I asked, reading his desire in his expression.

He nodded. "A decade or two ago, it would have been the furthest thing from my wishes. But life has been aimless since I quit the Generals. I had not realized how much I missed being part of the clan until I attended this Council. This would be the ideal way for me to re-establish myself."

"If you want it that much, go for it," I encouraged him.

"But what about you?" he asked. "As my assistant, you would have to remain here with me until you are old enough to venture forth by yourself. Do you relish the idea of spending the next thirty years of your life walled up inside this mountain?"

"Not really," I said. "I've enjoyed my stay — apart from the Trials — but I imagine it could grow boring after a couple of years." I ran a hand over my bald head and thought at length about it. "And there's Harkat to consider. How will he get back if we stay here?"

"I will ... stay with you ... if you decide ... to remain," he said.

"You will?" I asked, surprised.

"Part of ... my memory ... has come back. Much is ... still blank, but I ... recall Mr Tiny ... telling me the only ... way I could ... find out who I ... was before I died ... was by ... sticking with you."

"How can *I* help you find out who you were?" I asked.

Harkat shrugged. "I do not ... know. But I will ... stay by your ... side, as long ... as you will ... have me."

"You don't mind being cooped up inside a mountain?" I asked.

Harkat smiled. "Little People ... are easily ... pleased."

I lay back and considered the proposal. If I stayed, I could learn more about the ways of the vampires, perhaps even train to be a Vampire General. The idea of being a General appealed to me — I could picture myself leading a troop of vampires into battle with the vampaneze, like a pirate captain or an officer in the army.

On the other hand, I'd maybe never see Evra Von or Mr Tall or my other friends at the Cirque Du Freak again. No more travelling around the world, performing to audiences, or luxury comforts like going to the cinema or ordering a Chinese takeaway — not for thirty-odd years at least!

"It's a huge decision," I mused aloud. "Can I have some time to think it over?"

"Of course," Mr Crepsley said. "There is no rush. Seba expects no answer until after Council. We will discuss it in further detail when you have concluded your Trials."

"*If* I conclude them," I grinned nervously.

"*When*," Mr Crepsley insisted, and smiled reassuringly.

CHAPTER FIFTEEN

THE FOURTH Trial — the Blooded Boars.

It seemed liked half the vampires in the mountain had turned out to watch me take on the two wild boars. I learned, as I waited for the Trial to start, that interest in me was at an all time high. Many vampires had expected me to fail long before this. They were amazed that I'd survived the Hall of Flames. Already the storytellers of Vampire Mountain were busy turning my exploits into the stuff of modern legend. I heard one of them describing my Trial on the Path of Needles, and to listen to him tell it, I'd endured ten avalanches and been pierced clean through the stomach by a falling stalactite, which had to be cut out of me after the Trial!

It was fun listening to the murmured stories spreading through the crowds of vampires, even if most were hogwash. They made me feel like King Arthur or Alexander the Great.

"Don't go getting a swelled head," Gavner laughed, noting the way I was listening intently to the tales. He was keeping me company while Vanez chose my weapons. "Exaggeration is the key to every legend. If you fail in this or the final Trial, they'll make out that you were a lazy, stupid, good-for-nothing, and hold you up as an example for future vampires. 'Work hard, my boy,' they'll say, 'or you'll end up like that wastrel Darren Shan'."

"At least they won't be able to say I snored like a bear," I retorted.

Gavner grimaced. "You've been spending too much time around Larten," he growled.

Vanez returned and handed me a small wooden mace and a short spear. "These are the best I could do," he said, scratching the skin beneath his missing left eye with the tip of the spear. "They aren't much, but they'll have to do."

"These will be fine," I said, though I'd been hoping for something more deadly.

"You know what will happen?" he asked.

"The boars will be released into the ring at the same time. They might scrap with each other at the start, but as soon as they smell me, they'll focus on me."

Vanez nodded. "That's how the bear tracked you down on your way here, and why he attacked you. Vampiric blood heightens an animal's senses, especially its sense of smell. They go for whatever smells the strongest.

"You'll have to get close to the boars to kill them. Use your spear to stab at their eyes. Save your mace for their snouts and skulls. Don't bother with their bodies — you'd be wasting your energy.

"The boars probably won't coordinate their attacks. Usually, when one moves in for the kill, the other hangs back. If they *do* come at you together, they might get in each other's way. Use their confusion if you can.

"Avoid their tusks. If you get stuck on a set, get off them quickly, even if you have to drop your weapons to free yourself. There's only so much damage they can do if you steer clear of their tusks."

A bugle call announced the arrival of Mika Ver Leth, who would be presiding over the Trial. The black-garbed Prince bade me good evening and asked if I was ready to begin. I told him I was. He wished me luck and made the death's touch sign, checked to make sure I was carrying no concealed weapons, then swept away to take his position, while I was led into the arena.

The arena was a big round pit in the ground. A sturdy wooden fence had been built around it, to make sure the boars couldn't escape. Vampires stood around the fence, cheering like a crowd of Romans at the Colosseum.

I stretched my arms above my head and winced at the pain. Much of my flesh was tender and some of my wounds were already seeping beneath my bandages. My feet weren't too painful – a lot of the nerve endings had been burnt out, and it would be weeks, maybe months, before they grew back – but I stung piercingly everywhere else.

The doors to the pit swung open and two caged boars were dragged in by guards. A hush settled over the observing vampires. Once the guards had retreated and shut the doors, the locks of the cages were undone by overhead wires and the cages were lifted out of the pit by ropes. The boars grunted angrily when they found themselves in the open. They immediately head-butted each other, locking tusks. They were fierce creatures, a metre and a half long, maybe a metre high.

When my scent reached the pair, they stopped fighting and backed away from each other. One spotted me and squealed. The other followed the gaze of the first, set its sights on me, and charged. I raised my spear defensively. The boar turned several metres shy of where I was standing, and wheeled off to one side, snorting savagely.

The far-off boar trotted towards me, slowly, purposefully. It stopped a few metres away, eyed me evilly, pawed the ground with its hooves, then darted. I easily avoided its lunge and managed to strike one of its ears with the head of my mace as it sped past. It roared, made a quick turn and came at me again. I jumped over it this time, jabbing at its eyes with my spear, missing narrowly. When I landed, the second boar attacked. It threw itself at me, opening and shutting its jaws like a shark, twirling its tusks wildly.

I dodged the assault but stumbled as I did. Because of the destroyed nerve endings in my feet, I realized I couldn't rely on them as much as I used to. Numbness in my soles meant I could trip at any time, without warning. I'd have to tread carefully.

One of the boars saw me stumbling and rammed me hard from the side. Luckily, its tusks didn't catch, and though the blow drove the wind out of me, I was able to roll away and regain my balance.

I hadn't much time to get ready for the next attack. Almost before I knew it, a huge hunk of heaving flesh was coming straight at me. Acting on instinct, I stepped aside and thrust with my spear. There was a loud yelp and when I raised the tip of the spear it was red with blood.

There was a brief respite while the boars circled me. It was easy to spot the one I'd injured – there was a long gash down one side of its snout, from which blood was dripping – but it wasn't a serious injury and would do little to deter further attacks.

The bloodied boar half lunged at me. I waved my mace at it and it spun away, snorting. The other made a serious run, but lowered its head too soon, so I was able to avoid it by stepping smartly aside.

The vampires overhead were yelling advice and encouragement, but I drowned out the sound of their cries and focused on the boars. They were circling me again, raking up dust with their hooves, taking deep determined breaths.

The unharmed boar suddenly broke off circling and charged. I edged aside but it kept its head up and followed me. Tensing the muscles in my legs, I jumped and tried braining it with my mace. But I'd mistimed my jump and instead of connecting with the boar, the boar connected with me.

Its head and shoulders knocked my legs out from under me and I fell heavily to the floor. The boar turned quickly and was over me before I could get up, its hot breath clouding my face, its tusks flashing dangerously in the dim light of the pit.

I slapped at the boar with my mace but was in no position to make the blows count. It shrugged them off and worried me with its tusks. I felt one cut through the bandages around my belly and slice shallowly into the burnt flesh beneath. If I didn't get moving soon, the boar would do real damage.

Taking hold of the round ball at the end of the mace, I jammed it in the boar's mouth, muffling its eager snuffles. The boar retreated, grunting angrily. I scrambled to my feet. As I did, the second boar slammed into me from behind. I went tumbling over the first boar, rolled head over heels like a ball, and collided with the fence.

As I sat up, dazed, I heard the sound of a boar running straight at me. With no time to get a fix on it, I dived blindly to my left. The boar missed me and there was a ferocious clattering as it struck the fence full-on with its head.

I'd dropped my spear but had time to retrieve it while the boar tottered away, shaking its head, confused. I was hoping it would collapse, but after a few seconds it had recovered and looked as mean and purposeful as ever.

My mace was still stuck in the mouth of the other boar. There was no way to get it back, not unless it fell out.

Taking a firm grip on my spear, I decided I'd conceded enough ground to the boars. It was time to take the fight to them. Crouching low, holding my spear out in front of me, I advanced. The boars didn't know what to make of my behaviour. They made a couple of half-hearted lunges at me, then fell back warily. They obviously hadn't been infected with a large quantity of vampire blood, or they'd have attacked continuously, madly, regardless of safety.

As I herded them towards the far side of the pit, I focused on the boar with the bloody snout. It looked the less secure of the two, and retreated a bit quicker. There was a hint of cowardice about it.

I feigned an attack on the braver boar with the mace in its mouth, waving my spear in the air, so it turned and fled. As the other relaxed slightly, I changed course and leapt upon it. I grabbed the boar by the neck and held on as it roared and bucked. It dragged me on almost a full circuit of the pit before it ran out of steam and came to a stop. While it tried to snag me with its tusks, I dug at its eyes with my spear. I missed, cut its snout, sliced its ear, missed again — then struck true and gouged its right eye out.

The roaring when the boar lost its eye almost deafened me. It tossed its head about wilder than ever, and scratched my belly and chest with its tusks, but not seriously. I held on firmly, ignoring the pain in my hands and arms as burn wounds were torn open and blood flowed freely.

The vampires above me were greatly excited and cries of "Kill it! Kill it!" filled the air. I felt sorry for the boar — it only attacked me because it had been provoked — but it was him or me. This was no time for mercy.

I edged in front of the boar — a dangerous manoeuvre — and readied myself for a frontal attack. I kept to the right, so it couldn't see me, held my spear high above my head and waited for the right moment to strike. After a few frenzied seconds, the boar caught sight of me through its left eye and paused uncertainly, presenting a steady target. Bringing my arm down sharply, I drove the tip of the spear through the gap where the right eye had been, deep into the boar's crazed brain.

There was a horrible squishing sound, then the boar went mad. Rearing up on its hind legs, it let out an ear-piercing scream and dropped heavily downwards. I ducked out of its way, but as soon as it touched ground, the boar thrashed about like a bronco horse.

I hurried backwards, but the boar followed. It couldn't see me – it was past seeing anything – or hear me over the sound of its roars, but somehow it followed. Turning to flee, I saw the second boar preparing itself for a charge.

I halted, momentarily unsure of myself, and the dying boar crashed into me. I fell beneath it, losing my grip on the spear. As I tried to roll over, the boar collapsed on top of me, shuddered, then went still. It was dead — and I was trapped beneath it!

I strained to push the boar off, but its weight was too much. If I'd been in good physical condition, I could have done it, but I was bruised, burnt and bloody. I simply didn't have the strength to shift the massive animal.

As I relaxed, attempting to draw a decent breath before having another go at escape, the second boar drew up beside me and butted my head with its own. I yelped and tried scrambling away, but couldn't. The boar seemed to grin, but that might just have been the effect of the mace, which was still stuck in its mouth. It lowered its head and tried to bite me, but wasn't able, because of the mace. Growling, it took a few steps back, shook its head, retreated a few more steps, then pawed the ground, lowered its tusks... and charged dead at me.

CHAPTER SIXTEEN

I'D WRIGGLED out of some sticky situations in the past, but my luck had run out. I was trapped, at the mercy of the boar, and I knew it would show no more towards me than I had to its partner.

As I lay, waiting for the end, eyes locked on the boar, somebody shouted loudly above me. A hush had settled over the vampires, so the voice rang clearly through the cavern: "*NO!*"

A shadow leapt into the pit, darted forward into the space between me and the boar, snatched up the spear I'd dropped, jammed the blunt end into the ground and aimed the tip at the charging boar. The boar had no time to swerve or stop. It ran heavily on to the spear and impaled itself, then crashed into my protector, who dragged it to one side so that it didn't fall on me. The wrestling pair collapsed into the dust. The boar struggled weakly to get back to its feet. Lost control of its legs. Grunted feebly. Then died.

As the dust cleared, strong hands seized the boar lying on top of me and hauled its carcass out of the way. As the hands located my own and helped me to my feet, I squinted feebly and finally realized who'd leapt to my aide — *Harkat Mulds!*

The Little Person examined me to make sure no bones were broken, then led me away from the dead boars. Above, the vampires were speechless. Then, as we made for the doors, a couple hissed. Next, a few booed. Soon the entire Hall was filled with the sound of jeers and catcalls. "Foul!" they shouted. "Disgraceful!" "Kill them both!"

Harkat and me stopped and gazed around, astonished, at the furious vampires. A short while ago they'd been hailing me as a brave-hearted warrior — now they were baying for my blood!

Not all the vampires were in an uproar. Mr Crepsley, Gavner and Kurda didn't raise their voices or demand justice. Nor did Seba, who I spotted sadly shaking his head and turning away.

As the vampires yelled at us, Vanez Blane stepped over the fence and climbed into the pit. He raised his hands for silence, and gradually got it. "Sire!" he shouted to Mika Ver Leth, who was standing stony-faced by the fence. "I'm as appalled by this as any of you. But this wasn't planned and isn't Darren's doing. The Little Person doesn't know our ways and acted on his own. Don't hold this against us, I beg you."

Some of the vampires jeered when they heard that, but Mika Ver Leth waved sharply at them for quiet. "Darren," the Prince said slowly, "did you plan this with the Little Person?"

I shook my head. "I'm as surprised as anyone," I said.

"Harkat," Mika growled. "Did you interfere on your own account — or were you obeying orders?"

"No orders," Harkat replied. "Darren my ... friend. Couldn't stand by ... and watch ... him die."

"You have defied our rules," Mika warned him.

"*Your* rules," Harkat retorted. "Not *mine*. Darren ... friend."

The eagle-featured Mika looked troubled, and ran a black-gloved finger over his upper lip as he considered the situation.

"We must kill them!" a General shouted angrily. "We must take both to the Hall of Death and—"

"Would you be so quick to kill Desmond Tiny's messenger?" Mr Crepsley interrupted softly. The General who'd called for our heads lapsed into silence. Mr Crepsley addressed the Hall. "We must not act hastily. This matter must be taken to the Hall of Princes, where it can be discussed reasonably. Harkat is not a vampire and cannot be judged as one. We do not have the right to pass sentence on him."

"What about the half-vampire?" another General spoke up. "*He* is subject to our laws. *He* failed the Trial and must be executed."

"He didn't fail!" Kurda shouted. "The Trial was interrupted. He'd killed one boar — who's to say he wouldn't have killed the other?"

"He was trapped!" the opposing General bellowed. "The boar was about to make a fatal charge!"

"Probably," Kurda agreed, "but we'll never know for sure. Darren proved his strength and ingenuity on previous Trials. Perhaps he would have shrugged off the dead boar and avoided the charge at the last moment."

"Nonsense!" the General snorted.

"Is it?" Kurda huffed, jumping down into the ring to join me, Harkat and Vanez. "Are there any who can say for sure that Darren would have lost?" He spun slowly, meeting the eyes of all in the Hall. "Are there any who can say that he was in a truly hopeless position?"

There was a long, uneasy silence, broken in the end by a woman's voice — Arra Sails. "Kurda's right," she said. The vampires shifted uncomfortably — they hadn't expected the likes of Arra to side with Kurda. "The boy's situation was perilous but not necessarily fatal. He *might* have survived."

"I say Darren has the right to re-take the Trial," Kurda said, seizing on the uncertain silence that filled the Hall. "We must adjourn and stage it again, tomorrow."

Everybody looked to Mika Ver Leth for judgement. The Prince brooded on the matter in silence some moments, then glanced at Mr Crepsley. "Larten? What have you to say about this?"

Mr Crepsley shrugged grimly. "It is true that Darren was not actually defeated. But a breach of the rules usually implies a forfeit. My relationship with Darren compels me to speak on his behalf. Alas, I do not know how to make a case for mercy. Whatever the circumstances, he has failed the Trial."

"Larten!" Kurda screeched. "You don't know what you're saying!"

"Yes he does," I sighed. "And he's right." Pushing Harkat away, I stood by myself and faced Mika Ver Leth. "I don't think I'd have escaped," I said honestly. "I don't want to die, but I won't ask for any special favours. If it's possible to take the Trial again, I will. If not, I won't complain."

An approving murmur ran through the Hall. Those who'd been standing angrily by the fence settled back and waited for Mika to make his call. "You speak like a true vampire," the Prince commended me. "I do not blame you for what happened. Nor do I blame your friend — he is not one of us and cannot be expected to act as we do. There will be no measures taken against Harkat Mulds — that is a guarantee I am willing to make here and now, on my own."

Some of the vampires glared at Harkat, but none raised their voice against him. "As for *your* fate," Mika said, then hesitated. "I must confer with my fellow Princes and Generals before passing sentence. I don't think your life can be spared, but Kurda may have a point — perhaps it *is* possible to take the Trial again. To the best of my knowledge, it has never been permitted, but maybe there's an old law we can fall back upon.

"Return to your cell," Mika decided, "while I and the others seek council with our colleagues. You'll be informed of our decision as soon as we reach one. My advice," he added in a whisper, "would be to make your peace with the gods, for I fear you will face them shortly."

I nodded obediently to Mika Ver Leth and kept my head bowed while he and the other vampires filed from the Hall.

"I won't let you perish without a fight," Kurda promised as he slipped past me. "You'll get out of this yet, I'm sure of it. There must be a way."

Then he was gone. So were Vanez Blane, Mr Crepsley and the rest, leaving just me and Harkat with the dead boars in the pit. Harkat looked shameful when I turned and faced him. "I did not ... mean to ... cause trouble," he said. "I acted ... before I could ... think."

"Don't worry about it," I told him. "I'd probably have done the same thing if I was in your place. Besides, the worst they can do is kill me — I'd have died anyway if you hadn't leapt to my rescue."

"You are ... not angry?" Harkat asked.

"Of course not," I smiled, and we started for the exit.

What I didn't say to Harkat was that I wished he *had* left me to die. At least with the boar, my death would have been fast and easy to face. Now I had a long, nervous wait, which would almost certainly be followed by a gut-wrenching walk to the Hall of Death, where I'd be hoisted above the stakes and subjected to a messy, painful and humiliating finale. It would have been better to die nobly and quickly in the pit.

CHAPTER SEVENTEEN

HARKAT AND me sat on our hammocks and waited. The neighbouring cells were deserted, as were the tunnels. Most of the vampires had gathered in the Hall of Princes or were waiting outside for the verdict — vampires loved intrigue almost as much as they loved fighting, and all were anxious to hear the news firsthand.

"How come you leapt to my rescue?" I asked Harkat after a while, to break the nerve-wracking silence. "You might have been killed trying to save me."

"To be honest," Harkat replied sheepishly, "I acted ... for my own sake ... not yours. If you die, I might ... never find out ... who I used ... to be."

I laughed. "You'd better not tell the vampires that. The only reason they've gone lightly on you is that they respect bravery and self-sacrifice. If they learn you did it to save your own skin, there's no telling what they'd do!"

"You do not ... mind?" Harkat asked.

"No," I smiled.

"If they decide ... to kill you, will you ... let them?"

"I won't be able to stop them," I answered.

"But will you ... go quietly?"

"I'm not sure," I sighed. "If they'd taken me right after the fight, I'd have gone without a murmur — I was pumped up with adrenalin and wasn't scared of dying. Now that I've calmed down, I'm dreading it. I hope I'll go with my head held high, but I'm afraid I'll cry and beg for mercy."

"Not you," Harkat said. "You're too ... tough."

"You reckon?" I chuckled dryly.

"You fought ... boars, and faced ... fire and water. You didn't ... show fear before. Why should ... you now?"

"That was different," I said. "I had a fighting chance. If they decide to kill me, I'll have to walk to the Hall of Death *knowing* I'm a goner."

"Don't worry," Harkat said. "If you do ... die, maybe you ... will come back ... as a Little ... Person."

I stared at Harkat's misshapen body, his scarred, disfigured face, his green eyes and the mask he couldn't survive without. "Oh, that's a great comfort," I said sarcastically.

"Just trying ... to cheer you up."

"Well, don't!"

Minutes trickled by agonizingly. I wished the vampires would reach their decision quickly, even if it meant death — anything would be better than sitting here, not knowing.

Finally, after what felt like a lifetime, there came the sound of feet in the tunnel outside. Harkat and me tensed, rolled off our hammocks and jumped to attention by the door of the cell. We glanced nervously at one another. Harkat grinned weakly. My grin was even weaker.

"Here we go," I whispered.

"Good luck," he replied.

The footsteps slowed, stopped, then came again, softly. A vampire emerged from the gloom of the tunnel and slid into the cell — Kurda.

"What's happening?" I asked.

"I came to see how you were bearing up," he said, smiling crookedly.

"Fine!" I snapped. "Just dandy. Couldn't be better."

"I thought as much." He looked around twitchily.

"Have they ... decided yet?" Harkat asked.

"No. But it won't be long. They..." He cleared his throat. "They're going to demand your death, Darren."

I'd been expecting it, but it hit me hard all the same. I took a step backwards and my knees buckled. If Harkat hadn't caught and steadied me, I would have fallen.

"I've tried arguing them out of it," Kurda said. "Others have too — Gavner and Vanez put their careers on the line to plead for you. But there aren't any precedents. The laws are clear — failure to complete the Trials must be punished with death. We tried convincing the Princes to let you take the Trial again, but they turned a deaf ear to our pleas."

"So why haven't they come for me?" I asked.

"They're still debating. Larten's been calling older vampires forward and asking if they ever heard of something like this happening before. He's trying hard for you. If there's the slightest legal loophole, he'll find it."

"But there isn't, is there?" I asked glumly.

Kurda shook his head. "If Paris Skyle knows of no way to save you, I'm sure none of the others do either. If he can't help you, I doubt that anyone can."

"So it's over. I'm finished."

"Not necessarily," Kurda said, averting his eyes, strangely embarrassed.

"I don't understand," I frowned. "You just said—"

"The verdict's inevitable," he interrupted. "That doesn't mean you have to stay and face it."

"Kurda!" I gasped, appalled by what he was saying.

"You can get out," he hissed. "I know a way past the guards, a breach point I never informed anybody about. We can take seldom used tunnels down through the mountain, to save time. Dawn isn't far off. Once you get out in the open, you'll have a free run till dusk. Even then, I don't think anybody will come after you. Since you don't pose a threat, they'll let you go. They might kill you if they run into you later, but for the time being—"

"I couldn't do that," I interrupted. "Mr Crepsley would be ashamed of me. I'm his assistant. He'd have to answer for it."

"No," Kurda said. "You're not his responsibility, not since you embarked on the Trials. People might say things behind his back, but nobody would question his good name out in the open."

"I couldn't," I said again, with less conviction this time. "What about *you*? If they found out you'd helped me escape..."

"They won't," Kurda said. "I'll cover my tracks. As long as you aren't caught, I'll be fine."

"And if I *am* caught, and they worm the truth out of me?"

Kurda shrugged. "I'll take that chance."

I hesitated, torn by uncertainty. The vampire part of me wanted to stay and take what I had coming. The human part said not to be a fool, grab my opportunity and run.

"You're young, Darren," Kurda said. "It's crazy to throw your life away. Leave Vampire Mountain. Make a fresh start. You're experienced enough to survive on your own. You don't need Larten to look after you any more. Lots of vampires lead their own lives, having nothing to do with the rest of us. Be your own person. Don't let the foolish pride of others cloud your judgement."

"What do *you* think?" I asked Harkat.

"I think ... Kurda's right," he said. "No point ... letting them kill ... you. Go. Live. Be free. I will ... come with you ... and help. Later, maybe *you* ... can help *me*."

"Harkat won't be able to come," Kurda said. "He's too broad to fit through some of the tunnels I plan to use. You can arrange to meet somewhere else, when Council is over and he's free to leave without drawing suspicion to himself."

"The Cirque ... Du Freak," Harkat said. "You'll be able... to find it?"

I nodded. I'd got to know a lot of people across the world during my years with the Cirque, people who assisted Mr Tall and his colleagues when they came to town. They'd be able to point me in the direction of the travelling circus.

"Have you decided?" Kurda asked. "There's no time to stand and debate the issue. Come with me now, or stay to face your death."

I gulped deeply, stared at my feet, came to a snap decision, then locked gazes with Kurda and said, "I'll come." I wasn't proud of myself, but shame was a whole lot sweeter than the sharpened stakes in the Hall of Death.

CHAPTER EIGHTEEN

WE HURRIED through the deserted corridors, down to the storerooms. Kurda led me to the back of one, where we shifted aside a couple of large sacks, revealing a small hole in the wall. Kurda began to squeeze through, but I pulled him back and asked if we could rest for a couple of minutes — I was in a lot of pain.

"Will you be able to continue?" he asked.

"Yes, but only if we stop for regular breaks. I know time is precious, but I'm too exhausted to push on without pause."

When I felt ready, I followed Kurda through the hole and found myself in a cramped tunnel which dropped sharply. I suggested we slide to the bottom, but Kurda vetoed the idea. "We're not going all the way down," he said. "There's a shelf in the middle of this shaft which leads to another tunnel."

Sure enough, after several minutes we came to a ledge, swung out of the shaft and were soon back on level ground. "How did you find this place?" I asked.

"I followed a bat," he said, and winked.

We came to a fork and Kurda stopped to get out a map. He studied it silently for a few seconds, then took the turn to the left.

"Are you sure you know where you're going?" I asked.

"Not entirely," he laughed. "That's why I brought my maps. I haven't been down some of these tunnels in decades."

I tried keeping track of the route we were taking, in case anything happened to Kurda and I had to find my way back on my own, but it was impossible. We twisted and turned so many times, only a genius could have memorized the way.

We passed over a couple of small streams. Kurda told me that they joined up with others further ahead, to form the wide stream which had been used for burying the dead in the past. "We could always swim to safety," I suggested jokingly.

"Why not flap our arms and fly away while we're at it?" Kurda replied.

Some of the tunnels were pitch black, but Kurda didn't light any candles — he said the wax droppings would mark our trail and make it easy for pursuing vampires to track us.

The further we progressed, the harder it became for me to keep up, and we had to stop often in order for me to catch my breath and work up the energy to continue.

"I'd carry you if there was room," Kurda said during one of our rest periods, wiping sweat and blood from my neck and shoulders with his shirt. "We'll be entering larger tunnels shortly. I can give you a boost then if you'd like."

"That'd be great," I wheezed.

"What about when we get out of the tunnels?" he asked. "Do you want me to come with you some of the way, to make sure you're OK?"

I shook my head. "You'd be discovered by the Generals if you did. I'll be fine once I get outside. The fresh air will perk me up. I'll find somewhere to sleep, rest for a few hours, then—"

I stopped. Loose pebbles had clattered to the floor in one of the tunnels behind us. Kurda heard them too. He scurried to the mouth of the tunnel and squatted by the opening, listening intently. After a few seconds, he raced back to my side. "Someone's coming!" he hissed, dragging me to my feet. "Hurry! We must get out of here!"

"No," I sighed, sitting down again.

"Darren!" he screeched softly. "You can't stay. We've got to make a break for it before—"

"I can't," I told him. "Shuffling was hard enough — there's no way I can take part in a full-speed chase. If we've been found, that's the end. Go on ahead and hide. I'll pretend I acted alone."

"You know I wouldn't leave you," he said, squatting beside me.

We waited in silence as the footsteps came nearer. By the sound, there was only one person following us. I hoped it wasn't Mr Crepsley — I dreaded the thought of facing him after what I'd done.

The tracking vampire reached the mouth of the tunnel, studied us from the shadows a moment, then ducked forward and hurried over. It was Gavner Purl! "You two are in *so* much trouble," he snarled. "Whose dumb idea was it to run?"

"Mine!" Kurda and me said at the exact same time.

Gavner shook his head, exasperated. "You're as bad as each other," he snapped. "Come on — the truth."

"It was my idea," Kurda answered, squeezing my arm to silence my protestations. "I persuaded Darren to come. The blame is mine."

"You're an idiot," Gavner reprimanded him. "This will destroy you if word gets out. You won't just have to forget about becoming a Vampire Prince — chances are you'll be carted off to the Hall of Death to suffer the same fate as Darren."

"Only if you inform on me," Kurda said quietly.

"You think I won't?" Gavner challenged him.

"If it was your intention to punish us, you wouldn't have come alone."

Gavner stared at the senior vampire, then cursed shortly. "You're right," he groaned. "I don't want to see you killed. If the two of you come back with me, I'll keep your name out of it. In fact, nobody need ever know it happened. Harkat and I are the only ones who know at the moment. We can get Darren back before judgement is passed."

"Why?" Kurda asked. "So he can be taken to the Hall of Death and impaled?"

"If that's the judgement of the Princes — yes," Gavner said.

Kurda shook his head. "That's what we're escaping from. I won't let him go back to be killed. It's wrong to take a boy's life in such a heartless fashion."

"Wrong or right," Gavner snapped, "the judgement of the Princes is final!"

Kurda narrowed his eyes. "You agree with me," he whispered. "You think his life should be spared."

Gavner nodded reluctantly. "But that's my own opinion. I'm not about to disregard the ruling of the Princes on the strength of it."

"Why not?" Kurda asked. "Do we have to obey them even when they're in the wrong, even when they rule unjustly?"

"It's our way," Gavner growled.

"Ways can be changed," Kurda insisted. "The Princes are too inflexible. They ignore the fact that the world is moving forward. In a few weeks, *I'll* be a Prince. I can change things. Let Darren go and I'll get the ruling against him overturned. I'll clear his name and allow him to return and complete his Trials. Turn a blind eye just this once and I swear you won't regret it."

Gavner was troubled by Kurda's words. "It's wrong to plot against the Princes," he muttered.

"Nobody will know," Kurda promised. "They'll think Darren got away by himself. We'll never be investigated."

"It goes against everything we believe in," Gavner sighed.

"Sometimes we have to abandon old beliefs in favour of new ones," Kurda said.

While Gavner agonized over his decision, I spoke up. "I'll go back if you want me to. I'm afraid of dying, which is why I let Kurda talk me into fleeing. But if you say I should return, I will."

"I don't *want* you to die," Gavner cried. "But running away never solved anything."

"Nonsense!" Kurda snorted. "Vampires would be a lot better off if more of us had the good sense to run from a fight when the odds are stacked against us. If we take Darren back, we take him back to die. Where's the sense in that?"

Gavner thought it over in silence, then nodded morosely. "I don't like it, but it's the lesser of two evils. I won't turn you in. But!" he added, "only if you agree to present the truth to the others once you become a Prince. We'll come clean, clear Darren's name if we can, accept our punishment if we can't. OK?"

"That's fine by me," Kurda said.

"Your word on it?"

Kurda nodded. "My word."

Gavner let out a long breath and studied me in the gloom of the tunnel. "How are you anyway?" he asked.

"Not so bad," I lied.

"You look fit to drop," he noted sceptically.

"I'll make it," I vowed. Then I asked how he'd found us.

"I went looking for Kurda," he explained. "I was hoping we could put our heads together and figure a way out of this mess. His maps cabinet was open. I didn't think anything of it at the time, but when I dropped by your cell and found Harkat there by himself, I put two and two together."

"How did you track us through the tunnels?" Kurda enquired.

Gavner pointed to a drop of blood on the floor beneath me. "He's been dripping the whole way," he said. "He's left a trail even a fool could follow."

Kurda closed his eyes and grimaced. "Charna's guts! Espionage never was my strong suit."

"Too right!" Gavner snorted. "If we're to pull this off, we'd better move quickly. As soon as Darren's discovered missing, there'll be a team of trackers on his trail in minutes, and it won't take them long to find him. Our only chance is to get him outside and hope the sun deters them from continuing."

"My thoughts precisely," Kurda said, and started ahead. I followed as best I could, Gavner puffing along behind.

At the end of the tunnel, Kurda turned left. I headed after him, but Gavner grabbed my arm and stopped me, then studied the tunnel to his right. When Kurda realized we weren't at his heels, he paused and looked back. "What's the delay?" he asked.

"I've been in this part of the mountain before," Gavner said. "It was during my Trials of Initiation. I had to find a hidden jewel."

"So?"

"I can find the way out," Gavner said. "I know the path to the nearest exit."

"So do I," Kurda said, "and it's this way."

Gavner shook his head. "We *can* get out that way," he agreed, "but it'll be quicker if we take this other tunnel."

"No!" Kurda snapped. "This was my idea. I'm in charge. We don't have time to go wandering around. If you're wrong, it'll cost us. My way is certain."

"So's mine," Gavner insisted, and before Kurda could object, he ducked down the tunnel to the right, dragging me along after him. Kurda cursed loudly and called us back, but when Gavner ignored him, he had no option other than to hurry after us.

"This is stupid," Kurda panted when he caught up. He tried to squeeze past me to deal with Gavner face to face, but the tunnel was too narrow. "We should stick to the route on the maps. I know more about these tunnels than you. There's nothing the way you're going except dead ends."

"No," Gavner contradicted him. "We can save the better part of forty minutes this way."

"But what if—" Kurda began.

"Stop arguing," Gavner interrupted. "The more we talk, the slower we progress."

Kurda muttered something unintelligible, but said no more about it. I could tell he wasn't happy though.

We passed through a small tunnel that cut beneath a roaring mountain stream. The water sounded so close, I was afraid it might break through the walls of the tunnel and flood us. I couldn't hear anything over the noise of the stream, and it was so dark, I couldn't see anything either. It felt like I was all alone.

I was delighted to finally spot light at the end, and hurried towards it as fast as I could. Gavner and Kurda moved quickly as well, so they must have been anxious to escape the tunnel too. As we brushed the dirt from the tunnel off ourselves, Kurda moved ahead and took the lead. We were in a small cave. There were three tunnels leading out of it. Kurda went to the tunnel on the far left. "We're taking this one," he said, re-exerting his authority.

Gavner grinned. "That's the one I planned to take anyway."

"Then hurry up," Kurda snapped.

"What's wrong with you?" Gavner asked. "You're acting oddly."

"No I'm not!" Kurda glared, then smiled weakly. "Sorry. It's that tunnel under the stream. I knew we'd have to pass through it. That's why I wanted to go the other way — to avoid it."

"Afraid the water would break through?" Gavner laughed.

"Yes," Kurda answered stiffly.

"I was afraid too," I said, "I wouldn't like to crawl through a place like that too often."

"Cowards," Gavner chuckled. He started towards Kurda, smiling, then stopped and cocked his head sideways.

"What's wrong?" I asked.

"I thought I heard something," he said.

"What?"

"It sounded like someone coughing. It came from the tunnel to the right."

"A search party?" I asked worriedly.

Gavner frowned. "I doubt it — they'd be coming from behind."

"What's going on?" Kurda asked impatiently.

"Gavner thinks he heard something," I said, as the General crept across to explore the tunnel.

"It's just the sound of the stream," Kurda said. "We don't have time to—"

But it was too late. Gavner had already entered the tunnel. Kurda hurried over to where I was standing and peered into the darkness of the tunnel after Gavner. "We'd be better off on our own," he grumbled. "He's done nothing but slow us down."

"What if somebody's in there?" I asked.

"There's nobody down here apart from us," Kurda snorted. "We should head on without that fool and leave him to catch up."

"No," I said. "I'd rather wait."

Kurda rolled his eyes but stood sullenly beside me. Gavner was gone no more than a couple of minutes, but when he returned he looked years older. His legs were shaking and he sank to his bottom as soon as he emerged from the tunnel.

"What's wrong?" I asked.

He shook his head wordlessly.

"You found something?" Kurda asked.

"There's..." Gavner cleared his throat. "Go look," he whispered. "But be careful. Don't be seen."

"Seen by who?" I asked, but he didn't answer.

Intrigued, I crept along the tunnel, Kurda just behind me. It was short, and as I approached the end, I noticed the flicker of torches in a large cave beyond. I dropped to my belly, then edged forward so that I had a clear view of the cave. What I saw froze my guts inside me.

Twenty or thirty people were lounging around. Some were sitting, some lying on mats, some playing cards. They had the general appearance of vampires — bulky, rough features, crude haircuts. But I could see the sheen of their purplish skin and reddish hair and eyes, and I identified them immediately — our blood foes — *the vampaneze!*

CHAPTER NINETEEN

KURDA AND me retreated slowly and joined Gavner in the smaller cave. We sat next to him and nobody said anything for a while. Finally Gavner spoke in a dull, distracted tone. "I counted thirty-four of them."

"There were thirty-five when we looked," Kurda said.

"There are two adjoining caves of a similar size," Gavner noted. "There might be more in those."

"What are they doing here?" I asked in a whisper.

The vampires trained their sights on me.

"Why do you *think* they're here?" Gavner asked.

I licked my lips nervously. "To attack us?" I guessed.

"You got it," Gavner said grimly.

"Not necessarily," Kurda said. "They might have come to discuss a treaty."

"You think so?" Gavner sneered.

"No," Kurda sighed. "Not really."

"We have to warn the vampires," I said.

Kurda nodded. "But what about your escape? One of us can lead you to—"

"Forget it," I interrupted. "I'm not running away from something like this."

"Come on then," Kurda said, getting to his feet and making for the tunnel under the stream. "The quicker we tell the others, the quicker we can return and—" He was bending down to enter the tunnel, but stopped suddenly and spun to the side. Signalling us to stay where we were, he peered cautiously into the tunnel, then raced back. "Somebody's coming!" he hissed.

"Vampires or vampaneze?" Gavner asked.

"Too dark to tell. Think we can afford to wait and find out?"

"No," Gavner said. "We've got to get out of here." He studied the three exit tunnels. "We can get back to the Halls via the middle tunnel, but it'll take a lot of time. If they spot Darren's trail of blood and come after us..."

"We'll take the left tunnel," Kurda said.

"That doesn't lead up," Gavner frowned.

"According to my maps, it does," Kurda contradicted him. "There's a very small connecting tunnel, easy to miss. I only found it by chance."

"You're sure?" Gavner asked.

"Maps don't lie," Kurda said.

"Then let's go," Gavner decided, and off we dashed.

I forgot about my pain as we sped through the tunnels. There was no time to worry about myself. The entire vampire clan was under threat and all I thought about was getting back to the Hall of Princes and tipping them off.

When we reached Kurda's connecting tunnel, we discovered a cave-in. We stared at the pile of rocks, dismayed, then Kurda swore and kicked angrily at the blockage.

"I'm sorry," he sighed.

"It's not your fault," Gavner told him. "You couldn't have known."

"Where do we go now?" I asked.

"Back through the cave?" Gavner suggested.

Kurda shook his head. "If we've been discovered, they'll come after us that way. There's another tunnel we can use. It'll take us back in the same direction and it links up with tunnels leading to the Halls."

"Let's go then," Gavner barked, and we followed after Kurda as he led the way through the dark.

We spoke as little as possible, pausing occasionally to listen for sounds of pursuit. There weren't any, but that didn't mean we weren't being hunted — vampaneze can move as silently as vampires when they wish.

After a while, Kurda drew to a halt and pressed his head close to ours. "We're right behind the cave where the vampaneze are," he whispered. "Move slowly and carefully. If they spot us, fight for your lives — then run like hell!"

"Wait," I said. "I don't have a weapon. I'll need one if we're attacked."

"I've only got one knife," Kurda said. "Gavner?"

"I've two, but I'll need both of them."

"So what will *I* fight with?" I hissed. "Bad breath?"

Gavner grinned grimly. "No offence, Darren, but if Kurda and I can't fend them off, I don't think you can make much of a difference. If we run into trouble, grab Kurda's maps and head for the Halls while we stay and fight."

"I couldn't do that," I gasped.

"You'll do as you're told," Gavner growled, leaving no room for argument.

We started forward again, softer than ever. Sounds from the cave reached our ears — vampaneze laughing and talking quietly. If I'd been alone, I might have panicked and bolted, but Kurda and Gavner were made of sterner stuff, and their calm presence held me in check.

Our luck held until we turned into a long tunnel and ran into a lone vampaneze, walking towards us, fiddling with his belt. He glanced up casually as we froze, saw in an instant that we weren't vampaneze, and opened his mouth to roar.

Gavner darted forward, knives flashing. He stuck one deep into the vampaneze's belly, and slashed the other across his throat before he could make a sound and alert his companions. It had been a close call and we were all smiling weakly with relief as Gavner laid the dead body on the ground. But, as we were about to move on, another vampaneze appeared at the far end of the tunnel, saw us, and yelled for help.

Gavner groaned desolately. "So much for stealth," he muttered as vampaneze poured through from the cavern. He took a firm stand in the middle of the tunnel, checked the walls to either side, then spoke over his shoulder. "You two get out of here. I'll delay them as long as I can."

"I won't leave you to face them alone," Kurda said.

"You will if you've any brains," Gavner snarled. "This tunnel's narrow. One person can hold them off as capably as two. Take Darren and break for the Halls, as fast as you can."

"But–" Kurda started to say.

"You're arguing our chances away!" Gavner roared, flicking a knife at one of the nearest vampaneze, forcing him back. "Shift that dead vampaneze from behind me, so I don't trip over him — and scram!"

Kurda nodded sadly. "Luck, Gavner Purl," he said.

"Luck," Gavner grunted, and parried another attack.

We dragged the dead body out of Gavner's way and retreated to the mouth of the tunnel. Kurda paused there and studied Gavner in silence as he sliced at the vampaneze with his pair of knives. He was keeping them at arm's length, but it was only a matter of minutes before they swarmed over him, dispossessed him of his weapons, and killed him.

Kurda turned to lead me away, then stopped and dug out a map. "Do you remember the old burial chamber we visited?" he asked. "The Hall of Final Voyage?"

"Yes," I said.

"Do you think you could find your way back to the Halls from it?"

"Probably."

He stuck the map away and pointed down the tunnel we were in. "Go to the end of this," he said. "Take a right, another right, then four lefts. That'll bring you to the chamber. Wait a few minutes in case one of us comes. Get your breath back. Try re-bandaging yourself so that you stop dripping blood. Then go."

"What are you going to do?" I asked.

"Help Gavner."

"But he said—"

"I know what he said!" Kurda snapped. "I don't care. Two of us working together stand a better chance of holding them." Kurda gripped my shoulders and squeezed tightly. "Luck, Darren Shan."

"Luck," I replied miserably.

"Don't stay and watch," he said. "Leave immediately."

"OK," I agreed, and slipped away.

I got as far as the second right turn before I stopped. I knew I should do as Kurda said and flee for the Halls, but I couldn't bear the thought of leaving my friends behind. They were in this mess because of me. It would have been unfair to leave them to face death while I waltzed away scot-free. *Somebody* had to warn the vampires, but I didn't think it should be me. If I told Kurda I'd forgotten the way back, he'd have to go himself, meaning I could stay and fight beside Gavner.

I backtracked to the tunnel where the fighting was raging. When I got there, I saw that Gavner was still holding the vampaneze off single-handed. Kurda hadn't been able to move forward. The two were arguing. "I told you to leave!" Gavner roared.

"And I'm telling you I won't!" Kurda shrieked back.

"What about Darren?"

"I gave him directions to get back."

"You're a fool, Kurda," Gavner shouted.

"I know," Kurda laughed. "Now, are you going to let me in for a piece of this, or do I have to fight you as well as the vampaneze?"

Gavner stabbed at a vampaneze with a round, dark red birthmark on his left cheek, then dropped back a few steps. "OK," he grunted. "The next time there's a break in the fighting, shift up to my right."

"Agreed," Kurda said, and held his knife tightly by his side while he waited.

I crept forward. I didn't want to yell and distract them. I was almost upon them when the vampaneze fell back a metre or two and Gavner shouted, "Now!"

Gavner edged to his left and Kurda moved forward, filling the space beside him. I realized it was too late for me to take Kurda's place, so I started to turn away reluctantly. As I did, something crazy happened which stopped me dead in my tracks and held me rooted to the spot in stunned paralysis.

As Kurda stepped up beside Gavner, he raised his knife high and swung it down in a vicious arc. It cut deep into the belly of its intended target, slicing open the flesh, ensuring death. It would have been a lovely stroke to behold if it had been directed at one of the vampaneze. But Kurda hadn't stuck the blade into any of the purple-skinned invaders — he'd stuck it into *Gavner Purl*!

CHAPTER TWENTY

I COULDN'T understand what was happening. Neither could Gavner. He slumped against the wall and stared at the knife sticking out of his belly. He dropped his own knives, gripped the handle and tried to pull it out, but his strength deserted him and he slid to the floor.

Though Gavner and me were shocked, the vampaneze didn't seem the least bit surprised. They relaxed and those at the rear returned to their cave. The one with the red birthmark on his cheek stepped forward, stood beside Kurda, and studied the dying vampire. "I thought for a minute you were coming to his aid," the vampaneze said.

"No," Kurda replied. He sounded mournful. "I'd have knocked him out and bundled him away somewhere if possible, but others could have tracked down his mental signals. There's a boy up ahead, a half-vampire. He's injured, so he won't be hard to catch. I want him taken alive. They won't be able to track him."

"Do you mean the boy behind you?" the vampaneze asked.

Kurda swivelled sharply. "Darren!" he gasped. "How long have you been there? How much have you—"

Gavner groaned. I jolted into action, ducked forward, ignored Kurda and the vampaneze, and crouched beside my dying friend. His eyes were wide open but he didn't seem to see anything. "Gavner?" I asked, holding his hands, which were bloody from trying to take out the knife. The Vampire General coughed and trembled. I could feel the life slipping out of him. "I'm with you, Gavner," I whispered, crying. "You're not alone. I'll—"

"Suh-suh-suh," he stuttered.

"What is it?" I wept. "Don't hurry. You've got plenty of time." That was a bare-faced lie.

"Suh-sorry if muh-muh-my snoring ... kuh-kept you ... awake," he wheezed. I didn't know if the words were meant for me or someone else, and before I could ask, his expression froze on his face and his spirit passed on to Paradise.

I pressed my forehead to Gavner's and howled pitifully, clutching his dead body to mine. The vampaneze could have taken me easily then, but they were embarrassed and nobody moved forward to capture me. They just stood around, waiting for me to stop crying.

When I finally raised my head, nobody dared meet my gaze. All eyes dropped to the floor, Kurda's quickest of all. "You killed him!" I hissed.

Kurda gulped deeply. "I had to," he croaked. "There was no time to let him die a noble death — you might have got away if I'd left him for the vampaneze."

"You knew they were here all along," I whispered.

He nodded. "That's why I didn't want to take the route under the stream," he said. "I feared this would happen. Everything would have been OK if we'd gone the way I wanted."

"You're in league with them!" I shouted. "You're a *traitor!*"

"You don't understand what's happening," he sighed. "This looks terrible, but it's not what you think. I'm trying to *save* our race, not condemn it. There are things you don't know — things *no* vampire knows. Gavner's death is regrettable, but when I explain prop—"

"The hell with your explanations!" I screamed. "You're a traitor and a murderer — scum of the highest order!"

"I saved your life," Kurda reminded me gently.

"At the expense of Gavner's," I sobbed. "Why did you do it? He was your friend. He..." I shook my head and steeled myself before he could answer. "Never mind. I don't want to hear." Stooping, I picked up one of Gavner's knives and brandished it in front of me. The vampaneze raised their weapons immediately and closed in.

"No!" Kurda shouted, stepping in their way. "I said I wanted him taken alive!"

"He has a knife," the vampaneze with the birthmark growled. "Do you want us to let him chop off our fingers while we prise it away from him?"

"Don't worry, Glalda," Kurda said. "I'm in control of the situation." Spreading his hands he walked slowly towards me.

"Stop!" I yelled. "Don't come any closer!"

"I'm unarmed," he said.

"I don't care. I'll kill you anyway. You deserve it."

"Maybe so," Kurda agreed, "but I don't think you'd kill an unarmed man, no matter what he'd done. If I'm wrong, I'll pay for my error of judgement in the severest way possible — but I don't think I am."

I drew back the knife to stab him, then lowered my hand. He was right — even though he'd killed Gavner in cold blood, I couldn't bring myself to do the same. "I hate you!" I cried, then threw my knife at him. As he ducked, I spun and sped back up the tunnel, turned right and fled.

As the vampaneze surged after me, I heard Kurda roaring at them not to harm me. He told them I was injured and couldn't get far. One roared back that he was cutting ahead with a few others to block off the tunnels leading to the Halls. Another wanted to know if I was carrying any other weapons.

Then I passed momentarily out of earshot of the enemies and the traitor, and was racing through darkness, fleeing blindly, crying for my sacrificed friend — the poor, dead Gavner Purl.

CHAPTER TWENTY-ONE

THE VAMPANEZE took their time hunting me down. They knew I couldn't escape. I was injured and tired, so all they had to do was stay close and slowly reel me in. As I scurried and twisted through the tunnels, the roar of the mountain stream increased, and I realized my feet were guiding me to the old burial chamber. I thought about changing direction, to outwit Kurda, but I'd lose my way if I did and never make it back to the Halls. My only chance was to take the paths I was familiar with and hope I could block one off by bringing down the ceiling behind me.

I burst into the Hall of Final Voyage and paused to catch my breath. I could hear the sounds of the vampaneze behind. They were far too close for comfort. I needed to rest but there was no time. Struggling to my feet, I looked for the way out.

At first the cave seemed unfamiliar, and I wondered if I'd possibly wandered into the wrong one by mistake. Then it struck me that I was simply on the side of the stream opposite where I'd been before. Advancing to the edge of the bank, I looked across and saw the tunnel I needed to leave by. I also saw a very pale-skinned person, with white eyes and rags for clothes, sitting on a rock close to the wall — a Guardian of the Blood!

"Help!" I shouted, startling the thin man, who leapt to his feet and squinted at me. "Vampaneze!" I croaked. "They've invaded the mountain! You've got to warn the Generals!"

The Guardian's eyes narrowed and he shook his head, then said something in a language I didn't understand. I opened my mouth to repeat the warning, but before I could, he made a sign with his fingers, shook his head again, and slipped out of the cave, disappearing swiftly into the shadows of the tunnel beyond.

I cursed foully — the Guardians of the Blood must also be in league with the vampaneze! — then glanced down into the dark water at my feet and shivered. The stream wasn't particularly wide, and I could have jumped it with ease any other time. But I was exhausted, aching and desperate. All I wanted to do was lie down and let the vampaneze have me. Going on seemed pointless. They were sure to catch me. It would be a lot easier to surrender now and...

"No!" I shouted aloud. They killed Gavner and they'd kill the rest of the vampires — including Mr Crepsley — if I couldn't get to the Halls first and stop them. I *had* to go on. I took a few steps back, preparing for the jump. Looking over my shoulder, I saw the first of the vampaneze enter the cave.

I backed up a few more steps, then raced to the edge of the bank and leapt.

I knew immediately that I wasn't going to make it. There hadn't been enough pace or spring in my step. I flailed out with my arms, in the hope of catching hold of the ledge, but fell a good metre shy of safety, and dropped into the freezing water of the stream.

The current caught me instantly. By the time I bobbed to the surface, the mouth of the tunnel leading out of the cave and back underground was almost upon me. I threw out my arms, terrified, and caught hold of a rock jutting out of the bank. Using the last of my strength, I clawed my way to partial safety. Defying the flow of the water, I half-flopped on to the rock and grabbed hold of some deep-rooted weeds.

It was a perilous position, but I might have been able to scrape my way out of it — if not for the dozen or so vampaneze who'd crossed the stream and were standing overhead, arms folded, waiting patiently. One lit a cigarette, then flicked his match at my face. It missed, hit the water, quenched with a hiss, and disappeared at a frightening speed down the dark tunnel into the mountain.

As I clung to the rock, frozen and soaking, wondering what to do, Kurda pushed his way through the vampaneze and dropped to his knees. He extended a hand to help me up, but couldn't reach. "Somebody grab my ankles and lower me," he said.

"Why?" the vampaneze called Glalda asked. "Let him drown. It'll be easier."

"No!" Kurda barked. "His death serves no purpose. He's young and open to new ideas. We'll need vampires like him if we're to—"

"OK, OK," Glalda sighed, and signalled two of his men to take Kurda's legs and lower him over the edge, so that he could rescue me.

I stared at Kurda's hands as they stretched towards my own, then at his face, mere centimetres away. "You killed Gavner," I snarled.

"We'll discuss that later," he said, snatching for my wrists.

I pulled my hands out of his way and spat on his fingers, even though I nearly fell back into the water. I couldn't bear the thought of him touching me. "Why did you do it?" I moaned.

Kurda shook his head. "It's too complicated. Come with me and I'll explain later. When you're safe, dry and fed, I'll sit you down and—"

"Don't touch me!" I screeched as he reached for me again.

"Don't be stupid," he said. "You're in no position to argue. Take my hand and let me pull you to safety. You won't be harmed, I promise."

"You *promise*," I sneered. "Your word means nothing. You're a liar and a traitor. I wouldn't believe you if you said the world was round."

"Believe what you want," he snapped, "but I'm all that stands between you and a watery grave, so you can't afford to be picky. Take my hand and stop acting like an idiot."

"You haven't a clue," I said, shaking my head with disgust.

"You don't know a thing about honour or loyalty. I'd rather die than give myself up to scum like you."

"Don't be—" Kurda started to say, but before he could finish, I released my grip on the rock, pushed backwards with my legs, and let the water have me. "Darren — no!" Kurda screamed, making one last grab for me. But he was too late — his fingers clutched at thin air.

I drifted out into the middle of the stream, beyond the reach of Kurda and his vampaneze allies. There was a moment of strange peace, during which I bobbed up and down in the centre of the stream. Locking gazes with Kurda as I hung there, I smiled thinly and pressed the middle fingers of my right hand to my forehead and eyelids, making the death's touch sign. "Even in death, may I be triumphant!" I howled, adding a quick silent prayer that my curse would ring true, and that my sacrifice would encourage the gods of the vampires to extract a terrible revenge on this traitor and his allies.

Then, before Kurda could respond, the current took hold and swept me away in a brutal instant, out of his sight, into darkness, churning madness, and the hungry belly of the mountain.

DARREN SHAN
THE VAMPIRE PRINCE

THE SAGA OF DARREN SHAN
BOOK 6

For:

Martha & Bill - who fed a hungry half-vampire

OBEs (Order of the Bloody Entrails) to:
Katherine "kill-crazy" Tyacke
Stella "stabber" Paskins

Editors extraordinaire:
Gillie Russell & Zoë Clarke

Agent provocateur:
Christopher Little

PROLOGUE

BE CAREFUL who you trust. Even a supposedly close friend might be capable of betraying you. I found that out the hard way.

My name's Darren Shan. I'm a half-vampire. I was blooded when I was very young, and for eight years I toured the world with the Cirque Du Freak — a travelling circus of magically gifted performers. Then my mentor – Larten Crepsley – said I had to be presented to the Vampire Princes.

Most of the Princes and Vampire Generals gathered in the remote Vampire Mountain once every twelve years, for the Council of Vampires. After a long, tiring trek to the mountain with Mr Crepsley, Harkat Mulds (a Little Person who'd been brought back from the dead by a powerful man called Mr Tiny), Gavner Purl (a General) and four wolves (including a male I called Streak and a cub I nicknamed Rudi), I faced the Princes, who said I had to prove myself worthy of joining the ranks of the undead. They set me a series of harsh tests known as the Trials of Initiation. If I passed all five tests, I'd be accepted as one of them. If I failed, I'd be killed.

I passed the first three Trials, but the fourth ended disastrously — I fell foul of a wild boar and would have been gouged to death if not for Harkat, who leapt into the pit and killed the boar. The problem was, his intervention broke all the rules. While the vampires debated my fate, one sneaked into my cell and led me away to safety. He was a blond, slender, peaceful, highly intelligent vampire called Kurda Smahlt, and he was shortly due to become a Prince. I believed he was my friend.

While we were escaping, Gavner caught up with us and tried talking me into going back to face the verdict of the Princes. Kurda persuaded him to let me go. But, as we were closing in on freedom, we ran into a bunch of vampaneze — purple-skinned adversaries of the vampires, who kill humans when they drink from them — hiding in a cave.

That's when Kurda showed his true colours. He stabbed and killed Gavner, and I realized he was in league with the vampaneze. He tried taking me alive, but I ran and fell into a mountain stream. Kurda would have saved me, but I ignored his helping hand and surrendered myself to the vicious flow of the stream, which swiftly swept me away underground, into the belly of the mountain and certain death…

CHAPTER ONE

DARKNESS — COLD — churning water — roaring, like a thousand lions — spinning around and around — bashing into rocks — arms wrapped around my face to protect it — tucking up legs to make myself smaller, less of a target.

Wash up against a mass of roots — grab hold — slippery — the wet roots feel like dead fingers clutching at me — a gap between the water and the roof of the tunnel — I draw quick gasps of breath — current takes hold again — try fighting it — roots break off in my hands — swept away.

Tumbling over and over — hit my head hard on a rock — see stars — almost black out — struggle to keep head up — spit water out of my mouth, but more gushes in — feels like I'm swallowing half the stream.

The current drags me against a wall — sharp rocks cut deeply into my thighs and hips — freezing cold water numbs the pain — stops the flow of blood — a sudden drop —

plummet into a deep pool — down, down, down — held under by force of the falling water — panicking — can't find my way up — drowning — if I don't break free soon, I'll...

My feet strike a wall and propel me forward — drift slowly up and away from the pool — flow is gentle here — lots of space between water and top of tunnel — able to bob along and breathe — air's cold, and it stings my lungs, but I gulp it down thankfully.

The stream opens out into what sounds like a large cave. Roars from the opposite end: the water must drop sharply again there. I let myself drift to one side before facing the drop. I need to rest and fill my lungs with air. As I tread water near the wall in the dark, something clutches at my bald head. It feels like twigs. I grab at them to steady myself, then realize they're not twigs — they're *bones!*

Too exhausted to be scared, I grasp the bones as though they were part of a lifebuoy. Taking long, deep breaths, I explore the bones with my fingers. They connect to a wrist, an arm, a body and head: a full skeleton. This stream was used to dispose of dead vampires in the past. This one must have washed up here and rotted away over the decades. I search blindly for other skeletons but find none. I wonder who the vampire was, when he lived, how long he's been here. It must be horrible, trapped in a cave like this, no proper burial, no final resting place.

I give the skeleton a shake, hoping to free it. The cave erupts with high-pitched screeches and flapping sounds. Wings! Dozens or hundreds of pairs of wings! Something crashes into my face and catches on my left ear. It scratches and nips. I yelp, tear it loose and slap it away.

I can't see anything, but I sense a flurry of objects flying over and around me. Another collides with me. This time I hold on and feel around it — a *bat!* The cave's full of bats. They must nest here, in the roof. The sound of me shaking the skeleton disturbed them, and they've taken flight.

I don't panic. They won't attack me. They're just frightened and will settle down soon. I release the one I've caught and let it join the rush above me. The noise dies down after a few minutes and the bats return to their perches. Silence.

I wonder how they get in and out of the cave. There must be a crack in the roof. For a few seconds I dream about finding it and climbing to safety, but my numb fingers and toes quickly put an end to thoughts of that nature. I couldn't climb, even if I could find the crack and it was big enough for me to fit through.

I start thinking about the skeleton again. I don't want to leave it here. I tug at it, careful this time not to create a racket. It doesn't budge at first — it's wedged firm. I get a stronger grip and pull again. It comes loose, all at once, and falls on top of me, driving me under. Water gushes down my throat. *Now* I panic! The skeleton heavy on top of me, weighing me down. I'm going to drown! I'm going to drown! I'm going to—

No! Stop panicking. Use my brain. I wrap my arms around the skeleton and slowly roll over. It works! Now the skeleton's underneath and I'm on top. The air tastes good.

My heart stops pounding. A few of the bats are circling again, but most are still.

Releasing the skeleton, I guide it out towards the middle of the cave, using my feet. I feel the current take it, then it's gone. I hang on to the wall, treading water, giving the skeleton time to wash ahead of me. I fall to thinking while I wait: was it a good idea to free the skeleton? A nice gesture, but if the bones snag on a rock further along and block my way...

Too late to worry now. Should have thought of that before.

My situation's as desperate as ever. Crazy to think I might get out of this alive. But I force myself to think positively: I've made it this far, and the stream must open up sooner or later. Who's to say I can't make it to the end? Believe, Darren, *believe.*

I'd like to hang here forever — easier to cling on and die of the cold — but I've got to try for freedom. In the end, I force my fingers to unclench and let go of the bank. I drift out into the middle of the stream. The current bites at me and latches on. Speeding up — the exit — roaring grows furiously — flowing fast — angling sharply downwards — gone.

CHAPTER TWO

EVEN WORSE beyond the cave — makes the first half of the ride seem like a paddle in a swimming pool — sickening drops and turns — walls studded with jagged stones — water gushes wildly, madly — tossed about as though made of putty — impossible to exert control — no time to pause for breath — lungs bursting — hold my arms tight over my head — tuck my legs up as far as they'll go — conserve oxygen — bash my head on rocks — my back — legs — belly — back — head — shoulders — head...

Lose count of the collisions — can't feel pain any longer — eyes playing tricks on me — looking up, it's as if the rocks are invisible — I believe I can see the sky, the stars, the moon — this is the beginning of the end — senses in disarray, brain shutting down — out of luck — out of hope — out of life.

I open my mouth to take one long, last drink of water —

slam into a wall — air explodes out of me — force of crash pops me upwards — I break through to a small pocket of air between water and roof — lungs draw it in greedily, automatically.

I float here a few seconds, pressed against wall, gasping in air — current takes me again and drags me under — through a narrow tunnel — incredible speed — like a bullet — tunnel getting narrower — speed increases — my back scrapes along the wall — the rock's smooth, otherwise I'd be cut to shreds — feels like a water slide — almost enjoying this part of the nightmarish ride.

Tunnel evens out — running low on oxygen again — try forcing head up, to search for air — can't — don't have the energy to fight.

Water creeps up my nose — I cough — water pours down my throat — I'm losing the battle — roll over, face down — this is the end — lungs are filling with water — I can't close my mouth — waiting for death — all of a sudden: no water — flying — (*flying?*) — whistling air surrounds me — looking down at land — stream cutting through it — floating, as though I'm a bird or a bat — closer to stream — closer — are my eyes playing tricks again?

Turn over in middle of flight — look up — sky, *real* sky, open and bright with stars — beautiful — *I'm out!* — I'm really out! — I made it! — I can breathe! I'm alive! I'm...

Flight ends — hit water hard — impact shakes my guts to pieces and knocks brain out of order — blackness again, only this time inside my head.

CHAPTER THREE

CONSCIOUSNESS RETURNS gradually. Sounds strike me first: the roar of the water, much softer than in the mountain, almost lyrical. Slowly, my eyes flutter open. I'm staring up at stars, drifting along on my back. Luck or my body's natural defences? I don't know. I don't care. I'm *alive!*

The current isn't strong here. I could easily swim to the bank, pull myself to safety and begin the trip back to Vampire Mountain, which I spot in the near distance. Except I don't have the strength. I try rolling over to swim — can't. My legs and arms are like dead blocks of wood. I've survived the ride through the mountain, but the cost has been high. I'm completely limp and helpless.

I study the landscape while the stream sweeps me further away from Vampire Mountain. It's rugged and unspectacular, but beautiful after the darkness. *Anything* would seem beautiful after the darkness. I'll never take the countryside for granted again.

Am I dying? I could be — no feeling, no control, at the mercy of the stream. Maybe I'm dead already and just haven't realized it. No! Not dead. Water splashes up my nose and I splutter: proof I'm still alive. I won't give up, not after all I've been through. I have to summon strength from somewhere and make it to the bank. I can't drift along like this forever: the longer it drags on, the harder it will be.

I try willing energy into my exhausted limbs. I think about dying young and what a waste it would be, but that doesn't give me strength. I think about the vampires and the threat they face from Kurda and the vampaneze, but that doesn't work either. Finally, an old vampire myth succeeds in spreading a burst of fire through my icy bones: I recall the myth that a vampire who dies in running water is doomed to stick around as a ghost — no journey to Paradise for those who die in rivers or streams.

Strangely (as I never believed the myth), the thought spurs me into action. I raise a weak arm and flap feebly for the bank. The action doesn't do much, apart from spin me round a little, but the fact that I'm able to move at all fills me with hope.

Gritting my teeth, I face the bank and force my legs up behind me. They respond sluggishly, but they *do* respond. I try to swim freestyle — can't. I roll over on to my back, kick weakly with my feet, and guide myself with gentle hand motions. I slowly pull towards the bank. It takes a long time, and I'm swept much further away from Vampire Mountain, but finally I'm in shallow water, out of the current.

I half rise to my knees, then collapse. Lying face down, I turn my head sideways, splutter, then get back on my knees. I crawl out of the water, on to the snowy bank, where I collapse again. My eyes close. I weep silently into the snow.

I want to lie here and freeze: simpler than moving. But my feet are still in the water and I don't like the feel of them drifting behind me, so I pull them clear. The effort goads me into further action. Groaning, I prop myself up, then rise slowly and painfully to my feet.

Standing, I stare around as if I'm on an alien planet. Everything looks different. Day is breaking, but stars and the moon still shine lightly in the sky. After so long inside the mountain, I'd forgotten what daylight looks like. It's wonderful. I could stand here all day and just stare, except that wouldn't get me anywhere, and soon I'd fall, into the stream or the snow, and freeze.

Sighing, obeying some insistent inner instinct, I drag my feet forward a few steps, pause, shake my head, straighten up and lurch away from the stream, which froths and hisses angrily behind me — cheated of its victim.

CHAPTER FOUR

IT DIDN'T take me long to realize I couldn't make it very far if I continued in this state. I was soaked to the skin. My clothes were heavy with water and the air around me was bitterly cold. Mr Crepsley had warned me what to do if this ever happened: get rid of the wet clothes swiftly, or I'd freeze to death inside them.

It took a lot of effort to get out of my clothes. My fingers were numb and I ended up having to use my teeth to tear my way free. But I felt better when I'd undressed. A great weight had been lifted from my body, and though the full force of the cold hit me immediately, I set forward at a brisker pace.

It didn't bother me that I was wandering around as naked as the animals of the wild. There was nobody to see. Even if there had been, I wouldn't have cared — being so close to death, modesty was the last thing on my mind.

My brisk pace didn't last long. After a while, I began to

understand just how serious a mess I was in. I was stranded in the middle of nowhere, no clothes to protect me from the cold, beaten to a pulp, physically and mentally drained, with nothing to eat. It was a struggle just to keep moving. In a matter of minutes, I'd run out of energy and collapse. The cold would set in. Frostbite and hypothermia would finish me off.

I tried jogging, to warm myself up, but couldn't. My legs simply wouldn't work. It was a miracle they were able to support me at all. Anything faster than a slow crawl was beyond them.

I stopped and turned in a full circle, hoping to spot something familiar. If I was close to one of the resting places known as way-stations, used by vampires on their way to and from Council, there might be hope. I could hole-up, catch a day or two of sleep, and recover my strength. A good plan, with just one major flaw — I hadn't a clue where I was or if there were any way-stations nearby.

I weighed up my options. Standing still would get me nowhere. And scouting for a way-station was out of the question — I hadn't the strength or time. The first order of the day was to find somewhere sheltered to recuperate. Food, warmth and working my way back to Vampire Mountain could come later — *if* I survived.

There was a forest about a kilometre to my left. That was the best place to head. I could curl up at the base of a tree and cover myself with leaves. Maybe find some insects or small animals to feed upon. It wasn't ideal, but it made more sense than standing here in the open, or climbing slippery rocks in search of caves.

I fell many times on my way to the forest. That wasn't surprising — I was amazed I'd made it this far. Each time I lay in the snow a few minutes, gathering my diminished resources, then hauled myself to my feet and staggered on again.

The forest had assumed magical properties. I was convinced, if I could make it to the trees, everything would be fine. Deep inside, I knew that was nonsense, but the belief kept me going. Without it, I'd have been unable to continue.

I finally ran out of steam a hundred metres or less from the first trees of the forest. I knew in my heart, as I lay panting in the snow, that I'd reached the end of my tether. All the same, I rested a few minutes, as I had before, then made a valiant effort to rise — no good. I made it as far as my knees, then dropped. Another long rest. Again I tried to rise. Again I fell, this time face first into the snow, where I lay, shivering, unable to roll over.

The cold was unbearable. A human would have died from it long ago. Only the vampire blood inside my veins had kept me going. But even the powerful blood of the vampires had its limits. I'd pushed to the very end of mine. I'd no strength left, not even the tiniest morsel.

I was finished.

I wept pitifully as I lay there, tears turning to ice on my cheeks. Snowflakes drifted on to my eyelashes. I tried lifting a hand to brush them away, but couldn't. Even that small gesture was beyond me. "What an awful way to die," I moaned. Another hundred metres and I would have been safe. To collapse and die this close to the end was a shame. Maybe if I'd rested more in the cave in the mountain, I'd have had the energy to continue. Or if I'd—

A sharp, yapping sound jolted me out of my reverie. I'd closed my eyes and had been drifting off to sleep/death. At the sound, I cracked them open. I couldn't move my head, and the flakes of snow clouded my vision, but I was staring in the general direction of the forest and could see a vague shape making its way towards me, tumbling through the snow. Oh, great, I thought sarcastically. As if things weren't bad enough — now something's going to come along and eat me before I'm dead! Could things get any worse? Judging by what had happened to me recently — *yes!*

I shut my eyes as the creature came nearer and hoped I'd be too numb to feel its teeth and claws as it devoured me. Fighting back was out of the question — a squirrel could have knocked the stuffing out of me, the condition I was in.

Hot breath clouded my face. A long tongue licked around my nose. I shivered. It licked again, this time my cheeks and ears. Then it licked the snowflakes from my eyelashes.

I opened my eyes and blinked. What was going on? Was it cleaning me up before it killed me? That seemed unlikely. Yet what other explanation could there be? As I adjusted my vision, the animal nudged back a bit and came into focus. My jaw dropped. My lips quivered. And in a pained, shaky voice, I mumbled incredulously: *"Rudi?"*

CHAPTER FIVE

RUDI WAS the wolf cub who'd accompanied Mr Crepsley, Harkat, Gavner and me on some of the way to Vampire Mountain. He'd been part of a small pack, which included two she-wolves and a large male whom I'd christened Streak. They'd left us to unite with other wolf packs close to Vampire Mountain.

Rudi leapt around me, barking with excitement. He'd grown a bit since I'd last seen him: his fangs were longer and his fur was thicker than ever. I managed to lift my head and smile weakly. "I'm in big trouble, Rudi," I muttered as the cub licked my fingers. He cocked his ears and gazed at me seriously, as though he understood. "Big trouble," I repeated softly, then collapsed again.

Rudi rubbed his nose against my right cheek. It was wet and warm. He licked around my eyes and ears, then pressed his body against mine, trying to warm me up. When he saw how helpless I was, he took a few paces back and howled. Moments later, a second wolf emerged from the forest, larger, sleeker, every bit as familiar as Rudi.

"Streak," I whispered as the wolf advanced cautiously. His ears perked up when he heard my voice, then he bounded forward. Rudi carried on yapping until Streak snapped at him. The adult wolf sniffed me from head to toe, then barked at Rudi. They lay out flat beside me, Streak behind, Rudi in front, covering most of my body with theirs, transmitting their heat.

After a few minutes, warmth seeped through me. I flexed and unflexed my fingers and toes, working the worst of the chill out of them. I curled up into a ball, so the wolves could cover more of me, and buried my face between Rudi's hairy shoulders. We lay like that for ages, the wolves shifting position every so often to keep warm. Finally, Streak got to his feet and barked.

I tried getting up. Failed. Shook my head and groaned. "It's no use. I can't go on." The wolf studied me silently, then bent and bit my bum! I yelped and rolled away instinctively. Streak followed and I leapt to my feet. "Stay back, you no-good—" I shouted, then stopped when I saw the look on his face.

I stared down at my body, then at Streak, and grinned sheepishly. "I'm standing," I whispered redundantly. Streak howled softly, then nipped my right leg lightly and faced the trees. Nodding wearily, I set off for the forest and the wolves padded along beside me.

The going wasn't easy. I was cold and exhausted, and stumbled more times than I could keep track of. Streak and Rudi kept me going. Whenever I stalled, they pressed against me, or breathed warmly over me, or snapped to make me get up. At one stage, Streak let me grab the thick, long hair around his neck, and half-dragged me through the snow.

I'm not sure why they bothered with me — normally wild animals leave wounded companions behind if they can't keep up. Maybe they wanted to keep on the good side of the vampires, who put lots of scraps their way during Council. Or perhaps they sensed hidden resources within me and knew my cause wasn't hopeless.

After a long, hard walk, we entered a glade, where a large pack of wolves had gathered. There must have been twenty or thirty of the predators, lying about, eating, playing and grooming themselves, all different colours, builds and breeds. The wolves regarded me with suspicion. One, a dark, bulky male, padded over and sniffed me, then growled threateningly, raising its hackles. Streak met its challenge and growled back. The two stood snarling at each other for a few seconds, before the unwelcoming wolf turned its back on us and loped away.

Rudi ran after the dark wolf, yapping, but Streak barked angrily at the cub and he returned, tail between his legs. As I blinked owlishly at the wolves, Streak nudged me forward to where a she-wolf was suckling three cubs. She laid a protective paw over her cubs and growled at us as we approached, but Streak whined and dropped to his belly to show he meant no harm.

When the she-wolf had relaxed, Streak stood and locked gazes with the female. The she-wolf snarled. Streak bared his fangs and snarled back, pawed at the snow in front of her, then locked gazes again. This time, she lowered her head and didn't respond. Streak struck the backs of my legs with his snout and I dropped to the ground. As he nudged me on, I understood what he wanted me to do. "No!" I resisted, insides churning. "I can't!"

Streak growled and pushed me forward. I was too weak to argue. Besides, it made sense — I was cold and hungry, but too weak to eat. I needed to get something warm and nourishing down me, something that didn't need to be chewed.

I lay down and wriggled forward, gently shoving the three cubs to one side, making space. The cubs yapped suspiciously at me, then crowded round, sniffed me all over, and accepted me as one of their own. When my face was up close to the suckling she-wolf's belly, I took a deep breath, paused momentarily, then found a milk-engorged teat, closed my lips around it, and drank.

CHAPTER SIX

THE SHE-WOLF treated me the same as the three cubs, making sure I got enough milk, covering me with her paws to keep me warm, licking behind my ears and around my face to clean me (I crept away when I had to go to the toilet!). I remained with her for a couple of days, slowly regaining my strength, cuddling up to her and the cubs for warmth, surviving on her warm milk. It didn't taste good, but I was in no position to complain.

Pain racked my body as I recovered. Bruises covered every last scrap of me. My cuts weren't too serious — the cold restricted the flow of blood — but they stung like mad. I wished I had some of Seba's healing spider webs to apply to them.

The more I thought about my slide down the mountain stream, the more incredible it seemed. Had I really done it, or was this some crazy dream? If not for the pain, I might have believed it was the latter, but dreams are painless, so it had to be real.

More incredible still was that I hadn't broken any major bones. Three fingers on my left hand were broken, my right thumb was sticking out at an alarming angle, and my left ankle had blown up like a purple balloon, but otherwise I seemed to be OK. I could move my arms and legs; my skull hadn't been cracked open; my backbone hadn't been snapped in two. All things considered, I was in astoundingly good shape.

As the days passed, I stretched and tested myself. I still slept beside the she-wolf and drank from her, but I started getting up to take short walks, hobbling around the glade, exercising lightly. My left ankle pained me terribly, but the swelling subsided gradually and eventually returned to normal.

As my strength returned, Streak brought me meat and berries. I couldn't eat a lot in the beginning, but I sucked plenty of blood from the small animals he brought, and my appetite increased swiftly.

Rudi spent a lot of time with me. He was fascinated by my bald head – I'd had to shave my hair off after it caught fire during one of my Trials of Initiation – and never tired of licking it and rubbing his chin and nose over it.

After four days (possibly five or six — I hadn't kept a clear track of time) the wolves moved on to a new patch. It was a long march – seven or eight kilometres – and I lagged behind most of the way, helped along by Streak, Rudi and the she-wolf who'd been suckling me (she now regarded me as one of her cubs, and mothered me the same as the others).

As punishing as the trek was, it was beneficial, and when I awoke that night after a long, dreamless sleep, I felt almost as good as I had before my descent down the stream. The worst of the bruising had subsided, the cuts had healed, my ankle barely troubled me, and I was able to eat normally.

That night, I went hunting with the pack. I couldn't move fast, but I kept up, and helped bring down an old reindeer that several of the wolves were tracking. It felt good to be contributing to the pack after they'd done so much for me, and I gave most of my share of the meat to the she-wolf and cubs.

There was a nasty scene the next day. The dark wolf who'd objected to my presence when Streak brought me into the pack had never accepted me. He growled and barked whenever I came close, and often snatched food from my hands while I was feeding. I avoided him as much as I could, but that day, when he saw me playing with the cubs and handing meat out to them, he snapped.

He charged at me, barking wildly, meaning to drive me off. I backed away from him slowly, not showing any fear, but I didn't leave the pack — if I let him chase me out once, he'd never stop hounding me. I circled around the wolves, hoping he'd lose interest in me, but he followed, determined, snarling menacingly.

As I prepared to fight, Streak darted between us and faced the darker wolf. He raised his hackles to make himself look big, and growled deeply. It looked as though the dark wolf would back off, but then he lowered his head, bared his fangs and lunged at Streak, claws extended.

Streak met the challenge and the pair rolled away, biting and scratching at one another. The wolves around them hastily cleared out of their way. Some younger cubs yapped with excitement, but most of the older wolves ignored the fighting or looked on with only mild interest. They were accustomed to quarrels like this.

It seemed to me as though the wolves were going to tear each other to bits, and I ran around them worriedly, hoping to prise them apart. But as the fight progressed, I realized that, for all their barking, snapping and clawing, they weren't doing a lot of actual damage. Streak's snout had been scratched, and the dark wolf was bleeding from a couple of bites, but they weren't out to really hurt each other. It was more like a wrestling match than anything else.

As the fight wore on, it became obvious that Streak had the beating of the other wolf. He wasn't as heavily built, but he was faster and sharper, and for every swipe to the head he took, he delivered two or three of his own.

All of a sudden, the dark wolf stopped, lay down and rolled over, baring his throat and belly. Streak opened his mouth and clamped his teeth around the dark wolf's throat, then let go without breaking the skin and stood back. The dark wolf got to his feet and slunk away, tail between his legs.

I thought the wolf might have to leave the pack, but he didn't. Although he slept by himself that night, none of the wolves tried to chase him away, and he took his regular place in the hunting pack the next time they set out.

I thought about that a lot over the next day or two, comparing the way wolves handled their losers with how vampires handled theirs. In the world of vampires, defeat was a disgrace, and more often than not ended with the death of the defeated. Wolves were more understanding. Honour mattered to them, but they wouldn't kill or shun a member of their pack just because it had lost face. Young wolf cubs had to endure tests of maturity, just as I'd endured the Trials of Initiation, but they weren't killed if they failed.

I wasn't an expert on the subject, but it seemed to me that vampires could learn a thing or two from wolves if they took the time to study their ways. It *was* possible to be both honourable and practical. Kurda Smahlt, for all his treacherous faults, got that much right at least.

CHAPTER SEVEN

A FEW more days slipped by. I was so glad to be alive, I was savouring every moment of it. My body had healed almost completely, though faint bruises lingered in certain places. My strength had returned. I was full of vim and vinegar (one of my Dad's expressions; I never figured out what it actually meant), raring to go.

I took hardly any notice of the cold. I'd grown used to the nip of the wind and the chill of the snow. The occasional strong blast set me shivering, but most of the time I felt as natural wandering about naked as the wolves.

I'd been accepted as an equal member of the pack now that I was back on my feet, and I was constantly out hunting — since I was able to run faster than the wolves, my services were in great demand. I was gradually coming to terms with the way they thought and communicated. I couldn't read their thoughts but most of the time I had a good idea what they were thinking — I could tell by the way they hunched their shoulders, widened or narrowed their eyes, perked or dropped their ears and tails, growled or barked or whined. On the hunt, if Streak or another wolf wanted me to go to the left or the right, they only had to look at me and twitch their heads. If a she-wolf wanted me to play with her cubs, she howled in a certain soft way, and I knew she was calling me.

The wolves, for their part, seemed able to understand everything I said. I rarely spoke – there wasn't much need for words – but whenever I did, they'd cock their heads intently and listen, then reply with a yap or gesture.

We moved around a lot, as was the wolfen way. I kept an eye open for Vampire Mountain, but didn't spot it. That puzzled me — the reason the wolves met out here in the wilds was to converge on the mountain and eat the leftovers that the vampires threw to them. I decided to ask Streak about it, though I didn't think he'd be able to comprehend my question or fashion a reply. To my surprise, when I mentioned Vampire Mountain, the hackles rose on the back of his neck and he growled.

"You don't want to go there?" I frowned. "Why not?" Streak's only reply was another growl. Thinking about it, I guessed it had to be the vampaneze. The wolves must know about the purple-skinned invaders, or else they'd simply sensed trouble and were steering clear of the mountain.

I had to do something about the vampaneze, but the thought of going back to Vampire Mountain scared me. I was afraid the vampires would kill me before I had a chance to explain about the vampaneze. Or they might think I was lying and take Kurda's word over mine. Eventually I'd have to return, but I was delaying as long as possible, pretending to myself that I was still recovering and not fit to make the trip.

My three broken fingers had mended. I'd set the bones as best I could — *very* painful! — and wrapped the fingers together using long reeds and leaves. The thumb on my right hand still stuck out at an angle and hurt when I moved it, but that was only a minor irritation.

When I wasn't hunting or playing with the cubs, I thought a lot about Gavner. I got a pain in my belly whenever I recalled his death, but I couldn't stop thinking about him. The loss of a friend is a terrible, tragic thing, especially when it happens suddenly, without warning.

What really sickened me about Gavner's death was that it could have been avoided. If I hadn't run away, or if I hadn't trusted Kurda, or if I'd stayed and fought with Gavner — he'd still be alive. It wasn't fair. He didn't deserve to die. He'd been a brave, loyal, warm-hearted vampire, a friend to all.

Sometimes, when I thought about him, I was filled with hatred and wished I'd grabbed his knife and killed Kurda, even if it meant my own death at the hands of the vampaneze. Other times, a sweeping sadness would come over me and I'd cover my face with my hands and cry, wondering what prompted Kurda to do such an awful thing.

The wolves were puzzled by my behaviour. They didn't spend much time grieving for their dead. If they lost a partner or cub, they howled miserably for a while, then got on with their lives. They couldn't understand my mood swings.

To cheer me up, Streak took me out hunting with him late one evening. Normally, we never went hunting by ourselves, but the pack was settling in for the night, so we went without them.

It was nice to be on our own. A drawback to running with a pack is that you have to be very organized — if you make a wrong move that ruins the hunt, you're treated with disgust. Now that it was just Streak and me, we were free to lollop along as we pleased and make idle detours. It didn't matter whether we caught something or not — we were in search of sport, not prey.

We tracked a couple of young, frisky reindeer. We didn't expect to catch them, but it was fun to follow them. I think they sensed our harmless intentions because they kept turning back and running at us, then tossing their heads and fleeing. We'd been tracking them for almost a quarter of an hour when the two reindeer reached the top of a small mound and paused to sniff the air. I started after them, but Streak growled and drew to a halt.

I stopped, wondering what was wrong. Streak was standing stock-still like the reindeer. Then, as the reindeer turned and bolted back towards us, he nudged my legs with his snout and took off for a clump of bushes to the side. I followed quickly, trusting his more highly developed senses. We found a thick bush which afforded us a clear view of the mound, and lay low behind it.

A minute passed. Two. Then a figure appeared over the mound. My eyes were as sharp as they'd ever been, and I recognized the far-off vampire immediately — *Mr Crepsley!*

I started to get to my feet, overjoyed, and opened my mouth to roar a greeting. A low growl from Streak stopped me. The wolf's tail hung flat behind him, the way it did when he was anxious. I wanted to rush forward to greet my old friend, but I knew Streak wouldn't be acting this way without good reason.

Lying down flat beside the wolf, I kept my eyes on the mound, and soon the cause for his concern became obvious: behind Mr Crepsley marched five other vampires, and at the fore, carrying a sharp, polished sword, was the would-be Prince and traitor — *Kurda Smahlt!*

CHAPTER EIGHT

I KEPT close to the ground as the vampires passed, hidden behind the bushes, downwind so they couldn't smell me. Once they were out of immediate range, I turned to Streak. "We have to follow them," I whispered. Streak studied me in silence with his large, yellow eyes, then got to his feet. He slipped further back through the bushes. I trailed after him, trusting him not to lead me astray. A few minutes later, we circled around and caught sight of the vampires. We fell in behind them and matched their pace, careful not to get too close.

I examined the four vampires with Mr Crepsley and Kurda. Three were unfamiliar, but the fourth was Arra Sails. Her right arm had been in a sling the last time I saw her, but it was now hanging freely by her side. After a while, I noticed that two of the unfamiliar vampires were carrying swords like Kurda's, and were lagging a bit behind Arra and the other unarmed vampire.

It became clear what was happening. Mr Crepsley had decided to come looking for me. Arra and the other vampire had agreed to accompany him. Kurda, worried that I might have somehow survived, must have offered to assist, and brought the armed vampires with him. If they discovered me alive, the swords would flash, and that would be the end of myself, Mr Crepsley, Arra and the other vampire. Kurda was making sure word of his betrayal never made it back to the Generals and Princes.

I wasn't surprised by Kurda's devious plotting, but I was upset by the realization that he wasn't the only traitor. The two vampires with swords must have known the truth about him and the vampaneze, otherwise he wouldn't have been able to rely upon them. I suspected the Guardians of the Blood (weird humans who lived inside Vampire Mountain and donated their blood in exchange for the internal organs of dead vampires) of being part of the conspiracy, but I'd thought Kurda was the only vampire traitor — it looked like I was wrong.

If Mr Crepsley and Arra hadn't been concentrating so hard on the search, they'd have realized something was amiss — the sword-bearing vampires were edgy, all nervous glances and itchy fingers. I'd love to have jumped out and shocked Kurda — he was the edgiest of the lot — but common sense prevailed. If I was spotted alive, he and his men would kill me and the three true vampires. As long as they believed I was dead, they wouldn't do anything to give themselves away.

I spent a long time studying the faces of Kurda's

companions, committing them to memory. I wondered how many more were in on the plot to destroy the clan. Not many, I bet. The vampires with him were very young. Kurda most likely recruited them himself and talked them round to his way of thinking before they learnt the ways of the vampires. More experienced vampires, who valued honour and loyalty, would never dream of being in league with a traitor.

After a while, the group came to a halt in a small clearing, where they sat and rested, except Mr Crepsley, who spent the period anxiously pacing. I tapped Streak's shoulder, then pointed towards the clearing — I wanted to get closer. The wolf hesitated, sniffed the air, then led the way forward. We carefully crawled to within seven or eight metres of the clearing, where we stopped, hidden by a dead tree trunk. With my developed sense of hearing, I could eavesdrop perfectly from here.

Nothing was said for a number of minutes. The vampires were blowing into their cupped hands and tugging their jackets closer about themselves, shivering from the cold. I smiled as I thought how uncomfortable they'd feel if they were in my compromising position.

After a while, Kurda got up and walked over to Mr Crepsley. "Think we'll find him?" the traitor asked, feigning concern.

Mr Crepsley sighed. "Probably not. But I would like to keep searching. I wish to locate his body and cremate him fittingly."

"He might still be alive," Kurda said.

Mr Crepsley laughed bleakly. "We traced his path through the tunnels. We know he fell into the stream and did not emerge. You truly think he may have survived?"

Kurda shook his head, as though deeply depressed. The dirty swine! He mightn't think I was alive, but he wasn't taking any chances either. If not for that sword of his, I'd have—

I calmed down and tuned back into the conversation. Arra had joined the pair and was talking. "...saw wolf tracks further back. They might have discovered his body and devoured him. We should check."

"I doubt if they would have eaten him," Mr Crepsley said. "Wolves respect vampires, as we respect them. Besides, his blood would have poisoned them and we would have heard their mad howling."

There was a brief moment of silence, then Arra muttered, "I'd love to know what happened in those tunnels. If Darren had been by himself and fallen in, I could understand it, but Gavner has disappeared too."

My insides froze at the mention of Gavner.

"Either he fell into the stream trying to save Darren," Kurda said lightly, "or Darren fell in trying to save him. That's the only answer I can think of."

"But how did they fall in?" Arra asked. "The stream wasn't wide where they fell. They should have been able to clear it. Even if it *was* too wide for them, why didn't they just jump where it was narrower? It makes no sense."

Kurda shrugged and pretended to be as baffled as the others.

"At least we know that Gavner is dead," Mr Crepsley remarked. "Although we have not found his body, the absence of his mental signal means he breathes no longer. His death distresses me, but the uncertainty regarding Darren unsettles me more. The odds are stacked against his being alive, but until we have proof that he is dead, I shall not be able to accept it."

It was oddly comforting to know that even in the midst of worry, Mr Crepsley had lost none of his elaborate ways of talking.

"We'll go on searching," Kurda said. "If he can be found, we'll find him."

Mr Crepsley shook his head and sighed again. "No," he said. "If we do not locate his body tonight, we must abandon the search. There is your investiture to prepare for."

"Forget the investiture," Kurda snorted.

"No," Mr Crepsley said. "The night after next, you become a Prince. That takes precedence above all else."

"But—" Kurda began.

"No," Mr Crepsley growled. "Your investiture as a Prince is more important than the loss of Gavner and Darren. You have bucked tradition already by leaving the confines of the mountain so close to the ceremony. You must stop thinking about Darren. As a Prince, it is your duty to put the will and wishes of others before your own. Your people expect you to spend tomorrow fasting and preparing for the investiture. You must not disappoint them."

"Very well," Kurda groaned. "But this isn't the end of it.

I'm as upset by what's happened as you are. I won't rest until we know for sure if Darren is alive or dead."

The hypocrite! Standing there, acting innocent, pretending to be upset. If only I'd had a gun or a crossbow, I'd have shot him dead where he stood, the laws of the vampires — which forbid the use of weapons such as guns and bows — be damned!

When the vampires moved on, I stayed where I was, thinking hard. Talk of Kurda's investiture had disturbed me. It had slipped my mind that he was due to be made a Vampire Prince. But now that I thought about it, things took ominous shape. I'd thought the vampaneze just meant to kill as many vampires as they could and take over the mountain, but the more I considered it, the less sense that made. Why go to all that risk just to take over a bunch of caves they couldn't have cared less about? And even if they killed every vampire present, there were plenty more who could hurry to the mountain and fight to reclaim it.

There must be a logical reason for them being here, and I thought I knew what it was — *the Stone of Blood*. The Stone of Blood was a magical stone with which a vampire or vampaneze could locate the whereabouts of almost every vampire on the face of the planet. With the Stone, the vampaneze could track down and destroy vampires at will.

The Stone was also rumoured to be the only object that could save the vampires from being obliterated by the legendary Lord of the Vampaneze, who was supposed to arise one night and lead the vampaneze into a victorious fight with the vampires. If the dreaded Lord was coming – as Mr Tiny said – the vampaneze would naturally be eager to get their hands on the one thing which stood between them and total victory!

But the Stone of Blood was magically protected in the Hall of Princes. No matter how many vampires the vampaneze killed, or how much of the mountain they claimed, they'd never be able to enter the Hall of Princes and get at the Stone of Blood, because only a Vampire Prince was capable of opening the doors to the Hall.

Only. A. Vampire. Prince.

Like Paris Skyle, Mika Ver Leth, Arrow, or Vancha March. Or – the night after next – *Kurda Smahlt.*

That was the plan! Once Kurda was invested, he'd be able to open the doors to the Hall of Princes whenever he liked. When he was ready, he'd sneak the vampaneze up from the caves and tunnels – he knew ways into the Halls which no one else knew – lead them to the Hall of Princes, kill everyone there, and take control of the Stone of Blood. Once that was in his hands, vampires everywhere would have to do what he said — or perish disobeying him.

In less than forty-eight hours Kurda would be invested and the Hall would be his for the taking. Nobody knew of his treachery, so nobody could stop him — except *me.* Reluctant as I was to face the vampires who'd condemned me to death, it was time to return to Vampire Mountain. I had to warn the Generals and Princes before Kurda could betray them. Even if they killed me for it...

CHAPTER NINE

ONCE WE were back with the pack, I told Streak I had to leave for Vampire Mountain. The wolf growled and loosely grabbed my right ankle with his fangs, trying to keep me with him. "I have to go!" I snapped. "I must stop the vampaneze!"

Streak released me when I mentioned the vampaneze, snarling softly. "They plan to attack the vampires," I said quietly. "They'll kill them all unless I stop them."

Streak stared at me, panting heavily, then pawed the snow, sniffed the marks he'd made, and yelped. It was obvious he was trying to communicate something important to me, but I couldn't interpret his actions. "I don't understand," I said.

Streak growled, again ran his nose over the tracks he'd made, then turned and padded away. I followed wonderingly. He led me to a shabby she-wolf resting slightly away from the pack. I'd noticed her before, but hadn't paid much attention to her — she was old, not far from death's door, and hadn't much to do with the pack, surviving off scraps they left behind.

The she-wolf regarded us suspiciously as we approached. Struggling to her feet, she backed away cautiously, but Streak dropped to his belly and rolled over to show he meant no harm. I did the same and the she-wolf relaxed. When Streak sat up, he pressed close to the she-wolf, whose eyes weren't strong, and stared at her long and hard, growling softly, meaningfully. He made marks in the snow, similar to the ones he'd made for me, then barked at the old she-wolf. She peered at the marks, then up at me, and whined. Streak barked again, to which she replied with a louder, sharper whine.

As I studied the wolves, wondering what was going on, it suddenly struck me that Streak was asking the old she-wolf — I decided on an impulse to call her Magda (my grandmother's name) — to lead me to Vampire Mountain. But all the wolves knew where the mountain was. Why was Streak asking this ancient, pitiful she-wolf to lead me? It made no sense. Unless... My eyes widened. *Unless* Magda knew a way not just *to* the mountain, but *up* it!

"You know how to get inside!" I gasped, crouching forward with excitement. Magda stared at me blankly, but I knew in my gut I was right. I could find my way up the mountain by myself, using common, marked passages, except it would be very difficult to avoid detection that way. But if Magda knew of older, less-used passages, I might be able to sneak in!

I turned to Streak imploringly. "Can she take me there? *Will* she?"

Streak ignored me and butted Magda softly with his head, scratching at the marks he'd made in the snow. The she-wolf whined one last time, then lowered her head obediently. I wasn't happy that Streak had bullied her into obeying him, but my need to get safely to the Princes at the top of Vampire Mountain was paramount — if a bit of bullying was required to help me sneak past the vampaneze, so be it.

"How far up the mountain can she take me?" I asked. "To the top, the Hall of Princes?" But this was too much for the wolves to comprehend — I'd just have to let her lead me as far as she could, and make my own way from there.

"Can we go now?" I asked, eager to be under way — I wasn't sure how long the trek would take, and time was precious.

Magda struggled to her feet, ready to follow me, but Streak snarled at me, then jerked his head at Magda and led her through the pack to feast on fresh meat — he wanted to feed her up before we set off, which was a wise move, given the sorry state she was in.

While Magda fed, I hopped nervously from foot to foot, thinking about the journey ahead and if we'd make it in time; if Magda really knew the way into and up the mountain; and even if I made it to the top, past the vampaneze, how exactly I could contact the Princes, before some over-anxious guard or co-conspirator of Kurda's saw me and hacked me down.

When Magda had eaten her fill, we set off. Streak accompanied us, along with two other young male wolves —

they seemed to be tagging along for the adventure! Rudi followed us out of camp, yapping with excitement, until Streak nipped him sharply and sent him scampering away. I'd miss the young cub, but there was no place for him where we were headed, so I bid him a silent farewell and left him behind, along with the rest of the pack.

The going was good at first. Wolves can't run especially fast but are incredibly resilient, able to maintain a steady pace for hours on end. We surged through the forest, across snow and rocks, making great time.

Then Magda tired. The she-wolf wasn't used to matching the pace of young, tireless males, and wilted. The wolves would have run on ahead, leaving her to catch up later, but I didn't like the idea of abandoning her. When they saw me slow down to jog along beside her, they checked and circled back to join us.

We rested for a few minutes every hour or so. As day dawned and developed, I began to recognize my surroundings. By my reckoning, allowing for our pace and pauses, we should reach the tunnels a couple of hours before sunset.

It actually took a little longer than I thought. When the ground rose, Magda's pace slowed even further. We still made the tunnels an hour before the sun went down, but I was filled with pessimism — Magda was in very poor shape. If the route to the tunnels had left her panting for breath and shaking with exhaustion, how would she cope with a long, testing climb up the mountain?

I said to Magda that she could stay here and leave me to make my own way, but she growled stubbornly. I got the sense that she intended to press ahead, not for my sake — but her own. Old wolves were seldom given the opportunity to shine. Magda was relishing her role and would rather die on the climb than quit. As a half-vampire, I understood that, so even though I wasn't pleased about letting the she-wolf exhaust herself on my account, I decided not to deter her.

We spent the night waiting in the tunnel near the base of the mountain. The young wolves were restless and eager to proceed, but I knew that night was when the vampires and vampaneze would be most active, so I held my position and the wolves had no choice but to stay with me. Finally, as the sun rose on the land outside, I stood and nodded, and we climbed.

The tunnels Magda led us through were mostly narrow and unused. Many were natural tunnels, as opposed to the mainly vampire-carved tunnels which linked the Halls. A lot of crawling and slinking along on our bellies was required. It was uncomfortable (and painful in places for someone without any clothes!) but I didn't mind — since no vampires or vampaneze used these tunnels, nobody could catch me!

We stopped for regular rest periods. The climb was having a dreadful effect on Magda – she looked ready to topple over and die – but she wasn't the only one who found the going tough. All of us were sweating and panting, groaning from aching muscles and bones.

While we rested in a cave that was faintly lit by luminous lichen, I fell to wondering how Magda knew about these tunnels. I guessed she must have wandered in here when she was younger – perhaps lost, starving, separated from her pack – and found her way up through trial and error, to safety, warmth and food. If that was the case, she had a truly incredible memory. I was marvelling at this – and at the memories of animals in general – when Streak's nose lifted sharply. He sniffed the air, then got to his paws and padded to the mouth of the tunnel leading out of the cave. The younger wolves joined him, and all three bared their fangs and growled softly.

I was instantly alert. Picking up a sharp stone, I rose to investigate the cause of their concern. But as I was crossing the cave, focusing on the wolves, a slim figure dropped suddenly and silently from the shadows overhead, knocked me to the ground, and roughly jammed a large bone between my lips, choking me and cutting short my panicked cry!

CHAPTER TEN

As I raised my hands to fight, the three male wolves began to bark — but not at me or my assailant. They were focused on some other danger, further up the tunnel, and took no notice of the trouble I was in. Nor did Magda, who lay peacefully where she was and gazed at me with a curious but unalarmed expression.

Before I could strike, the person holding me said something that sounded like "Gurlabashta!" I tried to shout in response, but could manage only a muffled grunt because of the bone jammed between my teeth. "Gurlabashta!" my attacker snapped again, then eased the bone out and pressed a couple of dry fingers to my lips.

Realizing my life wasn't under threat, I relaxed and suspiciously studied the person who'd knocked me to the floor. With a start, I saw that it was one of the pale-skinned, white-eyed Guardians of the Blood. He was a thin, anxious-looking man. Putting a finger to his own lips, he pointed at the wolves — barking louder than ever — then up at the roof of the cave, where he'd dropped from. Pushing me over to the wall, he pointed out fingerholds in the rocks, then scrambled up into darkness. I lingered doubtfully a moment, then glanced at the agitated wolves and followed him up.

There was a crevice at the top of the wall, which the Guardian guided me into. He slid into a small hole close by. I waited in silence, my heart beating loudly. Then I heard a voice addressing the angry wolves. "Quiet!" someone hissed. "Shut up, you mangy curs!"

The wolves quit howling, but continued growling menacingly. They backed away from the tunnel mouth, and moments later I saw a purple-skinned face poke out of the shadows — a vampaneze!

"Wolves!" the vampaneze snarled, spitting on the ground. "Curse their eyes!"

"Leave them be," a second vampaneze said behind him. "They won't interfere with us if we keep out of their way. They're just scavenging for food."

"If they keep yapping, they could bring the vampires down on us," the first vampaneze murmured ominously, and I saw the blade of a sharp knife glint by his side.

"They're only barking because of us," his companion said, dragging him away. "They'll stop once we..."

Their voices faded and I heard no more of them after that.

When I was sure the way was clear, I looked over to where the Guardian of the Blood was hiding, to thank him for his unexpected assistance — but he wasn't there. He must have slipped away while I wasn't looking. I shook my head with confusion. I'd thought the Guardians were in league with the vampaneze, since one of them ignored my cries for help when I was fleeing from Kurda and his allies, and left me to them. Why help me now when they'd abandoned me then?

Mulling it over, I climbed down and rejoined the wolves. They were still sniffing the air guardedly, but had stopped growling. After a while, we followed Magda out of the cave as she resumed her way and led us further up the mountain. She slinked ahead even slower than before, though I didn't know if this was because of exhaustion or the threat of the vampaneze.

Some hours later, we reached the lower Halls at the top of the mountain, and skirted around them. We passed disturbingly close to the store-rooms at one stage. I could hear vampires at work behind the walls, getting ready for the large feast which would follow Kurda's investiture. I held my breath and listened for a few minutes but their words were muffled and I soon moved on, for fear one of them would discover us.

I kept expecting Magda to come to a stop, but she led us higher and higher, further up the mountain than I thought possible. I was beginning to think we must be almost at the very top when we came to a tunnel which cut upwards sharply. Magda studied the tunnel, then turned and gazed at me — I could tell by the expression in her eyes that she'd brought me as far as she could. As I dashed forward, eager to check where the tunnel led, Magda about-faced and limped away.

"Where are you going?" I called. The she-wolf paused and glanced back, tired resignation in her stare — she couldn't manage the climb. "Wait here and we'll collect you later," I told her. Magda snarled, pawed the ground and ruffled her fur — and I got the sense that she was going away to *die*. "No," I said softly. "If you just lie down and rest, I'm sure—"

Magda interrupted with a short shake of her head. Staring into her sad eyes, I began to comprehend that this was what she wanted. She'd known when she set out that the journey would prove too much for her. She'd chosen to undertake it all the same and die usefully, rather than struggle along after the pack for another season or two, perishing slowly and miserably. She was prepared for death, and welcomed it.

Crouching, I ran my hands over the tired she-wolf's head and gently rubbed the thin hairs on her ears. "Thank you," I said simply. Magda licked me, rubbed her nose against my left cheek, then hobbled away into darkness, to find a secluded spot where she could lie down and quietly leave this world behind.

I remained where I was a while, thinking about death and how the wolf had accepted it so calmly, remembering how I'd run when it had been my time to face it. Then, shrugging off such morbid thoughts, I entered the tunnel and climbed.

The wolves had a harder time on the final stretch than me. Even though they were great climbers, the rock was sheer, unsuited to sharp claws, and they kept slipping to the bottom. Finally, tired of hanging about, I slid down and let the wolves go ahead of me, using my head and shoulders to brace them when they lost their footing.

Several minutes later, we found ourselves on level ground, in a small, dark cave. The air here was musty, made worse by the strong stench of the hairy wolves. "You three wait here," I told them in a whisper, afraid their smell would carry to any nearby vampires. Shuffling forward, I came to a wall of thin, fragile rock. Dim light shone through several tiny holes and cracks. I pressed my eyes to the gaps but they were too small to see through. Inserting the nail of my right little finger into one of the larger cracks, I worked gently at the stone, which crumbled, widening the hole. Leaning forward, I was able to see through to the other side — and was astonished to find myself at the rear of the Hall of Princes!

Once I'd recovered from the shock — there was only supposed to be one way up to the Hall of Princes! — I began considering my next course of action. This had worked out far more neatly than I'd ever dared dream, and it was now up to me to make the most of my incredible good fortune. My first instinct was to burst through the thin wall and scream for the Princes, but the guards of the Hall or one of the traitors might cut me down dead if I did, killing my message with me.

Retreating from the wall, I returned to the wolves and led them back down the steep tunnel, where there was more space and air. Once comfortable, I lay down, closed my eyes, and fell to thinking about how to make contact with the Princes — while at the same time avoiding the spears and swords of the vicious traitors and well-meaning guards!

CHAPTER ELEVEN

I WISHED to speak to the Princes directly — but I couldn't just march up to the doors of the Hall and ask the guards to let me in! I could wait for one of the Princes to emerge and hail him, but they didn't leave the throne room very often. What if Kurda made his move before I could act? I thought about sneaking down to the doors and slipping in the next time they were open, but it was unlikely that I could evade the attention of the guards. Besides, if Kurda was inside and saw me, he might make an end of me before I had a chance to speak.

That was my greatest fear — that I'd be killed before I warned the Princes of the peril they faced. With this in mind, I decided it was essential that I contact somebody before approaching the Princes, so that if I died, my message wouldn't die with me.

But who to trust? Mr Crepsley or Harkat were the ideal choices, but there was no way I could make it to their cells undetected. Arra Sails and Vanez Blane also dwelt too deep within the mountain to be easily reached.

That left Seba Nile, the ancient quartermaster of Vampire Mountain. His cell was close to the store-rooms. It would be risky, but I felt I could get to him without being seen. But could I trust him? He and Kurda were close friends. He'd helped the traitor make maps of infrequently-used tunnels, maps which the vampaneze might be using at this very minute to advance on the Hall of Princes. Was it possible that he was one of Kurda's allies?

Almost as soon as I raised the question, I knew it was ridiculous. Seba was an old-fashioned vampire, who believed in loyalty and the ways of the vampires above all else. And he'd been Mr Crepsley's mentor. If I couldn't trust Seba, I couldn't trust anybody.

I rose to go in search of Seba, and the wolves rose with me. Crouching, I told them to stay. Streak shook his head, growling, but I was firm with him. "Stay!" I commanded. "Wait for me. If I don't come back, return to the pack. This isn't your fight. There's nothing you can do."

I wasn't sure if Streak understood all that, but he squatted on his haunches and remained with the other wolves, panting heavily as he watched me leave, his dark eyes fixed on me until I vanished round a bend.

Retracing the path by which we'd come, I climbed back down the mountain. It didn't take long to reach the store-rooms. They were quiet when I arrived, but I entered cautiously, taking no chances, through the hole which Kurda had revealed to me during the course of my escape.

Finding nobody within, I started for the door leading to the tunnels, then stopped and glanced down at myself. I'd grown so used to being without clothes, I'd forgotten how odd I'd look to non-animal eyes. If I turned up in Seba's quarters like this, naked, dirty and wild, he might think I was a ghost!

There were no spare clothes in this room, so I ripped apart an old sack and tied a strip of it around my waist. It wasn't much of an improvement but it would have to do. I tied another few strips around my feet, so that I could pad more stealthily, then opened a sack of flour and rubbed a few handfuls of the white powder over my body, hopefully to mask the worst of my wolfish smell. When I was ready, I opened the door and crept into the tunnel beyond.

Though it would normally have taken no more than two or three minutes to get to Seba's rooms, I spent nearly four times that getting there, checking each stretch of tunnel several times before venturing down it, making sure I had somewhere to hide if vampires emerged unexpectedly.

When I finally reached the old quartermaster's door, I was shaking with anxiety, and stood in silence a few seconds, collecting myself. When I'd recovered, I knocked lightly. "Come in," Seba called. I entered. The quartermaster was standing by a chest with his back to me. "Over here, Thomas," he muttered, examining the insides of the chest. "I told you not to bother knocking. The investiture is a mere two hours away. We do not have time for—"

Turning, he saw me, and his jaw literally dropped.

"Hello, Seba," I smiled nervously.

Seba blinked, shook his head, blinked again. "*Darren?*" he gasped.

"The one and only," I grinned.

Seba lowered the lid of the chest and sat upon it heavily. "Are you a vision?" he wheezed.

"Do I look like one?"

"Yes," he said.

I laughed and advanced. "I'm no vision, Seba. It's me. I'm real." I stopped in front of him. "Feel me if you don't believe me."

Seba reached out a trembling finger and touched my left arm. When he realized I was solid, he beamed and rose. Then his face fell and he sat again. "You were sentenced to death," he said dolefully.

"I figured as much," I nodded.

"You fled."

"It was a mistake. I'm sorry."

"We thought you drowned. Your trail led to the stream and ended abruptly. How did you get out?"

"I swam," I said lightly.

"Swam where?" he asked.

"Down the stream."

"You mean … all the way … through the mountain? That is impossible!"

"Improbable," I corrected him. "Not impossible. I wouldn't be here if it was."

"And Gavner?" he asked hopefully. "Is he alive too?"

I shook my head sadly. "Gavner's dead. He was murdered."

"I thought so," Seba sighed. "But when I saw *you*, I–" He stopped and frowned. "*Murdered*?" he rumbled.

"You'd better stay sitting," I said, then proceeded to tell him the bare bones of my encounter with the vampaneze, Kurda's treachery, and what happened after.

Seba was shaking with rage when I finished. "Never did I think a vampire would turn against his brothers," he growled. "And one so highly respected! It sickens and shames me. To think I have drunk blood to that sham of a vampire's good health, and prayed to the gods to grant him luck! Charna's guts!"

"You believe me?" I asked, relieved.

"I might not recognize treachery when it is skilfully concealed," he said, "but I know the truth when it is revealed. I believe you. The Princes will too." Rising, he strode for the door. "We must hurry to warn them. The sooner we–" He paused. "No. The Princes will see no one until the time of investiture. They reside within their Hall and will not open the doors until twilight, when Kurda presents himself. That is the way it has always been. I would be turned away if I went there now."

"But you'll be able to get to them in time?" I asked anxiously.

He nodded. "There is a lengthy ceremony before the investiture. I will have plenty of time to interrupt and level these grievous charges against our supposed ally, Kurda Smahlt." The vampire was seething with rage. "Come to think of it," he said, eyes narrowing, "he is alone in his chambers now. I could go and slit the villain's throat before—"

"No," I said quickly. "The Princes will want to question him. We don't know who else is working with him, or why he did it."

"You are right," he sighed, shoulders slumping. "Besides, killing him would be a mercy. He deserves to suffer for what he did to Gavner."

"That's not the only reason why I don't want you to kill him," I said hesitantly. Seba stared at me and waited for me to continue. "I want to blow the whistle on him. I was with Gavner when he died. He was down in the tunnels because of me. I want to look into Kurda's eyes when I expose him."

"To show him how much you hate him?" Seba asked.

"No," I said. "To show him how much pain he's caused." There were tears in my eyes. "I hate him, Seba, but I still think of him as a friend. He saved my life. I'd be dead now if he hadn't intervened. I want him to know how much he's hurt me. Maybe it doesn't make sense, but I want him to see that I don't get any pleasure out of exposing him as a traitor."

Seba nodded slowly. "It makes sense," he said, stroking his chin and considering the proposal. "But it is dangerous. I do not think the guards will kill you, but one of Kurda's allies might."

"I'll take that chance," I said. "What do I have to lose? I'll be killed afterwards anyway, because I failed the Trials. I'd rather die on my feet, thwarting Kurda, than in the Hall of Death."

Seba smiled warmly. "You are a true, courageous vampire, Darren Shan," he said.

"No," I replied softly. "I'm just trying to do the right thing, to make up for running away earlier."

"Larten will be proud of you," Seba remarked.

I couldn't think of anything to say to that, so I just blushed and shrugged. Then we sat down together and discussed various plans for the climactic night ahead.

CHAPTER TWELVE

I DIDN'T really want to involve the wolves any further – in case they were killed – but they remained seated, panting patiently, when I tried chasing them off. "Go!" I hissed, slapping their flanks. "Home!" But they weren't dogs and they didn't obey. I saw they planned to stick by me – the younger wolves even looked like they were relishing the thought of a fight! – so I gave up trying to drive them to safety, and instead settled back to wait for nightfall, judging the time by my internal body clock.

As the day was drawing to a close, we crawled back up the steep tunnel and made our way to the wall at the rear of the Hall of Princes. I set to work on the soft layer of rock and carefully carved out a gap big enough for us to squeeze through. I was surprised nobody had ever found this weak point before, but it was quite high up and from the other side the wall must have looked solid.

I paused briefly to consider the extraordinary run of luck I was enjoying. Surviving the gushing madness of the mountain stream; Rudi and Streak finding me when I was at my weakest; Magda leading me through the tunnels to the Hall of Princes. Even failing the Trials had been in one respect fortunate — I'd never have found out about the vampaneze if I hadn't come a cropper against the Blooded Boars.

Was it really just the luck of the vampires, or was it something more — like *destiny*? I'd never believed in preordained fate, but I was beginning to have my doubts!

Sounds of the approaching procession distracted me from my heavy thoughts. The hour of Kurda's investiture was upon us. It was time to act. Wriggling through the hole, I dropped to the floor, turned and caught the wolves as they slithered down. When we were all ready, we flattened close to the wall of the Hall and edged forward.

As we slipped around the curve of the dome, I saw the Generals who'd lined up to welcome Kurda Smahlt. They'd formed a guard of honour, stretching from the tunnel to the doors of the Hall. Almost all were armed, as were the rest of the vampires — the ceremony of investiture was the one time vampires could carry weapons into the chamber. Any one of the armed vampires could be a traitor, with orders to kill me on sight. I tried not to dwell on that horrible thought, for fear it might deter me.

The three Princes stood by the open doors of the dome, regally attired, waiting to blood Kurda and make him one of their own. I spotted Mr Crepsley and Seba close to the Princes. Mr Crepsley was staring in the direction of the tunnel – along with everybody else – but Seba had an eye out for me. When he caught sight of me, he nodded slightly. That meant he'd had words with a few of his staff and had positioned them nearby, with orders to stop any vampire who raised a weapon during the ceremony. Seba hadn't told his assistants about me – we'd agreed it was best to keep my presence a secret – and I hoped they wouldn't hesitate when I made my move, affording one of Kurda's men the chance to kill me.

The head of the procession entered the cave. Six vampires preceded Kurda, walking slowly in pairs, carrying the clothes which Kurda would slip on once he'd been invested. Next came two deep-voiced vampires, loudly chanting poems and stories, praising the Princes and Kurda. There were more of the chanting vampires behind, and their hymn-like cries carried up the tunnel and echoed round the cave.

Behind the first eight vampires came the vampire of the moment, Kurda Smahlt, hoisted aloft on a small platform by four Generals, clad in a loose white robe, blond head bowed, eyes closed. I waited until he was halfway between the tunnel and the Princes, then stepped out from the wall, strode forward – the wolves close on my heels – and shouted as loud as I could, "STOP!"

All heads turned and the chanting ceased immediately. Hardly any of the vampires recognized me at first – all they saw was a dirty, half-naked boy, covered in flour – but as I got closer, the penny dropped and they gasped and exclaimed. "Darren!" Mr Crepsley roared with delight and started towards me, arms outstretched. I ignored my mentor and stayed focused on the rest of the vampires, alert to signs of retaliation.

The traitors didn't delay. Two vampires in green uniforms raised their spears when they saw me, while another pulled out a pair of knives and moved forward to intercept me. Seba's men reacted splendidly, ignored the confusion, and darted forward to apprehend the spear-wielding vampires. They dragged them to the ground before they could launch their weapons, disarmed them and held them down.

But nobody could get to the vampire with the knives — he was too far ahead of Seba's assistants. He broke through the ranks of guards, pushed Mr Crepsley out of the way, and raced towards me. He threw one of the knives, but I ducked out of its way with ease. Before he could throw the other or get close enough to stick it into me, the two young wolves launched themselves at him and knocked him to the floor. They bit and clawed at him, howling with excitement and fury. He shrieked and tried fighting them off, but they were too powerful.

One of the wolves sunk its teeth into the vampire's throat and made a brutal end of him. I didn't mind — I was only concerned about not harming innocent vampires, and by the speed with which this one had reacted, and the determination he'd shown to kill me, he was without doubt one of Kurda's accomplices.

The other vampires in the cave had frozen with shock. Even Mr Crepsley stopped where he was, eyes wide, panting uncertainly. "Darren?" he asked shakily. "What is going on? How did—"

"Not now!" I snapped authoritatively, eyes peeled for traitors. There didn't appear to be any more, but I wasn't taking things for granted, not until I'd said my piece. "I'll tell you about it later," I promised Mr Crepsley, then calmly walked past him to face Kurda and the Princes. Streak padded along by my side, watching out for me, growling warningly.

Kurda had opened his eyes and raised his head at the start of the commotion, but had made no attempt to flee the platform or the cave. He stared at me with hard-to-read eyes as I advanced, more wistful than panicky, then rubbed the three small scars on his left cheek (made by the vampaneze when he was discussing peace terms with them some years before), and sighed.

"What's going on?" Mika Ver Leth roared, his expression as black as the clothes he wore. "Why are those vampires fighting? Break them apart immediately!"

"Sire!" Seba said quickly, before the order could be obeyed. "Those who raised weapons against Darren are not our allies. Those who hold them down do so at my command. I would strongly advise against releasing them until you have heard Darren out."

Mika stared hard at the calm old quartermaster. "You're part of this chaos, Seba?" he asked.

"I am, Sire," Seba said, "and proud to be."

"That boy fled from the judgement of the Princes," Arrow growled, the veins in his bald head throbbing thickly. "He is not welcome here."

"He will be, Sire, when you learn why he has come," Seba insisted.

"This is most objectionable," Paris Skyle said. "Never before has anyone interrupted the investiture of a Prince. I do not know why you are siding with the boy, but I think the two of you should be removed from the Hall until later, when we can—"

"No!" I shouted, pushing through the ranks of guards to stand directly before the Princes. Locking gazes with them, I growled so that all could hear: "You say nobody has ever interrupted the investiture of a Prince, and this might be true. But I say no one has ever sought to invest a *traitor* before, so it's time that—"

The cave erupted with furious roars. The vampires were incensed that I'd called Kurda a traitor (even those who hadn't voted for his investiture), and before I could make any moves to protect myself, a horde surged around me and started kicking, punching and tearing at me. The three wolves tried dashing to my rescue but were easily propelled by the sheer mass of vampires.

"Stop this!" the Princes roared. "Stop! Stop! Stop!"

Finally, the commands of the Princes seeped through, and those who'd surrounded me released me and shuffled backwards, eyes aflame with anger, muttering darkly. They hadn't hurt me — the press had been too tight for any of them to get in a decent blow.

"This is a grim night," Mika Ver Leth grumbled. "It's bad enough that a boy violates our laws and customs, but when fully-blooded vampires who should know better behave like a pack of barbarians in the presence of their Princes..." He shook his head, disgusted.

"But he called Kurda a traitor!" someone yelled out, and tempers flared again, as vampires hurled curses at me.

"Enough!" Mika bellowed. When silence had fallen, he fixed his gaze on me. He looked only slightly less enraged than those who'd attacked me. "Were it up to me," he snarled, "I'd have you bound and gagged before you could say another word. Then I'd see you hauled off to the Hall of Death, where you'd suffer the fate you deserve."

He paused and glared around at the vampires, who were nodding and murmuring approvingly. Then his eyes alighted on Seba and he frowned. "But one we all know, trust and admire has spoken up on your behalf. I have no respect for half-vampires who flee instead of standing to face their punishment, but Seba Nile says we should pay attention to what you have to say, and I for one am loath to disregard him."

"I agree with that," Paris Skyle grunted.

Arrow looked troubled. "I also respect Seba," he said, "but such a breach of decorum is deplorable. I think..." Looking hard at Seba, he changed his mind and nodded gruffly. "Very well. I'll side with Paris and Mika. But only for Seba's sake."

Turning to me, looking as kindly as he could given the circumstances, Paris said, "Say your piece, Darren — but make it quick."

"OK," I agreed, glancing up at Kurda, who was staring at me wordlessly. "Let's see if this is quick enough for you — Kurda Smahlt killed Gavner Purl." The vampires gasped, and looks of hatred were replaced with frowns of uncertainty. "At this very moment, dozens of vampaneze lurk in the tunnels beneath us, waiting to attack," I continued. Stunned silence greeted my words. "They were invited here by *him!*" I pointed at Kurda, and this time no voices were raised in anger. "He's a traitor," I whispered, and as all eyes locked on Kurda, mine dropped and a couple of confused tears rolled down my cheeks and fell to the dusty cavern floor.

CHAPTER THIRTEEN

A LENGTHY silence followed my accusations. Nobody knew what to say or think. If Kurda had vehemently denied the claims made against him, perhaps the Generals would have rallied to his side. But he just stood there, downcast, suffering their questioning stares without reply.

Finally, Paris Skyle cleared his throat. "These are grave charges to bring against any vampire," he said. "To level them at a Prince-to-be while he stands on the point of investiture..." He shook his head. "You understand what the consequences will be if you are lying?"

"Why would I lie?" I retorted. Turning, I faced the ranks of vampires. "Everyone knows I failed my Trials of Initiation and fled before I could be killed. By returning, I've condemned myself to execution. Do you think I'd do that for no good reason?" Nobody answered. "Kurda betrayed you! He's in league with the vampaneze. As near as I can figure, he plans letting them into the Hall of Princes once he's been invested, to seize control of the Stone of Blood."

There were cries of astonishment at that.

"How do you know this?" Arrow yelled over the noise. The bald prince hated the vampaneze more than most, because one of them had killed his wife many years ago.

"I'm only guessing about the Stone of Blood," I replied, "but I've seen the vampaneze. Gavner saw them too. That's why Kurda murdered him. He'd have spared *my* life, but I threw myself into the stream in the Hall of Final Voyage. I was sure I'd die, but I survived. Once I'd recovered, I came back here to warn you."

"How many vampaneze are down there?" Arrow asked, eyes blazing.

"At least thirty — possibly more."

The three Princes glanced at each other uneasily.

"This makes no sense," Mika muttered.

"I agree," Arrow said. "But a lie this outlandish would be simple to disprove. If he wished to fool us, he would have chosen a less fantastic story."

"Besides," Paris sighed, "look in the boy's eyes — there is nothing but truth in them."

A roar disrupted the conversation. One of Kurda's accomplices had broken free and had grabbed a knife from a General. Before he could get away, the guards closed ranks and encircled him.

"No, Cyrus!" Kurda bellowed, his first words since I'd disrupted the procession. The vampire's hand dropped and he looked to Kurda for guidance. "It's over," Kurda said softly. "Don't spill blood unnecessarily. That was never our aim."

The vampire called Cyrus nodded obediently. Then, before the circle of guards could close on him, he put the tip of the knife to his heart and made a swift, fatal stab. As the dead traitor fell to the floor, all eyes turned once again to Kurda, and this time the faces of the vampires were grim.

"What have you to say in rebuttal of Darren's claims?" Mika asked, his voice thick with emotion.

"At this moment — nothing," Kurda responded coolly.

"You don't deny the charge?" Arrow shouted.

"I do not," Kurda said.

A horrified moan swept through the cave at Kurda's admission of guilt.

"Let's kill him *now!*" Arrow growled, to a huge cheer of approval.

"With respect, Sires," Seba interceded, "would it not make more sense to focus on the vampaneze before we execute our own? Kurda can wait — we should deal with the intruders first."

"Seba is right," Paris said. "The vampaneze must be put to the sword. There will be time for traitors later."

Turning to a handful of guards, he told them to take Kurda and the other traitor away and hold them captive. "And under no circumstances let them take their own lives," he warned. "That would be the easy way out. Keep them alive until we have time to interrogate them."

Beckoning me forward, he addressed the massed vampires. "We will retire to the Hall of Princes with Darren. I ask the rest of you to remain here while we discuss the ramifications of this horrific turn of events. When we have decided on an immediate course of action, we shall inform you. There will be open talks later, when the present danger has been dealt with."

"And see that no one leaves the cave," Mika barked. "We don't know how deep this conspiracy runs. I don't want word of this reaching the ears of those who stand opposed to the welfare of our clan."

With that, the four of us entered the Hall of Princes, followed by several of the more senior Generals, as well as Seba, Arra Sails and Mr Crepsley.

Some of the tension seeped out of the air when the doors closed behind us. Paris hurried off to check on the Stone of Blood, while Mika and Arrow trudged disconsolately to their thrones. Seba thrust some clothes into my hands and told me to slip them on. I did so quickly, then let the quartermaster lead me forward to converse with the Princes. I still hadn't had a chance to have a word with Mr Crepsley, though I smiled at him to show that I was thinking about him.

I started by telling the Princes about my flight through the tunnels with Kurda, Gavner coming after us, changing direction, running into the vampaneze, Gavner making his stand, and Kurda's betrayal. When I got to the part about the stream, Paris clapped his hands loudly and grinned.

"I never would have credited it," the one-eared Prince

chuckled admiringly. "Young vampires over-eager to prove themselves used to go down it in barrels hundreds of years ago, but none ever tried—"

"Please, Paris," Mika complained. "Let's leave the reminiscences till later."

"Of course," Paris coughed meekly. "Do continue."

I told about washing up on a bank far away from Vampire Mountain, being found by the wolves and nursed back to health.

"That is not so extraordinary," Mr Crepsley interrupted. "Wolves have often given succour to abandoned children."

I described how I'd seen Mr Crepsley and Arra searching for me, but had kept my head down because of Kurda and the sword-wielding vampires.

"These two traitors," Mika said darkly. "Did you spot them in the cave?"

"Yes," I said. "They were two of the three who tried to kill me. The vampire stopped by the wolves was one. The other was captured and taken away with Kurda."

"I wonder how many more were part of this?" Mika mused.

"In my estimation — none," Paris said.

"You think there were only four of them?" Mika asked.

Paris nodded. "Vampires are not easily turned against their own. The three with Kurda were young and, if I remember correctly, all were blooded by him — the only three he ever blooded. Also, it is logical to assume that any in league with him would have been in the cave to witness his investiture. They would surely have acted along with the others to silence Darren before he could speak.

"I do not suggest we dismiss the possibility that there are one or two more we should be wary of," Paris concluded, "but it would be unhelpful to believe the rot is widespread. This is a time to pull together as one, not set in motion a series of unsettling witch hunts."

"I agree with Paris," Arrow said. "The suspicion must be stamped out before it has a chance to take hold. If we fail to re-establish trust swiftly, no vampire will be able to place faith in another, and anarchy will be rife."

I hurried through the rest of my story, bringing them up to date, telling them about Magda, my climb through the tunnels, how I contacted Seba to make sure word of Kurda's treachery wouldn't die with me if I was killed. I also mentioned the Guardians of the Blood, how one had failed to help when I cried out to him in the Hall of Final Voyage, but how another had come to rescue during my climb up the mountain.

"The Guardians of the Blood keep their own council," Seba said — he knew more about the Guardians than most. "They are loath to interfere directly in our affairs, which is why they would not have reported to us when they learned about the vampaneze. But indirect interference — such as hiding you when danger loomed — is permitted. Their neutrality is exasperating, but in keeping with their ways and customs. We should not hold it against them."

There was a long, thoughtful silence when I finished, broken eventually by Mika Ver Leth, who smiled wryly and said, "You put the clan's interests before your own. We cannot overlook your Trials of Initiation failure, or the fact that you ran from sentencing — but any dishonour you incurred has been cancelled out by this act of selfless dedication. You are a true vampire, Darren Shan, as worthy to walk the night as any I know."

I bowed my head to hide my shy smile.

"Enough of the praise," Arrow grunted. "There are vampaneze to kill. I won't rest until every last one has been hung over the stakes in the Hall of Death and dropped a dozen times. Let's storm down there and—"

"Easy, my friend," Paris said, laying a calming hand on the Prince's arm. "We must not rush into this. Our best trackers followed Darren's trail through the tunnels, passing close to the caves where the vampaneze were camped. Kurda would have thought of this and relocated them, so they would not be discovered. Our first priority must be to find them. Even after that, we must tread carefully, for fear they hear us coming and slip away."

"Very well," Arrow groaned. "But *I'm* leading the first wave against them!"

"I have no objection to that," Paris said. "Mika?"

"Arrow may lead the first wave," Mika agreed, "so long as I can lead the second, and he leaves enough for me to whet my blade on."

"It's a deal," Arrow laughed, the glint of battle lust in his eyes.

"So young and bloodthirsty," Paris sighed. "I suppose that means *I* have to stay behind and guard the Hall."

"One of us will relieve you before the end," Mika promised. "We'll let you mop up the stragglers."

"You are too kind," Paris grinned, then grew serious. "But that comes later. First, let us summon our best trackers. Darren will go with them to show them the inhabited caves. Once we—"

"Sires," Seba interrupted. "Darren has not eaten since leaving the pack of wolves, and has not partaken of human blood since departing Vampire Mountain. May I feed him before you send him off on so important a mission?"

"Of course," Paris said. "Take him to the Hall of Khledon Lurt and give him whatever he wants. We will send for him presently."

Though I'd have rather stayed and discussed the situation with the Princes, I was starving, and offered no protest as Seba led me away, through the cave of ogling vampires, down to the Hall of Khledon Lurt. In the Hall, I tucked into one of the most satisfying meals of my life, not forgetting to offer up a prayer of silent thanks to the gods of the vampires for helping me through my great ordeal — while asking them to guide all of us safely through the hardships still to come.

CHAPTER FOURTEEN

MR CREPSLEY brought Harkat to see me while I was eating. The Little Person hadn't been allowed to attend the Investiture — only vampires were permitted at the prestigious event — and knew nothing about my return until he walked into the Hall and spotted me shovelling food down my throat. "Darren!" he gasped, hurrying forward.

"'Lo, Harkat," I mumbled around a mouthful of fried rat.

"What are ... you doing ... here? Did they ... catch you?"

"Not exactly. I gave myself up."

"*Why?*"

"Don't ask me to explain it now," I pleaded. "I've just got through telling the Princes. You'll pick the story up soon enough. Tell me what's been happening while I was away."

"Nothing much," Harkat said. "The vampires were ... furious when they ... found out you'd fled. I told them ... I knew ... nothing about it. They didn't ... believe me, but I ... stuck to my ... story, so there was ... nothing they could ... do."

"He would not even tell *me* the truth," Mr Crepsley said.

I looked at the vampire, ashamed of myself. "I'm sorry I ran away," I muttered.

"So you should be," he grunted. "It was not like you, Darren."

"I know," I moped. "I could blame Kurda – I wouldn't have run if he hadn't talked me into it – but the truth is I was scared and seized the opportunity to get away when it presented itself. It wasn't just dying that I was worried about — there was also the walk to that horrible Hall of Death, then being hung above the stakes and..." I shivered at the thought.

"Do not chastise yourself too much," Mr Crepsley said softly. "I am more to blame for letting them subject you to the Trials in the first place. I should have insisted upon a suitable period of time to prepare for the Trials and the consequences of failure. The fault is ours, not yours. You reacted as anyone who had not been fully versed in the ways of the vampires would have."

"I say it was fate," Seba murmured. "Had he not fled, we would never have been alerted to Kurda's treacherous nature or the presence of the vampaneze."

"The hands of ... fate keep time ... on a heart-shaped ... watch," Harkat said, and we all turned to stare at him.

"What does that mean?" I asked.

He shrugged. "I'm not sure. It just ... popped into my ... head. It's something Mr ... Tiny used to say."

We looked at each other uneasily, thinking about Mr Tiny and the heart-shaped watch he was so fond of playing with.

"You think Desmond Tiny could have had something to do with this?" Seba asked.

"I do not see how," Mr Crepsley said. "I believe Darren had the natural luck of the vampires on his side. On the other hand, where that dark horse Tiny is concerned — who knows?"

While we sat puzzling it over — the meddling fingers of fate, or sheer good fortune? — a messenger from the Princes arrived, and I was escorted through the lower Halls and tunnels to link up with the trackers and set off in search of the vampaneze.

Vanez Blane — who'd trained me for my Trials — was among the five chosen trackers. The one-eyed games master took my hands in his and squeezed hard by way of greeting. "I knew you would not desert us," he said. "Others cursed you, but I was sure you'd return once you had time to think things through. I told them it was a poor decision made in haste, which you'd shortly set right."

"I bet you didn't *bet* on me returning," I grinned.

"Now that you mention it — no, I didn't," he laughed. Vanez examined my feet to make sure my padding was adequate. All the trackers were wearing soft shoes. He offered to find a pair for me but I said I'd stick with the scraps of sack.

"We must proceed with utmost caution," he warned. "No sudden movements, no lights, and no talking. Communicate by hand signals. And take this." He gave me a long, sharp knife. "If you have to use it, don't hesitate."

"I won't," I swore, thinking about the knife which had savagely cut short the life of my friend, Gavner Purl.

Down we went, as silently as we could. I'm not sure I could have found the way back to the cave on my own — I hadn't been paying much attention to the route that night — but the trackers had followed the trail I'd left when they came looking for me and knew which way to go.

We crawled through the tunnel under the stream. It wasn't as frightening this time, not after all I'd been through since last I passed this way. As we stood, I pointed wordlessly to the tunnel which connected the small cave to the larger one. Two of the trackers advanced and checked on the cave beyond. I listened intently for sounds of a struggle but there weren't any. Moments later, one of the trackers returned and shook his head. The rest of us trailed after him into the bigger cave.

My insides tightened when I saw the cave was deserted. It looked as if it had been empty since the beginning of time. I had an ugly premonition that we'd be unable to find the vampaneze and I'd be called a liar. Vanez, sensing this, nudged me gently and winked. "It'll be OK," he mouthed, then joined the others, who were exploring the cave cautiously.

It didn't take the trackers long to uncover evidence of the vampaneze and allay my fears. One found a scrap of cloth, another a fragment from a broken bowl, another a small pool of spit where a vampaneze had cleared his throat. When they'd gathered enough evidence, we returned to the smaller cave, where we held a quiet conversation, safe in the knowledge that the roar of the stream would cover our voices.

"It was vampaneze all right," one of the trackers said. "A couple of dozen at least."

"They covered their tracks admirably," another grunted. "We only unearthed them because we knew what to look for. We'd never have noticed if we'd been giving the cave a quick once-over."

"Where do you think they are now?" I asked.

"Hard to say," Vanez mused, scratching the lid of his blind eye. "There aren't a lot of caves nearby where that many vampaneze could comfortably hole-up. But they may have split into smaller groups and scattered."

"I doubt it," one of the others remarked. "If I was in charge of that lot, I'd want everyone to stick close together, in case we were discovered. I think we'll find them bunched-up, possibly close to an exit point, ready to fight or flee *en masse*."

"Let's hope so," Vanez said. "It could take ages to locate them all if they've split up. Can you find your way back to the Halls?" he asked me.

"Yes," I said, "but I want to come with you."

He shook his head. "We brought you down to show us the cave. Now that you've done that, there's no place for you here. We can move quicker without you. Return to the Halls

410

and tell the others what we found. We'll be back when we find the vampaneze."

Seba met me at the gate of entry and escorted me up to the Hall of Princes. Many Generals had filed in to discuss the emergency, but apart from those with special permission to run errands, none had been allowed to leave the cave around the Hall, so a lot stood or sat outside, waiting for news to trickle through.

Mr Crepsley and Harkat were inside. The vampire was talking with the Princes. Harkat was standing to one side, with Madam Octa's cage. He presented it to me when I joined him. "I thought ... you'd be glad ... to see her," he said.

I wasn't really, but I pretended I was. "Great, Harkat," I smiled. "Thanks for thinking of it. I missed her."

"Harkat has been taking good care of your spider," Seba said. "He offered to give her to me when you went missing, but I told him to hang on to her. I said one never knew what lay around the corner — I had a feeling you might be back."

"You may wind up with her yet," I said morosely. "I seem to have won back my honour, but there's still my failure in the Trials to account for."

"Surely they won't ... punish you for ... that now?" Harkat said.

I glanced at Seba's face — it was stern and he said nothing.

Vanez Blane returned a couple of hours later with good news — they'd discovered the whereabouts of the vampaneze. "They're in a long, narrow cave, close to the exterior of the mountain," Vanez explained to the Princes, wasting no time on rituals or pleasantries. "There's one way in and one way out. The exit tunnel runs straight to the outside, so they can make a quick getaway if they have to."

"We'll position men outside to catch them if they do," Mika said.

"That will be difficult," Vanez sighed. "The ground is steep where the tunnel opens out, and I'm sure they'll have sentries posted. I doubt that we'll be able to sneak men up there. It will be better to take them inside if we can."

"You think we cannot?" Paris asked sharply, alerted by Vanez's worried tone.

"It won't be easy, however we go about it," Vanez said. "No matter how delicately we mask our approach, we won't be able to surprise them. Once they become aware of us closing in, they'll throw up a rear phalanx to delay us while the majority escape."

"What if we block the tunnel from the outside?" Arrow asked. "Create an avalanche or something. Then they'd have to stand and fight."

"That's a possibility," Vanez agreed, "but blocking the tunnel may prove awkward. Besides, that would alert them to our presence and intentions, and they'd have time to prepare for us. I'd rather spring a trap."

"You think they might best us in a fair fight?" Arrow snorted.

Vanez shook his head. "No. We couldn't get close enough to make a full count, but I don't think there's more than forty vampaneze down there, probably less. I've no doubt that we'll beat them." The vampires cheered Vanez's claim. "It's not the winning that bothers me," he shouted over their excited clamours. "It's the losses we'll incur."

"Damn the losses!" Arrow growled. "We've spilt blood before, dispatching vampaneze — who here will hesitate to spill it again?" By the roars it was plain that nobody would.

"That's easy to say," Vanez sighed when the cheers had died down. "But if we barge in and take them on without some sort of a distraction, we're looking at the possible loss of thirty or forty vampires, maybe more. The vampaneze have nothing to lose and will fight to the bitter, bloody end. Do *you* want to take responsibility for those casualties, Arrow?"

Much of the vampires' joy abated at Vanez's words. Even the eager, vampaneze-hating Arrow looked hesitant. "You think we'll lose that many?" he asked quietly.

"We'd be *lucky* to just lose thirty or forty," Vanez replied bluntly. "They've picked their spot expertly. We won't be able to rush or overwhelm them. We'll have to advance a handful at a time, taking them on one-to-one. Our superior numbers will lead to eventual victory, but it won't be swift or easy. They'll hurt us — *badly*."

The Vampire Princes shared an uneasy look. "Those sort of figures are unacceptable," Paris stated bleakly.

"They *are* a bit on the high side," Mika reluctantly concurred.

"Is it possible to create a diversion?" Mr Crepsley asked, joining in the discussion. "Could we flood or smoke them out?"

"I've thought of that," Vanez said. "I don't see any way of pumping enough water down there to trouble them. Fire would be ideal, but the cave's well ventilated. The ceiling's high and full of tiny cracks and holes. We'd have to get inside the cave and light a huge bonfire to create enough smoke to bother them."

"Then it will have to be a full-frontal attack," Paris declared. "We will send in our best spearists first, who should eliminate many of them before we go hand to hand. Our losses should not be so great that way."

"They'll still be substantial," Vanez objected. "Spearists won't have much room to operate. They might take out the watchguards by the entrance, but after that…"

"What option do we have?" Arrow snapped. "Would you rather we went down with a white flag and discussed peace terms?"

"Don't bellow at me in that tone!" Vanez shouted. "I'm as anxious to get at them as any vampire here. But it will be a pyrrhic victory if we fight one-on-one."

Paris sighed. "If that is the only victory on offer, we must accept it."

In the short silence which followed, I asked Seba what a pyrrhic victory was. "That is when the price of winning is too high," he whispered. "If we defeat the vampaneze, but lose sixty or seventy of our own troops doing so, it will be a worthless victory. The first rule of warfare is never to weaken yourself irreparably whilst destroying your enemies."

"There *is* one alternative," Paris said hesitantly. "We could run them off. If we made a lot of noise approaching, I am sure they would scatter rather than face us. The vampaneze are not cowards, but nor are they fools. They will not stand and fight a battle they are sure to lose."

Angry mutters greeted this suggestion. Most vampires believed that would be dishonourable. The consensus was that they'd rather confront the vampaneze.

"It is not the most honourable of tactics," Paris shouted over the heated whispers. "But we could pursue and fight them on the outside. Many would escape, but we would capture and kill enough of them to teach them a harsh lesson."

"Paris has a point," Mika said, and the muttering ceased. "I don't like it, but if it's a choice between letting most go or sacrificing forty or fifty of our own…"

Heads began nodding, slowly, unhappily. Paris asked Arrow what he thought of the suggestion. "I think it stinks," he snarled. "The vampaneze aren't bound by our laws — they can flit once outside. We'd catch virtually none of them." Flitting was the super-quick speed vampires and vampaneze could run at. By tradition, vampires were not allowed to flit on the way to and from Vampire Mountain.

"Were I a General," Arrow went on, "I'd object most vehemently to letting them go. I'd rather fight and die than concede ground to the enemy in such a meek fashion." He sighed miserably. "But, as a Prince, I must put the welfare of our people before the stirrings of my heart. Unless somebody can think of a plan to distract the vampaneze and clear the way for an attack, I will agree to running them off."

When nobody spoke up, the Princes called their leading Generals forward and discussed the best way to drive off the vampaneze and where they should place their men on the outside. An air of disappointment hung heavily over the Hall and most vampires stood or sat with their heads bowed, disgusted.

"They don't like this," I whispered to Seba.

"Nor do I," he replied, "but pride must be checked in the face of such aggressive odds. We could not allow our men to perish in horrifying numbers, all for the sake of honour. Reason must be obeyed, no matter how galling it might be."

I was as upset as the rest of the vampires. I wanted revenge for Gavner Purl. There was no satisfaction in letting the vampaneze wriggle off the hook. I'd spoilt their plans to invade the Hall of Princes, but that wasn't enough. I could imagine the smirk on Kurda's face when he learnt of our diplomatic decision.

As I stood, pouting, a tiny insect flew into Madam Octa's cage and got trapped in a small web she'd spun in a corner. The spider reacted swiftly and advanced on the struggling captive, disposing of it presently. I watched, mildly interested, then stiffened as a crazy thought struck me.

Gazing at the feeding spider, I let my brain whirl wildly, and the plan formed within a matter of seconds. It was simple yet effective — the very best sort.

Standing on my tip-toes, I cleared my throat three times before I managed to attract Mr Crepsley's attention. "Yes, Darren?" he asked wearily.

"Excuse me," I called, "but I think I know how to distract the vampaneze."

All conversation ceased and every pair of eyes settled on me. I stepped forward unbidden, and spoke nervously. As I outlined my proposals, the vampires started to smile. By the time I finished, most were laughing outright and chortling gleefully at the wicked, cunning scheme.

Voting was brief and unanimous. My plan was put to the vampires and, as one, they roared their approval. Without any further ado, the Princes and Generals fell to organizing their attack forces, while Seba, Mr Crepsley and me slipped away to gather together our own army of troops and prepare for the first stage of what, in a war film, would probably have been called *Operation Arachnid!*

CHAPTER FIFTEEN

OUR FIRST stop was the cave of Ba'Halen's spiders, where Seba had taken me when I was suffering from burns after my Trial in the Hall of Flames. The quartermaster went in by himself, carrying Madam Octa in the palm of his left hand. He was grim-looking and empty handed when he emerged, eyes half-closed.

"Did it work?" I asked. "Were you able—"

He shushed me with a quick wave of a hand. Closing his eyes completely, he concentrated fiercely. Moments later, Madam Octa crept out of the cave, followed by a spider with light grey spots on its back. I recognized that spider — I'd seen it mooning after Madam Octa before.

Behind the grey-spotted spider came several more of the mildly poisonous mountain spiders. Others followed, and soon a thick stream of spiders was flowing out of the cave and gathering around us. Seba was directing them, communicating mentally with the wild, eight-legged predators.

"I am going to transfer control now," he told Mr Crepsley and me when all the spiders were in place. "Larten, take the spiders to my right. Darren, those to my left."

We nodded and faced the spiders. Mr Crepsley was able to communicate without the use of aids, as Seba was, but I needed my familiar flute to focus my thoughts and transmit them. Raising it to my lips, I blew a few practice notes. It was awkward, because of my bent right thumb – which still hadn't straightened out – but I quickly learnt to compensate for the damaged digit. Then I stood awaiting Seba's word.

"Now," he said softly.

Gently, I played and sent a repeated mental message to the spiders. "Stay where you are," I told them. "Hold, my beauties, hold."

The body of spiders swayed uncertainly when Seba stopped transmitting his thoughts, before fixing on mine and Mr Crepsley's. After a few confused seconds they clicked into sync with our brainwaves and resumed their solid shape.

"Excellent," Seba beamed, stepping forward, careful not to squash any of the spiders. "I will leave you with them and go find others. Escort these to the meeting point and wait for me. If any start to drift away, send Madam Octa to rally them — they will obey her."

We let Seba exit, then turned towards one another. "You need not play the flute continuously," Mr Crepsley advised. "A few whistles and commands once we get moving should be enough. They will fall into place behind us and advance naturally. Save the flute for stragglers or those of a rebellious nature."

"Should we lead or take the rear?" I asked, lowering my flute to wet my lips.

"Lead," Mr Crepsley said. "But keep an eye on them and be prepared to drop back if need be, ideally without interrupting the march of the others."

"I'll try," I said, then faced front and played.

Off I set, Mr Crepsley beside me, the spiders scuttling along behind. When we reached the larger tunnels, we moved further apart to form two separate files.

It wasn't as difficult to command the spiders as I'd feared. A few gave me problems – they fought with others or tried to edge away – but a quick intervention on the part of Madam Octa was enough to knock them back into shape. She was revelling in her role and even started patrolling the ranks of her own accord, without prompting. She'd have made a great General if she'd been a vampire!

Finally, we pulled into the large cave we'd established as our base. We arranged the spiders around us in a circle, then sat in the middle of them and waited for Seba.

He was leading an army of spiders almost half as large again as ours when he arrived. "Where'd you get them all?" I asked, as they encircled those already in the cave.

"The mountain is full of spiders," he said. "One simply needs to know where to look." He sat beside us and smiled. "Having said that, I have never in my life seen such a concentration in one place at one time. It is enough to unnerve even a hardened handler such as myself!"

"I feel that way too," Mr Crepsley agreed, then laughed. "If they have such an effect on *us*, what sort of terror will they provoke in the unsuspecting vampaneze?"

"That is what we shall shortly discover," Seba chuckled.

While we waited to be contacted by the Princes, Mr Crepsley took my flute from me and fiddled with it. When he handed it back, it no longer worked, and so couldn't alert the vampaneze. The fact that it had been muted didn't matter — the music itself made no difference to the spiders. I only used the flute out of habit, after years of performing with Madam Octa at the Cirque Du Freak.

After a long, uncomfortable wait, we spotted a platoon of vampires slipping by. Arrow shortly appeared and advanced to the edge of the eight-legged sea. He gazed uneasily around at the spiders and came no closer. He was gripping two heavy, sharp-tipped boomerangs, and had three more strapped to his waist. The boomerang was his weapon of choice. "We're ready," he whispered. "The vampaneze haven't left their cave. Our troops are in position. The sun shines brightly outside. It is time."

We nodded obediently and got to our feet.

"You know what to do?" Mr Crepsley asked me.

"I take my spiders out," I responded. "I get close to the mouth of the tunnel, taking care not to be seen. You and Seba will guide your spiders forward, using the tiny cracks and holes in the walls and roof of the cave. You'll hold them there until I make the first move. I'll send my spiders against the guards in the tunnel opening. When you hear the commotion, you'll order yours in — then the fun begins!"

"Allow us a decent amount of time to position our spiders," Seba instructed me. "They will be difficult to manoeuvre, since we cannot see where they are going. It will be a slow, painstaking process."

"I'm in no hurry," I said. "Will three hours be enough?"

"That should be plenty," Seba said, and Mr Crepsley agreed.

We wished each other luck, shook hands, then I summoned my troops — the smallest of the three clusters of spiders, since they'd have the least to do — and set off for the outside.

The sun shone wanly in a mostly cloudless sky, which was helpful — the vampaneze guards would keep well back from the mouth of the tunnel to avoid the deadly rays of light.

I emerged about forty metres up from the tunnel. I held my position until all my spiders were out in the open around me, then urged them forwards, slowly and carefully. We crept down the mountain until we were ten metres shy of the tunnel, sheltered by a large rock which jutted out of the mountain face, providing perfect cover. This was as close to the tunnel as I dared get.

Once in place, I lay down and watched the sun cross the sky. I'd been chosen for the external leg of the operation partly because it provided fewer problems than the pair working within the mountain would have to deal with, but also because I was immune to the sun. It was vital that we attack by day — the vampaneze would be loath to leave their sanctuary and face the sun — but the vampires would have been hampered by the solar giant as much as their foes. Only I could move about outside as freely as I pleased.

When slightly more than three hours had passed, I blew mutely on my flute and ordered the spiders to spread out wide, before advancing. Only the spiders moved forward — I stayed where I was, hidden by the rock. The spiders formed a ring around the mouth of the tunnel. From the outside they looked harmless, but when they entered the cave, they'd assume a different dimension — they'd look more numerous, and a lot more threatening. Cramped spaces have a way of magnifying one's fears. The vampaneze within would hopefully feel they were under siege, and panic accordingly.

A couple of minutes to make sure the ranks were orderly. Then I gave the signal to enter. They slipped in silently, covering not just the floor of the tunnel, but also the walls and roof. If everything went as planned, the vampaneze would think the tunnel was coming alive with spiders.

I was supposed to stay where I was, out of the way, but the temptation to sneak forward and observe the unfolding of my plan proved too great to resist. Lying flat on the rough face of the mountain, I slid down to the top of the tunnel and listened for the sounds of chaos within.

I could hear the heavy breathing of vampaneze, further back from the entrance than I'd expected. For a while, that was all I could hear, calm and regular. I was starting to wonder if maybe the spiders had slipped through cracks and deserted back to their natural habitat. Then one of the vampaneze grunted: "Hey! Is it my imagination, or are the walls moving?"

His colleagues laughed. "Don't be stu—" one began, then stopped. "What in the name of the gods…?" I heard him gasp.

"What's happening?" somebody shouted, alarmed. "What are they?"

"They look like spiders," one of his less-agitated comrades answered.

"There's millions of them!" a vampaneze whimpered.

"Are they poisonous?" another asked.

"Of course not," the unafraid vampaneze snorted. "They're just ordinary mountain spiders. They can't do any—"

Blowing hard on my flute, I sent the order to the spiders: "*Now!*"

Inside the tunnel, screams erupted.

"They're dropping!" someone howled.

"They're all over me! Get them off! Get them off! Get them—"

"Calm down!" the level-headed vampaneze yelled. "Just brush them off and — *ahhhhh!*" he screamed, as the spiders seized hold and sank their fangs in.

Individually, the spiders were harmless — their bites were only mildly irritating. But the simultaneous bites of hundreds of them… That was a different matter entirely!

As the vampaneze thrashed around the tunnel, slapping

and stamping at the spiders, screaming with pain and fear, I heard others advance from within the cave to see what was wrong. Darting into the tunnel, I crouched down low and ordered the spiders to surge on ahead. As they obeyed, panicking the newcomers and forcing them backwards, the cave behind echoed with the screams and writhing of the massed vampaneze, as Mr Crepsley and Seba's spiders slipped from the walls and roof and worked their fearsome charms.

The battle had truly begun.

CHAPTER SIXTEEN

I WASN'T supposed to join in the fighting, but the furore of the terrifed vampaneze excited me, and before I knew what I was doing, I'd sneaked forward to observe what was happening within the cave.

It was incredible to watch. Spiders covered the floor and walls and — most vitally — the rioting vampaneze. The purple-faced wretches were leaping around like cartoon figures, yelling and screeching, desperately trying to repel the attack. Some used swords and spears, which were no use against the tiny invaders, who easily ducked the wild blows and darted forward to sink their fangs into exposed patches of flesh. The vampaneze with the swords and spears were doing almost as much damage as the spiders. Lashing out blindly, they connected with their colleagues, wounding several, even killing a few.

Some of the wiser vampaneze were struggling to establish control, roaring at the others to form ranks against the spiders. But the pandemonium dwarfed their efforts. They were ignored, sometimes knocked out of the way when they tried to intervene.

In the midst of the panic, Streak and the two younger wolves bounded into the cave from the far entrance, yapping, howling and snarling as loudly as possible. I don't think anybody had invited the wolves along — they simply came of their own accord, eager to be part of the rout!

When the vampaneze saw the wolves coming, several turned and bolted for the exit. They'd had enough — even the lethal sunlight seemed a welcome prospect in comparison to this! I thought about standing aside and letting them pass, but the battle lust was strong in me and adrenaline was pumping through every cell of my body. I wanted to keep them here if I could, so that they might suffer along with the rest of their despicable tribe. At the time, revenge was all I could focus on. It was all that seemed to matter.

Looking around, I spotted a spear which one of the tunnel guards had dropped during the course of their hasty retreat. Picking it up, I wedged the end against a crack in the floor, then pointed the tip at the charging vampaneze. The lead vampaneze saw me and tried to veer out of the way of the spear, but those behind pushed him on unwillingly. Running on to the spear, he impaled himself without any help from me.

Standing, I roughly shoved the vampaneze off the spear, then bellowed at those behind him. They must have thought the way was blocked by a horde of savage vampires, because they immediately about-faced and retreated. I laughed triumphantly and started after them, meaning to add a few more scalps to my collection. Then I happened to glance at the vampaneze who'd run on to my spear, and came to a sickened halt.

He was young, his face only a light shade of purple. He was crying and making soft, whimpering noises. Unable to stop myself, I crouched beside him. "It ... hurts!" he gasped, clutching at the deep, wide hole in his belly. His hands were red and I knew his cause was hopeless.

"It's OK," I lied. "It's only a flesh wound. You'll be up on your—" Before I could say any more, he coughed. Blood pumped out of his mouth, a huge torrent of it. His eyes widened, then closed. He groaned softly, fell back, shuddered, then died.

I'd killed him.

The thought shook me to my very core. I'd never killed before. Even though I'd been looking forward to punishing the vampaneze for what they did to Gavner, it was only now that I considered the consequences of my actions. This vampaneze — this person — was dead. I had taken his life and could never restore it.

Maybe he deserved death. He might have been rotten to the core and in dire need of killing. Then again, maybe he'd been an ordinary guy, like me or any of the vampires, only here because he'd been following orders. Either way, deserving or not, who was I to decide? I didn't have the right to pass judgement on others and kill them. Yet I'd done it. Excited by the fear of the vampaneze, intent on revenge, letting my heart rule my head, I'd raised a weapon against this man and killed him.

I hated myself for what I'd done. I wanted to turn tail and run, get far away and pretend this never happened. I felt cheap, dirty, nasty. I tried consoling myself with the thought that I'd done the right thing, but how did one separate right from wrong where killing was concerned? I'm sure Kurda thought *he* was doing right when he stabbed Gavner. The vampaneze thought *they* were doing right when they drained people they fed upon. However I looked at it, I had the awful feeling that I was now no better than any other killer, one of a vicious, terrible, inhuman breed.

Only my sense of duty held me in place. I knew that vampires would be attacking any moment. It was my job to keep the spiders active until they did, so that the vampaneze couldn't regroup and meet the assault head on. If I deserted my post, vampires would perish in great numbers as well as the vampaneze. I had to concentrate on the bigger picture, regardless of how I felt inside.

Sticking my flute back between my lips, I played and urged the spiders to swarm over the vampaneze. The scene looked so different in light of the life I'd taken. I no longer enjoyed watching the vampaneze shriek and lash out blindly, or saw them as evil villains on the receiving end of their just desserts. Instead I saw warriors, terrified and humiliated, stranded far from their homes and allies, about to be ruthlessly slaughtered.

At the height of the hysteria, the vampires attacked, led by a bellowing Arrow, who tossed his sharp-edged boomerangs at the vampaneze, one after the other, drawing blood with each. Spearists were beside and behind him, and their hurled weapons caused much damage and claimed many lives.

As vampires poured into the cave, the spiders withdrew, urged to retreat by the unseen Mr Crepsley and Seba. I held my spiders in place a while longer, keeping the panic alive at this end of the cave.

Within less than a minute, the vampires had stormed the whole of the cave, those with swords and knives replacing the first wave of spearists. They hadn't come in great numbers — if too many had poured into the narrow chamber, they'd have got in each other's way — but the thirty who'd entered appeared far more in comparison with the stricken vampaneze. It seemed as though there were five vampires to every one of their foes.

Arrow was in the thick of the action, leading by example, as mercilessly efficient with his swords as he'd been with his boomerangs. Vanez Blane stood close by the Prince, knives flashing, backing him up. Alarmed as they were by the spiders and wolves, the vampaneze quickly realized where the real threat lay, and hurriedly backed away from the clinically murderous pair.

Arra Sails was also part of the initial assault. She was in her element, attacking the vampaneze with a short sword in one hand, a spiked chain in the other, laughing brutally as they fell beneath her. I'd have cheered her display a few minutes earlier, but now felt only dismay at the sheer joy she and the other vampires were taking in the destruction.

"This isn't right," I muttered to myself. Killing the vampaneze was one thing – it had to be done – but relishing their downfall was wrong. There was something deeply unsettling about seeing the vampires extract so much ghoulish satisfaction from the massacre.

Confused as I was, I decided I'd best wade in and lend a hand. The sooner we made an end of the vampaneze, the sooner I could turn my back on the horror. Taking a sharp dagger from the man I'd killed, I called off my spiders, then threw my flute away and stepped forward to join the press of battling vampires and vampaneze.

I kept to the edges of the fighting, jabbing at the feet or legs of vampaneze, distracting them, making it easier for the vampires they were facing to disarm and kill them. I took no pleasure from the success of my endeavours, only forged ahead, determined to help bring things to a quick conclusion.

I spotted Mr Crepsley and Seba Nile entering the cave, their red robes billowing behind them, eager to be part of the bloodshed. I didn't hold their eagerness to kill against them. I didn't hold it against any of the vampires. I just thought it was misplaced and unseemly.

The fighting intensified shortly after Mr Crepsley and Seba joined the fray. Only the toughest and most composed of the vampaneze had survived the first period of madness, and now they battled grimly to the finish, making their stands, some alone, some in pairs, taking as many vampires to the grave with them as they could.

I saw the first vampire casualties slump to the ground, bellies sliced open or heads bashed in, bleeding and sobbing, crying out loud with pain. On the floor, dying, covered in blood, they looked no different to the vampaneze.

As the front-runners of the second vampire wave trickled into the cave, Vanez slapped Arrow's back and told him to leave. "*Leave?*" the Prince snorted. "It's just getting interesting!"

"You've got to go," Vanez roared, dragging Arrow away from the fighting. "It's Mika's turn to blood his blade. Go back to the Hall of Princes and relieve Paris, as you promised. You've had your fair share of the killing. Don't be greedy."

Arrow left reluctantly. On his way, he passed Mika, and the two clapped each other on the back, as though one was a substitute replacing the other in a game of football.

"Not pleasant, is it?" Vanez grunted, pulling up beside me. He was sweating freely and paused to dry his hands on his tunic as the fighting raged around us.

"It's horrible," I muttered, gripping my knife before me like a cross.

"You shouldn't be here," Vanez said. "Larten wouldn't approve if he knew."

"I'm not doing it for fun," I told him.

Looking deep into my eyes, Vanez sighed. "So I see. You learn quickly, Darren."

"What do you mean?" I asked.

He gestured at the warring, whooping vampires. "They think this is great sport," he laughed bleakly. "They forget that the vampaneze were once our brothers, that by destroying them, we destroy a part of ourselves. Most vampires never realize how pointless and savage war truly is. You were smart enough to see the truth. Don't ever forget it."

A dying vampaneze stumbled towards us. His eyes had been cut out and he was moaning pitifully. Vanez caught him, lowered him to the floor, and finished him off quickly and mercifully. When he stood, his face was grim. "But, painful as war is," he said, "sometimes it can't be avoided. We didn't seek this confrontation. Remember that later, and don't hold our aggression against us. We were forced into this."

"I know," I sighed. "I just wish there'd been some other way to punish the vampaneze, short of tearing them to pieces."

"You should leave," Vanez suggested. "This is where the truly dirty work begins. Return to the Halls and drink yourself senseless."

"I might do that," I agreed and turned away, leaving Vanez and the others to round up the final stubborn vampaneze. As I was departing, I spotted a familiar face among the crowd — a vampaneze with a dark red birthmark on his left cheek. It took me a moment to recall his name — *Glalda*, the one who'd spoken with Kurda in the tunnel when Gavner was killed. He'd wanted to kill me as well as Gavner. Hatred flared in my chest, and I had to resist the urge to dart back into the action.

Edging clear of the fighting, I would have slipped away, except a crowd of vampires was blocking my path. They'd surrounded a wounded vampaneze and were taunting him before they closed in for the kill. Disgusted by their antics, I looked for another way out. As I was doing that, Arra Sails stepped forward to meet the challenge of the vampaneze called Glalda. Two vampires lay dead at his feet, but Arra pushed on regardless.

"Prepare to die, worm!" she yelled, flicking at him with her chain.

Glalda brushed aside the length of chain and laughed. "So the vampires send women to do their fighting now!" he sneered.

"Women are all the vampaneze are fit to face," Arra retorted. "You are not worthy of facing men and dying with honour. Imagine the disgrace when word spreads that you perished at the hands of a woman!"

"That *would* be a disgrace," Glalda agreed, lunging with his sword. "But it won't happen!"

The two ceased trading words and started trading blows. I was surprised they'd exchanged as much banter as they had — most of the combatants were too concerned with the business of trying to stay alive to stand about like movie stars and swap verbal insults. Arra and the vampaneze circled each other warily, lashing out with their weapons, probing for weak points. Glalda might have been surprised to come face to face with a woman, but he treated her with wary respect. Arra, for her part, was more reckless. She'd mown down several of the panic-stricken vampaneze early in the encounter and had come to believe that all would fall as easily as her initial victims had. She left clumsy defensive gaps and took perilous, needless risks.

I wanted to escape the confines of the cave and put the fighting behind me, but I couldn't bring myself to leave until I'd seen Arra's encounter through to the end. She'd been a good friend and had come looking for me when I went missing. I didn't want to slip away until I knew she was safe.

Mr Crepsley also stopped to observe Arra's battle. He was quite a distance away, separated from her by a pack of scuffling vampires and vampaneze. "Arra!" he yelled. "Do you need help?"

"Not I!" she laughed, driving her chain at the face of the vampaneze. "I'll finish this fool off before you can say—"

Whatever boast she was about to make was cut short. Ducking out of the way of her chain, Glalda brushed her defensive stroke aside, drove the tip of his sword deep into her belly, and twisted cruelly. Arra cried out with anguish and fell.

"Now, *woman*," the vampaneze sneered, straddling her and raising his sword. "Watch closely — I'll show you how we dispose of your kind!" Aiming the tip of his sword at her eyes, he brought it down slowly. Arra could do nothing but stare up at him hatefully and wait to die.

CHAPTER SEVENTEEN

I COULDN'T stand by and let Glalda kill Arra. Darting forward, I threw myself against the vampaneze and knocked him off-balance. He swore, fell heavily, and turned to deal with me. But I was quicker with my light dagger than he was with his heavy sword. Diving on top of him, I stuck it into his chest and by luck pierced his heart.

This vampaneze didn't die quietly like the first one I'd killed. He shook and gibbered madly, then rolled over, dragging me with him. He tried clambering to his feet. It was hopeless — it must have been clear to him that he was going to die — but he made the effort anyway.

When his legs gave out, he collapsed on top of me, almost spearing me with the handle of my own dagger. I gasped for breath beneath him as he convulsed and moaned, then managed to heave him off and slide out. As I got to my knees, I saw his face relax and the life leave his body. I paused and studied him. His expression was much like Gavner's had been — surprised ... annoyed ... afraid.

Gently, I closed the dead warrior's eyelids, then made the death's touch sign by pressing my middle fingers to my forehead and eyes, and spreading my thumb and little finger wide. "Even in death, may you be triumphant," I whispered.

Then I went to check on Arra. She was in a bad way. She tried getting up but I held her down and made her press her hands over the wound in her belly to stop the flow of blood.

"Will I ... die?" Arra gasped, her lips thin with pain.

"Of course not," I said, only for her to grab my hands and glare at me.

"*Will I die?*" she barked.

"I don't know," I answered honestly this time. "Maybe."

She sighed and lay back. "At least I will not die unavenged. You fight well, Darren Shan. You are a true vampire."

"Thanks," I said hollowly.

Mr Crepsley reached us and examined Arra worriedly. He rubbed spit around the edges of the cut, to stop the bleeding, but his efforts didn't make much of a difference. "Does it hurt?" he asked.

"Talk about asking ... stupid questions!" she gurgled.

"You always said I had a knack for putting my foot in my mouth," he smiled, tenderly wiping blood away from the corners of her lips.

"I'd ask you to kiss me," she said, "only I'm not ... in any shape ... for it."

"There'll be plenty of time for kissing later," he vowed.

"Maybe," Arra sighed. "Maybe."

While Mr Crepsley tended to Arra, I sat back and watched numbly as the battle drew to its bloody conclusion. No more than six or seven vampaneze were left on their feet, and each was encircled by several vampires. They should have surrendered, but I knew they wouldn't. Vampires and vampaneze only knew how to win and how to die. For the proud legions of the undead, there was no in-between.

As I watched, two vampaneze who'd been fighting back to back made a break for the exit tunnel. A pack of vampires moved to intercept them, Vanez Blane among them. They prevented the break-out, but one of the vampaneze threw his dagger in spiteful desperation before the vampires captured and killed him. It scorched through the air like a guided missile at its helpless target — *Vanez!*

The games master whipped his head backwards and almost avoided the dagger, but it was too swift, and the tip of the blade snagged on his one good eye. Blood spurted, Vanez screamed and covered his face with his hands, and Seba Nile hurried forward to lead him away to safety.

By the way he'd screamed, I knew in my gut that if Vanez survived, he would never again see the light of the moon or the twinkle of the stars. The vampaneze had finished the job which a lion had started. Vanez was now completely blind.

Glancing around miserably, I saw Streak chewing on the head of a still living vampaneze. One of the younger wolves was helping him. I searched for the other hot-blooded wolf and found it lying dead by a wall, belly ripped open, fangs bared in a vicious death-snarl.

Paris Skyle arrived and took Mika's place. The ancient Prince wielded a thick staff, both ends of which had been sharpened to stake-like points. He showed less taste for the fight than his younger brethren, but still fell in with the bloodshed and latched on to one of the last vampaneze. He made no calls for peace, nor did he tell his men to take these final hardy fighters alive. Perhaps it was best that he didn't. Those vampaneze who'd been taken intact – there were several – had only the Hall of Death to look forward to, where they'd be impaled on stakes in front of a crowd of jeering vampires. Given the choice, I was sure they'd rather die on their feet, with honour.

Finally, painfully, the fighting drew to a close. The last vampaneze was dispatched – he roared as he died, "May the demons take you all!" – and the clearing away of the bodies began. The vampires acted with mechanical efficiency. Generals who'd been swinging axes and swords mere moments before, now picked up wounded vampires and led them away to be nursed, chuckling as they did so, discussing the battle and making light of the injured party's wounds. Others collected the dead, first the fallen vampires, then the vampaneze. They made mounds of the bodies, which were collected by the ghoulish Guardians of the Blood (they must have been waiting outside the cave during the battle), who carried them away to be readied for cremation.

It was all done in good spirits. It didn't bother the Generals that we'd lost nine or ten of our own (the actual death toll, by the time those with fatal injuries succumbed, was twelve). The battle had been won, the vampaneze had been destroyed, and the mountain was secure. They thought they'd come out of 'the scrap' rather well.

A stretcher had to be brought for Arra — there was no way she could walk. She'd grown quieter while waiting, and stared at the roof of the cave as though studying a painting. "Darren," she whispered.

"Yes?"

"Do you remember … when I beat you … on the bars?"

"Of course," I smiled.

"You put up … a good fight."

"Not good enough," I chuckled weakly.

Coughing, she faced Mr Crepsley. "Don't let them kill him, Larten!" she hissed. "I was one of those … who insisted on his … death when he failed … the Trials. But tell them I said he should … be spared. He's a … worthy vampire. He's earned a … reprieve. *Tell* them!"

"You can tell them yourself," Mr Crepsley said, tears dripping down his cheeks, a display of emotion I never thought I'd see. "You will recover. I will take you to the Hall of Princes. *You* can speak up for him."

"Maybe," Arra sighed. "But if I don't … you'll do it for me? You'll tell them … what I said? You'll protect him?"

Mr Crepsley nodded wordlessly.

The stretcher arrived and Arra was loaded on to it by two

vampires. Mr Crepsley walked along beside her, holding her hand, trying to comfort her. She made a death's touch sign at me with her free hand as she left, then laughed – blood sprayed from her lips – and winked.

Later that day, shortly before the sun sank in the wintry sky, despite the best efforts of the medics, Arra Sails closed her eyes, made her peace with the gods of the vampires, breathed her last ... and died.

CHAPTER EIGHTEEN

HOURS LATER, when word reached me of Arra's death, I returned to the cave to try and make sense of it all inside my head. The vampires had departed. The dead bodies had been cleared away by the morbid Guardians of the Blood. Even the many trampled spiders had been removed. Only the blood remained, great ugly pools of it, seeping through the cracks in the floor, drying on the walls, dripping from the roof.

I scratched my cheeks — caked in dust, dried blood and tears — and studied the random patterns of blood on the floor and walls as it congealed, thinking back over the fighting and the lives I'd taken. As I listened to the echoes of the dripping blood, I found myself reliving the screams of the vampaneze and vampires, the moans of the dying, Seba leading the blind Vanez away, the relish with which the battle had been fought, Glalda's expression when I killed him, Arra and the way she'd winked at me.

"Mind if I join you?" someone asked.

Glancing up, I saw it was the aged quartermaster of Vampire Mountain, Seba Nile, limping badly from a wound he'd sustained during the fighting. "Be my guest," I said hollowly, and he sat down beside me.

For a few minutes we stared around the crimson-splashed cave in silence. Finally, I asked Seba if he'd heard about Arra's death.

"Yes," he said softly. He laid a hand on my knee. "You must not mourn too grievously for her, Darren. She died proudly, as she would have wished."

"She died stupidly!" I snapped.

"You should not say that," Seba admonished me gently.

"Why not?" I shouted. "It's the truth! This was a stupid fight, fought by stupid people."

"Arra did not think so," Seba said. "She gave her life for this 'stupid fight'. Others gave theirs too."

"That's what makes it stupid," I groaned. "We could have driven them off. We didn't have to come down here and cut them to pieces."

"If I remember correctly," Seba said, "it was *your* novel idea regarding the spiders which paved the way for our attack."

"Thanks for reminding me," I said bitterly, and lapsed back into silence.

"You must not take it to heart," Seba said. "Fighting is our way. It is how we judge ourselves. To the uninitiated this might look like a barbaric bloodbath, but our cause was just.

The vampaneze were plotting our downfall. It was us or them. You know that better than anybody — you were there when they killed Gavner Purl."

"I know," I sighed. "I'm not saying they didn't deserve it. But *why* were they here? *Why* did they invade?"

Seba shrugged. "Doubtless we will unearth the truth once we have had a chance to interrogate the survivors."

"You mean *torture*," I snorted.

"If that is what you want to call it," he replied bleakly.

"OK," I said. "We'll torture them and maybe learn that they attacked just for the hell of it, to knock us out of shape and take over the mountain. Everything will be fine then. We can walk around proudly and slap ourselves on the back.

"But what if that *wasn't* why they attacked?" I pressed. "What if there was a different reason?"

"Such as?" Seba asked.

"I don't know. I've no idea how the vampaneze think or why they do what they do. The point is, neither do *you* or the other vampires. This attack came as a surprise to everyone, didn't it?"

"It was unexpected," Seba agreed. "The vampaneze have never attacked us this aggressively before. Even when they split from us, they cared only about establishing their own society, not undermining ours."

"So why did they do it?" I asked again. "Do you know?"

"No," Seba said.

"There!" I exclaimed. "You don't know, I don't know, the Princes don't know." I got to my knees and locked eyes with him.

"Don't you think somebody should have *asked*? We stormed down here and tore them apart, and not once did any of us stop to question their motives. We reacted like wild animals."

"There was no time for questions," Seba insisted, but I could tell he was troubled by my words.

"Maybe there wasn't," I said. "Not *now*. But what about six months ago? A year? Ten years? A hundred? Kurda was the only one who contacted the vampaneze and tried to understand them. Why didn't others help him? Why weren't attempts made to befriend them, to prevent something like this from ever happening?"

"You are commending Kurda Smahlt?" Seba asked distastefully.

"No. Kurda betrayed us. There's no defending what he did. What I'm saying is — if *we'd* made the effort to get to know the vampaneze, perhaps there would have been no need for *him* to betray us. Maybe we somehow forced his hand."

"Your way of thinking puzzles me," Seba said. "You are more human than vampire, I suppose. In time you will learn to see things our way and—"

"No!" I shouted, jumping up. "I don't want to see things your way. *Your* way is the *wrong* way. I admire the strength, honesty and loyalty of the vampires, and want to fit in as one. But not if it means abandoning myself to stupidity, not if it means turning a blind eye to wisdom and common sense, not if it means enduring bloody messes like this just because my leaders are too proud to sit down with the vampaneze and thrash out their differences."

"It might have been impossible to 'thrash out their differences'," Seba noted.

"But the effort should have been made. The Princes should have *tried*."

Seba shook his head wearily. "Perhaps you are right. I am old and stuck in the past. I remember when vampires had no choices, when it was kill or be killed, fight or perish. From where I stand, today's battle was savage, but no worse than a hundred others I have witnessed over the course of my centuries.

"Having said that, I must admit that the world has changed. Perhaps it is time for us to change too." He smiled. "But who will lead us out of the darkness of the past? Kurda was the face of our future. He, perhaps, could have altered our ways of thinking and living. Now that he has shamed himself, who will dare speak up for the new world and its ways?"

"I don't know," I said. "But somebody should. If they don't, nothing will change, and today's debacle will be repeated, over and over, until the vampires wipe the vampaneze out, or vice versa."

"Heavy thoughts," Seba sighed, then stood and massaged his injured left thigh. "However, I did not come to discuss the future. We have a more immediate and less troubling decision to make."

"What do you mean?" I asked.

He pointed to the floor and I realized that Madam Octa and the spider with light grey spots on his back were squatting behind us. "Many of our eight-legged friends were crushed in the fighting," Seba said. "These were among the survivors. They could have slipped away with the rest, but remained, as though awaiting further orders."

"Do you think that guy's sweet on her?" I asked, pointing to the grey-spotted spider, momentarily forgetting my darker concerns.

"Most certainly," Seba grinned. "I do not think spiders know love as we do. But he remained by her side throughout the fighting, and did not leave when she decided to stay. I think they wish to couple."

I smiled at the absurd notion of Madam Octa walking down an aisle in a tiny white dress, Mr Crepsley waiting at the end to give her away. "You think I should put him in her cage?" I asked.

"Actually, I was thinking along the lines of freeing her, so that she could make her home with him. I am opposed to the captivity of wild creatures, except where strictly necessary."

"You want me to let her go?" I chewed my lower lip and thought it over. "What if she bites someone?"

"I do not think she will," he said. "With all the mountain tunnels to pick from, it is unlikely that she will choose to set up home where people might intrude."

"What about offspring? If she breeds, she could give rise to an army of poisonous spiders."

"I doubt it," Seba smiled. "Even if she could breed with Ba'Halen's spiders, her offspring would probably be no more poisonous than their fathers."

I considered it a while longer. Seba had suggested letting Madam Octa go before, and I had disagreed. But after all she'd been through, it seemed fitting to release her now. "OK," I said. "You've convinced me."

"You do not want to check with Larten?" Seba asked.

"I think he's got bigger things to worry about," I said, referring to Arra.

"Very well," Seba agreed. "Do you want to tell her the good news, or shall I?"

"I'll do it," I said. "Wait a minute — I'll fetch my flute."

Finding the flute where I'd dropped it, I hurried back, pressed it between my lips, blew soundlessly and sent the thought to Madam Octa: "Go. You're free. Leave."

The spider hesitated, then crawled away, the grey-spotted mountain spider in close attendance. Seba and me watched them until they slipped from sight through a crack in the wall. I'd never have fallen in with Mr Crepsley if not for Madam Octa. She'd played a key part in deciding my ultimate destiny. Though I'd never liked the spider since she bit my best friend, Steve Leopard, now that she'd slid out of my life forever, I felt strangely lonely, as though I'd lost a dear companion.

Shrugging off my peculiar mood, I laid my flute down — I wouldn't be needing it any longer — and told Seba I'd like to return to the Halls. Side by side, silent as a pair of ghosts, we turned our backs on the scene of the battle and departed, leaving the pools of blood to settle and thicken as they may.

CHAPTER NINETEEN

U̲p̲o̲n̲ ̲r̲e̲a̲c̲h̲i̲n̲g̲ my cell I fell into my hammock, fully clothed, still stained with the blood of the cave. After sleeping rough for so long, it felt heavenly, and I drifted off to sleep almost immediately. I slept right through the night and it was early morning when I awoke. The tunnels were quiet outside. Harkat was awake and waiting for me to get up.

"I heard ... you killed ... two vampaneze," he said, handing me a bucket of cold water, a rough towel, and a batch of fresh clothes. I grunted in reply, undressed and washed off the dried, flaky blood.

"The vampires ... would not let me ... join in. I was glad ... in a way. I do not ... enjoy the thought ... of killing."

"There's little about it to enjoy," I agreed.

"Was it ... awful?" he asked.

"I don't want to talk about it," I said.

"Very well. I will not ... ask again."

I smiled gratefully, dunked my bald head in the bucket, shook off the water when I came up, scrubbed behind my ears, then asked about Mr Crepsley. The green light in Harkat's round eyes dimmed slightly. "He is still ... with Arra. He is refusing ... to leave her side. Seba is with ... him, trying to ... comfort him."

"Do you think I should go and have a word?"

Harkat shook his head. "Not at the ... moment. Later, he will ... need you. For now, let him ... grieve alone."

Drying myself off, I asked about Vanez and the other vampires, but Harkat wasn't able to tell me much. He knew at least ten vampires had died and more were seriously injured, but word of who they were hadn't reached him.

Once dressed, I accompanied Harkat to the Hall of Khledon Lurt for a quick meal, then we wandered back to our cell and stayed there for the rest of the day. We could have mixed with the vampires in the Hall – they'd cheered loudly when they saw me coming in – but I didn't want to sit listening to them spinning wild tales about the battle and how we'd obliterated the vampaneze.

Finally, towards dusk, Mr Crepsley staggered into our cell. His face was paler than usual as he slumped into my hammock, lowered his head into his hands and groaned. "You heard the news?" he whispered.

"Yes," I said. Then, after a brief pause, I added weakly, "Sorry."

"I thought she was going to make it," he sighed. "I knew the wound was fatal, but she lasted such a long time, defying the odds, I began to believe she would live."

"Has she..." I cleared my throat. "Has she been cremated yet?"

He shook his head. "Nobody has. The Guardians of the Blood are holding the bodies aside for at least two days and nights, as is our custom. The vampaneze, on the other hand..." He lowered his hands and his expression was genuinely frightening. "*They* are being fed to the flames at this very moment. We took them from the Guardians and cut them up into tiny pieces, so their souls cannot escape the pull of the Earth — they will never make it to Paradise. I hope they rot here for all eternity."

I sensed this wasn't the right time to speak of the disgust I'd felt in the cave, or my belief that vampires needed to learn compassion, so I held my tongue and nodded quickly.

"What about ... Kurda and the ... other survivors?" Harkat asked.

"They will be dealt with later," Mr Crepsley said, eyes narrowing. "They will be questioned first, then executed. I will be there when they are. Do either of you wish to attend?"

"The questioning, yes," I said. "I'm not so sure about the executions."

"I will give ... both a miss," Harkat said. "I don't feel ... it's my place ... to watch. This is a ... matter for vampires."

"As you wish," Mr Crepsley said. "What about the funerals? Do you want to bid farewell to Arra?"

"Of course," I answered quietly.

"I would like … that," Harkat agreed.

Mr Crepsley's expression had softened as he mentioned Arra's name. "She did not say much once she left the cave," he whispered, more to himself than to Harkat or me. "Speaking was painful. She conserved her energy. Fought hard. She clung on to life as long as she could.

"The medics expected her to die. Every time her breath caught in her throat, they rushed forward, eager to clear the way for other wounded vampires. But she hung on. They got so accustomed to the false alarms that when she did eventually die, they did not realize, and she lay there twenty minutes, serene in my embrace, smiling blankly at me."

His eyes had filled with tears. I handed him a scrap of cloth as they began to drip, but he didn't use it. "I couldn't hear her last words," he croaked. "She spoke too softly. I think she was making some kind of reference to the bars."

"Have you had any sleep?" I asked, beginning to cry myself.

"How can I sleep?" he sighed. "There are the inquisitions to prepare for. I will not miss Kurda's sentencing, not if I have to forsake sleep forever."

"Don't be silly," I gently chided him. "When does the questioning start?"

"Midnight," he sniffed.

"Then you've plenty of time. Grab some sleep. I'll wake you before it starts and we'll go together."

"Promise?" he asked.

"I wouldn't lie to you about something this important," I replied.

He nodded, rose, and started for his cell. In the doorway, he paused and looked back. "You did well in the cave, Darren. You fought bravely. I was proud of you."

"Thanks," I said, choking on my tears, which were flowing freely now.

"Proud," he muttered again, then faced the corridor and shuffled off to his cell, carrying himself like an old, tired, broken man.

Later that night, Kurda Smahlt's trial began.

The Hall of Princes was packed with furious, bitter vampires, as was the cave outside. Virtually every vampire in the mountain wanted to be there to jeer at the traitor, spit at him, and cheer his sentence when it was announced. I'd come with Mr Crepsley and Seba Nile. We were seated in the front row. We hadn't thought we'd get so close — we arrived late — but I soon discovered that I was the flavour of the moment. The vampires attributed much of their victory over the vampaneze to my endeavours. They roared with rough delight when they saw me, and ushered me forward, pushing Mr Crepsley and Seba along with me, insisting I take pride of place. I'd have rather hung back and viewed the proceedings from afar, but Mr Crepsley was anxious to get as close to the platform as possible, and I hadn't the heart to disappoint him, not after what he'd been through with Arra.

The conspirators were to be brought forward one by one, for separate questioning and sentencing. If they spoke openly, and the Princes were satisfied with their answers, they'd be taken straight to the Hall of Death and executed. If they refused to co-operate, they'd be led away and tortured in the hope that they'd spill their secrets (but vampaneze, like vampires, could deal with enormous amounts of pain, and were almost impossible to break).

The first to face trial was Kurda. The disgraced General was dragged forward in chains, past the ranks of hissing and screaming vampires. Some brushed his guards aside and struck or kicked him. A few pulled at his blond hair and yanked fistfuls of it out by the roots. By the time he reached the platform, he was in a sorry state, his white robes ripped, his body bruised and bleeding. Yet still he held his head high, reacting to none of the abuse.

The Princes were waiting for him on the platform, flanked by four guards with long, sharp spears. He was placed before the trio, each of whom spat contemptuously on him. Then he was led to one side and turned around to face the assembled vampires. At first I couldn't bring myself to look him in the eye, but when I finally worked up the courage, I found he was staring down at me, smiling sadly.

"Order!" Mika Ver Leth shouted, silencing the booing vampires. "We have a long night ahead of us. We want to settle each case as quickly and effortlessly as possible. I know feelings are running high, but anyone who interrupts our interrogation of Kurda Smahlt — or the others — will be ejected immediately. Have I made myself clear?"

The vampires muttered sullenly and settled back in their seats. When peace had been restored, Paris Skyle rose and addressed the congregation. "We know why we are here," he spoke softly. "We have been betrayed and besieged. I am as eager as any to see the vile curs suffer for their crimes, but first we must learn why they attacked and if we can expect further assaults." Turning to Kurda, his features hardened. "Were you in league with the vampaneze we killed yesterday?" he asked.

There was a long pause. Then Kurda nodded and said, "I was."

Several vampires screamed bloody murder, and were swiftly escorted out of the Hall. The others sat white-faced and trembling, glaring hatefully at Kurda.

"Upon whose orders were you acting?" Paris asked.

"My own," Kurda said.

"Liar!" Arrow barked. "Tell us who set you up to this, or so help me, I'll—"

"I know what you'll do," Kurda interrupted. "Don't worry — I have no wish to be subjected to the rougher questioning of your professional torturers. I will speak the truth here."

"You'd better," Arrow grumbled, sinking back on his throne.

"Upon whose orders were you acting?" Paris asked again.

"My own," Kurda repeated. "The plan was mine. The vampaneze were here at my bidding. Torture me all you wish — my answer won't change because it can't change. It's the truth."

"*You* dreamt up this outrage?" Mika asked incredulously.

"I did," Kurda nodded. "I arranged for the vampaneze to

come. I provided them with copies of my maps, so they could slip in undetected. I—"

"Traitor!" a vampire howled, and tried to rush the platform. He was intercepted by a couple of guards and hauled away, kicking and screaming for all his worth.

"I could reach him," Mr Crepsley hissed in the midst of the commotion, his eyes pinned on Kurda. "I could leap forward now and make an end of him before anyone could stop me."

"Peace, Larten," Seba whispered, laying a soothing hand on the vampire's trembling shoulders. "Kurda is going nowhere. His death will come soon enough. Let us hear him out."

As soon as the screams of the irate protestor had subsided, Paris resumed the questioning. "Is it true that you planned to slip the vampaneze into the Hall of Princes once you had been invested, to seize control of the Stone of Blood?"

"It is," Kurda answered directly. "We would have waited for the Ceremony of Conclusion. Then, while you were drinking yourselves stupid, reminiscing about this Council and looking forward to the next, I'd have sneaked them up through secret tunnels, made short work of those who stood on guard, and taken over the Hall."

"But you could not have held it," Paris objected. "Surely you knew that Mika, Arrow and I would force open the doors and overwhelm you."

"That would not have happened," Kurda disagreed. "You wouldn't have been alive to force open the doors. I was going to poison the three of you. I'd six bottles of a very rare wine set aside especially for the occasion, each spiked with a particularly lethal concoction. I would have presented them to the three of you in advance of the Ceremony. You'd have toasted my good health, died an hour or two later, and the Hall would have been mine."

"And then you would have set about getting rid of the rest of our kind," Arrow growled.

"No," Kurda said. "I would have set about *saving* them."

"What do you mean?" Paris asked, surprised.

"Has nobody wondered why I chose such an inopportune moment to instigate an attack?" Kurda asked, addressing the question to the entire Hall. "Doesn't it seem strange that I opted to sneak in a horde of vampaneze during Council, while these Halls and tunnels were packed with vampires, when the chance of their being discovered was far greater than if they'd come in a few months' time?"

Paris looked confused. "I assumed you wanted to strike while we were all gathered together," he muttered.

"Why?" Kurda challenged him. "The plan was to sneak into the Hall and seize the Stone of Blood, not to engage the vampire forces. The more vampires in the mountain, the more difficult our task."

"You wanted to rub it in," Arrow snorted. "You wanted to show off and be able to say you took the Halls in the middle of Council."

"You think I'm that vain?" Kurda laughed. "You think I'd have risked my life just to look stylish? You forget — I'm not like most vampires. I act for the sake of results, not appearances. I'm a cold conspirator, not a hot-headed braggart. I was only interested in success, not showmanship."

"So why *did* you attack now?" Mika asked, exasperated.

"Because we'd run out of time," Kurda sighed. "It was now or never. As I said, I meant to save our race, not vanquish it. Our only hope lay in an immediate, pre-emptive strike. Now that it has failed, I fear we are doomed."

"What's this nonsense about pre-emptive strikes?" Arrow snapped. "We had no intention of attacking the vampaneze."

"It was not an attack by the vampires on the vampaneze I sought to halt," Kurda explained. "It was an attack by the vampaneze on the vampires."

"He talks in riddles!" Arrow exploded angrily. "He attacked *with* the vampaneze to prevent an attack *by* the vampaneze? Rubbish!"

"Perhaps he's mad," Mika murmured seriously.

"If only," Kurda chuckled darkly.

"This is getting us nowhere," Arrow growled. "I say we take him below and drain the truth out of him, drop by bloody drop. He's playing us for fools. We should—"

"Mr Tiny has visited the vampaneze," Kurda said, and though he didn't raise his voice, it was as though he'd roared. Arrow and the rest of the vampires lapsed into a sudden, nervous silence, and waited for him to continue. "He came three years ago," Kurda said in that same quiet but foreboding tone. "He told them that the Vampaneze Lord walked the lands and that they should search for him. When word reached me, I dedicated myself to the task of reuniting the vampires with the vampaneze. I hoped that if we bonded before they discovered their mythical leader, we could avoid the terrible consequences of Mr Tiny's prophecy."

"I thought you did not believe the myth of the Vampaneze Lord," Paris noted.

"I didn't," Kurda agreed, "until I saw how seriously the vampaneze were taking it. They'd never been interested in war with us, but since Mr Tiny's visit, they've been strengthening their arsenals and recruiting vigorously, preparing for their fabled leader's coming.

"And now he *has* come." A physical shock ran through the Hall. The vampires recoiled in their seats as though struck, and their faces became ashen. "Six months ago, the Vampaneze Lord was discovered," Kurda said, dropping his gaze. "He hasn't been blooded, but he's taken his place among them and is learning their ways. My act of treachery was the last desperate roll of the dice. If I'd gained control of the Stone of Blood, I might have been able to win the vampaneze over — not all of our blood-cousins are eager to engage in a war with us. Now that I've failed, the way is open for him. He'll be blooded, take control of the vampaneze, and lead them against us. And he'll win."

Lowering his voice, Kurda muttered ironically, "Congratulations, gentlemen. After today's *great victory*, nothing stands between your good selves and a futile war with the vampaneze. You've cleared the way for Mr Tiny's prophecy to come to pass.

"Enjoy your celebrations. This may be the last chance you get to bang your drums and brag about your valour. As of tonight, the clock is ticking. When it stops, our time is finished. Every vampire in this Hall – on this world – is *damned*."

Smiling bitterly, Kurda snapped loose the chains around his right hand, brought his fingers to his forehead and eyes, and made the death's touch sign at the Princes. Then he looked at me and repeated the gesture. "Even in death, may you be triumphant," he croaked sarcastically, and angry, desolate tears glittered in the corners of his sad blue eyes.

CHAPTER TWENTY

THE AWFUL hush which followed Kurda's proclamation seemed to last an eternity. Finally, Seba Nile rose slowly, pointed a trembling finger at Kurda, and hissed, "You lie!"

Kurda shook his head stubbornly. "I don't."

"You have *seen* this Vampaneze Lord?" Seba asked.

"No," Kurda said. "I would have killed him if I had."

"Then how do you know he exists?"

Kurda shrugged in response.

"Answer him!" Paris thundered.

"The vampaneze have a unique coffin," Kurda said. "They call it the Coffin of Fire. Mr Tiny bestowed it upon them many centuries ago, around the same time that he gave us this magical dome in which we stand. It has been guarded by a troop of vampaneze ever since, who call themselves the Carriers of Destiny.

"The coffin is like any other — until someone lies down

461

in it and the lid is put in place. Then the coffin fills with a terrible fire. If the person is destined to lead the vampaneze, he will emerge unscathed. Otherwise, he perishes in the flames.

"Over the decades, many vampaneze have braved the Coffin of Fire — and died. But six months ago a human lay down in it, faced the flames, and came out whole. He is the Lord of the Vampaneze, and once he has been blooded, every member of the clan will obey and follow him — to the death, if required."

The Princes stared at Kurda uncertainly, fearfully, until Paris asked in a whisper, "Were you there when this human was tested?"

"No," Kurda replied. "Only the Carriers of Destiny were present."

"Then this might be only a rumour," Paris said hopefully. "A fanciful lie."

"Vampaneze never lie," Kurda reminded him.

"Perhaps they've changed," Mika mused. "The Stone of Blood would be worth a few lies. They could have tricked you, Kurda."

Again Kurda shook his head. "Many vampaneze are as troubled by the coming of their Lord as we are. They don't seek a war. They fear the losses such a struggle would incur. That's why thirty-eight agreed to accompany me on this mission. They hoped to prevent total, all-out conflict, sparing their colleagues and friends."

"You keep talking about *preventing* a war and *saving* us,"

Paris noted. "I do not see how you thought betraying our cause could be of any help."

"I intended to force a union," Kurda explained. "When I heard that the Vampaneze Lord had been unearthed, I knew it was too late to put in place a fair peace agreement. Weighing up my options — which were few — I decided to chance a coup. Had I succeeded, vampires everywhere would have been at the mercy of the vampaneze. Those in the Hall of Princes could have communicated with their kin and, via the Stone of Blood, fed them the exact location of most living vampires. Our people would have had no choice but to agree to my terms."

"And what would *they* have been?" Paris asked contemptuously.

"That we join the ranks of the vampaneze," Kurda answered. "I'd hoped for an equal union, where vampires and vampaneze each made concessions. Given the change of circumstances, that was impossible. We'd have had to adopt the vampaneze ways and customs. But that would have been preferable to annihilation."

"Not for me," Arrow growled. "I'd have rather died."

"I'm sure others would too," Kurda agreed. "But I believe most would have seen sense. Even if they hadn't, and you all chose to fight to the death, at least I'd have tried."

"What was in it for *you*, Kurda?" Mika asked. "Did the vampaneze promise you a title? Are there to be Princes in the new regime?"

"The vampaneze made no offers," Kurda replied shortly. "Many wish to avoid a war, so a few dozen volunteers — brave men, who you killed like vermin — agreed to risk their lives and assist me. We had no ulterior motives. We did it for your sakes, not our own."

"Very noble of you, Kurda," Mika sneered.

"Nobler than you imagine!" Kurda snapped, losing his cool. "Have you no brains? Don't you see the sacrifice I made?"

"What sacrifice?" Mika asked, taken aback.

"Win or lose," Kurda said, "my reward would have been death. The vampaneze despise traitors even more than we do. Had everything worked out, I'd have remained within the Hall of Princes to oversee the merging of the clans. Then, when our people's future was assured, I'd have offered myself for sentencing and suffered the very same fate which awaits me now."

"You expect us to believe the vampaneze would have killed the man who presented their arch-enemies to them?" Mika laughed.

"You'll believe it because it's true," Kurda said. "Neither the vampires nor vampaneze will suffer a traitor to live. That law is written in the hearts of each and every member of the clans. The vampaneze who came with me would have been heroes — they'd broken none of their own laws, except trespassing on vampire turf — but *me*, a man who'd betrayed his own?" Kurda shook his head. "There was nothing 'in it' for me, Mika, and more fool you if you believe any different."

Kurda's words disturbed the vampires. I saw them gazing around at one another, ominous questions in their eyes and on their tongues. "Perhaps he wants us to reward him instead of dropping him on the stakes," someone cackled, but no one laughed.

"I expect and ask for no mercy," Kurda responded. "My only wish is that you remember what I tried to do in the difficult years to come. I had only the best interests of the clan at heart. I hope one night you see that and acknowledge it."

"If all you have said is true," Paris Skyle commented, "why did you not come to *us*? If we had known about the Vampaneze Lord, we could have taken steps to stamp him out."

"By killing every living vampaneze?" Kurda asked bitterly.

"If we had to," Paris nodded.

"That was not my wish," Kurda sighed. "I sought to save lives, not take them. Fighting won't save the vampires, not if Mr Tiny's prophecy is valid. But a *union* – before the threat could come to pass – might have been the saving of us.

"I can't say I was right," Kurda continued. "For all I know, my actions will provide the spark which leads to war and destruction. But I had to try. I believed it was in my hands to divert the course of fate. Right or wrong, I couldn't willingly surrender my people to Mr Tiny's grim prophecy."

Kurda trained his gaze on me. "I have few regrets," he said. "I took a chance and it didn't pan out — that's life. My one real source of sorrow is that I had to kill Gavner Purl. It was not my wish to shed blood. But the plan came first. The future of our people as a whole outweighed that of any individual. I'd have killed a dozen more like Gavner if I had to — even a hundred, if it meant safeguarding the lives of the rest."

With that, Kurda drew his case to a close and refused to speak any more of his betrayal. The Princes asked him if he knew where the Vampaneze Lord was, or what the vampaneze were planning, but in answer he just shook his head.

The Princes opened the questioning to the floor, but none of the vampires accepted the invitation to address the fallen General. They looked downcast and ashamed of themselves now. None of them liked Kurda or approved of what he'd done, but they had come to respect him, and regretted the way they'd treated him earlier.

When a suitable period of silence had elapsed, Paris nodded at the guards on the platform to position Kurda before the Princes. When he was standing in front of them, Paris reflected inwardly for a few minutes, gathering his thoughts. When ready, he spoke. "I am troubled by what you have said. I would rather you had been a nefarious traitor, out for profit and personal gain. That way I could sentence you to death with a clear conscience and no hesitation.

"I believe you acted in good faith. It may even be as you say, that by thwarting your plans, we have condemned ourselves to defeat at the hands of the vampaneze. Maybe it would have been for the best if Darren had not chanced upon your colleagues in the cave, or survived to carry news of them back.

"But you *were* discovered, you *were* revealed, and the vampaneze *were* dispatched by all bloody means possible. There is no way to change these things, even if we wished to. The future may be bleak, but we shall face it on our feet, as vampires, with firm hearts and wills, as is our way.

"I have sympathy for you, Kurda," he continued. "You acted as you thought you must, without consideration for yourself, and for that you are to be commended. However, you also acted without consideration for our laws and ways, and for that you must be punished. There is only one fitting punishment for the crime you have committed, and it is absolute — *execution.*"

A heavy collective sigh swept through the Hall. "Had I a choice," Paris went on, "I would grant you the right to die on your feet, as a vampire, with pride. You do not deserve to die ignominiously, bound and blindfolded, impaled on stakes from behind. I would let you embark on a series of harsh tests, one after the other, until you perished honourably. And I would drink a toast to your name as you were being cremated whole.

"But, as a Prince, I have no choice. Whatever your reasons, you betrayed us, and that harsh fact of life takes precedence over my own wishes." Rising, Paris pointed at Kurda and said, "I vote that he be taken to the Hall of Death and summarily executed. After that, he should be dismembered before cremation, so that his soul may never know Paradise."

After a brief pause, Mika Ver Leth stood and pointed as Paris was pointing. "I don't know if it's just or not," he sighed, "but we must obey the customs which guide and maintain us. I too vote for the Hall of Death and shameful cremation."

Arrow stood and pointed. "The Hall of Death," he said simply.

"Does anyone care to speak on behalf of the traitor?" Paris asked. There was complete silence. "We may be persuaded to reconsider our judgement if there is opposition," he said. Still no one spoke.

I stared at the pitiful figure in front of me and thought of how he'd made me feel at home when I arrived at Vampire Mountain, how he'd treated me like a friend, joked with me and shared his knowledge and years of experience. I remembered when he knocked Arra Sails off the bars, and how he'd offered his hand to her, the look of hurt on his face when she refused to take it. I recalled how he'd saved my life and gone out on a limb for my sake, risking even the success of his mission to help me out of a jam. I wouldn't be here now, alive, if not for Kurda Smahlt.

I started to rise, to speak up for him and request a less horrible form of retribution. Then Gavner's face flashed through my mind, and Arra's, and I stopped to think what he'd have done if Mr Crepsley, Seba or any others had got in his way. He would have killed all of them if he'd had to. He wouldn't have taken pleasure in it, but he wouldn't have baulked either. He'd have done what he felt needed to be done, the same as any true-hearted vampire.

Sinking back, I shook my head miserably and held my tongue. This was too big. It wasn't for me to decide. Kurda had fashioned his own downfall. He must stand alone to face it. I felt lousy, not sticking up for him, but I'd have felt just as lousy if I had.

When it became apparent that the judgement of the Princes was not going to be called into question, Paris signalled the guards on the platform, who surrounded Kurda and stripped him bare. Kurda said nothing as they robbed him of his clothes and pride, just gazed up at the roof of the Hall.

When Kurda was naked, Paris held his fingers together tight, dipped them in a bowl of snake's blood which had been hidden behind his throne, and ran his hand over Kurda's chest. Mika and Arrow followed suit, leaving three ugly red marks — the sign among the vampires for a traitor or one of bad standing.

Once Kurda had been marked, his guards led him away. Nobody spoke or made a sound. He kept his head bowed low as he exited, but I saw tears dripping down his cheeks as he passed. He was lonely and scared. I wanted to comfort him but it was too late for that. Better to let him pass without delay.

This time, as he was guided past the assembled vampires, nobody jeered or tried to harm him. There was a brief pause when he reached the open doors, to clear the way through the vampires packed beyond, then he was escorted out of the Hall and down through the tunnels to the Hall of Death, where he was caged, blindfolded, raised above the pit of stakes, then brutally and painfully executed. And that was the end of the traitor … *my friend* … Kurda Smahlt.

CHAPTER TWENTY-ONE

I DIDN'T go to watch Kurda being killed. Nor did I stick around for the trials of the vampaneze. Instead, I returned to my cell, where I remained until it was time, late the next night, for the funerals of Arra Sails, Gavner Purl and the others who'd died fighting to protect Vampire Mountain. Gavner's body had been recovered after the battle. Kurda told his guards where to find it and a search party soon located it, stuffed into a deep crack far down the mountain.

Streak and his fellow wolves had returned to the pack. They slipped away without a fuss, not long after the fighting had finished, leaving their dead companion behind. I never had a chance to bid them farewell or thank them.

I wondered if I'd ever run with the pack again. It seemed unlikely, even if my life was spared by the Princes. Now that Council was coming to an end, the wolves would be dispersing, to return to their usual hunting grounds. I'd probably seen the last of Streak, Rudi and the rest.

I spent the time between the trials and the funerals working on my diary. I hadn't touched it since coming to Vampire Mountain. I read back over my earlier entries, then described all that had happened to me since I left the Cirque Du Freak and set out for the mountain with Mr Crepsley. I managed to lose myself in the diary, so time flew by. I normally didn't enjoy writing – too much like homework – but once I started telling the story, the words tumbled out with hardly any effort. My pen only paused a couple of times, when I slipped away to eat and caught an hour or two of sleep.

I hoped the writing would help me get things straight in my head, especially with regards to Kurda, but I was just as confused by the end as I'd been at the beginning. No matter how I looked at it, I couldn't help feeling that Kurda had been both a hero *and* a villain. Things would be simpler if he was one or the other, but I couldn't pigeon-hole him. It was just too complicated.

Kurda had wanted to prevent the destruction of the vampires. To that end, he'd betrayed them. Was he evil for doing so? Or would it have been worse to act nobly and let his people perish? Should one stay true to one's friends, whatever the consequences? I found it impossible to decide. Part of me hated Kurda and believed he deserved to be killed; another part remembered his good intentions and amiable manner, and wished there'd been some other way of punishing him, short of execution.

Mr Crepsley came to fetch Harkat and me before I finished writing. I'd got most of the story down, but there was a bit left, so I stuck my pen between a couple of pages to mark my place, laid it aside, and accompanied the sorrowful vampire to the Hall of Cremation to bid farewell to our dear departed friends and allies.

Gavner Purl was the first to be cremated, since he was the first who'd fallen. He'd been dressed in a simple white robe and lay on a thin stretcher in the cremation pit. He looked peaceful lying there, eyes closed, short brown hair carefully combed, lips worked into a smile by the Guardians of the Blood who'd prepared his body. Though I knew the Guardians had removed all of Gavner's blood, along with most of his internal organs and brains, there were no visible signs of their macabre handiwork.

I started to tell Mr Crepsley what Gavner's final words had been, but as I did, I burst into tears. Mr Crepsley wrapped his arms around me and let me sob into his chest, patting me comfortingly. "Do you want to leave?" he asked.

"No," I moaned. "I want to stay. It's just ... hard, you know?"

"I know," Mr Crepsley said, and by the tears in his own eyes, I knew he meant it.

A large crowd had gathered to see Gavner off. Usually, only one's closest friends or colleagues attended a funeral. Vampires were different to humans — they didn't believe in showing up in large numbers to pay their condolences. But Gavner had been popular and had died to save others, so the cave was full. Even Paris Skyle and Arrow were present. Mika would have been there too, except one had to stay behind to guard the Hall of Princes.

There was no such thing as a vampire priest. Though vampires had their own gods and beliefs, they'd no organized religion. Paris, as the oldest vampire in the chamber, led the brief, simple ceremonies. "His name was Gavner Purl," he chanted, and everyone repeated the Prince's words. "He died with honour." Again we followed suit. "May his spirit find Paradise," he finished, and once we'd echoed his sentiments, the twigs and leaves beneath Gavner were lit by two Guardians, who made peculiar signs over his body, then moved back out of the way.

It didn't take the flames long to consume the General. The Guardians knew their business and had arranged things so the fire grew quickly and made short work of Gavner. I'd never been to a cremation before. To my surprise, I found it wasn't as upsetting as I'd thought it would be. There was something strangely comforting in watching the flames engulf Gavner, the smoke rising and slipping through the cracks in the ceiling, almost as if it was Gavner's spirit departing.

I was glad that I'd come, though I was grateful that we were ushered out of the Hall when it was time to extract Gavner's bones from the ashes and grind them to dust in the bowls which surrounded the pit. I don't think I could have stood by and watched the Guardians doing that.

Three more vampires were to be cremated before it was Arra Sails' turn. While Mr Crepsley, Harkat and me waited outside during the ceremonies, Seba Nile and Vanez Blane appeared, the limping quartermaster leading the blind games master. The pair greeted us and stopped to chat. They apologized for missing Gavner's cremation but Vanez had been undergoing treatment and couldn't leave until the dressing on his bad eye had been changed.

"How is the eye?" Mr Crepsley asked.

"Ruined," Vanez said cheerfully, as though it was no big thing. "I'm blind as a bat now."

"I thought, since you were having it treated..."

"The treatment's to stop infection setting in and spreading to my brain," Vanez explained.

"You don't sound too upset," I noted, staring at the large patch over his right eye, thinking how awful it must be to lose one's sight.

Vanez shrugged. "I'd rather have kept it, but it's not the end of the world. I can still hear, smell and feel my way around. It will take a while to get used to, but I learnt to adapt when I lost the first eye. I'm sure I'll be able to cope without the second."

"Will you leave Vampire Mountain?" Mr Crepsley asked diplomatically.

"No," Vanez said. "Any other time, I'd have gone out into the world and stumbled around until I met with a noble end, as is a blind vampire's way. But the coming of the Vampaneze Lord has changed all that. Paris asked me to stay. I can make myself useful, even if it's only helping out in the stores or kitchens. Right now, every vampire's needed. My remaining will allow some younger, fitter vampire to focus his energies elsewhere and carry the fight to the vampaneze."

"I too shall be staying," Seba announced. "My retirement has been put on hold. The world and its adventures will have to wait. The old and infirm must play their part now, selflessly. This is no time for putting one's best interests before those of the clan."

That phrase gave me a jolt. Kurda had expressed similar sentiments earlier during my stay. He thought it was wrong that crippled or old vampires were discarded by their colleagues. It was horribly ironic that his betrayal and death should serve as the spur to win other vampires round to his way of thinking.

"Does that mean the offer of a job no longer stands?" Mr Crepsley asked Seba — he'd been earmarked to take over as quartermaster when Seba retired.

"It does," Seba said, "but I am sure the Princes will find *some* use for you." He smiled briefly. "A sweeper of floors, perhaps?"

"Perhaps." Mr Crepsley also managed a fleeting smile. "Mika has already asked me about staying and perhaps resuming my official General duties, but I told him I did not wish to consider such things at the moment. I will decide later, when I have had time to mull the situation over."

"What about Darren?" Vanez asked. "Have the Princes declared his fate yet?"

"No," Mr Crepsley said. "Mika promised to reopen the debate first thing after the funeral ceremonies. I am sure he will be pardoned."

"I hope so," Vanez said, but he sounded unsure. "You do know that a death penalty has never been revoked? The Princes would have to alter the laws in order to spare Darren's life."

"Then alter them they shall!" Mr Crepsley growled, taking a step forward in anger.

"Peace, Larten," Seba interceded. "Vanez means no harm. This is an unusual case and it will require much thought before a final decision can be made, one way or the other."

"There is no 'one way or the other'," Mr Crepsley insisted. "I promised Arra I would not let Darren be killed. She said he had earned the right to life, and anyone who would argue with her dying wish will have *me* to deal with. We have endured enough death. I will not stand for any more."

"Hopefully, there will be none," Seba sighed. "I believe the Princes will be sympathetic. They may not wish to bend the laws, but in this case I think they will."

"They had better," Mr Crepsley said, and would have said more, except at that moment Arra was brought forward on a stretcher and carried into the Hall of Cremation. Mr Crepsley stiffened and stared after her longingly. I put an arm around him and so did Seba.

"Be brave, Larten," Seba said. "She would not have wanted emotional outbursts."

"I will conduct myself with all due decorum," Mr Crepsley said pompously, then added beneath his breath, "But I miss her. With all my heart and soul, I miss her."

Once Arra's body had been laid in place, the doors were

opened and we entered, Mr Crepsley in front, Seba, Vanez, Harkat and me just behind, to make our farewells. Mr Crepsley was every bit as composed as he'd sworn he would be. He didn't even shed a tear when the funeral litter was set alight. It was only later, when he was alone in his cell, that he wept aloud, and his cries echoed through the corridors and tunnels of Vampire Mountain, far into the cold, lonely dawn.

CHAPTER TWENTY-TWO

THE LONG wait between the cremations and my trial was grisly. Though Mr Crepsley kept saying I would be pardoned for failing my Trials of Initiation, and forgiven for running away, I wasn't so sure. Working on my diary kept my mind off the forthcoming trial, but once I'd brought it up to date and checked to make sure I hadn't left anything out, there was nothing to do but sit back and twiddle my thumbs.

Finally, two guards appeared and told me the Princes were ready to receive me. I asked for a few minutes to compose myself. They stood outside the door of my cell while I faced Harkat. "Here," I said, handing him a bag (which used to belong to a friend of mine — Sam Grest) with my diary and some personal effects. "If they decide to execute me, I want you to have these."

Harkat nodded solemnly, then followed as I exited the cell and let the guards guide me to the Hall of Princes. Mr

Crepsley also fell in behind, having been notified by a third Mountain guard.

We paused outside the doors of the Hall. My belly was rumbling with fear and I was trembling all over. "Be brave," Mr Crepsley whispered. "The Princes will treat you fairly. In the event that they do not, I shall come to your aid."

"Me too," Harkat said. "I won't let ... them do anything ... crazy to you."

"Thanks," I smiled, "but I don't want either of you to get involved. Things are bad enough as they are. No point all three of us winding up in the Hall of Death!"

The doors opened and we entered.

The vampires within looked solemn and their heavy gazes did nothing to ease my discomfort. Nobody spoke as we marched to the platform, where the Princes sat waiting, stern, arms crossed. The air seemed thin and I had to gasp deeply for breath.

Mr Crepsley and Harkat sat at the base of the platform, next to Seba Nile and Vanez Blane. I was led up on to it, where I stood facing the Vampire Princes. After a short period of silence, Paris Skyle spoke. "These are strange times," he sighed. "For centuries, we vampires have stuck by our old ways and traditions and looked on, amused, as humanity changes and evolves, growing ever more fractured. While the humans of this planet have lost their sense of direction and purpose, our belief in ourselves has never wavered — until recently.

"It is a sign of the times that one vampire would raise his

hand against his brothers, regardless of his good intentions. Treachery is nothing new to mankind, but this is our first real taste of it, and it has left a sour taste in our mouths. It would be easy to turn a blind eye to the traitors and dismiss them from our thoughts. But that would be to ignore the root of our problem and leave the way open for further acts of treason. The truth is that the changing world has made its mark upon us at last, and we must change if we are to survive within it.

"Whilst we have no plans to abandon our ways outright, we must face the future and adapt as required. We have been living in a world of absolutes, but this is no longer the case. We must open our eyes, ears and hearts to new ways of thinking and living.

"That is why we have gathered here tonight. In the normal run of things, there would have been no call for a meeting to decide Darren Shan's fate. He failed the Trials of Initiation — the penalty for which is death. He then fled from sentencing, a crime punishable in only one way — death. In the past, he would have been put to the stakes, and none would have intervened on his behalf.

"But times *have* changed and Darren has played an instrumental part in opening our eyes to the *need* for change. He has endured great pain and sacrificed his freedom for the good of the clan. He has fought bravely and proven his worth. Previously, his reward would have been a noble death. Now, however, pleas have been submitted, arguing for his right to live."

Paris cleared his throat and sipped from a glass of blood. The air in the Hall was alive with tension. I couldn't see the faces of the vampires behind me, but I could feel their eyes boring into my back.

"We have argued your case at great length," Paris recommenced. "In the world of humans, I imagine it would have been easy to reach a conclusion and you would have been openly pardoned. But we view justice differently. To clear your name and free you would mean altering the very fabric of our laws.

"Some have claimed that it is time to fine-tune the laws. They put forward a convincing case on your behalf. They said laws were made to be broken, a sentiment I do not agree with, but which I am beginning to understand. Others wanted the laws pertaining to the Trials of Initiation temporarily waived. In that case, you would have been cleared, then the laws would have been reinstated. A few called for permanent, outright changes. They felt the laws were unfair and – keeping in mind the threat posed by the coming of the Vampaneze Lord – senseless, in that they might work to rob us of new recruits and weaken our hand."

Paris hesitated and ran his fingers through his long, grey beard. "After lengthy debate, much of it heated, we decided against altering our laws. There may come a time when we will have to, but–"

"Charna's guts!" Mr Crepsley roared, and the next thing I knew, he'd jumped on to the platform and was standing in front of me, fists raised. Moments later, Harkat had joined him, and the two faced the Princes and glared. "I will not stand for this!" Mr Crepsley shouted. "Darren risked his life for you, and now you would sentence him to death? Never! I will not tolerate such bloody-minded ingratitude. Anyone wishing to lay hands on my assistant will first have to lay hands on *me*, and I swear by all that is sacred, I will fight them to my last savage breath!"

"The same goes ... for me," Harkat growled, tearing loose the mask from around his mouth, his scarred grey face even more fearsome-looking than usual.

"I expected more self-control, Larten," Paris tutted, not in the least put out. "This is most unlike you."

"Desperate times call for desperate measures," Mr Crepsley retorted. "There is a time for tradition, and there is a time to exercise common sense. I will not let you—"

"Larten," Seba called from the crowd. Mr Crepsley half-turned at the sound of his mentor's voice. "You should hear Paris out," Seba suggested.

"You agree with them?" Mr Crepsley howled.

"Actually," Seba replied, "I argued for change. But when the motion was defeated, I accepted it, as any loyal vampire would."

"The hell with loyalty!" Mr Crepsley barked. "If this is the price of loyalty, perhaps Kurda was right. Maybe it would have been for the best to turn this place over to the vampaneze!"

"You do not mean that," Seba smiled. "Step down, take your seat, and let Paris finish. You are making a fool of yourself."

"But—" Mr Crepsley began.

"Larten!" Seba snapped impatiently. "Down!"

Mr Crepsley's head dropped. "Very well," he sighed. "I shall bow to your will, and hear Paris out. But I am not leaving Darren's side, and any who tries to force me from this platform shall live to regret it."

"It is all right, Seba," Paris said as the quartermaster opened his mouth to argue. "Larten and the Little Person may remain." Once that had been settled, Paris continued with his speech. "As I said, we opted not to alter our laws. There may come a time when we have to, but we would rather not rush headlong into such a course of action. Change should be gradual. We must avoid panic and anarchy.

"Having agreed upon the need to be true to our laws, we searched for a loophole which Darren could take advantage of. Nobody in this Hall wished for his death. Even those most strenuously opposed to changes in the laws racked their brains in the hope that an escape clause would present itself.

"We considered the possibility of letting Darren 'escape' a second time, of relaxing the guard and allowing him to slip away with our unofficial blessing. But there would have been no honour in such a strategy. Darren would have been shamed; you, Larten, would have been shamed; and we who agreed to the compromise would also have been shamed.

"We decided against it."

Mr Crepsley bristled, then addressed the Princes in a hissed whisper. "Arra made me promise, on her deathbed, that I would not let Darren die. I beg you — do not force me to choose between loyalty to you and my vow to her."

"There will be no need to choose," Paris said. "There is no conflict of interests, as will become apparent as soon as you shut up and let me finish." He smiled as he said this. Then, raising his voice, he again addressed the Hall. "As those who were present during the debate know, Arrow was the first to suggest an honourable way out of our dilemma."

"I don't know how I thought of it," Arrow grunted, running a hand over his bald head, grimacing. "I've never been known as a great thinker. Normally, I act first and think later — if at all! — but a thought was swimming like a fish, deep within the ocean of my brain, and eventually it surfaced."

"The solution," Paris said, "is simplicity itself. We do not need to bend or change the laws to suit Darren's purposes. Instead, we need only place him above them."

"I do not understand," Mr Crepsley frowned.

"Think, Larten," Paris urged. "Who among us are immune to punishment? Who could fail the Trials of Initiation a dozen times and walk away untouched?"

Mr Crepsley's eyes widened. "You cannot mean...?" he gasped.

"We do," Paris smirked.

"But ... it is incomprehensible! He is too young! He is not a General! He is not even a full-vampire!"

"Who cares?" Mika Ver Leth chipped in, pulling a wry face. "We're not interested in the fine print. He's earned the right to bear the title. More than any of us here, perhaps, he is worthy."

"This is insane," Mr Crepsley said, but he was beginning to smile.

"Possibly," Paris agreed. "But it was put to a vote and all voted in favour of it."

"*All?*" Mr Crepsley blinked.

"Every single vampire in the Hall," Mika nodded.

"Excuse me," I whispered to Mr Crepsley, "but what's going on? What are you talking about?"

"Be quiet," he hushed me. "I will explain presently." He thought over the Princes' proposition — whatever it was — and his smile grew wider. "It makes sense, in a mad sort of way," he muttered. "But surely the title would be honorary? He knows so little of our ways, and he is so young and inexperienced."

"We would not expect him to engage in regular duties," Paris said. "He has much to learn and we will not rush his development. We will not even make a full-vampire of him — though we must share our blood, we will limit the amount, so he remains a half-vampire. But the appointment *will* be valid. He will not be a figurehead. He will hold all the responsibilities and powers of the post."

"Look," I grumbled, "tell me what's going on, or—" Mr Crepsley bent and whispered something in my ear. "What?" I snapped, and he whispered some more. "You can't be serious!" I yelped, feeling the blood rush from my face. "You're pulling my leg!"

"It is the only honourable way," he said.

"But ... I couldn't ... I'm not ... I never..." I shook my head and stared around at the vampires packing the Hall of

Princes. They were all smiling now and nodding at me. Seba looked especially pleased. "That lot agreed to it?" I asked weakly.

"Every one of them," Paris said. "They respect you, Darren. They also admire you. What you have done for us shall never be forgotten as long as vampires walk the earth. We wish to show our appreciation, and this is the only way we know."

"I'm amazed," I mumbled. "I don't know what to say."

"Say 'Yes'," Arrow laughed, "or we'll have to take you down to the Hall of Death and punch a few holes in you!"

Looking up at Mr Crepsley, I squinted, then smiled. "You'd have to obey me if I went along with this, wouldn't you?" I asked.

"Of course," he grinned. "I and all others."

"You'd have to do whatever I said?"

"Yes." He lowered his voice. "But do not think you could push me around. I will respect your standing, but I will not let your head swell unchecked. You will still be my assistant and I will keep you in your rightful place!"

"I bet you will," I chuckled, then faced Paris and drew myself up straight. I stood on the verge of a monumental decision, which would change my life forever. I'd have liked a few nights to think about it, and dwell upon the consequences, but there was no time. It was this or the Hall of Death — and anything was preferable to being dropped on the vicious stakes! "What do I have to do?" I asked.

"There is a lengthy, involved ceremony," Paris said, "but that can be postponed until later. Right now all you need do is accept our blood and offer some of your own to the Stone of Blood. Once you have been recognized by the Stone, the deed is done and it can never be reversed."

"OK," I said nervously.

"Step forward then," Paris said, "and let the pact be sealed."

As I advanced, Mr Crepsley told Harkat what was going on, and I heard him exclaim, "No way!" I found it impossible to hide my grin during the ceremony, even though everybody else in the Hall remained solemn-faced.

First, I removed my top. Then Arrow, Mika and me gathered around the Stone of Blood (only two Princes were required for the ceremony). Using my sharp nails, I cut into the fleshy tips of my ten fingers, drawing blood. Arrow and Mika did the same. When we were ready, Arrow pressed the bloody fingertips of one of his hands to mine, and Mika did the same on the other side. Then the pair laid their free hands on the Stone of Blood, which glowed red and emitted a low thrumming noise.

I could feel the blood of the Princes flowing into me, and mine into them. It was an unpleasant sensation but it wasn't as painful as it had been when Mr Crepsley first blooded me all those years ago.

The Stone of Blood glowed brighter the longer we remained joined to it, and the outer rim became transparent, so that I was able to see inside it and watch as my blood was added to that of thousands of other creatures of the night.

Stray thoughts zipped frenziedly through my mind. I remembered the night when Mr Crepsley blooded me. My first real drink of blood, when Sam Grest lay dying in my arms. The vampaneze I'd killed in the cave. The mad vampaneze — Murlough. Steve Leopard — my best friend when I was a human, who'd sworn to track me down and kill me when he grew up. Debbie Hemlock and the softness of her lips when we kissed. Gavner — laughing. Mr Tall directing his performers at the Cirque Du Freak. Harkat telling me his name after we'd killed the rabid bear. Truska (the bearded lady) fitting me out in a pirate costume. Arra — winking. Mr Tiny with his heart-shaped watch and loveless eyes. Kurda facing the hall of vampires. Annie and how she used to tease me. Sticking stamps into albums with Mum. Pulling weeds in the garden with Dad. Gavner, Arra, Sam Grest — dying.

I grew faint and would have fallen, but Paris darted behind me and propped me up. The blood was flowing rapidly now, and so were the images. Faces from the past, friends and enemies, moving as fast as the frames of a movie, then faster. Just when I thought I couldn't stand any more, Arrow and Mika removed their hands from the Stone of Blood, then broke contact with me, signalling the end of the ceremony. As I slumped backwards, Paris quickly rubbed spit on to the tips of my fingers to stop the bleeding. "How do you feel?" he asked, checking my eyes.

"Weak," I muttered.

"Give it a few hours," he said. "Once the blood kicks in, you will feel like a panther!"

The sound of cheering reached my ears and I realized all the vampires in the hall were hollering their heads off. "What are they shouting about?" I asked.

"They want to see you," Paris said, smiling. "They wish to grant their approval."

"Can't they wait?" I asked. "I'm exhausted."

"We shall carry you," Paris said. "It would not do to keep your subjects waiting ... *Sire*."

"'Sire'," I repeated, and grinned, liking the sound of it.

The three Princes lifted me up and placed me lengthways on their shoulders. I laughed and stared at the ceiling as they carried me forward, marvelling at this bizarre twist of fate, wondering what the future would hold and if anything could ever compare with this.

As they put me down, so that I could take the applause of the vampires on my feet, I gazed around and noted the beaming faces of Mr Crepsley, Harkat, Seba Nile, Vanez Blane, and the others. At the back of the hall, I thought I spotted the ghostly shades of Gavner and Arra, and – just behind them – Kurda, applauding silently. But that must have been an effect of the dizziness caused by the addition of the Princes' blood.

Then the faces blurred and I was staring out upon a sea of yelling vampires, one the same as the next. Letting my eyes close, I stood there, shaky on my feet, rocking from the vibrations of their roars, proud as a peacock, listening numbly as they chanted my name and cheered for me — me ... Darren Shan ... *the Vampire Prince!*

TO BE CONTINUED...

DARREN SHAN
VAMPIRE BLOOD TRILOGY

THE SAGA OF DARREN SHAN

No one expects to pay for
their mistakes in blood

But for Darren Shan, life as an ordinary schoolboy is over.
In *Cirque Du Freak*, Darren strikes a deal with
a creature of the night that will change his life for ever.
In *The Vampire's Assistant*, Darren joins the vampire ranks,
but fights the urge to drink human blood.
And in *Tunnels of Blood*, Darren will need all the luck of
the vampires to defeat a savage enemy.

Become a half-vampire
Explore the night
Feed

ISBN 0 00 714374-5

www.darrenshan.com

DARREN SHAN

VAMPIRE WAR TRILOGY

THE SAGA OF DARREN SHAN

Your life can change
in just one second

In *Hunters of the Dusk*, Darren Shan, the Vampire Prince,
must leave Vampire Mountain on a life or death mission. But
the road ahead is lined with the bodies of the damned. In
Allies of the Night, Darren faces his worst nightmare yet — school!
As bodies pile up, the past is catching up with the hunters fast.
And in *Killers of the Dawn* Darren becomes public enemy
Number One. Is this the end for Darren and his allies?

Become a half-vampire
Explore the night
Feed

ISBN 0 00 714375-3

www.darrenshan.com

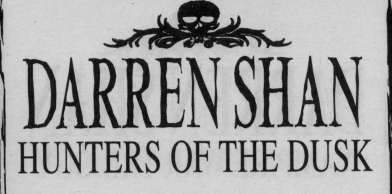

DARREN SHAN
HUNTERS OF THE DUSK

THE SAGA OF DARREN SHAN
BOOK 7

Darren Shan, the Vampire Prince, leaves
Vampire Mountain on a life or death mission.

As part of an elite force, Darren scours
the world in search of the Vampaneze Lord.
But the road ahead is long and dangerous
– and lined with the bodies of the damned.

ISBN 0 00 713779-6

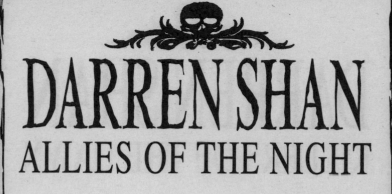

DARREN SHAN
ALLIES OF THE NIGHT

THE SAGA OF DARREN SHAN
BOOK 8

Darren Shan, Vampire Prince and vampaneze killer,
faces his worst nightmare yet – school!

But homework is the least of Darren's problems.
Bodies are piling up. Time is running out.
And the past is catching up with the hunters fast!

ISBN 0 00 713780-X

www.darrenshan.com

DARREN SHAN
KILLERS OF THE DAWN

THE SAGA OF DARREN SHAN
BOOK 9

Outnumbered, outsmarted and desperate, the
hunters are on the run. Pursued by the vampaneze,
vigilante mobs and the police, Darren Shan, the
Vampire Prince, is public enemy Number One!

With their enemies baying for blood,
the vampires prepare for deadly confrontation.
Is this the end for Darren and his allies?

ISBN 0 00 713781-8

www.darrenshan.com

DARREN SHAN

THE LAKE OF SOULS

THE SAGA OF DARREN SHAN
BOOK 10

"If you step through after Harkat,
you might never come back. Is your
friend worth such an enormous risk?"

A terrifying new world, a deadly new challenge
for Darren Shan, the Vampire Prince.

Darren and Harkat face monstrous obstacles
on their desperate quest to the Lake of Souls.
Will they survive their savage journey? And what
awaits them in the murky waters of the dead?
Be careful what you fish for...

ISBN 0 00 715919-6

www.darrenshan.com